D1169741

Judah the Hammer

The Second Book in The Judean Revolt Series

by

J.D. Sonne

Judah the Hammer

J.D. Sonne

Copyright © 2021 JD Sonne

All rights reserved

ISBN-13: 9-798-7750-6616-1

for all my students. . .who listened

Chapter One

Ephraim was a dwarf inside this cave. He had never been in anything this immense, man-made or otherwise. It seemed as if a large hand had hollowed the limestone into the massive natural fissure that easily had the capacity to house one or two thousand of their people.

Hezekiah watched Ephraim's reaction and said happily, "It is amazing, is it not? It is perfect for us. Father says we will be ready by next week. We will make our journey as soon as the priests light the mountain fires for the month of *Nisan*.

"What will it prove, our fleeing to a cave like so many rats?" Ephraim said as he inspected a corner of the cavern that seemed to open into another chamber. "Where does this go?" Without waiting for an answer, he edged into the opening and called, his voice echoing, "What good is our hiding here?"

"If enough Jews forsake their livelihoods," Hezekiah said, "the workings of the economy of Jerusalem will fall. At least that is what Father says. He thinks that economic duress will force the Greeks to ensure our rights again. That Antiochus will have to do as his father did: restore our rights and religious practices."

Ephraim was skeptical. "I do not know if that will work," he said. "Antiochus is not one given to persuasion and fiscal prodding."

"It is well known that he needs tribute for the Romans," Hezekiah said, fishing a flat of bread out of his pocket. He offered some to Ephraim who refused with a smile. "Economics may be the only thing that will 'prod' him, as you say. If our people will not work and the tax collectors have nothing to collect, then perhaps the Greeks will heed us."

"Antiochus does not need our paltry taxes," Ephraim scoffed. "Whenever he needs money, he simply raids another kingdom. I hear he is eyeing the eastern satrapies to wrest tribute from them. He has raided our temple; there is no treasure there anymore. No, I feel this will not work. Antiochus will simply order you all butchered to set an example for the rest of Judaea."

"Well, Father does not think so," Hezekiah said between bites, "and he has been working with the Greeks for a long time." He slid his back down a wall of rock until he was in a squat on his haunches. "I did not tell you, but he actually worked with Menelaus and the Greek generals, Nicanor and Apollonius for the annunciation last year."

"The annunciation? What is that?" Ephraim asked.

"It was the celebration of Menelaus' return as high priest. They held a service in the temple."

Ephraim in confusion said, "What do you mean? How could Nicanor and Apollonius—Oh no!" Ephraim stepped back in revulsion. "You mean the abomination of desolation—where they sacrificed a pig and held rites of prostitution on the altar? Your father had a hand in that blasphemy?"

"It saved many of our people," Hezekiah said defensively. "If Father had not assisted the Greeks and High Priest Menelaus, another slaughter, even more destructive than the parade of death, would have been ordered by Apollonius." Hezekiah looked at the last crumbling piece of bread unhappily. "At least that is what they threatened Papa with."

Ephraim squatted alongside Hezekiah. How could the temple high priest have set aside the laws of their fathers and the sanctity of the temple just to save a few lives? Jews had been dying for the law for centuries. Even now, Jews were dying all over Judaea rather than flout their beliefs and practices.

Ephraim saw that he had made Hezekiah uncomfortable. His large friend had actually put away the last bit of bread into his pocket, and Ephraim had never seen Hezekiah exercise any restraint regarding food. Then his stomach chilled. He realized that he understood too well the idea of placating the Greeks to save lives. Is that not what his father Naphtali did when he attempted to sacrifice a pig on the altar of Modiin's synagogue? Self-righteousness did not seem appropriate when his father's act was so like that of Hezekiah's father.

"I understand," Ephraim whispered. "I am sorry I sounded so proud. I do understand."

Hezekiah's face opened into a grin of relief. "I knew you would," he said, mistaking that Ephraim's epiphany had to do with friendship rather than an inner battle with hypocrisy. "The Kidron has a tributary right outside the cave. Let us fill our skins and return to Jerusalem. Mother is preparing for Shabbat. You will welcome the Queen of the Week with our family. Your uncle will not mind?"

"No," was all Ephraim said as they ambled toward the rock opening. "He will not mind."

Chapter Two

Menelaus blanched. "Would you repeat that, General? I could not have heard you correctly."

"The emperor would like his subjects to celebrate the upcoming Bacchanalia," Apollonius said again as he stared over the tablet at Menelaus, the High Priest of Jerusalem. "He feels that they would be less resistant to the other edicts if they engaged in a little, shall we say, provocative dancing and fraternization. They might find that they like the aesthetics of the celebration."

Menelaus shook his head emphatically. "They will never agree to that." He thought of the old temple high priest who had agreed to preside over the swine sacrifice in the temple only after Menelaus had overtly threatened the lives of the entire Jewish quarter. This Bacchanal could very well be the end of them all. "General, they will never agree," he repeated. "It will spark a riot, the like of which we have never seen."

Apollonius gazed at the high priest for a moment. "It is your job to persuade them to agree, High Priest," he said calmly. "Peaceful persuasion is still possible at this stage. By the time I implement *my* method of persuasion, it will be a very bloody proposition, I can assure you. It is not something that I take pleasure in," Apollonius said as he leaned forward over the small desk, his eyes finding Menelaus', "but I will have obedience on this issue. The emperor has ordered it, and I follow the emperor's orders."

Menelaus thought of the thousands who died in the destructive parade that Apollonius choreographed the year before. To punish the Jews for accepting the usurper Jason back to Jerusalem, the Greeks had polished their best armor, clad themselves in it and their parade dress and marched through the streets of Jerusalem.

As soon as thousands of Jews had emerged from their homes to watch the magnificent procession, the soldiers had turned their swords and pikes upon the spectators. Although impossibly brutal, the parade had proved to be thoroughly successful in quelling unrest for many months.

Menelaus studied Apollonius' hardened face for a moment and said, "I will make them see reason, General."

"I think that would be best, High Priest," Apollonius said in dismissal.

As Menelaus left the barracks and climbed into his litter, he reflected on the tales he had heard of the festival of *Bacchus*, as the Romans called him, or *Dionysus*, the Greeks' name for the god of wine. Even to his eclectic and liberal mind, these festivals sounded as if they appealed to the basest and most foul of human inclinations. From what Nadab had told him, the festivity would start with a feast of the most provocative and decadent delicacies: eels stuffed with breadfruit, an African root mixed with marine eggs that produced a pate with hallucinogenic qualities, countless pastries glazed with exotic sweets and other victuals that did not sound as if they could be edible however prepared. Because of the aphrodisiac effect of many of these foodstuffs, the culinary gluttony would invariably lead to gluttonies of a sexual nature, involving a mixing and matching of sexes and animals—Menelaus shuddered—and sometimes would even degenerate to sadism and masochism that would result in wildings, the collective murder by the revelers of one or more of the festival participants. He could not see the Jews of Jerusalem, except for the thoroughly Hellenized, contemplating such a festival, let alone participating in one. He wondered if he could convince them to at least playact. If he could not, there would be no one left to rule in Jerusalem.

Menelaus dismissed his litter bearers at the entrance to the palace and climbed the steps with a slow tread. Nadab came sweeping down on him, offering his arm to his weary superior. When the summons from Apollonius had arrived, he and Menelaus had wondered what the general had wanted with the high priest. Now, Nadab was deadly calm, questions on his face. He did not voice his queries but simply accompanied Menelaus to his atrium office.

After Menelaus informed Nadab of the new edict, Nadab sat down, settling his chin in his palm. He hunched in serious thought for many minutes and said, "Your honor, I think if we couch this celebration in one of our own, the people may not find it so objectionable. Your idea of play-acting may work. However, we must be careful how we approach the high council with the idea."

"Why not be direct, Nadab?" Menelaus asked. "They must simply be told that if they do not worship at the Bacchanal that they will die."

"Sire, the Jews will regard that as a challenge," Nadab said, "and a challenge in this culture almost always leads to the most stubborn resistance." He stood and wandered around the room. "No, we must proceed gently, very gently. If you will allow me, I will summon the temple high priest, Gideon. Did he not preside at the temple proceedings of the annunciation? He seems a pragmatist in these matters."

Menelaus attempted to arrange his desk, and distracted by the task, said absently, "Gideon has not been as pliant lately. In fact, he has become downright churlish at some of my requests regarding the new procedures governing temple rites."

"Nevertheless, I will send Janus to fetch him," Nadab said.

"As you wish," Menelaus said impatiently. "Only make sure he is quick about it. I must visit the aqueduct construction site and attend to the water allotments for the city. I have put off the engineer for too long."

* * * * *

Janus, Nadab's secretary, sniffed and peered through the door of the Hebrew temple offices. One of the Jew priests had directed him here to this obscure opening at the side of the temple. Previous to the annunciation of last year, he would never have been allowed this deep into the Hebrew temple complex. It seemed the Jews had finally relaxed their strictures regarding Greek attendance here. A direct order from General Nicanor had added teeth to the order of the emperor that Greeks have full access to all structures in Jerusalem. "High Priest Gideon?" Janus ventured. "Are you in here?"

* * * * *

Hezekiah looked up from the parchment he was copying and stood abruptly when he saw a thin, effeminate youth dressed in flashy Hellenic robes. It was still a shock to see Greeks on the temple grounds, edict notwithstanding, and he glared warily at the youth. "What do you want?" Hezekiah sounded gruffer than he felt.

"I am Janus, scribe to Menelaus, the High Priest of Jerusalem." Janus intoned imperiously. "The High Priest wishes a conference with Temple High Priest Gideon." When Hezekiah, unimpressed, sat back down and resumed copying, Janus added, "Immediately, Jew."

At the derisive lilt on the last word, Hezekiah stood again and moved toward the youth. He straightened to make his bulk more formidable and loomed over Janus in a threatening posture. "I will give him the message," his voice sturdy, yet calm. "I am his son."

Janus withered and backed out of the room. His courage seemed to return when five feet of courtyard separated him from the door and Hezekiah heard him squeak, "Well, see that you do!" The words were accompanied by the fey patter of his sandaled feet into the distance.

"What can the vulture want, now?" High Priest Gideon asked wearily when Hezekiah told him of Menelaus' summons. He had been in the adjoining room going over figures with his clerk and now moved to stand over Hezekiah's desk. Gideon leaned over the new draft of the Daniel scrolls and appraised his son's work. The words of Daniel were slowly spreading across Judaea. "Very well done, boy," he said. "That one will go to Ahaz of Bethlehem."

Returning to the topic of Menelaus' summons, Gideon asked, "has he not picked us to the bone? Does he want more tribute for the Crazy One?" The old priest absently fingered Hezekiah's writing reeds that were arranged on the table as he went on, "the temple is barely a skeleton as it is." Gideon walked to the rude wooden closet, opened it and stood for a long time sadly perusing its shelves. Only the barest of worship implements remained: a rough candelabrum, a linen cover or two, and the *Tanakh* scrolls that had survived the last raid only because Hezekiah had hidden them under his cloak when the defilers had ransacked the offices. He closed the closet and took his cloak off the back of his chair. "They are all defiled now. The temple itself is only a bare shell, not even fit for services after what went on during the annunciation last year. I wonder that we have even stayed this long." He donned his cloak against the cold Jerusalem winter. "I must go."

Hezekiah adjusted the cloak over his father's shoulders and walked him to the door. "Father, it is not your fault. You did what you could to preserve the law."

Gideon's old rheumy eyes fell on his son. "I think," he said wearily, "that it has not been enough. I have seen the total desecration of the Holy of Holies. Where now will the Lord G-d speak to his people? We have no serviceable tabernacle and I, as the keeper of the law, have allowed that to happen. All is defiled. All is impure."

Hezekiah watched the old man step out into the street and slowly pull the door shut behind him. He worried about his father, the once proud High Priest Gideon. Over the past three years, the strong and resolute leader had slowly devolved into a mere shadow of what he had been. The murders of the tens of thousands of Jerusalemites had been terrible, and Hezekiah knew his father had not recovered from the sight of prostitutes gamboling about the Holy of Holies the year before. Even now, the old priest spoke of his dreams streaming with swines' blood on the sacred altar. He even avoided the temple enclosure because the statue bearing Antiochus' likeness still loomed over the altar. And, worst of all, he told Hezekiah that he would be forever known as the High Priest who had presided over this terrible defilement that Jews throughout Judaea were now calling "The Abomination of Desolation." That term came directly out of the newly acquired Book of Daniel that Hezekiah was copying. The great prophet who oversaw the Jews in their Babylonian captivity had seen this abomination:

> *And they shall pollute the sanctuary of strength*
> *And shall take away the daily sacrifice*
> *And they shall place the abomination that maketh desolate. . .*

Hezekiah shook his head sadly and sat back down at his parchment and quills. As he sharpened the end of one of the reeds and dipped it in blacking, he did not like to think how his father's visit to Menelaus today would further alter the lives of Jews in Jerusalem and Judaea.

Chapter Three

Gophna, Judaea   The 19th day of *Adar II* 3594 (March 16th166 B.C.E.)

J udah patted the leader on the back. "Hillel," He said as he stood, "you and your men are welcome," then made sure his men made seating room for the new arrivals. "Now that the Greeks have left us, we can turn our attention to other matters. We were just discussing Lydda."

Hillel of Beit Ur had brought his men to the command tent where they milled about its entrance. This being their first invitation, they were not sure if they should enter or wait for Judah to usher them in. Finally, they pushed aside the flap and realized they need not have been hesitant, for the welcome they received was unrestrained.

"Lydda?" Hillel grunted as he sat down. His girth demanded that Avram and Eleazar make a little more room on either side for him, which they did with good grace. "What about Lydda? I hear more Greek soldiers are arriving every day. Not only that, but the Hellenized Jews are doing everything they can to welcome them."

"Exactly," Eleazar said. "If we are to truly rid Judaea of the Greeks, that means cleansing corrupt practices of the Law."

"I understand," Hillel said.

"Well, I do not." Asher shifted uncomfortably on the rug. "What exactly," he asked, "does that mean—'cleanse corrupt practices of the Law'?"

Judah saw his friend's discomfort but decided to be blunt. "It means that we must enforce the Law. It means that we must make sure that the ordinances of the Law are performed according to the written word."

As he watched Asher's face, Judah saw the wrestler, Eupolemus, emerge for a moment. Asher had made a great name, albeit a Greek name, for himself in the Hellenic world with his prowess as an athlete. In fact, he had been apostate for many years, having fled Modiin to follow Greek ways. His mother and seven brothers, however, had fallen victim to those very ways: they were tortured to death because they would not name the Greek emperor Antiochus as their god. From Shimon, the eldest, to Caleb, the youngest, not one of them would denounce the One G-d, the G-d of their Fathers. Asher's grief at the deaths and his failure to protect his family brought him back from the infidel ways of the Greek to fully embrace the faith of his youth once again. However, he had friends in Lydda where he had spent many years—friends, Hellenized Jew and Greek alike, who had been kind to him.

Studying their beards, hands or the dusty carpet, the men in the command tent avoided Asher's eyes as they could tell he was casting about for an alternative viewpoint, for Judah's implication was clear: Whoever shall not live by the Law, shall die by the Law.

"And how do we enforce the Law?" Asher said defensively. "By murder? By torture? Are we now to employ the tactics of our great enemy, Antiochus?"

Protests met his words, each man a loud voice proclaiming that no, it was not the same, that it was their land, that their Law was the Law and that their G-d was G-d. The men of Beit Ur joined in the verbal fray, adding their noise to the stifle of the tent. Judah said nothing but let the men argue for many moments.

At last Judah stood and the men quieted. He clasped his hands and rested them up under his beard as he thought about what to say. Walking around the outside of the circle of men, he was grateful for their silence as it gave him space to think.

"I want you all to think about what we have accomplished. Word is spreading that we defeated the Greeks in a great battle. That is the rumor." He waited for the chuckles to die down. "Of course, we know the truth. This army of Greeks was not very bright, and they underestimated us, figuring that they would just climb our little Gophna Hill and take our camp. That did not work out very well for them, but we also know that a smarter army will soon march on us and it will take every *yod* of our strength and wiles to stay alive. We are a small band, but because of these rumors, we are growing every day. Our people are gathering to us. The villages of Beit Ur, Gezer and Beit Horon are now among our number in these little hills of Gophna. Others are coming."

Judah stopped for a moment, raised Asher to his feet and put his arm around his shoulder. "However," he went on, "we need a cause. We need a standard for each Jew who is giving everything to join us. What better standard than that which makes a man a Jew? The Law. Many Jews have forgotten how to live the Law. We were stiff-necked from the very beginning. You would think that our bondage in Egypt would have relaxed our prideful necks. But, as you remember, we even gave our own Moshe quite a hard time." Another murmur of chuckles ebbed through the tent. "The Lord needed forty years in the wilderness to bend our necks. Well, the Greeks undid much of Moshe and even Yehoshua's work and Jewish necks have become stiff again. It is up to us, now, to act for the Lord and bend those necks. And, if we can do it without breaking them, so much the better."

Judah grasped the back of Asher's neck in a playful stranglehold. At this, the men laughed, and it did much to dispel the seriousness in the tent. He looked at his friend, who had suffered the hold with good grace, and said, "Asher, old friend, we will always use persuasion first. We will do our best to educate our errant brothers." Then Judah's face became as stone, "However, one way or the other, we will destroy that philosophy that led to the deaths of your mother, brothers and many other of our people. I—we—will wipe it out. That I promise you. And if it must start with Lydda, so be it."

Asher's head sank to his chest, but he said no more, seeming to accept the logic of Judah's speech.

Eleazar said eagerly, "Lydda is a great center of Hellenization. Do you remember, Judah, when we traveled there last year to find Asher—" He trailed off at the look on Judah's and Asher's face when he seemed to remember that trip had almost led to Asher's being stoned.

Asher had danced with Shoshanna at a Modiin wedding, a scandalous lapse of propriety, and had fled to Lydda. When Judah and Eleazar visited him the next day, they led Asher to believe that Shoshanna was in love with him. Asher returned to an angry village whose residents, to avenge the law of gender separation, were ready to pick up stones to kill him. Mattathias' intervention was the only reason that Asher was alive today.

Eleazar ploughed ahead, "Ah—anyway, if we could remove the Hellenizing influences of Lydda and bring their Jews over to our cause, that would be a great defeat for the Greeks. We could even destroy the heathen temple and gymnasium there."

"Destroy them? I have seen that temple and gymnasium," Avram said, "and I do not see how we could destroy them. How do you demolish such a structure? The stones are massive, and the Greeks are very tidy masons."

"We will borrow an elephant or two from the Greeks," a voice said in the back. "Perhaps Antiochus can spare a couple of beasts." The men turned and murmured welcome's to Mattathias. He had risen from his sick bed to attend the meeting.

Mattathias was getting too old and stiff to sit on the rugs any longer, so Judah ran outside and fetched a stool for him. He placed the stool directly in front of him so his father could be at the center of things. As Judah watched Mattathias ease carefully down to the stool, sadness overcame him for a moment at the turn of events that had forced them into the hills. His father had not been well since leaving his estate in Modiin. Living in the hills was a drag upon his health. Judah thought he should be living out these days in comfort in his house, not in barbaric conditions such as these. His hatred of the Greeks intensified every time he looked at his father's debilitated shuffle and he felt he could not wait to sink his sword into Greek flesh again.

"Father, what think you of our attacking Lydda?" Judah asked. "Our plan is to turn it into a Jewish center as it was before the Greeks. We will drive out all Hellenists, Greek and Jew alike, unless they come over to us. We will purge the city of its infidel leanings."

Mattathias did not answer right away. He fiddled with his robe so that it fit more snugly around his cold legs, looked up and smiled. "It is a good plan, but are you ready?"

The men nodded, the carriage of their bodies becoming stout, some voicing their affirmations of readiness until he interrupted them.

"I mean," he asked quietly, "are you ready to kill Jews? Oh, yes," Mattathias said as he slowly surveyed their startled faces, his eyes making a deliberate sweep of the tent. "You will have to kill Jews. You must realize that not all our Jewish brothers will want to forsake the Greek way. Are we to do as Yehoshua did and kill those who will not follow the Law?"

He shifted a little upon the stool. "I do not say it is right; I do not say it is wrong. I only say that you have some decisions to make. Whatever you decide, you must steel yourselves to complete the task, whatever you determine it is."

Asher's concerns on the matter of killing Greeks had not bothered any of them, and they had ignored his allusion to their Jewish brethren whose necks Judah wanted to bend. They understood his concern but did not share it. But, the reality of the situation being voiced by Mattathias brought the matter home to them: killing their own, killing Jews. The tent's silence signified that a convulsion of principle wracked the men.

"Perhaps no Jews need die," Eleazar said, hope in his voice. "Perhaps Judah is right about the rumors. They may open a way for more Hellenists to flock to our cause."

"Like so many geese," Judah said. He smiled, then sobered. "We must realize that with all these geese may come infiltrators. We must guard against those who would spy upon us." Judah stroked his beard as he thought.

The men were quiet for only a moment, then the noise of discussion enveloped Judah. He did his best to filter out the various conversations so he could learn what to do. Listening for quite a while as he strolled through the discussions, he crouched from time to time upon hearing engaging points or ideas. Finally, his pithy "Enough!" stopped the exchanges and the men lifted their eyes to him.

"We may not know what to do at this moment. I am not ashamed to admit that I am uncertain what to do with unrepentant Jews. Unrepentant Greeks? Now, that is no problem!" and the men reacted with a thunderous guffaw when he etched his thumb across his throat. After the laughter receded, he said, "As always, I believe that when the time comes, we will know what to do. We must rely on the Lord G-d. We are living His Law; therefore, He-of-No-Name is bound to us. He will tell us what to do when the time comes. *Nu*," Judah clasped his hands together to signify an end to the weighty subject, "Let us plan our assault on Lydda. Let us be resolute against the Greeks, and who knows?" He clapped the seated Eleazar on the back, then playfully slapped the back of his head-covering, "Perhaps Eleazar is right, errant Jews may flock to us like so many geese. Now, our approach to Lydda must come from the East. The Jewish quarter is located there and that will preserve our surprise approach against the Greek quarter in the center of town."

The men were so steeped in their heed to Judah that no one noticed Asher's departure from the meeting. No one, that is, except Judah. He could spare only a moment for a look of worry at the tent flap, then put his full attention back into the planning of the assault on the Greek center of Lydda.

Chapter Four

Jerusalem, Judaea   The 19th day of *Adar II* 3594 (March 16th 166 B.C.E.)

G ideon stood outside Menelaus' enclosure, trying not to act restive. Ever since Menelaus had forced the annunciation on the Temple High Priest, Gideon refused to enter the chambers or offices of the High Priest of Jerusalem. So now he stood, looking up at the shimmering cloud wisps that were blowing in from the south. The breeze was warm. Winter was loosening its grip on the city so that the sun was no longer frustrated in throwing its rays against the streets and their inhabitants. Feeling the warmth through his cloak, the Temple High Priest shifted his shoulders, lifted his face and smelled spring. The ground seemed to be yielding somewhat, anticipating the new growth of the approaching season. The trees, their skeletons stretching over the arbors in the courtyard, were showing signs of life in the small buds on their bony fingers.

A stately procession of two, Menelaus and his counselor, Aminadab, came out of the enclosure and bowed to Gideon, who bowed back. The three moved beneath one of the arbors and sat down, each taking his own stone bench, Gideon and Menelaus facing and Nadab off to the side of Menelaus.

"Thank you for your condescension, High Priest," Menelaus said unctuously. "We appreciate your visiting us here."

"I come when summoned, High Priest Menelaus," Gideon said. "What is it you want?"

"The aqueduct construction is coming along," Menelaus said. "I thought you would like to know how the water was to be allotted this quarter. The elders of Bethlehem will be pleased that it is first on the rotation, after that will come Mizpeh. Perhaps you would like to tell the priests at your next gathering."

"They will be pleased, Excellency," Gideon said. "Will that be all?"

As Gideon watched Menelaus' face, he knew that he had not been summoned here because of the water allotments. Menelaus usually sent a messenger regarding logistical matters such as these. No, there was another reason for the summons and the discomfort in Menelaus' face did not indicate positive news.

"Well," Menelaus said, glancing aside at Nadab. "There is something else."

Gideon rose. "What is it? If it is bad news, you must out with it. What is it?"

Menelaus told him. It did not take long, and at the end of the message, Gideon hastily excused himself and fled the courtyard.

Gideon came out of the palace gate into the street, overhead, the clouds not so wispy, the sun no longer warm. He felt cold and sick. Staggering, he stopped and had to lean against a stone wall in a side alley. "How will I tell them?" He murmured, his cheek pressed into the stone. "This cannot be. All of the *Tzadikim* will die. The Greeks will take all the Pious Ones in death. They will never agree to such blasphemy. They will all die."

He pushed away from the wall. He must meet with the families. They must leave Jerusalem for the caves. They must not wait. His resolve propelled him along and he wondered if he should even tell them of the edict. Many of them did not even know what the Bacchanal was. He, of course, had never seen one, unless one could count Menelaus' annunciation of the previous year. He stopped and closed his eyes against the horrific vision of the prostitutes, the swine on the altar.

* * * * *

Hezekiah had not been able to concentrate on the copywork during his father's absence. He spent most of the time pacing, arranging and rearranging the writing reeds, blacking and parchment, not using any of them, his nerves spiking. When he heard the door open, he stopped. "Father," he said. Gideon's ashen face stunned him, and he knew. "It is bad news."

Moving about the room, Gideon seemed to be gathering, inventorying. He also muttered from item to item, until he could ignore the persistence of Hezekiah's questioning no longer.

"We must leave Jerusalem," Gideon said.

Hezekiah took his father's arm to stop his random movements. "Father," he said, forcing Gideon to look at him. "You must tell me what happened."

On the nearest table, Gideon dropped the detritus that he had been collecting and slumped into a chair. He leaned on the table with his elbow and buried his face in one hand.

Hezekiah watched his father sob for a few moments, then sat next to him and said, "Father, it will be all right. We are leaving for the caves next week."

Gideon raised his old, tear-stained face to his son and said, "We cannot wait. We must assemble our people and leave today, tomorrow at the very latest." He wiped his eyes with both hands, despair settling over his weary body, and said, "Antiochus has decreed that we participate in the Bacchanalia. Our people must fully engage in the festivities, or they will be put to death."

Hezekiah knew enough Hellenized Jews in Jerusalem to know what a Bacchanal was. His mouth gaped, slack with horror. This was even worse than the abomination of desolation. It was one thing to defile a structure, even a temple; it was another and more serious matter to defile one's body. That was what the Bacchanalia was all about, the debauching of body, spirit, soul and everything else that made a righteous, pious man. "What do you want me to do, Father?" He asked.

"You must spread the word for the heads of households to come to me. I will inform them of the edict and of our revised departure plans. I believe that most of them are almost ready. If it is a matter of some families not having foodstuffs for the journey, there are many of us who have an excess that we can share. Now go, Son. Tell them to hurry. In all things they must hurry."

Hezekiah embraced his father and hurried out into the Jewish Quarter to gather the men.

Chapter Five

Gophna, Judaea   The 18th day of *Adar II* 3594 (March 16th 166 B.C.E.)

J udah said, "You spend so much time watching her," Quietly, he had approached Eleazar from behind. "Why not speak to her?"

Eleazar did not even turn to look at Judah. He had been leaning idly on his axe amid his chore of wood chopping and resumed at once. "The chopping block is here," he said, "the shearing tent is there. It is not your business."

"One of my fighters is distracted. That is my business." Judah turned his gaze to the raggedy tent used for processing the sheep, catching Shoshanna's eye. She looked away in embarrassment, resuming the frenetic clapping of the wool cards, ignoring Judah's scrutiny. He watched Shoshanna for a moment and listened to his brother's axe strokes bite into the block, the rived logs shearing off on either side.

Now she was laughing with the other women as she worked the serrated blocks against each other to thin out the fleecy residue of shearing. Her face was animated and happy at the moment, but there was still a shadow of sadness that often fleeted across her features. Even amid the laughter, Judah could see trauma in her face. Aloud he said, "She is still lovely."

Eleazar did not answer and Judah could tell that he wished to be alone, but he felt rather impish at the moment. He wanted to goad Eleazar into a reaction about his betrothed—for that is what she still was—even though his elder brother was shunning the woman.

"Well, perhaps if you do not want her, Asher will step up. He has always been rather interested in Shoshanna. Now that he is one of us, perhaps Esther the matchmaker will make a contract, since," Judah said, toeing the dust, his face a mask of innocence, "you do not wish to take her to your marriage bed."

If Judah wished a reaction, it was the right thing to say. Eleazar bellowed and dove at his younger brother who stepped aside, using his attacker's blind rage against him. Eleazar plunged into the dust at Judah's feet to the delight of all the female onlookers in the shearing and carding area, except Shoshanna. She, unlike the others, turned her head aside as if to avoid becoming a voyeur to an intimate family argument. She was fully aware of the reason for the fight, and although she was indirectly involved, it seemed indecent to view Eleazar's inner turmoil so exposed.

Judah was not angry, but knew he needed to put a stop to Eleazar's moon calving over Shoshanna. He pulled his brother from the ground and shook him. "I am weary of your attacking me every time I bring up her name. This is getting ridiculous. I have the Greeks to fight—I do not want to fight you, too. This is for your own good!"

After hitting Eleazar once in the jaw to stun him, Judah dragged his brother behind a copse of Cedars and left him there.

The women saw Judah emerge from the copse and move toward them. Shoshanna stood, making her way toward Judah. The other women watched her go, their amusement in the fight having dwindled after Judah hit Eleazar. They whispered together, scandalized at the violence, and wondered aloud to each other why Shoshanna was going to Judah and what she was going to say to him. What they saw next made them all gasp as one. They watched in horror as Shoshanna, a woman, lifted her hand against a man, and not just any man, but against Judah the Maccabee, the commander.

Judah parried Shoshanna's slap by simply grabbing her wrist. He then commenced to drag her behind the copse of trees as well. The women rose at this spectacle and yelled shrill and self-righteous catcalls at the boorish behavior, urging Judah to stop or "They were going to tell his father—and his mother."

Judah heard none of the rebukes, however. The blood pounding in his ears reduced the civilized speech he had in his head into a rant.

Thrusting Shoshanna at Eleazar, Judah said, "I will stand for no more of this ridiculous behavior from you two." At Shoshanna's expression of outrage, Judah amended, "Well, not you." He nodded toward Eleazar, "But, this great oaf, here! Do not glare at me, Oaf!"

Eleazar tried to scramble to his feet at this affront, but Judah simply kicked him in the chest so that his brother fell on his back. The displacement of dust from Eleazar's undignified landing made them all cough.

"What do you mean by ignoring this woman? She is my sister! Maybe not officially because of your immature behavior, but she is the only sister I have ever known." Judah strode back and forth, his feigned anger now becoming real as he verbalized Shoshanna's ill treatment. "So perhaps she was used by the infidel Greek!" He paused at Eleazar's gasp but went on, "Could she help that? Are you, are we as a village, going to make her a victim again?" Judah walked threateningly up to Eleazar, splayed in the spent needles of the cedar that loomed over him, and kicked him hard in the arch of the foot. "Yes, yes, I've heard the elders talking—that they do not know what to do with her. That perhaps she is defiled, that perhaps you should take another.

Well, I am the commander of this camp and I command you two to honor your betrothal contract. I do not care what anybody else says."

He stopped when he heard weeping. Shoshanna was sitting, hunched into herself, her arms wrapped around her knees. She rocked softly, having drawn her head covering over her face.

Abashed, yet fascinated, Judah watched her uncontrolled sobbing and felt ashamed. Who was he to dredge up the horrors she had experienced? Who was he to tell her and Eleazar what to do in this intricate and complicated matter of their relationship? He backed away and fiddled with the corner of his head covering, not knowing what else to do.

Eleazar got to his feet and after shooting Judah a look of revulsion, he edged his way over to the weeping woman. "Shoshanna," he said. "Shoshanna."

Shoshanna's face appeared from beneath her head shawl, her eyes illumined with tears. "Eleazar."

It was enough. Eleazar put his arms around his betrothed, sat next to Shoshanna in the dust and rocked with her. Tears coursed their way down his face in concert with her renewed sobbing and the two buried themselves in each other in a fervent embrace, then a kiss.

Judah reeled from surprise, having thought that he had made a terrible mistake in attempting to stage this reconciliation. Luckily the attempt had not gone as awry as he feared, and he thought as he crept away, May all my conquests, however clumsy, end like this one. He turned and watched the kiss for another moment, then smiling, considering, decided to go see what Miriam was up to.

Chapter Six

Jerusalem, Judaea   The 19th day of *Adar II* 3594 (March 16th 166 B.C.E.)

E phraim had removed his sandals, silencing his feet as he sought out the last families. Hezekiah had given him the assignment to tell those nearest the Greek quarter of Gideon's planned march next nightfall and of Antiochus' edict about the Bacchanalia. He willed his eyes to widen so his sight could drink in as much light from the sinking moon as possible. But the persistent black of the night assailed his vision, and his feet were getting cold as he padded along on the ice-cold cobbles. Winter was moving along, but the cold, dark season had not yet fully yielded to spring.

Finally, his last whispered message having been delivered to the Bar Moshe's, he eased his gait into a more relaxed stroll, thinking to preserve his strength for the march tomorrow night. The caves were not that far away, perhaps half a day's journey, but there was much to carry in the way of supplies that would make the trek even more arduous. They had been instructed not to use carts and they would not be allowed to bring animals; they would be their own beasts. High Priest Gideon wanted them to avoid Greek eyes as they escaped Jerusalem, a difficult proposition at best—with the noise of carts and animals, impossible.

A sudden burst of clattering impelled Ephraim to ally himself with the stone wall of the alley he was navigating toward his uncle's house. A Greek patrol had rounded the corner ahead of him and the thuds of their synchronized marching echoed around the niche in which he was hiding. Frozen in fear, he considered his situation. If he ran, there was a chance he could get away from them in one of the many incongruities of roads and alleys that was Jerusalem. However, if they caught him out on the streets this late at night flouting the Greek curfew law it would go very badly for him. The patrol would take him to the barracks, and he would probably never be heard from again. Not only that, if they tortured him, they may be able to extract information about the departure plan of those who were heading for the caves tomorrow night.

The patrol's insistent feet were nearing, and he did not know what to do until they were only cubits from him. Suddenly, an impossible alternative presented itself among his choices and he quickly acted upon it.

"Sirs! Sirs!" He yelled, rushing at the patrol.

Immediately, they stopped and spread out in a defensive formation, drawing their swords and holding aloft their shields. The leader bellowed, "Halt, you! Stand aside!"

"Sirs! I saw them! Insurgents are lying in wait up yonder!" Ephraim gabbled in excitement, making up the tale as he went. He then lowered his voice to a whisper. "They are planning to attack any patrol that comes this way."

The leader of the patrol barked an order to two of his men. "Timon! And you, Hipponax! Lead the men on and foil the attack, if there is one," he said, a cynical note directed at Ephraim. "You, Telemon, take this Jew back to the barracks for questioning."

"But I am a loyal subject of Antiochus!" Ephraim protested. "I follow the Greek way!"

"Not a likely story, Jew," The leader said. "For that is what you are. You are not dressed like a Greek."

"My father makes me dress like this!" Ephraim retorted as the patrol moved down the alley toward the phantom insurgents.

The leader did not answer as he and his men trotted away.

Telemon said, "Come on, you," disappointment in his voice at being left behind with the prisoner. He still had his sword drawn and waved it in the direction of the barracks, the opposite direction of Ephraim's uncle's dwelling. "Go ahead of me—that way."

As Ephraim scurried out of the sword's reach ahead of his captor, his mind was working a little more fluidly than it was a moment before when he first saw the patrol. He was proud of himself for increasing his odds of escape. Yet, he was no warrior and suddenly he wished that he had kept up on the training that Judah had initiated in Modiin a lifetime ago. He decided to attempt conversation with the Greek.

"Telemon, is it?"

"Quiet!"

"I was just going to ask you, sir, from where do you hail?"

Ephraim felt the sword prick the flesh of his back through his robe as Telemon said, "If you do not hold your tongue, I will cut it out, Jew! Now be still."

Ephraim forsook the conversational approach and tripped instead. The sprawl was complete. "Sorry! he said and slowly rose to his feet. On his way to regaining an upright stance, he ducked under the Greek's sword, launching himself at the soldier's midsection.

An involuntary grunt accompanied the Greek's loss of balance and the two men's feet caught against a stone kennel whereupon they both smashed into the alley's wall. Ephraim hit his forehead, but it was only a glancing blow compared to the full force with which the back of the Greek's helmet connected with the stone. Shots of light darted through Ephraim's vision, but he was able to struggle back to his feet. The Greek groaned weakly only for a moment before he faded into unconsciousness as a result of horrific jarring of his helmet and head meeting the unyielding street.

As he retreated, Ephraim whispered, "I am sorry, Telamon. But thanks be to G-d that I escaped you." He hurried off into the night, careful to vary his way from that of the patrol seeking the phantom insurgents.

Chapter Seven

Jerusalem, Judaea   The 20th day of *Adar II* 3594 (March 17th 166 B.C.E.)

Apollonius carefully edged along the huge stones that formed the tower core of the Akra. The outside ramp was taking shape and he marveled at its workmanship, the stones impossibly smooth under his ascending feet, but the outside stone railing still existed only as a draft on the head mason's building plan. The mason, who was accompanying the general during his inspection, gestured with rough hands at the workings of the pulleys hefting the huge blocks of stone to the Akra's present height of forty-five cubits.

Apollonius kept his back pressed against the comforting stone of the tower core and looked over the vista before him that stretched to the north of Jerusalem. His heart blanched a little when he realized how like home the topography here was. The hills were covered with the same green scrub as Carrhae. Arid, its shabby foliage elegant in its scarcity, this desert landscape could be the very view from the front door of his estate. He sighed and his mind thought on his wife managing the planting of the spring wheat. Would she contract with his favorite seed broker to get the best price? While he was ruminating on his future harvest two thousand furlongs away, his eye caught a distant glint undulating on one of the mounds of desert green north of the city. A few, then many edged into his vision and he remembered that his scouts had told him that Timotheus was to arrive at the Jerusalem barracks the next few days.

Apollonius dismissed the mason and hurried down the ramp, finding it difficult to keep his eyes off the vista. He thought of his sons, still away keeping order in Egypt, and hoped they were well. Perhaps he should bring them to Judaea to serve with him, then realized that the only reason he was in this corner of the kingdom was that

Judah the Hammer

Antiochus had ordered it. Perhaps he was getting too used to being in this backwater of a country that was full of unenlightened rebels. No, he would not bring his sons here.

It seemed that he had not been the only one to notice the return of Timotheus' cohorts, for there was a general hubbub both out on the parade grounds and in the corridors outside his temporary office. "Bring Philo to me," he said to one of his lieutenants who was hovering near his desk. "Gather the dispatches for Timotheus," he said to another. "I want to give them to him as soon as he arrives. Also, call the clerk so he can log the report during Timotheus' debriefing."

Apollonius sat back in Commander Philo's chair and barked one of his knees under the desk. The desk was too small for his large build, but he needed a center of operations while he was here in Jerusalem. Not only did he have to prepare the campaign against Gophna now that Timotheus had utterly failed in his campaign, but he must also now enforce Antiochus' edict that the Jews observe the Bacchanal. Philo had graciously agreed to move to his second's desk, thus starting a displacement ripple throughout the barracks. Apollonius nonchalantly rubbed his knee. As he watched the lieutenants clatter off to expedite his orders, he stood to fetch another missive that he had placed on a chair against the wall. When he sat back down, he banged his knee again.

"Zeus! Antiochus and Epiphanes!" He said, the epithet bouncing off the stone walls of the inner barracks. "I do not care if I am only going to be here for a while. I am going to commission a new desk." At that moment Philo walked in.

"General Apollonius, you sent for me?" The amused smile on Commander Philo's face indicated that he had heard the general's interesting profanity the moment before.

"Yes, Commander," Apollonius said, keeping his features firm. "Timotheus and his cohorts are outside Jerusalem. I would like the palace cohorts to turn out and welcome him properly."

"What do you mean, 'properly,'?" Philo asked slyly.

"I mean," Apollonius said, trying to keep the dark glee out of his voice, "a welcome fit for a commander who loses 500 of his men without killing or capturing even one of the enemy."

Philo considered this, then said, "Yes, I understand. I will see to it, General. It will be a most fitting welcome."

Apollonius again sat back in his chair at Philo's knowing grin, but did not acknowledge it with one of his own. As he watched the other general's curt exit, he leaned back, the desk assaulting his knee again. He confined his reaction to a ragged sigh but cheered up at the thought of whetting Timotheus' troops against the Jerusalem pacifists. Even though the Gophna Jews had given the fool and his men a thorough drubbing up north, after Timotheus had been treated to an appropriate 'welcome', he would be even more effective against the Jews who had fled Jerusalem.

"Nicanor will be pleased," He said aloud listening to his voice echo against the stone of Philo's office, then went on with his thoughts. I wonder if Menelaus has a new report on the pacifists' movements. Was not there something about their fleeing to caves— where——in the Kidron? I shall have to speak to the high priest soon.

21

Apollonius bellowed for his slave, "Demos! I hunger. Bring me food."

Chapter Eight

The Road from Gophna to Lydda, Judaca   The 22nd day of *Adar II* 3594 (March 19th 166 B.C.E.)

J udah had not been out of the hills for many weeks and the heady freedom that always accompanied him when he was mounted on his beloved *Tiklit* was not diminished this day. If anything, it was more pronounced, and he had to restrain himself from removing his head covering to lay his head bare to the wind. Eleazar raced alongside him on *Bakayan*, and as the two horses plummeted down the road to Lydda, Judah could almost imagine that he was still a simple blacksmith apprentice in Modiin, not the commander of a growing rebellion, and that he and Eleazar were embarking on a simple visit to a relative.

As the familiar outskirts of Lydda appeared ahead of them, however, he was reminded of the realities of their present existence. Greek soldiers had set up a barricade about twenty cubits away just outside their Cousin Benyamin's house and were detaining travelers entering Lydda for questioning. A small crowd of men, women and a few children now lounged at the side of the road awaiting their interview with the Greek soldiers.

Judah reined up on *Tiklit* immediately, and Eleazar did the same. The two sat and stared at the scene.

"I did not expect this," Eleazar breathed. "What do you think is going on? I thought only we in the hills were at war. Has it spread?"

While he had been isolated in Gophna, his head full of war and strategy, Judah had not given much thought to what was happening in the rest of Judaea. He had been so intent in harassing the Greeks encamped in the valley below their hills that he had not considered what was happening to his countrymen. Oh, he had heard some reports from refugees that had gathered to their hills, but he felt a little ashamed at his myopia regarding their lot. He discovered from these reports that the rest of the Jews were suffering privations just as he and his people were, but they did not have the benefit of hill ridges to shield them. As he gazed at the crowd, he was sure that the barricade up ahead was only a small measure of what his fellows were enduring. There were things much worse than being detained while traveling.

Eleazar said, "Do you think we had anything to do with this?"

Judah scoffed, "What? Our stand in Gophna? Do not be ridiculous. I doubt anyone knows about that, here. This is Lydda, a Greek center. No one has heard of our little rebellion."

"Well," Eleazar said as he yanked *Bakayan* up into the scrub at the side of the road, we obviously cannot go that way. I know a path that leads behind those trees that we can use to get to Cousin Benyamin's house."

The two had to lean low over the saddles to get through the trees. Judah tried not to curse when a particularly weighty branch almost knocked him from his mount. At last, they saw Benyamin's sheep enclosure and guided their mounts to the horse stalls beside them.

"Look, there is Cousin Anna," Judah whispered as they dismounted. "Let us scare her!"

"With the soldiers so close? No, Judah," Eleazar urged. "That is not wise!"

But Judah was already making his stealthy approach toward his portly cousin. He liked many things about Anna, her cooking, her sense of humor, but his favorite trait was her skittish nature—she scared well. He edged along the house until he was almost close enough to scatter the chickens she was feeding. Suddenly, a massive Greek soldier emerged from around the house. He was holding a ladle full of water from his cousin's well at the front of the house.

His and Judah's eyes met and they both froze. Cousin Anna was crouched against the house retrieving some firewood and slowly looked up. She did not seem shocked at the Greek soldier's presence at her front door; however, when she followed the Greek soldier's eyes and saw Judah, a scream appeared on her face but did not sound. She backed away from the two men until her ample body had nowhere to go, wedged as it was against the side of her house.

The soldier threw aside the ladle and drew his sword. "This must be the Maccabee." He circled to the left of Judah. "So, Jew. Have you come a-visiting your lovely cousin here?"

Judah felt like looking around at Eleazar in his confusion but dared not draw his gaze from the soldier. How did this Greek know his name? Then it came to him. This Greek outside his cousin's house was here because him. The thoughts spun through his head as he tried to make sense of this situation. Eleazar was right—the news of the rebellion must have spread, and the Greeks had positioned guards at his cousin's house thinking he would eventually come to visit. As implausible as that thought seemed even as it streamed across his mind, he could think of no other reason for this soldier's familiarity with the name, "The Maccabee."

His training and strategizing did not allow him to reply to the Greek's taunt. At all costs this soldier must be subdued, and quickly, or he would alert his companions that must be in and around Benyamin's house. Faster than thought, Judah shot across the yard, scattering the cackling chickens, even kicking one so that it flew in an explosion of feathers and squawks at the soldier's face. His legs propelled him off the ground in a massive spring. Airborne, he found a strange moment when he as looking down into the Greek's face: bald surprise lined the soldier's features. Even in the blur of the event, Judah realized that this surprise was the reason the soldier had not responded. He had not moved a muscle from the time Judah began the charge. Thought did not stop Judah, however, and he plunged his sword downward into the neck of the soldier, killing the Greek where he stood. The next instant he was beside his aunt, holding her mouth to keep the scream inside her throat. She had been valiantly quiet up to this point, but Judah did not want to press his luck.

Suddenly another person emerged from around the front of the house from where the Greek had come and Judah looked up, ready to react again. It was only Eleazar, his sword drawn, eyes wild.

"Cousin," Judah whispered to the woman, whose terrified eyes were unblinking above his hand, "are there others?" She nodded. "Are you all right?" She nodded again.

Anna pulled Judah's hand away and said softly, "We do not allow them in the house, but they use our well when they thirst. Hurry in! There you will be safe!"

"First, we must attend to him," Judah said, glancing at the corpse.

"Throw him in those tall weeds over there. You can bury him tonight in the coop," Anna whispered. "They will not start looking for him until tomorrow morning. They often escape their posts to go drinking and whor—er, I mean other things, in Lydda."

Judah and Eleazar looked at her in surprise. To hear their gentle aunt refer to whoring (although she had stopped herself from completing the utterance) and make such a matter-of-fact suggestion about the disposing of the body lying at her feet in her chicken enclosure tested their reason.

She saw their startled faces and smiled. "You, Judah the Maccabee, are not the only rebel in Judaea!"

Judah said urgently, "Yes, Cousin! That is what I want to ask you. We had no idea that people knew—"

"Tend to the body," Anna interrupted, "then we will talk. I will watch to make sure no more Greeks approach. Hurry!" She hissed at their hesitant faces as she took up a vantage at the corner of the house. "We shall also have to think up a story when his comrades come asking about him."

Judah and Eleazar looked at each other, shrugged, and with difficulty hefted the body, Judah at the head and Eleazar at the feet, and bore it in the direction of the weeds

When they finally entered the house, Anna said authoritatively, "Sit and rest. Benyamin will not be home for many hours."

"Cousin—" Judah began as she poured a gourd of water over his and Eleazar's hands. The liquid that collected in the earthen bowl was red with blood.

"Here is a cloth. Eat first, then talk," Anna said, then pulled at the neck of Judah's tunic. "See, you have blood on you," she clucked. "Give me your tunic so I can wash it out. I'll give you one of Benyamin's. You do not want to appear in town like that."

"How did you know I want to appear in town?" Judah asked, bemused.

"Well, don't you?"

"Yes," Judah said uncertainly. "But I do not know exactly how to—"

"Eat!" she repeated. "Then talk."

Obediently, Judah and Eleazar tore at the bread and mutton she had placed before them. Anna brought the clean tunic, withdrew for a moment so Judah could change then sat down at the table.

She watched them, satisfaction on her face. "It is lucky we slaughtered that old ewe yesterday," Anna said. "The Lord G-d of Hosts knew you were coming. We have not killed a sheep for months and months."

Finally, when the two men could eat no more, they sat back and looked at Cousin Anna expectantly.

"Yes, now we can talk," she said. "You were asking—"

"So, you have heard about our doings in the hills of Gophna?" Eleazar said, sucking meat juice off his fingers.

"We hear of almost nothing else. *Maccabee* this, *Maccabee* that. You have made quite a stir with your exploits." As she cleared the wooden plates, she *tsked* happily, "Imagine repelling that immense Greek army and not one of your men perishing in the process."

"You know about that?" Judah asked. "We did not know that word was getting out."

"Yes. In fact," Anna said as she cleared the rest of the table, "These Greek soldiers are part of that army. General Timotheus left them behind. Spies must have studied our town and found out that we are your cousins." Anger filled her voice. "Likely one of those filthy apostates who left our congregation told them. They will pay," she added grimly.

Again, Judah and Eleazar looked at each other. This was not the gentle Cousin Anna that they remembered. She was the one at the family gatherings who quailed with revulsion during a sacrifice for worship or a slaughter for a meal. An adept peacemaker, she could always break up arguments and outright battles with her gentle entreaties of reason. Now she had more the qualities of the Amazons that Asher often spoke of in the heathen mythologies. Gentle Anna had turned into a warrior.

The front door slowly opened. Judah and Eleazar jumped to their feet, their hands going to their sword hilts. The creased worry on Anna's face relaxed when Benyamin entered.

"Husband, you are home early," Anna said with relief and rushed to embrace him. "See who is here!"

"Judah! Eleazar!" Benyamin removed his cloak and sat down beside them on the rugs, pushing the cushions aside. "But how did you get past the Greeks?" He thumbed outside.

"Judah cut his way through them, or, at least, one of them," Anna said proudly.

Benyamin stared at his wife, then at the two men. "Explain," he said.

Benyamin's eyes reflected his grim delight when told of Judah's dispatch of the Greek soldier. Anxiety replaced it when he asked, "But, what is your plan? They are here looking for you."

"Never mind that, Cousin," Judah said. "I want to know what the people are saying. I want to know who will stand with us, if any."

"Oh, there are many who will stand with you," Benyamin said. "Many are already conducting raids against the Greeks stationed here, harassing them, killing them when they can."

"What about those who flout the Law?" Judah asked.

"There are many of those as well. They are almost all on the Greek side of Lydda now. None of them attend synagogue anymore," he said sadly. He pulled his head covering down slightly almost as if mourning. Judah knew that Benyamin would take the defection of the congregation almost as badly as the high priest, as he was the caretaker of the synagogue. He sat up, however, pride on his face and said, "But you Judah, you are famous here. Refugees both from Modiin and Beit Ur have been coming here for months and many have relatives up in Gophna. One mother I spoke with just today has a son who is fighting with you. They are from Beit Ur."

"I am just getting to know the fighters from that village. What is his name?"

"Moshe Bar Levi."

"I do not know him, yet," Judah said regretfully. "But most of them have the beginnings of being good fighters."

Benyamin went on, "And the southern ridge assault where you smashed the Greeks with rocks and arrows—well, people are rallying to the rebellion because of these stories. The conversion of Eupolemus back to our ways is a favorite, and I am happy to say that some have come back to the congregation because of his return."

Judah and Eleazar's features alternated between disbelief and joy at the news of their notoriety. It was a good feeling to know that they were not alone in their fight.

"Nu, Judah," Benyamin continued, "Why are you here? What can I do to help? And, there are many others who would be honored to further the cause of the Maccabee."

"I need to speak to the community," said Judah. "I need to warn them that the time for infidelity to the Law is past."

"I doubt that the infidels will gather to hear you," Benyamin said, shaking his head. "A few may come out of curiosity, but the great bulk will be people who are already true to the Law."

"I expected that," Judah said, leaning forward eagerly. "But if I know our people, they will make sure that the apostates get the message."

"And, what would that message be?" Benyamin ventured. "What are you planning to do?"

Judah hesitated for a moment and looked over at Eleazar who had his head down. He and his men had discussed this issue over and over, but that did not mean it made it any easier to verbalize the plan. "We are planning to do as Yehoshua of old. We will cleanse Lydda."

Benyamin stood and looked at Anna, whose face had turned ashen. "What do you mean?" He asked, although by the look on his face, Judah knew he fully understood what he meant. Every Jew knew the story of Yehoshua and his utter destruction of the city of Jericho. Every Jew also knew that the Lord had commanded Yehoshua to destroy every man, woman, child and beast within its walls.

"I mean that the only people left living in Lydda will be those who will live by the Law. The rest will die by the Law."

Benyamin and Anna were silent. He stroked his beard; she stood and moved to put away the kitchen things.

"There is precedent," Eleazar finally said. "The Lord often demands a cleansing. There is not only Yehoshua and Jericho. Think of Ashdod's demise after their theft of the Ark and the Covenant. Think of Gideon's destruction of Midian."

Benyamin moved to his wife's side and clutched her arm. "What about the children?"

Judah paused, then said, "The parents are responsible for what happens to their children. Their decision will determine whether their lineage will continue. I will warn them; that is all."

"Judah," Benyamin said. "Judah, you cannot mean this. Surely the Lord does not intend this! The children?"

"Cousin, it is indeed harsh, but the Lord G-d is harsh with those who will not believe. And he will be harsh with those who molest and murder the Children of Israel. I am but his instrument. They will have ample warning." Judah stood and walked to where his cousins stood and put his hand on Benyamin's shoulder. "I will give them every chance to come back. They will even have time to flee if that is what they wish. But Lydda will be a stronghold for those who follow the Lord." He patted Benyamin's shoulder and said, "And *only* for those who follow the Lord. Now gather the people in the synagogue. I would speak to them."

Chapter Nine

Jerusalem, Judaea   The 23rd day of *Adar II* 3594 (March 20th 166 B.C.E.)

T he flying vegetables and filth were as thick as migrating birds as Timotheus and his troops marched into Jerusalem. The ringing catcalls berating their lineage and skill were impossibly cruel. From two miles outside of the Jerusalem gate, the Palace Guard had formed as spectators to the disgraced cohort and filled the air with derision as befitted those who had been beaten by mere Jews. Timotheus and his men stayed ramrod straight in their saddles amid the missiles of refuse; for all the grudging respect this demeanor inspired, it was not enough to mitigate what became known as the "Gophna Debacle."

As Apollonius watched the parade of disgrace, he smiled grimly. Timotheus and his men would need an outlet for the fury and shame they were now experiencing at the hands of their comrades. What better target for their venting than the Jews down in the caves of Kidron? Reports were reaching him of their migration and his scouts said that the Jews were well ensconced in their refuge of natural stone. The red faces of Timotheus' marching cohorts told him that they were becoming sufficiently whetted for blood, especially Jewish blood.

The march finally ended with the cohorts filing in and forming endless rows on the parade ground before the barracks. They stood, still ramrod straight, their horses having been taken away by slaves to the stables.

Apollonius ascended the wooden platform outside the entrance to the barracks and looked out over the mortified cohort.

"So, the Jews gave you a drubbing," Apollonius shouted, derision flattening out his voice, which nevertheless carried to every member of the cohort. "It is good that our beloved emperor is not here, for oh, what would come of your failure? Can such inferiority be allowed to continue? I feel we must thin out the ranks of such a band of misfits and sluggards."

He watched the men carefully. For all his derogation, admiration filled him that not one of them blanched; not one of them did so much as glance at his neighbor. They stood and bore the weight of his invective.

"And the Jews," he spat, immediately quelling his admiration for them. "It was the bastard Jews who bested you. They are a race that has not risen from the dust of tyranny for centuries. They are a race that has been carried away into captivity again and again by nations far less civilized than we. What, are the Jews not subject to our emperor? What, are the Jews allowed to flout His law with impunity?" Apollonius paused, his chin on his chest as he considered, his mouth working its grim line as he thought. "I have heard reports that many of you feel that Ares forsook you." He went on, "that you feel the God of War was with the Jews." Apollonius brought up his hands in entreaty. "Is it possible? Have you so lowered yourselves that you consign your gods to the enemy?" He glowered in revulsion.

It was then that Apollonius noticed a slight vapor of movement through the stalks of men. He stayed silent and even turned to Philo, engaging him in a token conversation so that the men would not feel his furious eye on them. He wanted them to ruminate and even agitate on his words. The vapor soon erupted into murmured protest and he turned his eye on them, at which moment the men quieted.

"Perhaps you think I am too harsh?"

Cries of "No, No!" erupted throughout the ranks, the soldiers knocking the air above them with their protesting fists. Apollonius did not allow himself to smile although the soldiers were delighting him with their predictability. It was when he started hearing, "What can we do? How can we atone?" that he permitted a slight arc to form on his lips and held up his hands to quiet them.

"The Jews," Apollonius said, "are attempting to flout an edict of our beloved emperor once again. It was not enough that they cling to this bastard religion of theirs, eschewing the brightness and glory of our gods for their dark and solemn Jehovah, but now they are even refusing to celebrate the festival of our great God Bacchus."

The men shifted and murmured, digesting this impossibility.

"Therefore, you will join the palace cohorts in rooting out those Jews who resist participation in the Bacchanal, meting out a punishment that befits sacrilege against Bacchus and the One True God, Epiphanes."

Nodding and loosening their bodies in their approval at Apollonius' command, the men's faces, though grim, reflected cheer.

"Further, General Timotheus, who, I am sure, is anxious to show that his men can still dispatch unruly Jews, will take the Second, Fourth and Seventh Cohorts down to the valley Kidron where there is a network of caves. Many Jews from Jerusalem are living in those caves, hiding from their responsibilities here in Jerusalem. Timotheus will teach these Jews a lesson of obedience to their emperor. That lesson, I am sure, will not be lost upon those Jews who remain in Jerusalem for us to rule. General

Timotheus, do you accept this assignment?" At Timotheus pious nod, he said, "And do your men accept?"

The tumult released by these words of Apollonius swirled into the air. Apollonius bowed slightly. He left the platform and entered the barracks followed by Philo.

Apollonius sauntered into his office and sat down. This time, however, he anticipated the puny depth of the desk and avoided bumping his knee. Although Philo was silent all the way into the office, Apollonius knew the commander well enough to see that he was anxious to speak regarding the command he had just given to the Timotheus' cohorts.

After hunching over some of the requisitions and reports on the desk, he glanced up at Philo and said, "Well, out with it. You disapprove of my command?"

Philo puffed himself out in protest and said, "I would not say that, General—"

"Philo, Philo. Candor, please. I do not have time for a coy display. As you can see, I have much work to do. And the sooner I complete it, the sooner you will get your desk back and I can return to my *kotaikai* in Samaria."

"Very well," Philo said uneasily. "I question the deploying of so many cohorts to deal with a few pacifists in a cave. One could dispatch a thousand Jews in a cave with fifty men. I wonder at the superfluity."

"It is simple, Philo," Apollonius said as he pressed his seal into one wax tablet after another. "Timotheus and his men are valuable as military servants to the empire. I do not want to shame them too much. They, of course, made a royal botch of the affair in the north, but that does not mean I want to grind them up. Give them some Hebrew blood to drink; that is what I say. A nice slaughter does a man good once in a while. These men need it."

Philo nodded as if this made sense then said, "But the men, will they not feel it is beneath them?"

"They will not care. They want to kill Jews. They are good men and feel that they have let us down. I want to give them the opportunity to make things right, and if all that takes are the head of a few Jews on pikes, what is that to me? We will send them out tomorrow."

"I suspect that they are ready to go right now. You made them thirst for Hebrew blood; perhaps they should march immediately," said Philo.

"Nonsense. They need food and a day's rest. I am not inhuman, after all."

Philo, bowed and turned to leave, but Apollonius said, "One more thing, Philo."

"Yes, General?"

"I want ten patrols formed to help keep rebel activities in the north to a minimum. The patrols are to man every thoroughfare and road to keep those dissident Jews up in the hills. Set up a rotation so that every three days, fresh patrols are dispatched to various destinations in the north around Gophna. Let us see how much the Jews like their beloved hills when we force them to stay wedged in their ridges. That will be all."

Apollonius, out of courtesy, watched Philo's salute and departure, then settled back into the repetition of seal against wax.

Chapter Ten

Gophna, Judaea   The 25th day of *Adar II* 3594 (March 22nd 166 B.C.E.)

J udah stood to the right of the wedding canopy, the *chuppah,* as his father intoned the *Ketubah,* the groom's contract to the bride. He bowed his head as if contemplating the stipulations of Eleazar's intent to care for and protect Shoshanna but was actually carrying on a clandestine conversation with Asher. With the imminence of Eleazar's and Shoshanna's wedding upon his return, he had not had a chance to debrief his men about his experience in Lydda.

"So, they know of us?" Asher whispered. "And Greeks are there? They were waiting for you?"

Off to the left of the *chuppah,* Hannah's eyes caught Judah's as he turned to answer Asher. Her look of reproof forced him to cast his eyes down and he did not answer.

"Well?" Asher hissed, poking him. "Tell me!"

Judah poked Asher back and jerked his head toward Hannah. Asher leaned out and earned the same look of admonishment from Judah's mother. He eased back out of the line of her sight.

Finally, Mattathias made an end, and Eleazar held up a gold coin and pressed it into Shoshanna's trembling hand.

Shoshanna closed her hand, drawing it into her chest, bowed her head and nodded, mute as brides always were under the canopy.

Silence fell on the celebrants as Mattathias read the first blessing of *Nisuin* and Judah thought back to his own wedding. He searched the ranks of women to his left and found his wife. She felt his look and joined his gaze, her eyes twinkling and a slight smile forming on her lips. I used to despise her, Judah thought as he smiled back. During a large part of his youth, for he had been thirteen when betrothed, he had cursed Esther the Matchmaker for bringing Miriam to his parents' attention. She was the daughter of the wealthiest family in Modiin, but although only twelve, already known as the village shrew. His schoolmates and brothers had made great fun of Judah when the betrothal contract had been made public. But now, he wondered at her shrewish reputation, for she was a capital wife. She was an opinionated woman, to be sure, but marriage seemed to have rounded her edges and he found her quite agreeable and warm. Asher poked Judah again. Mattathias' expectant gaze was upon his son and everyone was waiting for Judah to recite the first wedding blessing.

Judah harrumphed in embarrassment and intoned, somewhat shakily at first, "Blessed art Thou Lord our G-d, King of the Universe, who created all things for . . ."

As Judah finished the recitation and Mordechai Baruch began the second blessing, Judah wished he could pound Asher to get him to stop his silly sniggering. Asher was finding great sport in Judah's forgetfulness and wandering attention. As it was, Judah had no choice but to stand with as much dignity as possible hoping that Asher would quiet down. As the third, fourth, fifth and sixth blessing were read, he also prayed that Asher would not trouble this wedding of his brother and Shoshanna as he did the wedding at Modiin the year before.

"I hope you do not try to dance with any of the girls this time," he said under his breath to Asher after the seventh blessing had been recited by Avram the blacksmith. "It almost got you killed last year."

"I will not sully this day," Asher murmured back. "I am no longer infidel, and besides that, I don't want to be stoned. But, look at them, Judah! Finally, some happiness for our Shoshanna and Eleazar."

Judah watched Asher's face carefully and to his relief, saw only a modicum of wistfulness there. There would be no scandalous behavior from him today. "Yes," Judah said, "They seem happy."

And indeed, the faces of the groom and bride, as they sheepishly led each other into the small tent for their *Yichud* or seclusion that was set up next to the *chuppah*, exuded joy and a little embarrassment. Shoshanna's discomfiture was not apparent because of the veil covering her face, but Eleazar's face was alight with a blush under his bearded cheeks. They disappeared into the tent for their first few wedded moments together while the women of the wedding party dashed about to lay the wedding tables with feast and wine.

Asher pulled Judah aside for a serious talk. "Now you must tell me. With all the wedding preparation, I have not had a chance to talk to you of Lydda. Were the people receptive?"

Judah reached for a fig on the wedding table, his mother swatting away his hand as she hurried by with a vessel of wine.

"Wait for the couple," she said. "It will not be long. That goes for you, too, Asher."

Asher said, his smile impish, "Yes, Aunt Hannah." She swept away and he reached for a fig as well. "Well? Judah. The people?"

"The congregation was very receptive. But the devout were the only ones there. I do not know how the rest of the city will react to the news." The residual smile directed at his mother a few moments before disappeared and he said, "I am afraid, brother, that many will have to die."

Asher did not speak for many moments and finally said, "I will follow you, Judah Maccabeus. But this is a terrible thing that you ask of me."

"It will not be easy for any of us," Judah answered. "We do not know what horrors we will be forced into that day we ride into Lydda. All I know is that it is necessary. And I know that—"Judah hesitated on his next utterance, "The Lord commanded it."

Asher's reaction was exactly as Judah expected. "The Lord? He speaks to you? So, you are not only our commander, but our prophet as well? How can the Lord want us to kill our own? Who appointed you prophet?" His voice rose, "Who ordained you Moshe? What, are you going to lead us against the Greeks for the next forty years?"

Judah took Asher's arm and led him farther away from the wedding guests, their argument starting to attract attention. "We have been through this many times, Asher," Judah growled, finally letting go of his friend when they found a secluded tree amid some large rocks. "I cannot have this argument every time we discuss Lydda. I understand everything you have said. I understand all of your objections. But you know that the Jews who follow Greek ways have polluted themselves. Either they must make themselves clean or we must cleanse them with the ultimate purge."

"That of death?" Asher said, thrusting his chest against Judah's. "And the Lord G-d said, 'Thou shalt not kill.' But he tells *you* to kill? How? When? Did you climb Sinai as Moshe did?"

"'And the Lord G-d told Moshe,'" Judah retorted, "'Thou shalt have no other gods before me.' And those who have become Greek are whoring after other gods. Asher, you are my best friend. But we have been over and over this. I do not want to discuss it again. Do what you must do. Go with us to Lydda, or stay here. You must do what you will. I know it will be difficult for you to carry out this mission against your old friends," Judah laid his hand on Asher's shoulder, "but I need you with me. However," Judah's earnest eyes pierced Asher's. "I will understand if you cannot participate. There will be no dishonor in such a case." He viced Asher's shoulder. "I mean it."

Asher disengaged from Judah's grip and paced back and forth for many moments. In concert with his harried footsteps, he exhaled, his mind doing battle with his heart. He gave up the pacing and sat down on a rock, his head in his hands. "Let me think, Judah. I need to be alone."

Judah approached Asher and gave him an awkward pat on the shoulder. "Whatever you decide will be right." He left Asher, hearing more exhalations from him as he went.

Judah plunged through the trees back to the clearing where the wedding had been set up, but something was wrong. By now, the couple should have emerged from the wedding tent and the celebration should have begun. The cheers, singing and friendly murmur that was usually present as an undercurrent in such festivities did not assault Judah's ears as he approached the strangely silent revelers. However, not all was silent. A shrill keening, muted by the folds of the wedding tent, etched into the air of the clearing.

"*Eemah*," Judah asked. "What—"

"*Shah*, it is Shoshanna," Mother said, the fingertips of her hands resting against her forehead. "She is not right."

"What do you mean?" Judah whispered. When his mother did not answer, he said solemnly, "It is the Greek, is it not? And his use of her. It has come to the marriage bed."

"Judah!" Mother said, utterly shocked at her son's bald speech. "You should not speak of such things, especially in the hearing of your mother."

"Mother, listen to her. It is hardly a secret."

The wailing in the tent intensified and no one knew what to do. They did not know if they should disperse or administer somehow to the newlyweds. The women wanted to help Shoshanna but were loath to intrude upon the intimacy of the *Yichud*. It was evident on the men's faces that they would rather face the emperor Antiochus himself than have anything to do with what was going on between Eleazar and Shoshanna.

Eleazar appeared at the door flap, his face anxious and taut. "Mother, please!"

Mother had grasped Judah's hand at an especially loud moan from Shoshanna and now disengaged her fingers from his as she rushed into the tent.

The villagers moved away from the tent but did not go near the food tables. The musicians sat idle, yet restive. A pall weighed down the celebrants until the setting was more funereal than nuptial.

Judah stood well away from the tent and felt someone enter the space beside him. It was Asher. Judah did not look at him.

"What is it?" Asher asked. "What is wrong?"

"Your precious Greeks did this to Shoshanna," Judah said quietly. "Do you hear her? It is that pig who took her by force. He ruined her for my brother. I wish he were still alive so I could kill him again."

Asher said, "Did Eleazar try to consummate?"

"I do not know," Judah said derisively, finally looking at Asher. "That is his right."

"But usually not in the tent right after the ceremony. He should have been more—"

"More what?" Judah asked. "It is his right," he repeated, but with not much conviction.

"Zeus, Judah. You are married. Did you not give Eleazar any advice on how to approach Shoshanna?"

More wails issued from the tent and Asher paused, looking down at his feet.

"Do you still wish to preserve the Greeks? Judah asked. "Do you still nurture a care for their filthy lives? Listen to her." He gritted his teeth and made a fist at his side. "My G-d, my G-d, grant that I may avenge her virtue. Killing Apelles was not enough!"

The sounds issuing from the tent were becoming more muffled and finally stopped. Judah's mother came from the tent, a tremendous weariness covering her features, and went to Mattathias. She drew him away from the crowd, both of them huddling against each other in serious discussion.

Judah, shaking, saw that the villagers were no longer silent but were starting to discuss the event. He also found that many eyes were on him, eyes that were imploring, questioning, lost.

"Judah." Asher was nudging him. "You must speak to them."

"I?" Judah asked, a little too loudly. "I—I do not know what to say to them. Why me?"

"Because you are the commander. Because you know what to do. Now go on," Asher said, giving Judah a resolute push toward the crowd. "And," he said, "because you have finally convinced me that you are right about Lydda."

Judah looked back in surprise at Asher, straightened his robe, nodded and started to form the words he would say to his people.

Chapter Eleven

The Kidron Caves of south of Jerusalem, Judaea   The 1st day of *Nisan* 3594 (March 27th 166 B.C.E.)

T he air in the cave, while cool, was gritty. The tiny particles of rock, stirred up by the occupants, invaded everything: eyes, noses, skin, clothing, food; sand swirled in the bottom of every gourd or jug.

Ephraim sat on his haunches in his small makeshift domicile in a corner of the cave and watched Deborah. She was helping her mother with the bread. They could not cook in the cave, as the fire was too greedy, robbing the human occupants of air, so makeshift ovens had been constructed of rock just outside the cave's mouth. The ovens were rather elegant as many masons had fled with the refugees. Ephraim had counted all the souls living here in the large cave and in smaller adjoining chambers and as near as he could tell, there were one thousand and twenty-six people making their unlikely home here.

Deborah's hair escaped from her head covering and she tucked it back under the cloth quickly. Every movement of her hand reminded Ephraim of the swans he had seen when he and Hezekiah had spied over one of the palace walls into Menelaus' gardens. The whiteness of her skin, its soft, downy—

Ephraim groaned and turned away. Hezekiah had tried many times to facilitate a conversation between his sister and his friend, since Deborah was not betrothed as yet, but Ephraim's clumsy rhetoric always failed him.

Once, at such a time, Hezekiah had dragged Ephraim to the ovens, ostensibly to reset a stone that had sloughed off during a rainstorm. Deborah was taking her family's turn at the oven. It had been a clear night, stars glinting in the blue-black vault above them. It was during the dark hours that the time allotments for cooking were arranged so the Greeks could not detect the smoke during the day. When the two men arrived at the ovens, Deborah had been friendly with Ephraim, eager even, until he said, "What is that smell? Whew! It smells like you are cooking a skunk. Is that kosher?"

Now, Ephraim shook his head and squinted with his whole face at the horrible memory. He looked over at her again, and ducked his head, for Deborah was striding toward him, the set of her face rather forbidding.

He looked this way and that, feeling like something hunted. She was very close; there was nowhere for him to go, so he sat and tried to assume nonchalance. He did not feel that it was working, because he was shaking.

"So, what are you looking at?"

Ephraim looked up at the girl, sweat pouring off him, though outside a cold *Nisan* had just begun. He pressed as far into the rock at his back as he could and tried to shrug but his body was too rigid. "Nothing. I—"

She looked behind her, her eyes furtive and whispered, "I would like to talk to you. Meet me at the ovens tonight. Perhaps my cooking will not smell so much like skunk."

Ephraim's face grew hot. He looked about him, dropped his eyes from hers and said, "We should not be speaking, your mother and father will be angry."

She drew away from him and said quietly, "Meet me at the ovens, at the beginning of the last watch."

Ephraim watched her go, his jaw gaping, his entire body a shudder. "This is ridiculous," he said to himself. "She is just a girl. Why does she affect me like this?"

In Modiin, he had never had this problem. He was able to talk to many of the girls and even joke with them, within the confines of religious protocol and good taste, of course. But this girl—she was different. She was very young; Did Hezekiah say she was thirteen? He was nearly twenty. His betrothal was just being arranged when the horrendous events took him from Modiin, so he was unattached. Because of the upheaval of moving from Jerusalem, he wondered if the protocols of matchmaking had been suspended. But, even if they were not, he did not know how to go about arranging a match. His father had been directing all the arrangements. His death and Ephraim's swift departure had stopped all of that.

At the thought of his father, he sank into the darkness of soul that often claimed him these days. He sat unmoving for a long time.

He must have dozed, for the cave was dark except for a few lamps pulsing their light against the walls hewn by the destructive seasons. It seemed very late; he likely had missed the meeting with Deborah. He wavered to his feet and found the mouth of the cave, careful not to disturb the sleeping forms lying about in the dust.

The women were thrusting the flats of bread into the oven with wide baking paddles. They stood around and gossiped about the day with their neighbors, their throaty rich murmurs making the night more vibrant, yet calm.

No men were about except for one old priest who stood as a guard. Ephraim nodded at him and wandered out past the ovens. He did not know what watch it was and did not feel like asking anybody, so he simply sat down and enjoyed the novelty of breathing in air that was not tinged with dust. He was almost glad he had missed the appointment.

"So, you came."

Ephraim started then forced himself to relax. Obviously, his sense of time was not as nebulous as he thought. Perhaps his inner mind did want him to keep the appointment. She is only a girl, he reminded himself. To Deborah he said only, "Yes," because that was all he could think of to say.

"I know I am not supposed to talk to a man who is not a relative," Deborah said, sitting down next to him, "but I am sick of rules and I am sick of being cooped up in such a place."

"It is for your own safety," Ephraim pointed out as he eased slightly away from her. "Jerusalem is becoming very dangerous for those who follow the Law."

"The Law, the Law. Does anybody think of anything but the Law?" Deborah said in exasperation. "I want to be out in a field—like that one yonder."

"I cannot see a field," Ephraim said.

"That is because it dark. But I know it is there. I have seen it."

"You should not be out of the cave for any reason during the day," Ephraim said, alarmed. "A report came to us yesterday that Philo and Apollonius are trying to determine our whereabouts. If they see you—"

"They will not see me," Deborah laughed. "And if they do, I will just tell them that I am Bedouin."

Ephraim laughed in spite of his discomfort. Deborah looked anything but Bedouin. As the daughter of the temple high priest, she was dressed in finery that no Bedouin would wear. Even now, amid the dust and rustic conditions, Deborah's clothes still had the sheen of cleanliness, as did her face. Ephraim looked down at his own robes and saw that they were sullied with dust and grime. Feeling self-conscious, he attempted to pat some of the dirt out of the cloth, all in vain.

"My mother and father have been speaking of my betrothal," Deborah said. "Your name has been coming up in their talks with the matchmaker."

Ephraim's heart crashed against his chest and his stomach turned cold at her matter-of-fact tone. He scrambled away from her, leaving a cloud of dust where he had been sitting.

While coughing and waving the dust away, she asked, "What is the matter?"

Ephraim blurted, "What is the matter? This is how I find out that your parents are considering me for your husband?" In shock, he assessed her frank grin. What kind of a girl was this? "Not only that," he went on, "but I have nothing. They do not even know my family as both of my parents are dead."

"I overheard my father talking of your father, Naphtali," Deborah said, seeming amused at Ephraim's strong reaction. "Naphtali of Modiin was known as a good man. You could not help it that your rebels killed him."

Ephraim stared at her. It appeared that he had been the subject of conversation in Deborah's family for some weeks. "How is it that they would want to arrange for your *Kidushin* in such a place?" he asked. "Betrothal is a serious and complicated matter. It is not something one would want to conduct in a cave, of all places."

"Why not in a cave?" Deborah asked impatiently. "Father says that he wants our lives and ceremonies to go on as usual. 'Otherwise, the Greeks win,' he says."

"I must leave." Ephraim said struggled to his feet. "It is wrong for me to be talking to you, especially if what you say is true."

"So, you do not object to me as your bride?" Deborah said, mischief in her voice.

"Do not be ridiculous," Ephraim scoffed, looking down at her. "It is not up to me. If a contract is made, that is one thing—but—" In frustration, he waved his hands at her. "I do not even know what I am saying. This is crazy!"

Ephraim stalked back to the ovens and into the refuge of the cave, hearing Deborah's gentle laughter behind him. As he settled into his corner of the cave, lying down on his blanket, he smiled in spite of his confusion.

Chapter Twelve

Miriam yawned. "So, husband. Tell me more of Lydda. With the wedding and what-not, I have not had a report. Did you convince them?"

Arching his back to ease out his muscles after the long ride from Lydda, Judah reveled in the gourd of cold water that Miriam plied upon him. He then lay back on the cushions as she poured the water he had not drunk into a bowl and washed his feet. "It was only a very small step in getting the word out to the Jews in Lydda." He grunted as she cracked one of his toe joints. "Careful, wife. I will need that toe on patrol."

"Answer my question, Judah," Miriam said. "Did they listen to you?"

"Yes, but the faithful did not need convincing. I am relying upon them to convince their neighbors that if they do not come to the Law, the Law will come to them."

"What exactly does that mean?" Miriam asked, and cracked another toe, smiling as Judah howled. "The great Maccabee," she said, pursing her lips to keep the smile off her face. "Quiet, or the neighbors will hear."

"They hear everything anyway, wife," Judah said as he yanked his foot away. "Our house is made of cloth." He leaned into her playfully and bussed her cheek. "And, I mean, *everything*."

"That is enough!" Miriam gasped through the kiss that had moved from her cheek to her mouth. "It is mid-day." She looked around, scandalized. "Really, Judah."

"Wife, I am only trying to keep you happy according to *Tanakh*." He put amorous arms around her and spoke into her ear, "I am only performing my conjugal duty as your husband."

Luckily, the neighbors were attending to their afternoon chores, or they would have heard a very respectable conjugal performance as they had passed by the Maccabee's tent. As it was, however, Judah and Miriam were very much alone during their marital duty and when they were finished, they lay together and talked quietly.

"Are you frightened, Judah?" Miriam asked, her head against his barrel chest. Immodest though it was, she enjoyed their nakedness after lovemaking. Her mother had always warned against this intimacy, saying that women should always be covered even during the act. Such modesty, however, did not make sense to Miriam, and Judah did not seem to mind.

"Sometimes, *Susah Katan*" Judah said, using his pet name for her, Little Mare, "But—and you will be surprised by this—all I do in such instances is think of you and what you would do, and it fortifies my spine. I rarely feel fear during such times."

Miriam pushed up from his chest so she could look at Judah's face. "Do not bait me, husband. I will not be fodder for your jokes."

The dead seriousness she saw on Judah's features, however, mollified Miriam immediately, for she settled back into his arms and soon dozed.

As Judah watched Miriam sleep, he marveled at the contentment he felt. Here he and his people were, living like outlaws in the hills of Gophna, and he felt utterly at peace. It was just a matter of time before the Greeks returned and in frightening force, yet he felt no worry, no angst. The only worry he felt was that he felt no worry. He shook his head and almost laughed out loud, but Miriam's soft snores reminded him to stay quiet.

The next moment, however, Miriam was awake anyway, for Avram's muffled voice urged Judah through the tent wall, "Commander? I would speak with you."

Judah scrambled up, mumbling an apology to Miriam, who, having rolled off Judah, was clutching her robe to her body as she yelled at Avram. In spite of themselves, they laughed when they heard Avram's voice become faint and apologetic as he moved away from the tent to escape Miriam's epithets.

When Judah emerged from the tent, Avram was skulking on the other side of the campfire, looking down in embarrassment. At Judah's smile, he approached, still wary, and said, "Commander, you sent out the Bar Moshe brothers as scouts yesterday. They have reported back and would speak with you."

"Already?" Judah said, irritated. "They were to stay out a week. I wanted them to cover all of the area round about Jerusalem."

"I think you will not be angry when you hear what they have to say," Avram said with a noncommittal shrug.

Avram was right. Judah was far from angry, and the feral grin that surfaced on his face during the brothers' report infused his followers who had gathered in the command tent with eagerness. That look meant that their idleness atop this ridge would soon end.

"So, Greeks are sending out small patrols?" Judah said, his face lighting up. "The Lord of Hosts with us! How many in their patrols?"

"Not more than ten, sometimes twenty," Hosea said, acknowledging his elder brother's glare with "Well, you gave the whole long-winded report, Yacob. I think I can give the count."

Judah grinned and patted Yacob's shoulder to keep him from clubbing Hosea. "I am pleased. Father, I think we should harass these patrols. What do you think?"

The men nodded and murmured their approval at Judah's deference to Mattathias, who rarely spoke these days. The growth in his belly was sapping his strength and it was all he could do to say, his voice faint, "It shall be as you say, Judah. But not on Shabbat."

"Of course, Father. Not on Shabbat. Eleazar, pick ten men, well-horsed. We will ride tonight. Include Yacob and Hosea so they can show us where they last saw the patrol. We will make the Greeks think twice about underestimating us. A patrol of twenty," he said merrily, "will make good sport."

"Father," Judah said after the others had left the command tent, "How are you feeling?"

"I am well," Mattathias said.

Judah stooped and arranged more cushions around his father to ease his body away from the hard ground of the tent. Mattathias' gray face belied his calm words, and pain migrated across his features as Judah fussed with the cushions.

"That is enough, son," Mattathias said kindly. "Just let me rest here for a moment. Then I will go back to my tent."

Judah sat back. "Father, perhaps we should take you and mother out of the hills. You are not comfortable here." As he looked at his father's ashen face, he wondered at the feeling of well-being he experienced a few moments before in Miriam's arms. That feeling was gone, now. "I am worried about you."

"Comfort is not to be had anywhere in Judaea as long as the invader holds sway," Mattathias said, trying to keep the pain out of his voice. "I will stay with my people."

The resolute voice did not invite debate, so Judah kept quiet. As he sat, listening to the labored breathing of his father, the old despair of his inadequacy assailed him, and he quailed under its strength. Would he be able to vanquish the recurring black feeling if his father died? His father had been the only one in the past who had been able to talk Judah out of the darkness. He gripped his hands together. The range of emotions from the calm moments before to the despair he felt now meddled with his psyche until he felt himself shake. What could he do?

Seeming to sense the emotions that ravaged his son, Mattathias grasped Judah's forearm. "Son. Hold on." Mattathias' eyes teared at the distress in Judah's. "You must not be afraid. Soon I will go the way of all the earth, and the fight will be left to you." The old man lifted his eyes wearily, seeming to focus on the tent's undulation caused by the beginnings of an early spring gale. "Again, I must remind you. Judah will be victorious. The commander, Judah, and the land, Judah, will ride the wings of victory." Mattathias lowered his eyes into his boy's face. The black eyes were steady as he said, "Never despair, my son. Now, tend to those Greek patrols."

Judah lay his head on Mattathias' chest as if to weep, then after many minutes, stood, his eyes dry. He helped his father to his feet and ushered him carefully back to his tent.

Chapter Thirteen

E phraim's head spun. A contract had been made and he had a family once again. The betrothal had great force in the community and many male hands welcomed him, patting him on the back and embracing him in familiar bear hugs after the simple ceremony. The groom's offering had been dispensed with because of the unusual living conditions and Ephraim's bereft circumstances, but the bride's dowry ensured a comfortable beginning for him and Deborah, if they ever got out of the cave, that is.

He now sat with her family. It was Shabbat. He and Hezekiah lay on their sides, facing each other as they quietly discussed politics. Every so often, however, Ephraim would look up and scan the cave for Deborah. As the wedding approached, he found more and more pleasure in simply sitting by and watching her, preferably unseen. Her lithesome movements stirred him, and he found he was having a difficult time controlling the yearning in his loins as he anticipated their eventual release after the *chuppah* ceremony.

This Shabbat was especially languid. Families lounged about the cave, adults discussing the community and country, children at quiet and restrained play.

Hezekiah was steeped in a monologue detailing the evils of Antiochus. For a while, Ephraim attended his friend's arguments, but soon his mind drifted back to his impending nuptials. The wedding was to be as festive an event as the caves would allow and much activity was being devoted to the 30th day of *Nisan*, that being the designated date for the wedding, deemed auspicious by Deborah's family. The day before, Ephraim had even been fitted for a wedding robe, as the community tailor shared their exile in the cave.

Yesterday, as the tailor had *tsked* and muttered over Ephraim's tall frame, his mind had gone back to Modiin, the site of the last wedding he had attended. Judah, Eleazar, Shoshanna, his own father Naphtali: all of them rushed back into his memory unbidden. He tried to close his thoughts to Modiin, but it did not work. As the tailor had arranged the folds of the new robe about him, his mind set to wondering about the fate of his former friends.

If Modiin had indeed fled to Gophna, how did it fare? What weddings had it seen solemnized? Babies born? Deaths? Ephraim frowned and tried to bring his attention back to Hezekiah who was now issuing a harangue on the evils of Greek philosophy. He decided he did not want to think upon Modiin—the memories were too painful.

An agreeable roar always was present in the cave, except perhaps in the dead hours of early morning or on Shabbat. To Ephraim's ears, the Shabbat hum of this day sounded especially benign. The effect was enhanced by Deborah's sudden appearance. She had been assisting a sick family and seemed drawn and tired. But something else was wrong.

"*Abba! Abba!*"

Deborah's voice sounded unnaturally shrill. Gideon, who had been studying the new scroll of Daniel that Hezekiah had copied the week before their exile to the caves, stood in alarm at his daughter's harried approach. "What is it, *Taleh Raq*, Lambkin?"

"The lookout says they are coming," Deborah gasped. "It is a huge force of Greeks. Reuel saw them afar off. He said their armor glinting in the sun made them look like walking pillars of fire."

"Well, it is not as if we had not expected their coming," Gideon said, exchanging a look with his wife, his face a mask of calm.

"What shall we do, *Abba*?" Hezekiah asked.

"Why, nothing," Gideon answered. "It is Shabbat."

"But, *Abba*," Hezekiah and Deborah said together, their voices frightened.

"Children!" Their mother, Judith, said, "Keep your voices down. Your father is right. Let us go back to what we were doing."

Gideon repeated his wife's admonition so the families around him would hear and spread his words, "Everyone! Let us go back to our Shabbat observance. Do not panic. *Ha kohl bah seder.* Everything is as it should be."

As a wave, the inhabitants of the cave ebbed back into an agitated version of their former activity. Deborah alone could not settle, and she paced back and forth until her mother, and finally, her father spoke to her with sharpness. It was only then that she reluctantly sat at Judith's feet, laying her head against her mother's knee, eyes fearful.

Ephraim wished he could be the one comforting her, but it was not his place, at least, not yet, and as he gazed around the cave, he realized that the friendly hum of the cave had ceased. All was quiet.

Pressed against each other, providing solace even in their silence, families found calm in their shared memories of household. The Queen of the Week, Shabbat, was upon them and she did her part: rest vanquished panic. Even the young children and babies were at repose in the arms in their parents or older siblings.

The flood of calm rippled only once; Reuel, the lookout for that day, dodged through the recumbent forms throughout the cave calling for High Priest Gideon.

"They are approaching, Your Honor! They are not two furlongs hence. What would you have me do?"

"See to your family, Reuel," Gideon said quietly. "There is nothing to be done."

Fifteen minutes passed, then a half-hour, then an hour. The first watch of night had almost begun when the voice was heard.

"Jewish citizens of Seleucia!"

A faint murmur mulled through the crowd in the cave as people sat up, straining to hear.

"I say, Jewish citizens of Seleucia!" The voice, its owner now closer to the maw of the cave, boomed an echo. "By the grace of the Great God Antiochus, you are granted a reprieve. Although you flout his commands and even flee from his presence, he is a generous god. If you will but live according to the commandments of the Great Antiochus, you shall live. It shall suffice! Come out and you shall live."

Gideon rose and adjusted his robes and head covering. He moved among the people, some clutching at his hem, some simply nodding in respect as he passed. All heads followed his progress until he stood at the mouth of the cave.

The sun had not set on the Shabbat; the death of the Queen of the Week was less than a half-hour away. With dusky shades of golden red, the late afternoon sun fell upon the high priest under the vault of rock. The aura defined his priestly robes, creating a crimson vision.

"We will not come forth, neither will we do the king's commandment, to worship a false god or to profane our Shabbat."

Having delivered the terse message, Gideon turned slowly and returned to the shadows of rock. He sat down with his family and waited.

* * * * *

Timotheus turned to Demetrius, his second lieutenant. "Good god, what a stubborn people," the general said. "Well, it is all to the good. My men need sport. Give the command."

Demetrius saluted Timotheus and turned to the lieutenants. He raised his arm, sword in hand, and abruptly lowered the steel.

It was the signal. The waiting troops exhaled battle cries and a destructive cloud of infantry rushed toward the mouth of the cave. Some of the stouter soldiers kicked over the stone ovens, idle on the day of rest.

Despite the cries, this was no battle, this, for the Greeks moved against the Jews without opposition. Those at the mouth of the cave lay down under the swords and submitted to the slaughter. A few of the children cried out until the Greeks silenced them.

Ephraim was the only one who stood when the Greeks began their onslaught. "Father Gideon! We must defend. Why did you not order the rocks down?" Ephraim lifted his eyes to the net of rocks that hung suspended above the cave's mouth. The net had been strung for such a time as this, yet the rocks hung idle. At Gideon's silence, he shook the old high priest and yelled, "Someone must get to the ropes!"

Gideon gathered Judith, Hezekiah and Deborah to him and beckoned to Ephraim to come to the embrace. "Son, we will die in innocence. Heaven and earth will testify for us that the Greeks do put us to death wrongfully, for we will not lift our hand on Shabbat."

A rush of fear infused Ephraim with sick dread when he realized that Gideon meant for all of them to die, no opposition being offered to the Greeks. Then he saw Naphtali, his father, in a terrible vision.

The scene at the altar of Modiin opened to him as if he had never been away. He saw Naphtali raise the sacrificial ax to appease the Greek. Just as clearly, he saw the sword arm of Mattathias descend, the blade cutting into the neck of his father yet again. The memory only lasted seconds, but it was long enough for him to cry, "No!" and grab Deborah from Gideon's embrace and yank her brutally away from him. "Not again! I will not see this again," he raged and dragged Deborah away from the carnage that was beginning to bleed from the mass at the mouth of the cave.

Deborah resisted his grasp at first, crying for her father and mother. Her innate sense of survival, however, quelled her struggle, and, docile, she allowed herself to be led by her betrothed through the pack of humanity to the back of the cave.

"We can get out through one of the smaller openings at the west end of the cave," Ephraim rasped as he stumbled over recumbent bodies, dragging Deborah with him.

Not far behind them, the Greek soldiers sliced and butchered their way through human flesh until they found themselves against the cave walls. Then they turned and made their way back, listening carefully for the groans of those still stirring and putting an end to the sounds with their chopping swords.

For all Ephraim's speed, quickened by fear even as he pulled Deborah along, he was not far ahead of the butchers. The quicksilver slashes of their blades moved against human flesh as if against air. However, an eerie silence settled over the murders, the slaughter that followed at their heels creating little outcry from the Jews now. Even the children were meeting the blades in silence.

Pacifism for them must be as a sleeping drought, Ephraim thought wildly as he dragged Deborah along toward the back of the cave. But I, for one, am going to stay awake.

Ephraim found a small, jagged alcove and pushed Deborah inside. He covered her body with his and whispered into her ear, "I cannot remember where the other cave opening is."

Too shaken to speak, Deborah gave a jerk of her head over Ephraim's left shoulder. He immediately put his arm about her waist and propelled her toward the direction she indicated. Before they faded back into the cave, however, the voyeur in them forced their attention back at the unspeakable scene that they fled. At that moment, one of the Greeks cut through a mother and the infant she was holding with one lethal swipe.

Ephraim and Deborah froze at the deprecating leer on the soldier's face as he gazed down at the dismembered bodies. Deborah vomited.

The Greek looked up at the sound and saw them. Ephraim clutched at Deborah and tried to pull her into the recesses that led to the smaller entrance, but she pushed him away, not seeing the danger.

The Greek yelled something and two of his fellows appeared at his side. Deborah finally saw them and forgot her embarrassment about the bile now dripping from her face. As Ephraim drew her back, neither one of them took their eyes from the three soldiers who were advancing, joy on their faces at the promise of new sport—one that might be more entertaining than simple slaughter.

Aside from a sneering first glance at Ephraim, not one of the soldiers were looking at him now. All their attention was upon Deborah and as they shouted and heckled each other, Ephraim wished he had learned more Greek. Not that he had any doubt about their intentions.

* * * * *

"Let me have her first," the first Greek said. "After all, I saw her first. She is young." He licked his lips. "I must sacrifice to Venus when we return to Hierosolyma (Jerusalem)."

"Well, hurry up," the second soldier snarled. "We still have to mop up. There are a few alive. Timotheus will not wait for your rutting if he gives the order to depart."

"It will not take long," the first soldier said as he set aside his sword and shield, lifted his tunic and moved toward Deborah.

"It never takes you long," chuckled the third soldier. "But, what about him?"

"The smelly Jew? Make him watch. But do not let him run. He looks like he is ready to bolt. Take care of him, but do not kill him. He looks like he needs an education in matters such as these."

* * * * *

The blow was so quick that Ephraim went down before he realized he had been clubbed in the face with the sword hilt of the third soldier. The pain in his nose and forehead was so severe that he could barely see. Deborah's scream pierced his ears. A thud silenced her and through a dizzy haze he saw the two soldiers hold her down while her attacker crouched over her as he fumbled beneath his tunic.

Ephraim tried to keep his senses but felt himself drifting. He must have lost consciousness for a moment, but only for a moment, for when he woke, the Greek was still moving back and forth atop Deborah. Ephraim was swimming in sweat. This must be a nightmare. But no, the terrible animal sounds coming from Deborah were too real to be part of a dream. His vision fluttered and he found that his eyes could focus once again. Casting his gaze about, he forced himself to avoid the horrific scene, looking instead for some way out of this, some way to save his betrothed. The sword. It lay, a discard at the side of the Greek. He summoned his wits, still numb, and rolled his body toward the sword. The two who had been holding Deborah had stood and were now lounging against the rock wall as the girl was completely subdued. They did not react to Ephraim's movement, their attention riveted on the amusement at their feet and the anticipation of their use of the girl. Ephraim knew his prowess with the sword was not enough to best the armed spectators, but he saw something he could do. His hand grasped the sword hilt, and he stood up quickly, closing the opposite hand over the hilt so that his command of the weapon was two-fisted. He raised the sword over his head and with a jolting arc downward, he severed the head of the rapist."

The shock on the two Greeks' faces told him that he had another opportunity. He brought the sword up again and gazed at the unspeakable trauma on Deborah's face. She was drenched in the rapist's blood. Her eyes were empty, the body nude and ravaged, her robe having been pushed up, no longer a protection. Then she seized, but even during the convulsion, her modesty surfaced, pulling her hands over her privates. Ephraim brought the sword down with a sob.

It was impossible, but the two Greeks still did not react, their shock at the death of their friend and of the girl too great for them to yet do anything but stare at the tall Jew.

Ephraim ran. He edged into a slim recess, luck helping him find the opening into a tunnel that led to another cave. The Greeks by now were clambering into the same recess, their swords clanging against the rock.

Ephraim thanked Him-of-No-Name for the maze that fell away before him and his familiarity with its narrow caverns and ledges that the pursuing Greeks did not share. Ahead, he saw the faint red of sunset entering a fissure of rock. He moved toward it quickly, the noise of the Greeks only a muted distraction trapped in the rock behind him.

The Queen of the Week had expired and the dark red of her death provided a protective mantle for Ephraim as he ran from the cave hunting for a hiding place. A tell of rock rose to his left, but he did not head for it, too obvious a lair. Instead, he ran for some low scrub that had spread itself over a small ravine to the right of the rock mound, crawling beneath its dense, scraggly undergrowth. He grabbed great fistfuls of rough earth and rubbed it over his face, neck and robe so he would blend in with the scrub.

The Greeks clattered across the rock outcropping that Ephraim had shunned and spent many minutes wearing themselves out climbing among the rocks searching for their quarry. Finally, they came off the rocks and made a cursory sweep of the scrub, but by now, they were spent and discouraged. Swearing, they forsook the search and went back to the cave for orders and to retrieve the body and head of their friend.

Ephraim did not stir until well after the Greeks left. Insensible of the thicket of scrub piercing his flesh with its brambles, he lay still as death for many hours. Finally, he crept out of the thicket, it tearing at his body and robes, and pulled himself to a rock and sat down. The sun had set on the Shabbat and dumbly he looked into the west, squinting for some fleeting sign of the retreating Queen of the Week. She was gone. She would be gone for a long time. He curled himself around the rock and pressed his forehead against its hard surface.

Chapter Fourteen

The Road to Beit Horon, Judaea   The 2nd day of *Nisan* 3594 (March 28th 166 B.C.E.)

Syrus eased his rump off the saddle, grateful that his men would not notice as they were engaged in a healthy exchange of gossip. The foray the night before into the temple of Ashtaroth had chafed his loins to the point that sitting a horse was untold misery. How his men would have laughed had they known. As it was, however, they were merry in their disregard as they regaled each other with the latest stories about palace intrigues that had trickled down to Judaea from Antioch.

"Our dear emperor has actually taken to dressing as Diana, the goddess of the hunt," one of the privates offered.

"Rumors," another ventured. "He is too busy getting ready to raid the Parthian treasury. He has no time for that nonsense. He has to gather tribute for the Romans, or he will lose his divine skin."

As much as Syrus would have liked the gossip to continue, distracting the men so he could nurse his rump, he knew his duty was to keep the talk clean of disrespect for their emperor. Reluctantly, he settled back into his saddle and said, "All of you, quiet, or I will gut you and leave your entrails for the dogs of the next village. You will show respect for our divine emperor."

"Yes sir," the two privates mumbled and continued their plodding way in silence. The others in the patrol who had been about to join the jocular observations about their emperor added themselves to the silence. Now the only sound in the ear of the patrol was the muted cadence of shuffling hooves along the road to Beit Horon.

The hills about them could barely be called hills. Their guileless slopes presented rare evidence of fauna and none of human life. Although spring had arrived, it had not taken hold here and the low foliage about them was still encased in the rigor of winter.

Syrus again shifted impatiently in his saddle. He knew he was too far south to encounter any rebels. The rises of Gophna were barely visible to the north and he regretted his decision of a few hours before to turn south at the deserted village of Modiin. One of his men had mentioned that Modiin was the backwater town where this ridiculous rebellion of the Jews had started and had retold the story of Apelles' botch.

Suddenly, Syrus sat up and raised his hand over his head. Instantly, the patrol stopped, and the horses nosed toward the edges of the road where unruly spikes of tundra beckoned their appetites. However, it took only a small nudge against their bridles to discipline their noses upright. The men watched Syrus and waited.

The leader of the patrol sniffed and pulled his weight up into a kneel over the saddle of his horse and straightened his legs into a rather unsteady stand. This time it was not to assuage the pain in his backside, but rather to get a better look at the curl of smoke, its burn blending into the afternoon clouds.

"Agias."

Syrus' second cantered his horse up to the lieutenant and inclined his ear. "Yes, sir?"

"Agias, your eyes are better than mine. How close would you say that smoke is?"

The second squinted and shielded his brow with his cupped right hand. "I should say not more than a furlong."

Syrus leaned around in his saddle and said, "We shall dismount. Be wary. I do not know what should be afire here on this Zeus-forsaken road, but we must be ready. Advance."

For a while, the smoke taunted them, seducing the patrol with its proximity, then wafting out of reach. Finally, their slow tread made headway and the smoke spiraled down into a violence of red and orange flame.

Hardened gazes fell on a burning carcass, the blackened flesh of what must have once been a horse was crackling, its juices seeping into the dust of the road. The fire spinning around the mass was mesmerizing to the men, not only because it was an exquisite scene of holocaust, but also because it blotted the more disturbing sight of the Greek patrol strewn about in various poses of death.

Syrus skirted the burning carcass, avoiding the boiling flames and stooped over one of the corpses. It was the body of a fellow lieutenant, Polydeuces. He pulled a pike from the chest of the lieutenant and brandished it as if to throw. But it would do no good. The rebels were long gone. They had used the lieutenant's own pike to finish him; the strike in his neck must not have been enough.

Although he knew it to be a vain endeavor, Syrus ordered his men to search all of the bodies for life. He did not put the pike down but clutched it obsessively as his men moved from body to body.

It was not customary for the leader of a patrol to carry a phalangite pike, even the short ones like this were unwieldy at their five-cubit reach. However, Polydeuces always took it along, to "instill fear into the locals." He had told Syrus as much the day before when they had assembled in the barracks yard in Jerusalem to embark on their respective patrols to the north.

"Well," Syrus addressed the pike facetiously, "It looks like you were an instrument of "fear" as Polydeuces intended, after all." He threw the weapon down and walked over to the body of the lieutenant. Stooping, he looked into its face. "Vain fool. You did as all of us have done. You underestimated the Jews." He stood when his second approached him.

"Shall we take the bodies back, lieutenant?"

"No," Syrus muttered. "We will bury them."

"But, lieutenant," the soldier said, scandalized. "It is standard procedure for us to bear back the bodies of our fallen."

"Do you want to end up like these men, Agias?" Syrus asked. "Operating by standard procedure has not gotten us far in this accursed conflict with the Jews."

"We must at least burn them," the soldier persisted. "It is a disgrace to bury them like so much rubbish."

"And bring these rebels down on us in the same manner? More smoke will attract them, idiot." Syrus looked around at the other men who were watching the exchange with great interest and said loudly, "No, we will bury them, and quickly, too. Philo ordered me to bring back a report after our patrol. I cannot very well do that if we are all slain, now can I?"

This seemed to make sense to the men, and they moved to their horses for their shields and daggers.

"Make the graves shallow; we do not want to tarry here. Hurry!"

As the men hollowed out the earth with their daggers and scooped it aside with their shields, Syrus turned away from the digging and kept his eyes on the guileless terrain around them.

Chapter Fifteen

Road from Beit Horon to Gophna, Judaea   The 2nd day of *Nisan* 3594 (March 28th166 B.C.E.)

Pale, Eleazar rode alongside Judah.   His lack of color did not keep him from shouting at his younger brother. "Why did you taunt him, brother? He almost killed you, *teepaysh*."

"I wanted to let him know that his fierce pike was not so fierce, after all," Judah said dismissively and pulled *Tiklit* back into a slow canter. "The stupid Greeks and everyone else I talk to, for that matter, are always lording their fierce phalanx pikes and pikemen over us. 'What are you going to do against those pikes, Judah? How will you fight against the Greek phalanx, Judah?'" He leaned forward and tousled *Tiklit's* forelock. "I am weary of hearing about their pikes. Not only that, why would they bring them out on a patrol? That's extra weight on the horse. Well," he said, thinking of the dead soldier, "That's the price he'll pay for showing off."

Judah turned his mount aside and led Eleazar and the rest of the men to a creek he knew of outside the village of Beit Horon. As they watered their horses, Judah leaned over toward Eleazar and said quietly, "Why are you so upset? All ended well. And, you should not yell at me in front of the others, even if I am your younger brother."

"I do not want to have to tell mother of your death," Eleazar whispered in frustration. "You must be more careful, Judah; that is all."

"I am very careful. I did not taunt the Greek until after I got him in the neck," Judah laughed, then harumphed the laugh into a cough at Eleazar's expression.

"It is no laughing matter," Eleazar snapped. "He almost got you with his dagger when you made your little speech as you waved the pike over his head."

"What? You did not like my little speech about how the Greeks would have to take their pikes and. . ."

"Please, Judah," Eleazar said wearily. "Do not repeat your vulgarity. It is bad enough you said it once, and to an infidel."

"That infidel is dead. He will carry no tales of my 'vulgarity.' What, were you afraid he would tell mother?"

Eleazar turned his horse abruptly away from Judah and galloped back to the road. Judah clucked to *Tiklit* and beckoned Avram and the others in the party. "Hurry," he said, "we are far from Gophna and must make it back by nightfall. I want to see how the other parties led by Asher and Aulus did."

The other parties, as it turned out, were as successful as Judah's in dispatching Greek patrols. As they gathered in the command tent, they clapped each other on the back in congratulation.

"They were not very vigilant," Asher said, shaking his head. "We simply waited until they stopped to relieve themselves. They did not post a guard."

"My Greeks were almost the same," Aulus said. "They were riding along as if they were on holiday. Not once did they lift their eyes from the road and their chatter. My archers made worms' meat of them in a hurry." He shook his head. "It was almost too easy."

Judah looked up from the map. "I assure you that next time, it will not be. The Greeks have not been quick learners thus far because they have not had to be. After their defeat at Magnesia against the Romans," he nodded toward Aulus, "they have been content to do battle against a defenseless foe: our women and children." Here he inclined his head at Asher whose face turned grim at the memory of his mother's and brothers' deaths. "Now, however, they have to contend with a real enemy," he looked at his commanders who were gathered around the map in the command tent. "Thank Him-of-No-Name that we turned out to be real enemies." Laughter filled the tent and he peered at the map once again. "I think that after we are rested, we should set out again." He placed his finger just above Jerusalem. "I would like to see us strike even closer to Jerusalem. That would stir—"

Outside the tent, a voice keened happily, and the men looked up. The woman's voice called, "Judah! He is come back! He is come back!"

Judah pushed away from the parchment and pushed through the flap, his men eagerly following after. Miriam and Shoshanna were at the head of a large contingent that was now pressing against the outside of the command tent.

Judah cried, "What is it? What has happened?"

"I have returned."

The male voice came from behind the two women and at its familiar sound, Judah staggered. He pulled at his beard in great agitation and actually tried to back into the command tent but could not because of the press of his men behind him.

Ephraim, son of Naphtali, emerged from the mill of people and a great silence crushed all talk and movement. His face was still, unreadable; he stood in front of the crowd for what seemed to Judah an eon. An uncertain step carried him toward Judah, then another, until he was face to face with the rebel commander.

The people of Modiin, now Gophna, fastened their attention upon the two men, once best friends, now rived apart at the event forced upon them by the Greek invader: the terrible death of Naphtali.

"Ephraim! Ephraim!"

The voice was faint, but unmistakable as it carried over the heads of the crowd, who, in its entirety, turned away from Judah and Ephraim and waited. Mattathias finally labored his way through the human barrier and put one firm hand on Judah's shoulder and the other, a little more tentative, on Ephraim's.

Awash with red, Mattathias' old eyes brimmed over so that the rivulets ran into the white fall of his beard. The sobbing was so faint that only Judah and Ephraim could hear its anguish, nevertheless, the two young men bowed their heads.

"Can you ever forgive me?" Mattathias said to Ephraim. "Son, I am sorry. I am sorry." The words were but a whisper, but it seemed that their entreaty carried its spirit over the crowd, for there was great weeping among the women and tears were starting in the eyes of almost every man.

Mattathias sank to Ephraim's feet, his hands clutching at the hem of his robe, his voice still a faltering hiss, the crowd murmuring at the old leader's frail obeisance.

Ephraim followed Mattathias' crouch and stooped with the old man for a time, letting the grief spend itself. Then he stood, bringing the old man up with him, the embrace eloquent in both its sorrow and penitence. Judah's arms joined those of Mattathias and Ephraim, the scene so poignant the onlookers felt as if they were a part of the circle.

Later, the command tent smelled of mutton, Miriam having ordered the slaughter of her prized ram in honor of Ephraim's return and repatriation with their people. As the commanders hunched around the meat, Judah watched Ephraim's face for a clue explaining his return. The face had aged, as had his own, but he still had no idea why Ephraim had come back. The debriefing with his old friend had not occurred yet, as custom dictated that food be served before business discussed.

Finally, the joint was picked over, the bread no more than a paltry discard of crumbs. Sluggish with food, the men nevertheless were alert with expectation, and it was difficult for them to wait politely for Ephraim to initiate his tale. But wait they did until Ephraim seemed to take note of their eagerness and spoke. He did not seem eager, however.

"I have a terrible report, brothers," he began, "and I do not know where to begin."

Judah leaned over to Ephraim and said, "If you are not ready, we understand."

"No, this cannot wait," Ephraim said. "My feelings do not matter in such a case." His hands trembled.

Their faces stone, the men sat quietly until Ephraim gathered himself. He continued, "Armageddon is upon us. I tried to follow peace. That is why I left Modiin after—" Ephraim broke that sentence and began another. "Against such an enemy, there is no seeking peace." He bowed his head and whispered, "We face a monster."

"What happened, brother?" Judah urged quietly.

"It was Shabbat. Shabbat. And they killed them all." And Ephraim told the men of Kidron Cave.

As Judah's men listened, their limbs quaked with revulsion and rage. Many of them rent their garments in shock; their trembling took root in the earthen floor of the tent until its very walls seemed quake.

"I alone escaped," Ephraim cried. "My betrothed and her family were among those who were butchered. High Priest Gideon would not defend. He would not fight because it was the day of rest—" He stopped, and his breath would only come in great rasping gulps.

Mattathias was the first to speak after giving Ephraim a moment to rest his grief. "What are we to do?" he asked. "If we do as our brethren have done and fight not for our lives and Law against the heathen, they will quickly root us out of the earth. What are we to do?"

The tent was heavy with grief and the quandary of the problem at hand. Shabbat observance was the very touchstone of the law. It was the tenet that the Lord and Moshe had been very clear about, relegating those who broke the commandment to punishment by stoning. For many moments, the men were silent, not knowing what to say. There was a problematic solution in the thoughts of almost every man in the tent. But none dared speak it. Finally, Judah broke the silence, voicing a proposition.

"Father," Judah said, his hand on Mattathias' arm. "We must suspend adherence to the Law so we can defend ourselves on the Shabbat. The Lord does not mean for us to die as they did in the caves. If we all die keeping the Shabbat there will no one left to keep the Shabbat. We must live to keep the Law. After all, it was just a matter of time before we would have had to face this issue. We are lucky no assaults by the Greeks in Gophna took place on Shabbat, or we would have died as well. And now the Greeks know."

New tears came into Mattathias' eyes. A battle raged on his face for many moments until he finally said, "It shall be as you say: whosoever shall come to do battle with us on the Shabbat day, we will fight against him. Neither will we die all, as our brethren that were murdered in the caves." The decree, however, seemed to sap him, and he leaned heavily against Judah. His breath did not come easily, and the men looked at each other in great alarm.

"I will take him back to his tent," Judah said. "Eleazar, Avram. Assist me."

Tenderly, the huge Avram lifted the wizened Mattathias, as if a child in his arms, and bore him out of the tent with the supported aid of Judah and his brother. The men of Modiin and Beit Ur watched, reverence on their faces, and prayed.

Chapter Sixteen

Jerusalem, Judaea   The 3rd day of *Nisan* 3594 (March 29th 166 B.C.E.)

S yrus' rump still was tender, but the pain fled when he sat in the chair facing the severe General Apollonius. General Nicanor sat in another chair to Apollonius' right. Syrus knew that Nicanor was the ranking officer here, but the old, hardened warrior seemed to defer to Apollonius. He allowed the junior commander to direct the inquiry, only interposing occasionally.

"So, Lieutenant. You buried them?" It was more of a statement than query, for Apollonius was squinting at the parchment upon which the scribe had etched notes during the initial debriefing.

"Yes, General. As I indicated, the slaughter was fresh enough to indicate the Jews had just left. I did not want our presence known."

Apollonius said nothing as he read the parchment. Suddenly he discarded it, leaned over Philo's desk and stared at Syrus.

Syrus became alarmed as the stare lasted almost a full ten seconds, then relaxed when Apollonius picked up the parchment again and turned to Nicanor. "It says here that Lieutenant Syrus feels that we are underestimating our foe. That the Jews have full run of the north because of our lack of vigilance. Are those your words, Lieutenant?"

Syrus became uneasy again at the scrutiny directed at him by Antiochus' two lead generals. "Yes, sir. But I did not mean to imply that command was at fault—"

"Of course, of course, soldier," Apollonius said impatiently. Then to Nicanor, "I think Lieutenant Syrus is right." He smiled as Syrus relaxed in his seat. He looked at the report again. "Are you aware, Lieutenant, that yours is the only patrol that returned?"

Syrus was too well-trained to gape at the words, but he could not control his stammer as he asked, "Of the three dispatched to the north? We are the only ones?"

Syrus fiddled with his helmet. "What about the seven who stayed closer to Jerusalem? Did they return?"

"Yes, all quite whole. But I suspect that if the—" He turned to Nicanor. "What was the rebel's name? I can never remember. The *Macc*, the *Macca*—"

"The Maccabee. He also goes by the name, Judah Maccabeus," Nicanor said.

"Yes, thank you, Excellency," Apollonius said. "If Judah Maccabeus sends his patrols farther to the south, we could be in trouble." He peered at the parchment again. "Well, Lieutenant Syrus, it was your training and command skill that brought you back whole. We will send you out on patrol again, but only after you debrief the rest of the lieutenants on new protocols for dealing with the insurgents: vigilance and seriousness in dealing with the enemy, and burial rather than bearing the bodies back for the pyre for the dead. You are dismissed."

Syrus sat up straighter in his chair, delighted with the prospect of leading a debriefing. "Yes sir," he said and stood. He saluted and exited Philo's barracks' command office.

* * * * *

"He was just lucky, you know," Nicanor said with a smile. "It was not his training and command skill that brought him back. It was blind luck."

"I know that, old friend," Apollonius said as he peered at an illegible document. "Who in Hermes' name wrote this? But, I have to do what I can to promote morale in this ridiculous situation. Philo is an idiot. And he and Timotheus are on their way to a royal botch, once again. It is their arrogance and disdain for the Jews that keep them from defending our interests in Judaea."

"You are right as always, Apollonius," Nicanor said. "And it is time we put your military rectitude to full use. You are to take your Samarian *kotaikai* to Gophna and take care of this situation with the Jew rebels once and for all. The Jerusalem guard is useless for this conflict. They are inculcated with Timotheus' and Philo's complacence. We have danced around the problem for months. We need to take the Jews seriously, as our little Syrus said. It seems lieutenants can often see what our esteemed commanders cannot."

"Well, we were all lieutenants once," Apollonius said. "Some a little more dim than others, but—"

"I remember the time in Magnesia," Nicanor said, "Right before we were to go into battle against the Romans, you as a lieutenant actually told your men to be sure to wash their undertunics the night before so that the corpse detail would not have to do it after they were dead. And, they actually carried out your order!"

"I know, I know! The order did not make any sense as their bodies would have been burned—dirty undertunics and all—but it gave them something to do, taking their mind off the slaughter we were facing the next morning," Apollonius said gruffly, but with a reminiscent smile. "I thought the pragmatic approach to death would keep my men from obsessing about its horrors." He laughed. "It worked, too. They were actually cheerful as they bent at the stream like a bunch of old washerwomen, cracking dirty jokes about their wives and sweethearts and playing in the water like children."

"That was quite a sight," Nicanor said, chuckling. "My men were actually jealous. And, most of your men survived that butchery, if I remember correctly."

"They did not want to get their carefully laundered tunics dirty, I suppose," Apollonius said. "However, many of your men survived also."

"That is correct, but only because we cowered behind that dead elephant to shield the members of our chariot corps from the Roman archers. Ares smiled upon us that day."

"Yes, anyone who survived that day had the hand of Ares, and indeed that of Athena upon them," Apollonius said. "I did not think we would ever recover from that vainglorious defeat,"

"Perhaps we have not." Nicanor rose and strolled around the room. "If you think about it, all we have succeeded in doing is angering the Romans because of Antiochus' silly incursions into Egypt and now, we have stirred up this nest of Jews because of our emperor's ham-handed dealings with them. All I can hope is that the Jews do not think of allying themselves with the Romans. That could be disastrous for us, that is, if we survive more of Antiochus' inflammatory edicts. Do you realize that we have not managed to conquer any new territory since the battle of Magnesia? In fact, we have lost territory." Nicanor shook his head. "No, my young friend. I am afraid that we are entering into the last days of our glorious empire."

Apollonius stood up and hit his knee. Cursing, he stacked the documents and tablets on his desk. "Well," he said. "I hope you are wrong. I still have many payments to make to the usurers back home on my new property in Antioch. And the wife is becoming impatient with my long absence. She will not be pleased when the courier gives her word of this new assignment you have given me up north. Tell me more about this Judah Macca—, Macca—"

"Maccabeus," Nicanor said patiently. "Judah Maccabeus. And you should order a new desk. That one is too small for you."

"I am not staying here for long. I must return to my *kotaikai* in Samaria if I am to direct this campaign against Maccabeus."

"And I am summoned to Antioch," Nicanor said. "The emperor wishes my report on the Jews to be delivered within the month.

The two generals walked through the busy barracks' corridors, answering the numberless soldiers' salutes they encountered with cursory gestures so they could concentrate on their discussion about the Jewish rebel.

"So, you say that this Maccabeus came from the village where Apelles was killed?" Apollonius said.

"Yes, he was among the rebels of the first group that resisted. "In fact," Nicanor said as he grabbed a soldier whose cuirass strap was awry, "—fix that, private—it is said that this Judah is actually the one who killed Apelles."

"As I recall, Apelles was on his way to becoming a commander. Philo spoke highly of him. Where are we going?"

"Yes, he was very good. But like everyone else who has come up against the Jews, he underestimated them. We are going to my stables."

Apollonius sighed. The elephants, again. Well, if he were going to find out more about this Maccabeus fellow and his assignment up north, he would have to tag along and play with Nicanor's damned animals.

"Did I tell you that Aphrodite is with child? Look at her. She is beautiful, is she not?"

By this time, they had arrived at the elephant camp and were leaning against the tall corral fence that enclosed Nicanor's herd of war elephants. As Apollonius gazed at the gray behemoths, he decided that beauty was too strong a word to describe the beasts, but he played along in deference to his friend. "Yes, she is magnificent. An absolute minx. She glows."

Nicanor looked sharply at Apollonius for a moment, then laughed. "Oh, I know you are patronizing me, old friend. But she was impregnated by my superb bull I had brought here from Apamea just last month. We will have to wait a while, to be sure, but that calf will be as the progeny of Zeus, himself."

"Are you sure it was not Zeus, himself, who sired the calf? He is given to such flights of love."

"Do not be blasphemous," Nicanor said idly as he watched the cow graze on a scattered mound of straw. "It is too bad that the child will not be ready for battle for fifteen seasons."

"By Ares and Eris! I hope we are not fighting the Jews for that long!" Apollonius said as he eased off the fence. "But, back to this—Maccabeus. Is he the author of the debacle at Gophna?"

"Actually, Timotheus is the author of the debacle at Gophna," Nicanor said, balancing on the fence and turning so he could face Apollonius. "The Jew was merely in the right place at the right time, fighting Timotheus' inept cohorts."

"And, if you remember, those cohorts paid for it dearly," Apollonius said. "It was necessary for me to humiliate them when they returned from Gophna. To this day, they still have to bear the harangues of their peers. Not even their victory at the caves of Kidron has helped their reputations."

Nicanor scoffed. "Victory? Really. You mean killing a thousand unarmed Jews did nothing to enhance their reputation? That is shocking!"

Apollonius said nothing and Nicanor turned back to watch the elephants. "Well, I wonder how this Judas Maccabeus will do against my children?" How will he and his unwashed rebels fare against the slash of sharpened tusk?" A slave handed him his riding crop and he beat it against the fence to attract Deucalis, his favorite bull. As Deucalis sidled up to the fence so Nicanor could scratch him on the massive nob between his eyes, he said cheerfully to Apollonius, "And, you, my friend, will figure out a way to entice this Jew from his hilly stronghold. Then he will have to face my elephants and your Samarians. Now, that will be a battle. Come and say hello to Deucalis."

When the elephant approached, Apollonius had moved well away from the fence and that is where he now stood as he listened to Nicanor. He had seen these beasts at work during battle and their ferocity and unpredictability on the field filled him with great awe. So much so that he disliked being in the vicinity of any of them. "Oh, I am well here. I will watch from afar."

But Nicanor would have none of it. "I insist. He has been pining for you. Look at him. He is upset that you never come to visit. There, there, Deucalis, you great lout. He is here, at last. Come on, come on, Apollonius. He will not hurt you."

Apollonius thought he did indeed see a red cast to the elephant's eye, but he did not think it was because, as Nicanor said, the animal was pining for him, but rather that he could sense Apollonius' abject fear. The soldier in him forced his approach to the fence, and he idly wondered if elephants were like dogs and could smell fright. If that was so, he was in deep trouble. He leaned warily into the enclosure and touched Deucalis once on the trunk with a wary index finger. "There," Apollonius said, "I have said hello." He made as if to jump off the enclosure.

"No, no," Nicanor said jovially. "You must put your cheek against his, like this." Nicanor climbed the fence and rubbed his grizzled cheek right above the tusk of the big pachyderm. The elephant seemed to enjoy it.

"Oh, all right," Apollonius said gruffly, climbing up the fence so that his rump perched on the top railing.

Nicanor withdrew his head from above the tusk so Apollonius could do honor to the elephant. Apollonius put his head over the tusk to briefly lay his cheek against Deucalis' own, when suddenly the elephant reared away from the fence. The only thing that saved Apollonius from being gored by the huge tusk was his soldierly instinct. That instinct told him to swing his legs up to grasp the tusk at its base and hang on, doing his best to hug the tusk to his chest.

The elephant stomped about and the blast of its trumpeting almost dislodged Apollonius with the sheer force of sound, but he hung on. The elephant then began tossing its head to shake off the unwelcome passenger, but Apollonius hung on.

Nicanor and the slave handlers were through the fence by this time and waved their hands as they rushed at the huge bull. This only served to plunge the male into more fury and he began to charge them, slashing at them with his huge ivories.

During the flailing of the elephant, Apollonius was surprised that he still had the capacity for thought. "If I survive this 'hello,'" he said to himself, "anything the Jews throw at me will seem like a nice evening with a whore."

"Stop!" Nicanor ordered the handlers. It was obvious that all the waving and shouting was inflaming Deucalis. They withdrew, putting the fence between them and Apollonius and the elephant.

The snuffling rants and slashes that had escalated into stupendous trumpetings finally diminished as the elephant calmed down. But as the beast paused, then stopped, Nicanor and the rest were astonished that Apollonius did not let go immediately. They also heard a strange guttural rumbling, and to their astonishment, they discovered that the strange rasping baritone they heard was Apollonius singing to the elephant.

Deucalis stood, his massive tree legs still somewhat restive, but he had stopped his charge. Apollonius let go of the tusk with one hand and reached up to the massive nob between Deucalis' eyes to stroke the leathery grey flesh. Now,the elephant's only movement was a slight sway back and forth.

Finally, Apollonius dropped away from the beast and strolled over to where Nicanor and the handlers were standing, their mouths open, and eyes widened in alarm.

"What in Hermes' name was that?" Nicanor sputtered. "What was that? Singing? If one can even call it that."

"Just a lullaby I used to sing to my sons. It seemed to calm him."

"Old friend, I am sorry. . ."

"Say nothing of it," Apollonius said cheerfully. "Deucalis and I seem to have reached an understanding." The bull approached the fence once more and this time it was Apollonius who reached through the fence and scratched the grey hide under one eye. At Nicanor's startled expression, he chuckled and said, "Oh, I do not pretend to know what that understanding is. Let us just say that two warriors have an agreement."

Nicanor could do nothing but stare.

Chapter Seventeen

Jerusalem, Judaea   The 11th day of *Nisan* 3594 (April 6th 166 B.C.E.)

N adab dismissed the scout after directing him to the paymaster. "So, the old man died," He said thoughtfully and returned to Menelaus. resuming his place at the high priest's side, as he waited for his instructions for the day. Menelaus was too disorganized to ever give any coherent instructions, but Nadab waited anyway, as he did every morning.

"I wonder if that will change things," Menelaus said as he pushed papers and tablets around his desk in a semblance of work. "They say that if you cut off the head, the rest of the body is useless. Perhaps the rebellion will die now. Ah, engineer. I have been waiting for you. We must discuss the aqueduct."

Nadab stayed silent as Menelaus turned his attention to the water engineer and his plans for the aqueduct and turned away to cough so he could roll his eyes undetected. As always, Menelaus managed to misread the obvious politics presented to him. Everyone knew that it was Mattathias' son, Judah Maccabeus, who was the heartbeat of the rebellion. Mattathias' death would be felt, yes. But the rebellion would continue in very good health.

"A premature thought, I believe, Excellency," Nadab said carefully. "We must wait and see, but the Maccabee is the one who drives the uprising."

"So that is what he is calling himself? *The Hammer*. Well, I have heard that he is rather brutish," Menelaus said. "That he is unschooled and rather stupid. Now, if we reroute this canal to the Greek quarter. . ."

Nadab idly sorted the items on Menelaus' desk and wondered where the high priest was getting his intelligence. Whoever the source, he was being paid far too much. The information was entirely false. All one had to do during the last few months is watch events unfold in the north to understand that this Judah the Maccabee was a genius of a tactician. First, General Timotheus had returned in disgrace, having lost 300 men with not one rebel death to show for it. Now, the Greek Patrols that Apollonius was sending up north were being decimated at a very healthy rate. As Menelaus' representative, Nadab had attended a military briefing by one Lieutenant Syrus the week before, and it was apparent that the Jew chieftain was succeeding in forcing the Greeks to take him seriously. This Syrus had urged the patrols to be wary and vigilant. That they should never let their guard down and that the villages round about were undoubtedly giving comfort to the rebels.

Now as Nadab listened to Menelaus discuss the rerouting of the aqueduct to accommodate the construction of the Greek Akra, he thought more on the rebellion. This Maccabee has enticed an entire population into thinking that they could be wolves rather than the sheep they have been for centuries—like the sheep that had been slaughtered in the Kidron caves the week before.

As Nadab wandered around Menelaus' room, his thoughts were busy with one another, ebbing and circling until he stopped, mid-step and mid-thought. The pacifists. They must have been the group that—what was the young man's name that had come to visit him earlier this winter? Eli? Ephraim? Ephraim. That was it. Ephraim spoke of a group who was engaged in passive resistance. Were they the ones who perished in the caves of Kidron? And this Ephraim hated Judah Maccabeus. Nadab's stomach turned cold when he realized he had missed a vital opportunity. He had not had Ephraim followed, thinking the young man would come back as he had again and again before Nadab's audience with him. But, he had not. Nadab plunged his fist into his other hand and uttered an epithet.

Nadab came out of his reverie and noticed that the engineer and Menelaus both had their eyes on him.

"I am sorry," Nadab bowed. "I just realized that I forgot to attend to one of my duties this morning. With your permission?"

Menelaus impatiently waved him out of the room and returned to this discussion with the engineer.

As Nadab walked quickly through the corridors he said aloud, "Was he with those who were in the caves? Did he perish? I must find him, this Ephraim."

As Nadab slowed to a stroll, he muttered to himself, clicking and *tsking* his way along the atrium hall to his small office. Citrus trees hung over the way, creating a canopy of fruit-laden foliage, but he hurried under, heedless of the beauty. The more he thought about losing Ephraim, the more depressed he became. Finally, the heaviness induced him to sit on a bench beneath one of the Eucalyptus trees in the atrium courtyard.

He could not shake the chagrin he felt at the loss of this opportunity. If he could have employed Ephraim, the benefits to his career would have been great, indeed. As a Jew who had thrown in his lot with the Greeks, Nadab's position was compromised by this dangerous rebellion. Although the Greeks did not particularly like him or Menelaus, the Jews hated them even more, viewing them as collaborators and even traitors. He and Menelaus would be among the first to be ousted or even killed in the event, however unlikely, that the rebellion succeeded. If Nadab could appropriate Ephraim's allegiance, or even just trick him into giving him information on the Maccabee and his rebels, he could stay the rebellion and keep his position secure in the Greek hierarchy of affairs.

After a few deep breaths, he forced himself to rise and plod away to his office. His clerk, Janus, was figuring away on the palace payroll accounts when he entered, and the abacus continued to whir as Nadab wandered out to the north balcony to watch the construction of the Akra.

The tower loomed over the palace and temple complex in stultifying ugliness. Unlike other Greek architecture that stunned with its marble elegance and beauty, this structure was entirely graceless and squat for all its height.

"Ugly, yes," Nadab said aloud, "but it will likely save our hides one day." He pictured himself cowering in one of its turrets with Menelaus and coughed out a laugh.

"Advisor? May I serve? Are you well?"

"Perfectly well, Janus," Nadab said as he walked back into the office and sat down.

The abacus popped and clicked as Janus returned to his figures and did not stop when Nadab asked, "Janus, I need an agent. Are there any available in Jerusalem?

Janus' eyes followed the colored beads as he manipulated them back and forth, but he said, "Let me see, let me see. Yes, I believe one just returned from Rome. One of our best."

"I need him to find a Jew for me. I am afraid he may have been one of those who died in the caves at the hands of Timotheus. However, if he is still alive, I must know of it."

"If anyone can find your Jew, it is Barbatus."

Nadab stood, almost upsetting the chair behind him. "Barbatus?"

"Yes, advisor. He is your man. I've never seen anyone so dogged as he. Barbatus can find anybody."

Nadab was glad that Janus was so obsessed with his figures that he did not notice the sweat dampening his brow. He had picked up one of Janus' parchments, ostensibly to inspect his cipherings, but his trembling fingers could not hold the document and it drifted out of his grasp. Yes, he was aware of Barbatus' talents. Menelaus had sent Barbatus after Jason the year before, and Nadab had not forgotten the frightening aura that surrounded the assassin, or 'agent' as Janus now referred to him. Barbatus had not only killed Jason, the former high priest, but also his wife and two young sons.

Nadab struggled over to his chair and sat down roughly. He said, "Summon him."

"Barbatus, your honor?"

"Yes," Nadab whispered. "As quickly as possible."

Chapter Eighteen

Road to Lydda, Judaea   The 22nd day of *Nisan* 3594 (April 6th166 B.C.E.)

J udah watched Asher carefully. His formidable body was resolute and confident. Asher's knees were sure against the saddle and his sitting of the mount was that of an expert horseman. The face, however, was woeful and agitated as Judah and his men galloped toward Lydda.

Mattathias' death had shrouded them all with a debilitating sadness, it was true, but Asher's depression was something more. Although Judah had finally talked Asher into the necessity of cleansing the villages and towns of their Hellenic influence, his friend was not happy about it. He knew Asher dreaded the possible clash with former friends and even family here in Lydda.

Judah had determined that the day after Shabbat would be the day to carry out their raid on the city. He had chosen Lydda because it was the Hellenic center with which he was most familiar, having spent much of his childhood here visiting his uncle, aunt and cousins. They would arrive in Lydda today, the day before Shabbat; however, he and his men would not attack during the reign of the Queen of the Week. He wanted to allow the town a couple of days to mull over his rumored arrival. Perhaps the presence of the Maccabee and his men would induce more Lyddans to observe the Shabbat than would otherwise. They could then decide who needed teaching, who needed circumcision and who needed killing to ensure the keeping of the Law in Lydda.

This contingent was the largest that Judah had ever amassed from among the men of Modiin and Beit Ur. The fleet of two hundred riders sounded thunderous to him as the equine mass rolled toward the town.

The year before, this very road had felt the hooves of *Tiklit* and *Bakayan* as Judah and Eleazar had ridden to Lydda to trick Asher into coming back to Modiin to be stoned. He had been the enemy apostate Greek then. Perhaps that was another reason that Asher rode along so sullenly now— he remembered that day also.

Judah bivouacked his men well outside the Greek town. Two hundred could not easily infiltrate the Greek center, but two could. After he made sure his men were well ensconced in the grove of cedars about two furlongs from his Uncle Benyamin's house, he took Aulus, and the two hiked into Lydda, leaving the horses behind with the other men.

"Judah," Aulus asked as they walked along, "are you sure you should not take Asher? He knows the town far better than I and he has more contacts."

"His are not the contacts I need. I am afraid that his contacts, that is, his former associates, are beyond persuasion. For all intents and purposes, they are full Greek. Moreover, those who lean toward us might regard the former Eupolemus as an infidel and not trust us."

"But Judah," Aulus persisted. "If they saw that the famous wrestler, Eupolemus, was back with you, would they not cling more fully to your cause? I would think that you could even gather a few who you say are 'beyond persuasion' because they esteemed Asher when he was the Great Eupolemus. Your logic is faulty."

Judah believed that his logic was faulty also, but what he did not want to tell Aulus was that he did not trust Asher this day. Asher's strange silence bothered him, and he wanted to make sure that his friend stayed safely in camp. Another thing that Judah did not tell Aulus is that he assigned Avram and Eleazar to keep close watch on Asher to make sure that he did nothing to compromise the mission in Lydda.

"Also, Judah, if the local Jews know of your arrival, the Greeks will too," Aulus pointed out. "They will come looking for us. I hope you made arrangements to make our camp mobile every night."

"Old friend, we are of the same mind," Judah said, smiling. "After night falls, Eleazar will move the camp across the road to a well-hidden ravine we know of. The night before the attack we will move to the hills above the Greek quarter."

Aulus nodded in approval. "Are we not stopping at your uncle's?" he asked as Judah walked resolutely past the little estate on the eastern edge of town.

"No," Judah said, pulling a hood over his head. "I am afraid that the house is being watched, and I do not want to endanger my uncle and aunt any more than I already have."

"Should I conceal also? Aulus said, his hand on his hood.

"No. You are a Roman merchant. I am your slave."

Aulus chuckled. "Oh, that is right! I am going to enjoy this!"

Although Judah did not want to stop at his uncle's house, that did not mean that he would not contact him. He hoped to see Benyamin at the temple high priest's dwelling closer to the Greek side of Lydda. He felt that the word of his and his men's coming would spread faster from the center of town.

Many Greek soldiers were patrolling the streets, especially in the Jewish Quarter. This gave Aulus a chance to cuff Judah repeatedly across the head and yell "*Serve improbe! Noli mihi dicere!*" Evil slave! Do not speak to me!" Judah took the pounding with good grace, cowering as a slave should, but vowed he would take each strike out of Aulus' hide the next time they sparred in training; however, Judah and Aulus' discretion allowed them to avoid all Greek patrols.

When the high priest's home came into view along with the marble columns of the Greek section of Lydda, Judah noticed that there were more Greek buildings than the last time he was here. The Hellenists had made incursions into the Jewish section of the town. He wondered if they were buying the land from the Jews or if the Greek officials were simply confiscating estates that served their territorial needs. He set his mouth. If the latter were true, that would stop.

He and Aulus walked around the back of the house and knocked quietly at the door that led out to the garden, the tendrils of old growth erupting with the immature growth of early spring. The door opened and the high priest's wife peered out.

"The Maccabee!" she exclaimed and slammed the door shut.

Judah and Aulus heard her through the door, the voice a shrill whisper, "Husband! It is the Maccabee. He is here!"

From behind the door, the high priest thundered, "Well, why did you slam the door in his face?" The door opened and they heard the voice in all its volume, "Are you crazy, woman?" The face calmed, however, and a smile beckoned with a clandestine look this way and that. "Come in, come in," the high priest of Lydda whispered.

Judah and Aulus entered the house. "Sit, sit," the high priest said. "It is good to see you, Judah! So today is the day? But the Queen of the Week arrives at sundown. That is only a few hours away," he said. "Wife! Food and drink!"

"Thank you for your welcome," Judah said with a slight bow and sat down on the rug where the high priest indicated. "This is my friend, Aulus."

"Yes, the Roman! I have heard of you. Infidel that you are, you are still welcome in my house. It was not always so, but these are strange times."

Aulus nodded awkwardly and sat down next to Judah.

"*Adohni*, we will wait until the day after Shabbat for our raid. We want news of our arrival to spread, so that those who are of our cause will have a chance to be prepared and let their intentions be known. And Moshe said, 'The Lord will not suffer the destroyer to come in unto your houses to smite them.' I do not want to hurt any who are with us. But," Judah said, "if any be against us, they shall not stand.

"I will let it be known that you are here," the high priest said.

As the high priest called for his young son, Judah thought back to his last visit here. In his speech in the synagogue, he had made it clear to the people that they were to be exact in observing the Law and that they must do their best to convince their neighbors to do the same. Those had been friendly faces, faces that were with him and the cause. There were many, however, who had not been there. Those Jews who had cleaved to the Hellenic life would likely not listen to him. He could only hope that their neighbors, friends and relatives by now had convinced them to come back to the Law.

As the high priest instructed his son, Judah could see that the boy did his best to attend his father's words, but his distracted eyes kept darting back and forth between his father and Judah. Finally, the high priest had to gently pat his son on the side of the head to make sure he was listening to the instructions.

"Shlomo! Listen! Do you understand?"

"Yes," the boy said breathlessly, now looking fully at Judah. "I am to go to Reuven's, Shishak's and all the shops where we trade and tell them that the day after Shabbat is the Day of the Maccabee."

The high priest looked at Judah and said, "It will not take long for the word to spread throughout the town to Jew and Greek alike that the day of Greek rule in Lydda is done. From now on we will be part of a Jewish realm."

Judah glanced over at Aulus briefly then said uneasily, "A Jewish realm, your honor? I only wish to teach the people that they must follow the Law—"

"Judah, this is much bigger than that. If you succeed in limiting the Greek influence in a town like Lydda, more people are going to start thinking about wresting power away from the Greeks and setting up their own king." The high priest quoted, "'And they anointed David King over Israel.' David was thirty years old when he began to rule, and he reigned for forty years. How old are you, Judah?"

Judah felt Aulus' eyes on him as he sputtered, "With all due respect, your honor, what on earth are you talking about? A Jewish king? Me? Ridiculous!"

"Not so ridiculous, Judah. At least, the Lord G-d and the prophet Samuel did not think so when they anointed Jesse's son."

"I am worried about subduing this town, not ruling it," Judah protested. He stood. "It is time we leave. I thank you for your hospitality and the good food."

"G-d go with Judah the Maccabee," the high priest intoned, "and with his Roman friend as well."

Aulus bowed as he followed Judah out. When they were back on the road, he said, "From a slave to a king—all in one day. Your god must be collaborating with Zeus. Such power!"

"Quiet, you," Judah growled from beneath the hood. "Let us go back to camp and make ready."

"Careful how you talk to your master, slave," Aulus said, cuffing Judah in the side of the head once again.

The words flew about the town like the desiccated leaves of a fall long past. "The Maccabee is here" and "Judah has arrived with his Men of Modiin," (for his men were becoming almost as famous as Judah, himself) and "Judah is here to banish the Greeks." A bustling rumor even proclaimed that Judah had already declared himself king and that the seat of his throne was to be in Lydda—to be renamed *Beit Judah*, "The House of Judah."

The Greeks heard it too, but their response was different. "The Maccabee? What is that? A disease?" "No, it is a Jewish warrior." "Is that not the same thing? Well, our soldiers will make short work of his rag-tag band." "He is warning us to follow Jewish ways." "He thinks to convert us? A Greek pike will convert him!"

When Judah and Aulus gave the word, from the copses to the ravine, the men of Modiin scrambled to set up camp so that they not desecrate the Queen of the Week more than was needful. They had resolved to defend themselves even on Shabbat but did not want to tempt the Lord of Hosts too far beyond the Law. Therefore, after they settled down under the gibbous moon of Shabbat and were finally at rest, they allowed themselves the comfort of hope. Hope that they were up to the task of scouring the Greeks from Lydda.

Chapter Nineteen

Lydda, Judaea   The 13th day of *Nisan* 3594 (April 8th 166 B.C.E.)

T he day after Shabbat, the devout stayed in their homes, signifying that they would offer no opposition to the Maccabee. Judah's emissary, his Uncle Benyamin, the caretaker of the synagogue, had assured them of their safety in synagogue the day before. If the priests and elders would but attest to their sons' circumcisions, Judah and the Men of Modiin would pass by their dwellings in their cleansing of Lydda.

Judah started his men out early. The two-hundred rode over the town at dawn, the first task to be the breaking down of the altars of false gods located throughout the Greek quarter of Lydda. Marble would fall, stone friezes would crumble under their clubs and any who stopped them would fall by the sword. Any who were not circumcised could enter the synagogue and have the ordinance performed by the high priest of Lydda. No one, no matter how old, no matter how sinful, would be turned away who wanted to adhere to the Law. All would be welcome as G-d's people.

The heathen altars were toppled by horse and rope. Any humans who interfered were just as easily subdued. As Judah and his men moved their numbers through the Hellenic quarter, however, they were surprised at the lack of resistance. Only two priests and three female acolytes of Aphrodite emerged from her temple. Their shrieks trailed after them as they fled town and Judah's sword. As Judah's men, amused, watched the worshippers flap away, they stayed wary. They were sure that the Greek contingent of soldiers that was stationed here would soon show itself and would be a major factor in their success or failure in gaining Lydda. As it turned out, it was not a factor at all. The contingent simply faded away.

Asher, who had convinced Judah at the last minute to allow him to ride into Lydda with the others, had ridden down one of the alleys of the Greek quarter with a small patrol to flush out any stragglers; he and the patrol now clattered toward Judah, Asher's face alight with joy, the others looking more solemn.

"It seems impossible," Asher said, breathless with happiness, "but everyone from the quarter is gone. The word of our arrival must have spread." He shook his head. "Why would the Greeks run without a fight?"

Judah shared a smile with Asher. He had been worried that Asher would have to face old companions, either accepting them into the congregation or smiting them if they shunned the Law. It could have been a very ugly situation. "Asher," Judah said meaningfully, "The Lord of Hosts is with us!"

"The Lord of Hosts is with us!" Asher returned solemnly, turning his horse to gallop down another alley.

"It looks like they left everything behind," Avram said, coming out of an abandoned bakery, his hands and pockets full of leavened booty. "They even left coins in the till."

"Avram, are you sure the bread is that of the Law?" Judah said, laughing. "I would not have you become unclean, or we may have to banish you."

"Have no fear," Avram said through the large wad of dough. "They were Kosher enough to have the prayer in their doorpost. They must have served the Jewish quarter."

To Eleazar, who had ridden up and halted beside him, Judah said, "Brother, go and tell the entire company to stay alert. We do not know if this is a trap." With a pointed look at Avram, he continued, "And there is to be no looting. If anyone is to benefit from the merchants abandoning their concerns, it is to be the Jewish inhabitants of Lydda.

Judah watched Avram skulk away and almost grinned. He did not begrudge the blacksmith his bread, but he also did not want anarchy to sully their victory, no matter how easily won. The word to be careful spread among the two-hundred, but in the end it was unnecessary. The fighters encountered no one who was willing to stand up for their Hellenic gods or Greek practices. They had fled instead.

"Judah!" The reapproach of Eleazar's *Bakayan* covered *Tiklit* and Judah with an explosion of dust. "You must see this!"

Judah urged *Tiklit* to follow *Bakayan*. The two brothers slowed when they came upon a quiet herd of horsed men. At Judah's touch, Tiklit merged into the mass. These fifty fighters had just finished their sweep of the Jewish quarter and now, along with Judah, their ears and eyes strained toward the sound.

Finally, they discerned a faint enunciation of song:

> *Saul has slain his thousands,*
> *And David his ten-thousands.*

The women of the Jewish quarter, no longer cowering in their homes, no longer afraid of the Greek beast, were marching toward the fighters. Women had sung this song once before back in the days of King David when he had slain an entire army of Philistines. The melody lilted and flowed down the street toward Judah and his men. They dismounted and moved slowly down the street in the direction of the music.

> *Saul has slain his thousands,*
> *And David his ten-thousands.*

The tune was familiar and the men, in spite of being encumbered by helmets, armor and weapons, found themselves swaying that soon escalated into a celebration of dance.

Judah did not dismount with the others, knowing how Aulus would chide him later for not acting the commander and joining in the celebration. As he leaned on the pommel of *Tiklit's* saddle and watched, he marveled at the ease of their victory here. And today, the priest had not had to force circumcision of even one infant or adult male. Any who had wanted to repent had submitted to the ceremonial knife of the priest as soon as the Shabbat sun had descended the day before. Judah smirked a little when Benyamin told him that none of the newly converted were with them to celebrate in the streets today. They were home nursing their privates.

The women sang and Judah's men danced until midday. The women set out food as at a wedding, and all sang and danced some more. Those who had decided to return and throw their lot in with the Maccabee thronged in the street until it became strained with humanity. At last, the final glow of day disappeared behind the ruined marble of the Greek quarter and the weary, but still teeming numbers wandered toward the synagogue at the center of the Jewish quarter. The high priest and Benyamin unlocked the doors and let them in. Some who had not frequented the house of worship for years leaned upon the arms of those who had, and the spirit of tolerance and camaraderie filled the holy structure. Later it was said that many beheld the ghostly presences of cherubim and seraphim wafting among the human worshippers. And others swore that they had heard a great rushing wind accompany the words of the high priest as he conducted the impromptu service.

Before the Queen of the Week made another visit to Lydda, the marble reliefs of buildings left standing had been etched free of all the human forms that the infidel Greeks had so blatantly carved into their pediments and columns. All the statues of the heathen gods and demigods had been crushed into rubble that would be used for the mortar of new Jewish homes. The remaining Greek structures would come down as time and the seasons would allow.

Judah and his men stayed for a week. They wanted to ensure that Lydda, now endowed with the good Semitic name of Lod as in the days of Shemed the Benyaminite, was now a Jewish holding and would ever stay that way.

Chapter Twenty

Jerusalem, Judaea   The 15th day of *Nisan* 3594 (April 10th 166 B.C.E.)

This time there would be no leniency. Apollonius had all the commanders of the Lydda contingent put to death in the yard of the palace barracks, their heads buried separate from their bodies.

"I want to make sure that they have a very hard time finding their way to Hades," Apollonius said to Philo as they conversed out in the yard after the executions. "I want the lord of the underworld to spew them out of his mouth. Let them wander in oblivion for eternity. The cowardly fools. Have their subordinates scourged—fifty lashes each—and throw them into the Akra."

"Commander," Philo said, "I am not sure the Akra has enough completed cells at the moment to accommodate all of them."

"Then double or triple them up," Apollonius snapped. "Cram them together like olives in an urn. Just house them!"

Philo turned to Syrus and nodded. The newly promoted colonel strode away to instruct the executioner and his scourgers.

As Apollonius idly watched Syrus converse with the lieutenant of the death cohort, he muttered, "This is getting ridiculous. Here is another cohort that I may not be able to use if it is so easily convinced to desert its post. Handing over Lydda to the Jews," he said in vehement disgust. "Oh, for the days of Alexander where all who served were true Macedonian, and not these indigenous bastard Bedouin. I swear to Zeus that they do not know the meaning of tenacity."

"Quite right," Philo agreed. "Ever since we allowed the recruitment of the natives, however necessary, the quality of the cohorts has diminished. Now, as to the Jews, what have you been authorized to do?"

"I am waiting for final word from Nicanor," Apollonius said as he watched the last of the headless bodies borne from the grounds amid the grunts of those receiving their lashes. "I have my orders, but I am not to march upon Gophna until Antiochus has been notified of our plan."

"Which of my cohorts from Jerusalem would you like me to make ready?" Philo asked.

"None of them," Apollonius answered and stood with his arms folded as if daring Philo to react. "I am using my Samarian cohorts. They will deal with the problems from now on."

Philo did react, but only in a slight reel backward as if struck. He said nothing, bowed backed away respectfully from his superior and left the yard. He did not even remain to witness the rest of the beheadings and scourgings.

Those who fled Lydda are part of the Hieropolis/Jerusalem cohort, Apollonius thought. And Philo is responsible for their cowardice. Disciplining his commanders was never pleasant—well, once in a while it was—but he knew that refusing to use Philo's Hieropolis cohorts for the campaign up north was a severe blow to his ego. But how in Ares' name could he keep sending the same troops that the Jews kept routing? Certainly, morale of Philo's cohort would drop when they found out he was not using them to march on the Jews of Gophna, but it was worse for morale that the empire kept losing men to this ridiculous conflict with Jewish farmers and merchants. He was lucky that Antiochus seemed occupied with his preparations for the campaign to Parthia. If the monarch had been paying more attention to the Jewish problem, Apollonius probably would have lost his head by now.

He became aware of someone standing nearby and his whirring thoughts ceased. Although his new adjutant did not speak and stood deferentially off to the side of the commander, Apollonius sensed a question and turned toward him immediately.

"Lieutenant Syrus, is it not?"

"Colonel now, sir."

"Ah, yes. You are he who commanded the only patrol to escape the Maccabee last week. Congratulations on your promotion."

"Thank you, sir." Syrus did not smile but straightened his shoulders beneath the praise.

"How can I help you, Colonel?"

Syrus paused for a moment then said, "Sir, not to sound presumptuous, but am I to go with your Samarians up north? I would like to be of service."

"That remains to be seen, Colonel," Apollonius said noncommittally. "I will assess my need but keep acquitting yourself as you did with your patrol, and I will probably be able to use you."

The soldier kept a straight face, commending him further, Apollonius thought. Syrus saluted as if to leave, thinking himself dismissed, but Apollonius asked, "I wonder, Syrus, did you have an ear to the cohort who fled the Jews?"

Syrus stopped mid-salute and considered the question, then said carefully, "I heard some talk among those who fled, yes, commander."

Apollonius cocked an expectant eyebrow.

Syrus rushed on, "Well, sir. The men I talked to were a superstitious lot, and they were saying that they heard and saw things in Lydda that frightened them."

"Nonsense. What could they have seen?" Apollonius started walking toward Philo's office in the barracks. A slight incline of his head invited Syrus to accompany.

"You are right, sir. It is nonsense and I hesitate to repeat it. But they said that there were—apparitions."

"Apparitions. You mean ghosts?" Apollonius asked, straightening to keep his dignified bearing.

"That is what they said, commander. Ghostly beings appeared to many in the cohort. The men said they spoke a strange language that sounded like otherworldly music."

"Otherworldly music?" This time Apollonius shook the semblance of dignity and gave full vent to disbelief, his voice harried. "How in Hades' name would those louts know what 'otherworldly music' sounded like?"

"It does sound absurd," Syrus agreed. "Not only that, but the night before they were expecting the Jewish attack, the rumor being that the Maccabee was in town, a loud rushing wind kept them awake all night. That frightened them because no trees bent in the supposed gale and they insisted that no clouds heralded a storm. One of the men said that it seemed that these things proved that the Hebrew god was more powerful than our own pantheon, and what could they do but retreat? As they had heard that the Jews were going to launch the attack at dawn, the cohort crept out before sunup. The Greek civilians heard the retreat and fled with them. Those refugees are starting to drift into Hierosolyma even now. "

Apollonius stood at the entrance to the barracks and thought for a moment. Finally, he gazed at Syrus and said, "I want the name of that man who blasphemed against our gods, saying that the Hebrew god was more powerful." He thought for another moment, then said, "And, I want you to arrange for me to meet with Menelaus, the High Priest of Jerusalem. See if he will meet me here in the barracks—I cannot keep straight which ones will 'dirty' their feet in a visit to our grounds, and which ones refuse. I do not care about that. I need more information on this Maccabee, and Menelaus with his connections is the one to get it. That will be all."

After Syrus left, Apollonius sat down and shuffled his tablets and papers around for a moment. He needed intelligence on this Jew, and worry filled his mind as he thought of the drubbing the Greeks had suffered yet again at this rebel's hands.

"Nicanor. Where are you when I need you?" Apollonius sighed and stood. Nicanor had left the week before to return to the emperor in Antioch. What would he have thought of these ridiculous stories of otherworldly beings? Apollonius harrumphed. Nicanor would have added twenty lashes to each man for being drunk on duty. Feeling a little better having channeled his old friend, he picked up one of the parchments on his desk. As he looked over the report on the Akra progress, he thought of his Samarians and relief further warmed him. He must return to Samaria within the month to prepare his assault on the rebel stronghold in Gophna. That was just what he needed: a tangible plan of action to get at the problem. He would go ahead and gather all the intelligence that he needed on this Judah the Maccabee, and his Samarians would return the drubbing to the Jews with a usurer's interest. He sat down and unhappily returned to the pile of work on Philo's desk. This time he did not bang his knee.

Chapter Twenty-one

Gophna, Judaea   The 20th day of *Nisan*, 3594 (April 15th 166 B.C.E.)

I t was not acceptable to show it, but the women of Gophna worried. They never spoke of their anxiety in large groups, but rather waited for the intimacy of two or three before they spoke openly, and even then, they were not as open as their thoughts.

Shoshanna and Miriam clapped the carding blocks together and culled the thatches of yellow wool into manageable tufts.

As Miriam worked over one particularly knotty clump, she said, "You and Eleazar seem to be enjoying married life. It shows in your faces."

"It was difficult at first, but Eleazar was kind—and patient."

Miriam said nothing, but nodded. It was noised about Gophna that Shoshanna and Eleazar's marriage bed had been troubled because of the way Shoshanna had been used by the barbarian Greek. In fact, there were many who disapproved of Eleazar's decision to honor the betrothal after Shoshanna's defilement. It did not matter that she had been carried off by force; she was still a damaged woman.

Any who had been brave enough to voice their criticism to Eleazar soon regretted their audacity, for he sent them away with their ears ringing with epithets and threats. Even Judah, who was uncertain about Eleazar's decision to marry Shoshanna, had had to fight off Eleazar a year ago when he had told his brother that he should forget Shoshanna. Now he spoke of his reservations about the match to Miriam, but no one else. "I fear for them," he had said to Miriam after the contract was renewed, overseen by Esther the matchmaker. "I do not know if Eleazar will be able to shake the image of Shoshanna having been with the Greek. I know I would not."

Judah's remark had chilled Miriam, and she could not help but think that perhaps, had she been in Shoshanna's place that Judah would have put her away. Now as

Miriam watched Shoshanna's expert hands pull and separate the unruly strands of wool, she was glad that Eleazar was able to discard the traditions and mores that would have allowed him to discard Shoshanna. There was even an undercurrent of thought among the most rigid that explored the possibility of stoning Shoshanna. Both Judah and, before his death, Mattathias, for all his orthodoxy, had stepped in and squelched all talk about stoning. They strengthened the point that Shoshanna had no choice in the matter of her use, having been carried off against her will.

"If all our men die, what will become of us?" Shoshanna's voice was matter-of-fact.

It was an unusual question for Shoshanna, and Miriam stared for a moment before remembering her manners. The question made her think hard, given her thoughts of a moment before. She said, "I heard Judah say that perhaps we could flee to Rome. There are communities of Jews there who might accept us."

"Rome?" Shoshanna asked. "I hear the Romans are brutal. In some cases, even worse than the Greeks."

"Not if they are our allies," Miriam pointed out. "But it will never come to that. We are gaining in numbers. Entire villages now are joining us, no more just a trickle of refugees. And, the men say that the rebellion is gaining strength in word and deed throughout Judaea. Pockets of resistance are forming outside of Judah's sphere on the strength of his name alone." She patted Shoshanna whose carding blocks were now idle, her thoughts obviously having arrested her work. "We have nothing to fear."

The ashen lines in Shoshanna's features reflected her skepticism. She clapped the blocks against each other as she raked out more wool. "That is what I always used to think," she said sadly.

The women carded the mounds of freshly sheared wool in silence for many hours. Shearing occurred earlier on Gophna than it would have in Modiin. Although the full warmth of spring was not expected for another two weeks, the need for wool outweighed the sheep's comfort. The weather was temperate enough that the sheep would not freeze, for they were a valuable commodity, but the daily current of refugees compounded the urgency for clothing and blankets.

The cry of "They are back from Lydda!" induced the women to throw aside their carding blocks and run toward the command tent. That is where the returning men would congregate and report their success or failure, the latter of which there had not been many, Miriam thought with relief as she ran along, pulling wisps of stray wool from her clothing and head scarf. She aided Shoshanna in the same way as they ran along to join the crowd that was forming around the command tent.

"This does not look like all the men," Shoshanna observed as the warriors wearing the grit of travel thundered into camp. "Some are missing!"

"Judah was planning on leaving half of the men in Lydda to help in administering its affairs and to train more men for the rebellion," Miriam said. "But where are Judah and Eleazar?"

Whereas before, the returning warriors would make a ceremony of reporting to Mattathias, now it was Shoshanna's father, Mordechai Ben Baruch, to whom they delivered their debriefing. Mordechai had never been foremost in the village hierarchy as he was often thought shallow and weak. However, as Mordechai was the most senior of the high priest council, Judah felt that his stepping into the role of receiving the reports as Mattathias had done would provide the people with a familiar continuity.

Miriam and Shoshanna stood side-by-side, both mourning the recent loss of their father-in-law, Mattathias. Shoshanna, however, was proud of the new stature, albeit mostly figurative, of her beloved father. They were outside the main body of the mass, and Miriam stood on tiptoe when she finally heard Judah's baritone delivering the report. She saw that he had climbed atop one of the logs by the campfire so he could be better heard by the crowd.

* * * * *

". . .As improbable as it seems, we encountered no resistance to speak of in Lydda," Judah announced breathlessly. "A few fat priests and priestesses of Bacchus and Aphrodite waddled out when we pulled down the statues of their deities, but all we had to do was wave our swords at them and they fled the town right quickly."

The laughter that this remark inspired was a welcome vent for the anxiety of the village. Many had felt that Lydda would be a frightening contest that would test the fortitude of their fighters, and that they might fail. They had faced so many terrible obstacles, but virtually all had melted before them as wax. Now another great victory graced their community, and again not one drop of Jewish blood was lost. "The Lord of Hosts with us," the crowd shouted. "The Lord G-d is Great! He is the Master of the Universe!"

As Judah gave them time to react to his speech, his eyes searched for Miriam. He widened his periphery to include the outskirts of the crowd and at last found her. Their eyes glinted with relief that they still had each other. Buoyed by her gaze, he interrupted the crowd, hushing them good-naturedly.

"I know I keep telling you that the ease of our victories up to now will soon end— "He held out his hands for quiet. "But the time will come," he said, "when our blood and that of our children will sweeten the land for which we fight. Will you say that the cost is too high? Will you say that we must speak peace with our enemy? Will you say that the fight has been long enough and that we must lay down our arms?"

The crowd was not silent for long. A cry of "No!" sheared the quiet and another and another until the air was rent with shouts that shunned weakness and banished indecision.

As was a commander's wont, Judah felt compelled to sober the crowd further by being more specific about the dangers to come. "We have been lucky so far, but I assure you that the time will come when we will be tested and tried," he said. "We have been fighting the Jerusalem cohort up to now. They are not as formidable as the other cohorts in the various *kotaikai* round about. I am talking about Apollonius' Samarians, of course."

The crowd, restive and good natured up to now, immediately became solemn at the mention of the Samarians. These were Apollonius' chosen cohort, rumored to be cruel and hard. They knew all about Apollonius by now, too. He had been the author of the parade of death in Jerusalem. There was barely a family in Modiin and Beit Ur who had not lost loved ones in that butchery. Such a foe could not be taken lightly.

When Judah saw the disconsolate faces, he saw that he had achieved his objective of exorcising their idea of unopposed victory. He did not want to leave them thus, however. He thumped his brother, John, on the shoulder and said, "But, be not sad, my people! Lift up your heads. The Greeks are formidable, but not unbeatable. And, do not forget! We have the Lord of Hosts with us! For if he be with us, who can stand against us?"

"No one!" the village of Gophna cried. "No one!"

Judah jumped down from his log perch by the campfire and ploughed through the furrows of robes until he came to Miriam. Their greeting was sedate, but as Judah led her away to their tent, the conjugal gleam in their eyes made those nearby exchange merry looks.

* * * * *

Miriam leaned up on her elbow and watched Judah as he dozed. Such moments were as rare as gold and as precious—these times when she had the commander of the rebellion all to herself. He had become harder in body than when they were first betrothed as teenagers. All of them had been softer, then. She had not brought her mirror with her to Gophna, an oversight that she cursed every day, but she was sure if she looked into the polished metal, she would see a different image as well. Her clothing was loose, and her cheeks and chin felt like they protruded more than usual. Yes, they had all changed, she thought, watching Judah's shoulder ripple as he stretched in his sleep. Living out-of-doors, milking goats, shearing sheep, repairing fences, in fact, doing almost everything that they were used to having done for them by servants had hardened them all.

This wilderness living was not anything like the world in which she had been raised, but she found that it suited her. She enjoyed working outdoors and learning how to work with her hands. Not that she had been pampered before. As much as her father and mother had wanted to pamper her as befitted the daughter of a wealthy businessman, they failed. The more they admonished her over the years to be more feminine, to sit more demurely, to keep her voice down, to not be so sarcastic and insulting, to stay indoors and work at the loom, the more Miriam fled from the tenets of their advice. All during her childhood she had enjoyed being outdoors, her hands in the dirt, grooming her horse, climbing a tree or even throwing rocks at the neighborhood boys, or girls, for that matter. Her father had only once put his foot down regarding her behavior. It was in her thirteenth year. He found her crouched under the belly of her horse, pounding a nail into the shoe on its hoof under the expert but uneasy eye of the family groom.

Miriam grinned at the memory, her eyes shining in the dark. Judah exhaled and rolled toward her. Although he did not wake, he reached over her body and clutched at it until she rolled toward him. Now she was married to the commander of Israel. Her arm dimpled with goosebumps when she thought back to all the other biblical generals in her people's ancient writ: Moshe, Yehoshua, David. Bathsheba came to her mind. Did not David's ill-gotten consort wash herself naked on her roof? Miriam's laugh blurted only for a moment; she stifled herself so she would not wake Judah. Even so, he shifted and groaned.

She burrowed into his chest, and chuckled softly to herself, "David and Bathsheba : Judah and Miriam."

This time, she had to crawl out of the tent to keep from waking her husband.

Chapter Twenty-two

Gophna, Judaea   The 22nd day of *Nisan* 3594 (April 16th 166 B.C.E.)

Ephraim chuckled. "*Nu*, you finally married Eleazar."

Shoshanna looked up in surprise at Ephraim, smiled, and laid her cheek back against the goat's flank and resumed milking. Her family had been close to Ephraim's and they had played together as children. It was pleasing to see him again among the people. "I was kept from my beloved," she said. "Things happened."

"Yes, I heard." Ephraim had just fetched water for his tent. He set the two buckets outside the stall where Shoshanna was working. He entered the small enclosure and crouched beside the goat. The gentle ping, shush, ping of the milk stream rattling the pail was a comforting sound. It reminded him of his childhood. He was wistful as he said, "Many things have changed for us. But here we all are together. That is something."

Shoshanna wiped her hands on her apron and drew the pail out from under the goat. "Yes, that is indeed something. I am sorry for your loss. I heard about your betrothed being murdered by the Greeks."

Ephraim blanched. He had ever maintained his lie that Deborah had been slain by the Greeks and not by his own hand, and hearing the lie still shocked him. He did not know what to say.

Shoshanna glanced away from his pale face and whispered, "I am sorry. I should not have mentioned it."

Ephraim straightened and said, "Think not of it. You are very kind to acknowledge my grief. Her brother and family were also lost. They were dear to me also. Hezekiah and I were best friends." He barely was able to articulate this last utterance. He missed

Hezekiah almost more than he did Deborah. After all, he and Hez had known each other better, his relationship with Deborah was new.

Shoshanna put her hand on his arm, ignoring the custom that a woman not touch a male not of the family. "I know. I lost many close to me." She did not elaborate further.

Ephraim wondered if she were referring to Jews or Greeks. After all, she had spent a lot of time in the company of the enemy. It would be plausible that she had formed— relationships.

"So, are you going to let Shoshanna do all the work?"

Shoshanna and Ephraim turned. Judah had just washed his face in one of Ephraim's buckets. Water was still pouring from his beard and he sopped it into the front of his mantle.

"I worked hard to heft that water up here!" Ephraim protested. "But I will overlook your greed just this once, only because you are the great warrior and commander."

Judah and Ephraim watched Shoshanna pour milk through the straining cloth. Judah said, "Well, I am gathering our men for a command meeting. Shoshanna, do you know where your husband is?"

Shoshanna wrung out the cloth into the dirt. "I believe he is over that bluff yonder. He said something about gathering better wood for the arrow shafts. The fletchers were complaining about the green wood they had to use for the last batch of arrows."

"Ever the carpenter, that one," Judah said, laughing. "Ephraim. I need you at the meeting, too. Come. Stay well, sister."

"Go with G-d, brother."

The sky was glorious that day. The sparse clouds of the early spring drifted across the blue. As Ephraim and Judah gathered the commanders, all commented on the sky and decided that instead of meeting in the command tent, they would build a fire against the chill and meet outside.

Around the fire, the men alternated between loose discussions about the victory of Lydda the day before, and the success of the patrols in killing Greeks. Judah brought the last of the men to the fire.

"Perhaps the Lord wants the world to know that he is with us," Avram was saying when Judah arrived. "Perhaps none of us will ever fall."

Most of the men scoffed at this. Amid derisive yet good-natured snorts and catcalls, Eleazar said, "Perhaps. And perhaps, Antiochus will embrace Moshe as his own. I, for one, would volunteer to circumcise the emperor."

Laughter crackled into the flames and Judah smiled. He said into the remaining deep rumbles, "We must send out more patrols tomorrow. I would like most of you to concentrate your vigilance closer to Jerusalem. I hear we are having an effect. More and more refugees are finding their way to us and they are telling me that there are not as many Greeks being sent out."

Today, in honor of the unexpected ease of their victory in Lydda, Judah had allowed some of the younger men to join them around the campfire. These included his younger brothers, John and Shimon. They sat, trying not to fidget.

"Remember that we must slay every member of every patrol that we come across," Judah said. "The Greeks must understand that patrolling our country is going to be costly with their blood. If they keep finding Greek bodies strewn about on the roads that they are attempting to patrol, we may be able to gain control of the hills outside of Jerusalem.

Shimon raised his hand. Judah ignored him.

"So. Who? Where?" Judah asked.

"I will take the region of Gath," Schmuel, Judah's overseer, said.

"And I, Ashdod," Avram said.

Shimon's hand was still raised.

Judah looked at the hand. He was clearly irritated with his little brother. At least Shimon did not speak. Finally, Judah decided to reward Shimon's verbal restraint by letting him voice his question or comment. "Yes, Shimon. What is it?"

"Forgive me, Commander, but I have a suggestion."

The men coughed and straightened their faces at the piped "Commander."

"What is it?" Judah repeated.

"Well, sir. You just said that the attacks on the patrols are having an effect on the Greeks. And, remember that merchant last night who spoke of the Greek soldier who feared going out on patrol because of us 'dirty murdering Jews'?"

The men smiled again, and Judah said impatiently, "Yes, yes. I remember. Get on with it, Shimon."

Shimon went on, unaffected by Judah's grumbling demeanor. "Well, I think that we can scare the superstitious Greeks even more if, after we kill them, we hide their bodies."

The men did not smile, but neither did they protest. Even Judah, who had opened his mouth to slam Shimon's suggestion, closed his mouth after he had thought for a moment.

Shimon, seeming to sense acquiescence, went on eagerly, "Think how confused the Greeks would become if they never knew what happened to their patrols? That those who were sent out simply disappeared? I think that will make the infidels even more fearful because they will have no idea what we did to them."

"That is a lot of trouble, Shimon," Eleazar growled. "You do not know what we are up against during a patrol. Dragging bodies about would make our job more difficult."

"But, not impossible," Judah mused. "I think it is worth a try. Morale is everything in this conflict. We do not have the numbers, at least not yet, to engage the Greeks in a pitched battle. But we do have our wiles. That we have been lucky against the Greeks thus far can work well in our favor; Shimon's trick of hiding the bodies may diminish their morale even further."

Shimon's eyes shone with pride. Judah's other sibling, John, looked grudgingly impressed. John, two years older, was sturdier than Shimon, but Judah knew that even he recognized that Shimon had more brains. He also knew that John disliked Shimon's getting all this attention.

"John, I want you to increase the number of look-out points among our hills here," Judah said. "We have more refugees from which to draw the youth for look-out duty. The Greeks, I am sure, are amassing some kind of force, I just wish I had more details about who is leading them and when they plan to attack. Shimon, I want you to help your older brother."

As he watched John scramble away with Shimon, Judah noted with satisfaction John's relieved expression that he was not forgotten. Ever since Judah had assumed command of this rebellion, he had paid more attention to politics in the world and here in the camp. He knew that family rivalries were probably the most destructive force that faced any kingdom or potentate. The Egyptians, Persians, even the Greek empire all had split in civil war and had dynasties obliterated because brother fought brother, father fought son, or even sister fought brother to gain power. He wanted to avoid those terrible nepotistic struggles if possible. He could see a real rivalry brewing between Shimon and John, for all that they were inseparable, and he did not want to fuel it in any way.

The command circle still hunkered around the campfire, whose embers were settling, dwindling into ash. He stared at the coals. Returning to his concern about where and when the Greeks would attack, he said, "We need to start gathering intelligence. I need to know more about the Greeks. Although it was disconcerting to have them camped in the valley below, at least I knew what they were up to. Now I feel like I am blind, and I do not like the feeling."

* * * * *

Ephraim, who had been silent during the entire exchange around the campfire, straightened somewhat. He had been feeling out of sorts among all his former friends and neighbors with all their talk of war and implements of war. He was not a warrior and he felt it no more keenly than now. He worried that he had nothing to contribute, nothing to offer, until this moment.

"Judah," Ephraim said, "I would have a word with you, alone."

The men looked over at Judah and at his nod of dismissal, gratefully rose and retired to their tents and wives. As they drifted away from the dying campfire, Ephraim moved over and sat next to Judah. "Judah, I may be able to help in the area you speak of."

"What area?" Judah asked, his expression absent with weariness. Obviously, his mind had already moved on to a more familiar topic than intelligence as he was hunched over a rough map of the hills. Ephraim guessed he was now wondering how he would set up training venues with the new refugees that were ever streaming into the hills of Gophna. He had heard Judah mention as much to Eleazar a few moments before.

"Intelligence, brother. Intelligence."

Judah's eyes immediately lost their glaze and he regarded Ephraim with real interest. "Speak on."

"I only just recently remembered a strange exchange I had with the advisor to Menelaus in Jerusalem—"

"You had contact with Menelaus?" Judah interrupted.

"No, I did not say I had contact with Menelaus, but with his advisor. Listen, would you?"

"Sorry," Judah said. "Go on."

"Nadab is Menelaus' advisor. I went to visit him a number of times trying to get an audience with him. I finally succeeded."

"Why were you so intent upon gaining an audience with those infidels? They are scum."

Ephraim hesitated, then decided that the truth was best. "You must remember how angry I was when I left Modiin. The only thing I was interested in was revenge. I wanted revenge against you and your family because of. . . " Ephraim voice trailed off.

"Your father's death at the hands of my father," Judah finished for him. "I understand."

An uncomfortable silence rested between the two men for a moment. Judah said, "You have nothing to fear from me, Ephraim. You have indeed suffered greatly because of my family, and for that I am sorry."

Ephraim considered this. Mattathias had apologized, and although Judah's was implied, it was good to hear the words. "Thank you, Judah," he said, willing the tears away. After controlling himself, he went on with the story. "Nadab was more interested in the pacifists who were of my acquaintance than he was in you at that time. Your notoriety had not yet spread, though he did want to speak further of you in a future audience. I never went back, however—"

"But, you could, now," Judah said thoughtfully. "If you returned to Jerusalem and sought another audience with him, you could be very helpful to our cause. Could you not feed him false information?"

"I could, but Nadab is cunning. I can tell you that he is very adept at gathering and sifting intelligence. I would have to be careful. Whatever I feed him, at least in the beginning, has to be absolutely truthful."

Judah shook his head. "I do not know. Maybe it is too dangerous."

"Judah, are you keeping your friends from going out on patrol because it is too dangerous? Are you sparing your women from living in the wild because it is too dangerous? Your rebellion is no longer an infant. It could grow into an unruly adolescent unless it acquires a brain and maturity. You need intelligence and it seems that I am the one to gather it. I can insinuate myself into Nadab's confidence. Yes, it will be a dangerous business, but I have already paid the price for being a Jew in my own country." Grief took him again for a moment as he thought of Hezekiah and Deborah. Then, sturdying his face, he said, "It is time for the Greeks and their collaborators to pay as well."

Judah stood up. "Well," he said. "It seems I have my first spy. I do not know, though, if it is a time for congratulations."

Ephraim rose and embraced Judah, laughing. "I always have had a gift for extracting information from the unsuspecting. Remember when we were boys, Eleazar came to my house to fetch you for a whipping?"

"I remember it well," Judah said, laughing. "While I hid in your storage room, you plied him with your mother's sweetmeats until you got him to tell you his reason for being there. After you sent word to me via your little brother, Gad, I was able to sneak away. I was still punished, but at least I succeeded in putting it off for a few hours. Not only that, but you were always the one who instigated our pranks with the high priest while he taught us *Tanakh*. The rest of us were always caught, but you always escaped."

The two shared a pleasant and long laugh. After the mirth faded, Judah said, "It is about time we had a spy. Did not the Lord send Caleb and Yehoshua to spy among the Canaanites? Even Moshe employed spies."

"Well," Ephraim said, "If Moshe could have a spy, then we can too."

"It is only fitting," Judah agreed.

Chapter Twenty-three

Antioch, Syria   The 30th day of *Nisan* 3594 (April 25th 166 B.C.E.)

General Seron luxuriated as he watched the shimmering water displace the geometry of the the cunning blue mosaic bath. Interrupted by the courier delivering the message from Teman, he forced himself to breathe slowly, holding his composure until the courier left. Raising his shaking hands high above him, he brought them down against the water with a vehement splash. Damn. Nicanor had returned to Antioch from Judaea and would attend his audience with Teman.

Until now, Seron had enjoyed full and exclusive access to Teman, the emperor's advisor, and even found his way to the emperor occasionally. He had filled Teman's ear with suggestions about prosecuting the war against the Jewish rebels, and he was sure that some of the advice had reached the royal ear of Antiochus, himself. The invitation had come this morning for an individual audience with Teman, and Seron had congratulated himself that his plan of worming his way into the emperor's inner circle was proceeding nicely, until now. Nicanor's presence in the royal palace could ruin everything for Seron. And now there was water all over the floor with no one to mop it up as Panus had stepped out to fetch some towels.

"Panus!"

The slave, eyes widened in terror, burst through the tiled archway, towels piled high in his arms. "Sir!"

"Get me out of here! And clean up that water."

Quickly the slave laid down a thick, absorbent towel over the water, then another, and with great solemnity and grace, draped a larger brocaded towel over Seron's naked torso, all the while clucking and muttering apologies.

Seron had outgrown his governorship in Gaza. That province of Judaea had been lucrative enough with his skimming of revenues from the Frankincense that traders brought from the mountains of southern Arabia, but now he had elevated designs. His picked troops of native Thracians had kept order in Gaza well, and he felt that he was infinitely qualified to help bring order to other unruly provinces, the larger Coele-Syria, perhaps. It was true that his Thracian contingent was mercenary in nature and therefore subject to ridicule from the home-bred Macedonian troops, but he would put them up any day against any cohort in Judaea, Macedonian or Greek.

After this second courier from the palace delivered the message that the audience with Teman would include Nicanor, Seron spent the rest of the morning yelling at his slaves. He even beat one for being too slow to accommodate his hasty timetable for meeting Antiochus' advisor: the slave had been unable to find his favorite robe in a timely manner.

The ride in his litter through the streets of Antioch did not go much better. Between the stench of the open sewers that ran down the middle of the stone throughways and the aggressive hawkers of wares that his bodyguards continually had to repel, the twenty-minute ride seemed to last more like twenty hours.

When Seron finally arrived at the palace, things were even more fraught. First, he was kept waiting by Teman, a terrible snub that others in the court were sure to notice. Second, he found that his dresser had forgotten to affix the brooch that had been given him by the emperor. And, third, an urge to relieve himself surfaced when Teman finally deigned to offer him audience.

"Come in, come in, Commander," Teman said, bustling past him, looking out into the corridor, then retreating into the office, shutting the door. "We will start without Nicanor. He is late, the rogue."

As Seron squirmed in the proffered chair to ease the pressure on his bladder, he attempted to look dignified.

Teman wasted no time. "So, Commander, how goes it in Jerusalem? Are we having success?"

Seron was not stupid enough to think that Teman was unaware of the debacle in Judaea. The advisor knew of every patrol that was decimated by the Jews, of every failure of the Greeks to subdue the rebels in the hills of Gophna. Teman certainly had as good, if not better, intelligence than Seron. The advisor to the emperor had more resources than he, a provincial governor, and that of lowly Gaza, had.

Seron, to test the counselor's information, replied, "Timotheus has had some success, advisor. Why, just a few weeks ago, he managed to defeat one-thousand rebels in the Kidron caves outside of Jerusalem."

"Ah, yes, the unarmed men, women and children that our valiant troops managed to, shall we say, subdue? They attacked on the Jew Shabbat, a day forbidden to them for defense." Teman fingered the large gold ring on his right hand and said absently, "A brilliant strategy authored by Timotheus. A glorious victory for the empire. A glorious victory for our emperor."

So Teman knew about the slaughter, and Antiochus certainly knew, by extension. But Seron found that he had tired already of the political undercurrent of this conversation and while Teman continued his observations of the Judaean affair, Seron's thoughts wandered to the beach of Gaza where his guard was housed, and his palace was being built. In his mind, he saw its spacious balcony that overlooked *Mare Nostrum*, as the audacious Romans called the great ocean that stretched from the shores of Tyre and Sidon to the Iberian Peninsula.

Our Sea,indeed. Seron glowered. He preferred the old Greek name, *Ho Pontos*, which meant "road or passage." Many nationals like himself persisted in this appellation rather than accede to the Latin as almost everyone else was doing.

His mind returned to the palace and he relaxed. It was to be a beautiful and lavish edifice and he hated the thought of leaving it, better post notwithstanding, but his ambition demanding it. Amid Teman's didactic remarks that were becoming more and more critical of the Greek commanders in their treatment of the Jewish "problem," he heard echoing footsteps on the polished Thassos marble. The cadence belonged to Nicanor's brisk and heavy stride. Any relaxation Seron may have felt evaporated at the sight of the hardened visage of the provincial governor of Judaea.

But Nicanor's face opened with delight as he approached Seron.

"It is good to see another Greek face after dealing with so many Jews! So, General," Nicanor said, patting Seron hard on the bicep, "I am glad to see you here in Antioch. How is your lovely wife? My woman speaks highly of her."

"Demeter is well, I thank you," Seron said, adjusting his shoulder armor, askew from Nicanor's thump. "So, you left Apollonius behind?" He asked politely.

"That is my prerogative as "the old man," Nicanor chuckled. "I made him stay to take care of the troublesome Jews. He is taking a large contingent of his Samarians to deal with this Judah Maccabeus. That fellow has been leading us on a merry chase, to say the least."

Both men ignored Teman, who was not taking the snub with good grace. He coughed and cleared his throat to remind the two generals that he was the one with the emperor's confidence. They continued to ignore him.

Finally, Nicanor brought Teman into the conversation by asking, "So, our emperor is well, I trust? Will we have the honor of an audience this day? And, how are you, counselor?"

"I am well enough," Teman said sourly. "How much information can you give me about this Jew—what did you call him?"

"Judah Maccabeus," Nicanor said good-naturedly. "He is proving very elusive, but Apollonius can take care of him, I will wager."

"Our emperor will not be pleased that a mere Jew is making sport of his royal armies," Teman said.

"No, but this Jew is a good strategist, and I am afraid that the combination of his wiles and our lack thereof has been a detriment to our strength in Judaea," Nicanor observed easily.

"Do not let the emperor hear you say that," warned Teman. "He will not be pleased."

"Let me hear what?"

All three men turned and bowed immediately. Antiochus had entered Teman's office.

"My lord," Nicanor said as he sank to one knee, with Seron hastening to follow his example. "It is good to see you again."

"Rise, rise," Antiochus said happily. "I do not usually darken Teman's dank office, but I heard you had arrived." Antiochus extended his hand imperiously and Nicanor laid the flank of his cheek against it. The emperor nodded at Seron and simply said, "General."

Seron stayed on his one knee and fumed that Nicanor had earned the emperor's hand. He glanced over at Teman and saw that the advisor was angry as well at Nicanor's usurpation of the emperor's attention.

Finally, Antiochus said, "All of you, come to my lovely atrium and let us sit and discuss Judaea. I hear that we are having a little trouble."

Teman and Seron obediently rose and followed Antiochus and Nicanor, the emperor having pulled Nicanor near, entwining his arm through the general's own. The three men and the emperor sat cordially together, the latter encouraging the men to discuss their families, children, home life, mistresses, favorite deities and then, after all other topics were spent, Jerusalem.

"Sire," Nicanor was the one to open the subject of the Judaean conflict. "The Jewish rebellion has a figurehead. His name is Maccabeus. The Hammer."

"How charming," Antiochus said, leaning forward. "However did he get that name?"

"I am not sure," Nicanor said. "I regret to say I have never seen him. But the Jews have elongated craniums. Perhaps his head is shaped that way."

"Like a hammer?" Antiochus giggled. "Oh, I hope he is captured soon. I will have his head sent here so our scientists can study it. Rapture! They are close to apprehending him, I trust?"

"I will not lie to you, Highness," Nicanor said. "This rebel has given us some trouble. However, I have put Apollonius in charge. He will get results, I can assure you."

"Whatever shall I do with my Hebrew children?" Antiochus sighed, *tsking* his confusion. "Why cannot they recognize the one true God: Me? I have given them chance after chance. I have done my best to educate them in the true order of religion and they shun me time after time. 'For, I am a jealous God and will have no other gods before me.'"

The three men stared at each other. The emperor was embarking upon a new tenor promoting his self-deification: he was taking on the verbal attributes of the god worshipped by the very Jews he was trying to exterminate. Seron and Nicanor recognized the verbiage, having fought among and against Jews for so long. And

Teman's education as a noble included a wide exposure to the world's religions, of which the monotheism of the Jews was one.

Seron knew that Nicanor was the only one brave enough to engage the emperor, so he stayed silent, waiting for the old general to speak. He knew enough about the emperor that these descents into strange fancies often were clues as to how to expedite Antiochus' royal business.

"My Lord, what would you have us do, concerning your children, the Jews? How should we proceed?" Nicanor asked.

Antiochus's head dipped almost to his lap and he was silent for a full minute. Teman seemed poised to stand and revive him when the emperor stirred and said, "Soon I go into the east on a godly mission. I must retrieve my gold and silver that has been extracted from my earth by the Parthians. They go after foolish and vain gods and do not know me. Therefore, I will appear to them. They will understand, then."

Seron inwardly sighed. Many men would be squandered on this "mission." The Parthians were a formidable foe. Although many of their practices seemed Greek and they used the Hellenic military hierarchy to organize their forces, their temperaments were more like the fierce Dahae from whom they descended. The Dahae had almost repelled the great Alexander when he ventured east into India.

"General Nicanor." Antiochus said.

"Yes, my lord?"

"You, my son, are to send every Jew to me."

Nicanor seemed to strain in understanding. "Forgive me, Great Epiphanes. I am slow of intellect. Would you explain so my inferior mortal ears are able to understand? Send the Jews to you? You would like them relocated in our satrapy? In Antioch?"

Antiochus closed his eyes as if humoring a child. He smiled kindly at Nicanor. "The human mortal is so literal, bless him," the emperor said. "No, my dear Nicanor. You are to send them to *me*.

"Of course, divine one." Nicanor nodded, seeming to understand.

"Go about your business, all of you," Antiochus said. "I must make ready for the journey."

Seron and Teman openly gawked, not even attempting to cover their astonishment at the strange exchange between their emperor and his general. They watched Nicanor stand, bow and exit the atrium before taking the opportunity offered by Antiochus' dismissal to follow the general. Soon they were beside him increasing their strides to keep up.

"What did he mean? What did he mean?" They chorused.

Nicanor stopped mid-stride and looked at them airily. "It seems that Antiochus is to deal with his Parthian children, and I am to take care of his Hebrew children."

"But what did he mean, 'send them to him'?" Seron asked. "It would take a monumental migration to get all the Jews up here. Not only that, but they will not come quietly. It would make the Babylonian conquest seem like a day on the Euphrates. What can it mean—" Suddenly, Seron's face darkened in understanding. "Surely, he does not mean—he cannot intend—"

Nicanor pursed his lips for a few moments and said, "Oh yes, General Seron, that is exactly what he means. He wants the Jews sent to him, to God, the one God. He means for me to exterminate them as a race. He will school them in worship—in the afterlife."

Nicanor left Teman and Seron. He exited the atrium.

As the two watched Nicanor disappear into the palace corridors, Teman said. "A daunting task, to be sure," he said.

"Daunting, of course," Seron answered. "But if anyone can exterminate an entire race, it is Nicanor." He thought, And, please Ares, may he botch the job so that I can take over the task.

Chapter Twenty-four

Jerusalem, Judaea   The 30th day of *Nisan* 3594 (April 25th 166 B.C.E.)

A dministrator Menelaus," Apollonius said. Reluctantly he stood up as if acknowledging respect for the reigning high priest. It was a gesture he did not feel the high priest deserved. For all that Apollonius was carrying out a war against the Jews, this fellow was at least part Hebrew and as far as Apollonius was concerned, a traitor to his people. That his treason helped Apollonius' cause was beside the point; the man was slimy. And so was the lackey who stood off to the side.

"General Apollonius. As always, it is a pleasure."

"I know you are busy, high priest, so I will come straight to the point. I need to know about the man, Judah the Maccabee or Maccabeus—or whatever he is called. He is having too much of an impact on our affairs here, and I do not believe that the influence of any Jew should be felt by our great empire. What can you tell me about him?"

As usual, Menelaus assumed a blank look, recovered and turned to his lacky. When Apollonius saw the focus of the high priest's gaze, he too turned to the oily little man and waited with a surly, cocked eyebrow.

The advisor cleared his throat and said, "I know that his father, Mattathias, started the rebellion in Modiin where Commander Apelles met his end. Judah, being younger and stronger, seems to have taken the reins from his father—in fact, we just heard a report that the father has died—so the Maccabee is now the undisputed leader of the rebellion. He seems to have a charismatic mien that naturally inspires allegiance, for many are flocking to the Gophna hills to join him."

"That is disturbing," Apollonius said. "But it will not last long. I am soon taking a force up north to deal with this Maccabee once and for all. My Samarians are preparing for the campaign even now. I am leaving within a matter of days to join them.

However, before I leave, I need more information on the doings of this Judah and his rebels. What more can you tell me?"

The lacky eyed Menelaus who nodded for him to continue. "We just dispatched agents throughout Judaea who will report to us on the general movements of the rebels. However, we just sent an extremely reliable man up north to secure an intelligence source that we believe will be even more helpful in the months to come. As soon as we hear from him, we will contact you."

"Why was this not done already?" Apollonius asked. "The incident in Modiin happened four months ago."

Menelaus merged back into the conversation, "Most thought that the attack on Apelles was a mere anomaly," he said. "No one realized that the tiny rebellion was a threat. Certainly, we did not hear about them massing in Gophna until many months later. I can assure you, though, that I will procure the information needed to defeat them."

"I certainly hope you do, high priest. The tales of the Maccabee's exploits, inflated though they are, are reaching the ears of our emperor. I just received a missive from him, and I can assure you, he is far from pleased. He will find another prop to fill your position unless you prove more useful to us in this endeavor."

"I am always honored to serve the emperor and his subjects," Menelaus said silkily. "We will soon have our reports on the Maccabee in hand, if not the Maccabee, himself."

"See that you do, high priest. There are plenty of Jews who can easily replace you."

As Apollonius watched the door close upon their departure, he returned to his work, thinking, what a useless conversation—in fact, what a useless backwater is Judaea!

Chapter Twenty-five

Lydda, Judea   The 1st day of *Iyar* 3594 (April 26th 166 B.C.E.)

B arbatus muttered, "These Jews have turned into a suspicious lot." He dug for the fifth time into his satchel for his papers. Luckily, he was fluent in Aramaic, or he would never have gotten through all the sentries that the rebels were posting at their new holdings they had taken in the north. He had not realized the extent of Jewish control up here. Greek patrols that ventured north of Jerusalem were disappearing at a steady rate, and more and more Greek refugees were drifting into Jerusalem. The Jewish grip on northern Judea was drawing tighter, he was sure, than his employers in Jerusalem were aware.

On his last trip to Judea years before, he had remembered Lydda as a beauty of a city. Its gymnasium was a wonder that had not an equal north of Jerusalem. Once he had even seen the famous Eupolemus wrestle here. Nadab had informed him before he set out on this mission that Eupolemus had become one of Judah Maccabeus' closest military advisors. Now having taken back his Hebrew name of Asher, he had shaken off his Hellenic leanings and was cleaving once again to the orthodoxy of the Jews.

Barbatus looked at the city with distaste. The impressive marble edifices were pockmarked, vandals having scoured the carvings of their aesthetics. The magnificent statues that had adorned the pediments of the temple and the gymnasium were gone, their absence leaving a great void atop the buildings. Now, instead of the square and disciplined Greek soldiers that had once patrolled the streets of Lydda, scruffy Jewish freedom fighters outfitted with an unruly hodge-podge of armor prevailed.

"The Jews may have more freedom," Barbatus scoffed aloud as he watched a platoon of Jews march past, ridiculous in their shabby get-up, "but it is too bad they have not been able to acquire a tasteful eye along with it."

During the last three weeks, he had stopped at many towns in his mission for Nadab. This Ephraim was not directly known to many, that was clear, and Barbatus was beginning to get discouraged. A few knew the story third, fourth and fifth-hand about his father's murder at the hand of Mattathias and of his disaffection with the Maccabee. Fewer knew that he was part of the rebellion again, but beyond that, Barbatus heard no new information about either his leanings or his whereabouts.

He began to make discreet inquiries throughout the Jewish shops that lined the streets where before there had been Greek whorehouses and taverns. He had once been very familiar with this area of town and it made him indescribably sad to see the wholesome concerns take over the enterprises of vice. Traditional clothing shops and bakeries now stood where his favorite brothel had once graced the main road of Lydda. He sighed and made another inquiry.

"Do you know of Ephraim of Modiin, son of Naphtali?" Barbatus lounged against the rickety booth belonging to the female fruit vendor and looked over the dried pomegranates with a shudder. He took one anyway and laid a coin down.

The woman warmed a little at the sight of the coin and said, suspicion still in her voice, "I may have. Who are you? You are not from around here."

At least the suspicion took a simple and direct route. "I am his cousin from Jerusalem. My name is Yitzak. I have not seen him since our mothers suckled together. You see. . ."

The woman opened up a little more at the plausible story Barbatus spun about his and Ephraim's pleasant childhood together during Ephraim's visits to Jerusalem. At the end of the tale, the vendor was eager to share all the gossip within the reach of her memory.

"My tale is not as happy as yours," the woman said sadly, "Like you and Ephraim, he and the Maccabee were childhood friends of the closest sort. Then at the beginning of the rebellion, the Maccabee's father, Mattathias, killed Ephraim's father, Naphtali, or was his name Natan? Well, anyway, Ephraim fled Modiin and then came back after the terrible slaughter of the innocents in the Kidron Caves. He seemed one with the Maccabee, again. Then it is said that he and the Maccabee had another fight after which he left for good. I think he is on his way to Jerusalem. He just passed through here yesterday to gather supplies for his journey."

Barbatus, since he already knew the story about Ephraim, had trouble keeping his eyes focused during the woman's windy narrative, but when she mentioned the Jew's presence here in Lydda just the day before, he perked up. "You say he was here? I am so sorry I missed him. Where did he go while he was here?"

"Maybe the baker's, the forge or the tanner's—"

"Where are these concerns located?"

The woman leaned out of her stall and pointed east toward the old Jewish quarter. "That way. He did not spend much time down here at all. He even eschewed my lovely pomegranates. Well, they may not be so lovely, but they are here and off-season, too. An Egyptian merchant came through here last week and I was lucky—"

"Thank you for your time, woman," Barbatus interrupted and laid down another coin. "You have been most helpful."

As Barbatus hurried off, he cursed himself for not being here the day before. He would rather miss a contact by a month than a mere day. However, he was intrigued by the news that Ephraim and the Maccabee were estranged. That would make his job much easier. If he exercised enough finesse, he would have no problem bringing Ephraim into Nadab's web. The strong smell of lime and tallow assaulted his nostrils and he knew the tanner was near. Sure enough, he saw skins and various cuts of leather strung outside a concern that had once been a Greek statuary shop. The statues that had once lined its frontage were broken off at the knees and feet, their jagged marble stumps an atrocity when the mind recalled their former elegance.

Yes, Ephraim had been here, the shopkeeper with the filthy apron said. No, no one else was with him. All he bought was a saddlebag for his horse. And, no, he did not stay long. He said he was on his way to Aijalon where he needed to conduct business, then on to Jerusalem.

The terse interview allowed Barbatus to leave Lydda with plenty of information and plenty of light left in the day. As he galloped toward Jerusalem, the thought crossed his mind that all of this had been a little too easy, and ease of any type made him suspicious.

Chapter Twenty-six

Jerusalem, Judaea   The 2nd day of *Iyar* 3594 (April 27th 166 B.C.E.)

A pollonius eagerly broke the seal of the parchment.

> *Old friend. As always, I hope to find you and your*
> *Military enterprises well. Are the Jew behaving themselves?*

"Do the Jews ever behave themselves?" Apollonius held the letter up, shaking it playfully as if addressing its author. "Are you crazy, old man?"

> *Antiochus has authorized me to take care of the Jewish problem, once and for*
> *all. (He couched the command in deific terms: "That all his 'children, the*
> *Jews' be sent to him. Of course, this means death for all of them—or as many*
> *of them as we can get our hands on. I suppose I do not have to spell it out for*
> *you, old friend, as I know you understand our emperor's vernacular as well as*
> *I.)*

At this Apollonius chuckled, knowing that instead of what Nicanor really wanted to say, rather than the 'emperor's vernacular,' was the 'emperor's flights into fanciful insanity,' as he often termed Antiochus' forays into his divine roleplays.

> *As per this 'extermination order,' you are free to do with the Jews as you wish.*
> *I   believe your campaign up north to dispatch the Maccabee and his*
> *followers would be an   appropriate beginning.   Consider this your*
> *authorization. I wish I could have delivered the order in person, but I have*
> *pressing business in Antioch. Seron and I have been thrown together by the*

emperor to iron out our empire's military problems on her frontiers, especially to the East. In other words, Antiochus wants a path blazed for him into Parthia so he can recover more gold. Seron and I must draw up the most profitable route lined with temples and treasuries so Antiochus can gather as much wealth as possible on the way to Parthia's capital. The Roman tributum payment is past due. I feel like a damned money broker. Stay well.

In the Service of Our Divine Antiochus Epiphanes,

Nicanor of Apamea

P.S. Look in on my elephants, would you?

"Of course, I will look in on your elephants, old friend," Apollonius said to the parchment. "I will not get close enough to ride them, pet them or smell them, but I will look in on them, from afar off. Perhaps I can simply climb the Akra to 'look in on them.' It has reached its full height, after all." He smiled and put the letter on Philo's desk. For all his recent "understanding," with Nicanor's old bull, Deucalis, Apollonius' aversion to the beast still was quite strong.

A knock on the door sounded and Apollonius said to it, "Come."

Colonel Syrus entered, saluted and announced, "You wanted to know when the new brace of patrols had gone out. They just left, sir. They should be back in two days."

"Thank you, Colonel. I also want reports upon their returns. We must monitor our patrols with more vigilance. The Jews must not get the idea that they can wipe out our men with impunity. If we lose any more patrols, I need to know immediately so I can gauge my dealing with the Jews when I defeat them in Gophna."

"Yes, Commander. It shall be as you say."

"Oh, one more thing, Colonel."

Syrus turned again to face the general. "Yes, sir?"

"When are the other patrols due back from the north? Did we not send them out two days ago?"

"That is correct, General—two days ago. They are due back at sundown today."

"I'll want a report before they retire."

"I'll see to it, General."

"That will be all." Apollonius turned to his other missives. He would have just enough time to start packing for his return to Samaria. As soon as he debriefed Philo on the patrol rotation, he would be free to give his full attention to the Gophna campaign. Perhaps when the patrols returned tonight, they might have information on the Maccabee's movements. With such information, he could be very close to marching on the Jews in those damn hills, very close, indeed.

Chapter Twenty-seven

Road to Gezer, Judaea   The 2nd day of *Iyar* 3594 (April 27th 166 B.C.E.)

J udah dragged the last Greek corpse into the underbrush. "See?" He grunted, dusting his hands together. "That was not so bad."

"I still think that it would achieve the same effect if we just left them," Eleazar grumbled as he took off his cloak and dusted it over the Greek body, a customary and ancient form of cursing. "Not only that, but there is a better chance of our being caught by another patrol while we are out here exposed."

"Do not fret, elder brother," Judah said cheerfully. "I am always watching your back. I will not let the Greeks get you."

"Be still, Judah," Eleazar warned, yet grinned, "or I will tell *Eemah* that you got blood on your cloak that she wove for you." He reached for and lifted the lapel of the fine homespun of his brother's cloak and looked at it with distaste. "You should not have worn it out on patrol."

"And I will tell her that you were being loud with Shoshanna the night before."

Eleazar blushed, the downward cast of his eyes serving as a weak comeback, and mounted his horse. Loudly, he formed up the men to get them to the cover of the hills above the road.

As their horses negotiated the winding path above the road to Gezer, the men spoke in the whispers they used while on patrol.

"*Nu*, Judah, it is too bad that you and Ephraim could not mend your differences," Eleazar said, edging Bakayan closer to Tiklit so that he could keep his voice low. "When did he leave?"

"Four days ago," Judah said. "He said he would never see me again and that he hoped Mattathias was being punished by the Great-I-Am on the other side for his murder of Naphtali."

"He said that?" Avram rode his mount closer so he could join in the sotto voice exchange. "He must have been angry to speak such a curse."

Judah was sorry that the cover story for Ephraim's departure caused so much consternation among the ranks of his men, and indeed throughout the entire camp, but there was no help for it. If Ephraim's cover were to be maintained, he and Judah were the only ones who could know the truth. He only hoped that the story of their quarrel would find its way quickly to the courts of Jerusalem so that Ephraim could more easily wedge himself into Menelaus' and Nadab's circle.

"Yes, he was angry," Judah said, "but we are better off without him."

"What caused the argument?" Schmuel had ridden up also.

"Keep your voices down!" Judah hissed. "He wanted me to parley with the Greeks. He would have me go to Jerusalem and speak to Apollonius face to face."

"Apollonius? The author of the Parade of Death?" Avram's jowls shook with outrage.

"The very one," Judah murmured.

"Impossible!" Schmuel said. "How does one parley with the dark one? Apollonius is of the adversary!"

They all nodded agreement and made the sign to ward off the evil eye. Eleazar said, "You did right, Judah. Anyone who wants to consort with Apollonius—" he did not finish voicing the thought, as if it were too horrendous to contemplate.

"Enough talk," Judah whispered. "I would that we return to Gophna in one piece. Maintain silence, now."

As the patrol plodded on, Judah thought, because of this ruse, Ephraim is as the blowing dust. He will have no people and nowhere to lay his head in safety for some time to come. I hope we did not make a mistake. I wonder if freedom is worth the heavy coin that we will all ultimately pay.

The purple sunset washed the hills, making the terrain swim in a Tyrolean haze. Juniper and desert grass hunkered below its heavy colors, sending flaccid reflections back to the sky in their long shadows.

He made his men stop and watch the sun's descent behind the hills of Gezer. "That," Judah announced, forsaking the whisper of patrol, "is what you are fighting for." He wanted to add, "And why Ephraim is putting himself in extreme danger, spying for us," but he restrained himself. He said aloud, "Do not forget that the Lord G-d wants this to be our land. But we must be willing to spill blood and have our blood be spilt."

The men did as Judah asked and watched the fading sun for a few moments then urged their mounts forward, anxious to make camp, for they were tired. Later they would think about the land that they were fighting for. Maybe tomorrow, after a good sleep.

Chapter Twenty-eight

Jerusalem, Judaea   The 2nd day of *Iyar* 3594 (April 27th 166 B.C.E.)

A pollonius growled, "What do you mean, none of them has returned?"

"The patrols were supposed to check in with the barracks lieutenant," Syrus said uneasily. "He has had no one report in."

"How is that possible?" Apollonius snapped. "How many patrols were there?"

"We sent out ten," Syrus said.

"Ten patrols vanished into thin air, Colonel? That report is unacceptable. This should not be a mystery. See to it!"

"Yes, sir!" Syrus turned on his heel and did not bother to conceal his sprint with a more dignified and nonchalant trot.

Apollonius, for his part, was beginning to cultivate a grudging respect for the rebel commander. How could a mere Jewish farmer disrupt the patrols of the Greek empire? "Are you sure not even one has returned?"

But Syrus had disappeared. There was no one to answer him.

Apollonius wandered into the corridor outside Philo's office to see if he could scare up a lieutenant for an errand. It was silly of him to send Syrus away before giving him all the dispatches that needed to go out before day's end. He looked up at the sunset. Damn.

Finally, he found a particularly young lieutenant whose eyes widened at the specter of the general out in the corridor without his adjutants. "Lieutenant!"

"Yes sir!" The young man's voice was a little too shrill, but his salute was snappy.

"I want you to take these letters and deliver them for me. The one I need to reach its destination first is the one to Menelaus. The others can follow the course of the logic of your travel through the city."

"Right away, General! I am honored!"

"Yes, yes, of course," Apollonius murmured. "You are dismissed."

"Thank you, General, thank you!"

"DISMISSED, Lieutenant!"

As he watched the youth swing the leather case with the dispatches over his shoulder and hurry off, Apollonius thought, Menelaus had better have some answers for me about Judah the Maccabee or there will be Hades to pay.

He sat back at the desk and riffled through the detritus that covered his desk. "I cannot do this, now!" he announced to himself. As he stood up, he gaped and stretched, trying to loosen the tightness in his neck and back and decided to walk off his frustration before his meeting with Philo. Tonight was as good as any to give command back to the former commander of Jerusalem. He was sick of worrying about the accursed patrols. Let Philo worry about them for a change. Then Apollonius could start planning the Gophna campaign and get back north to his Samarians.

So many soldiers were in the barracks corridor and yard that Apollonius stopped saluting and gave a nod to every acknowledgment instead. Even so, with all that nodding, by the time he returned to his office his neck was in need of work.

Perhaps tonight I will call for Alexandria, he thought. I need a release of my loins and a good massage. He sighed. He must be getting old. The massage sounded more inviting than the other.

"Ahem."

"General Philo," Apollonius said to his colleague who was idling in the doorway. "Come in, come in." Usually, he was not this happy to the see the commander of the Jerusalem guard, but now that he was about to relinquish the reins to the austere commander standing before him, Apollonius' face was a study in delight. "I am hereby ordering you to take back your desk, general. After I show you the patrol rotations, this office is yours once again. I am returning to Samaria within the next few days."

Philo's expression did not change, but he said, "As you wish, sir. Did you hear that the patrols have not returned?"

Apollonius turned solemn. "Yes. Colonel Syrus is seeing to that, attempting to find some answers. I wonder if there are any answers to find?" Apollonius stood up from the desk and suffered a final assault on his knee. He swallowed the epithet. Although this transfer of command was an informal moment, it was still a moment that demanded a certain decorum. "Sit here, general. The desk seems to like you better than it does me."

Philo eased into the desk and the relief on his face almost made Apollonius smile. It had been a difficult few months for everyone. The antics of this Maccabee had put a strain on the very command structure in Judaea. Thwarted assaults, lost Hellenic strongholds like Lydda and now disappearing patrols had undermined Greek hubris. Apollonius straightened. Once he returned to Samaria, all would be well. The momentum of the conflict would shift back to the Greek side where it belonged, his Samarians vanquishing the rebels once and for all.

Chapter Twenty-nine

Jerusalem, Judaea   The 3rd day of *Iyar* 3594 (April 28th 166 B.C.E.)

Nadab strode through the palace courtyard, his annoyance with Menelaus escalating. "The old devil is so afraid of Apollonius, that he sends me alone to give him the report, or to report the lack of a report. The weasel."

Feeling the cold of the cobbles under his feet, Nadab cursed that he had worn his elegant, brocaded slippers rather than his more substantial boots. The sun of spring was not incessant enough to warm the stones and Nadab shivered. He did not know what he was going to say to the fierce Greek commander. The author of the parade of death in which so many Jews had died would probably have no compunction about slaying a little advisor to the high priest. He exhaled, feeling rattled. He had expected the return of Barbatus by now.

In the past, Nadab's timing in such matters had fallen on the positive side of luck. Not this time. The absence of Barbatus was a terrible miscarriage of timing. The only thing that might save him was Apollonius's perception of Nadab as the mere mouthpiece of Menelaus. That may spare him a sword through the vitals, but not a severe tongue-lashing and demotion that could seriously limit his political options with the Greeks. The more he thought about the meeting, the sicker his stomach became.

Nadab turned down the alley that led to his favorite market area in the Jewish quarter. He had not been here for a long time. If Apollonius were to have him killed, he wanted to visit his old, comforting haunt, in case it was for the last time.

"Where have you been, old friend?" Shem's booming voice greeted Nadab well before he reached the small concern. "Sit down, sit down. Ruth, look who is here!"

"Silvanus!" Ruth said, delighted. "It has been a long time. I still remember your 'usual.' Shall I?"

"Thank you, yes." Nadab relaxed, happy to hear his alias, Silvanus, again. It was the one he employed during his forays, more infrequent lately, into the Jewish quarter. The food and drink served here were not good enough for Nadab's expensive palate, but over the years the information gleaned under Shem's little awning had more than compensated for its culinary shortcomings.

"So, old friend," Shem said as Nadab sipped the lemon drink, "your merchandising travels have kept you far away from us. You have exotic tales to share, I daresay."

As Shem had no idea as to Nadab's true identity, Nadab simply nodded. At the couple's expectant gaze, he said only, "I have been very busy, it is true." He continued, hoping to deflect their curiosity, "But you! You seem to be prospering! I see you have added a number of tables."

"Yes," Shem agreed. "We have been doing very well. Our quarter has been spared the purges that the rest of the city has seen—thanks be to G-d—and we have experienced an increase in our coin."

Nadab idly nursed his drink and politely commiserated with Shem on his good fortune before his mind returned to its quandary. How was he to escape reporting to Apollonius? As Nadab's worries darted in and out of Shem's friendly monologue, the advisor found it harder and harder to smile during the course of the conversation. Shem did not seem to notice, however, and it was not until another customer drew his attention that he left Nadab alone.

This street was truly Jewish in its character. No Hellenic apparel or dress of any other nationality, for that matter, appeared among the Hebraic robes that flowed over its cobbles. In fact, because of the anonymity of the Semitic mass, and wonderful seduction of the lemon drink before him, he almost missed the two figures that walked by Shem's enterprise. He stood. There was something familiar about the stealthy gait of the shorter man. He followed them, leaving his lemoned drink on Shem's table.

"Barbatus?" Nadab asked tentatively.

The two figures turned and Nadab, contrary to his usual diplomatic nonchalance, stepped back and gasped, "And, is it not—Ephraim?"

Ephraim smiled widely and grasped the arm of the advisor to the high priest while Barbatus smirked. "Yes, advisor," Ephraim said, "I have come back, and I have some information from Gophna that may interest you."

"It is good to see you, Ephraim Bar Naphtali," Nadab said warmly, clasping Ephraim's shoulder. "I wonder at your absence this past year. Your friend Judah—"

"He is not my friend." Ephraim's tone belied his polite smile.

"Your acquaintance, then," Nadab said easily, darting a look at Barbatus, "is leading the Greeks about by their noses. Quite a feat, if you ask me. He is flouting the skill of the entire Seleucid army. But, perhaps," Nadab said as he waited for the servant to open the gate to the palace complex, "you are approving of his actions."

"I neither approve nor disapprove," Ephraim said, shrugging. "What Judah the *Maccabee* does," his emphasis on the new surname was derisive, "is not my affair."

"Indeed," Nadab said with a faint smile, "your indifference is obvious."

Barbatus followed the two Jews, staying out of the exchange. When they arrived at Nadab's office, the agent seated himself in a corner chair, laid his head back and seemed to doze.

"So, Ephraim, how did you two cross paths?" Nadab asked, nodding at Barbatus.

"He introduced himself as one of your agents," Ephraim said, "and said you were looking for me. How he knew who I was, I do not know."

"Barbatus is extremely resourceful," Nadab said, chuckling uneasily. "All that matters is that he found you. Since our talk last year, I have been wondering how we could help each other."

Ephraim said nothing.

Nadab leaned back in his chair. He could see that Ephraim still tended his animosity toward the Maccabee with great care; nevertheless, it was obvious that he also cultivated a healthy mistrust for Nadab and all things even vaguely Greek. But Ephraim's very presence here indicated that the hatred superseded the mistrust, and Nadab wanted to harvest that hatred before it became overripe and useless to him. If Ephraim became foolhardy in his anger, he would be of little use to someone like Nadab, who liked his espionage to remain subtle.

At that particular moment, Ephraim did not seem reckless or anxious in the least; that calm made for a useful agent. Nadab, however, must proceed with great caution. He did not want to frighten Ephraim back into hiding. That was a real danger. Nadab had recruited some spies who had seemed solid, but once or twice he had pressed too hard or too soon, and he had lost them. Ephraim was too important for Nadab to be foolish in his recruiting. He decided to play coy and dismiss Ephraim today before either one of them broached the subject of espionage. He did not want to seem too eager. "But, my manners! You seem tired, *Adohni* Ephraim. I will not keep you. I am sure that you need to rest. Tonight, come dine with us. We observe all dietary laws," Nadab said, raising his voice slightly at Ephraim's facial demur. "Our table is not sullied with unclean creatures. You have nothing to fear."

"You are observant?" Ephraim's stoic mask fell for a moment. "You adhere to the Law?"

"Let us just say that I am a Jew who observes the important tenets of the law. And let us just say that my mother and father's training in culinary habits, merged as they were with guilt, die very hard indeed."

"I remember before, when we spoke," Ephraim said cautiously, "that you saw much of worth in Greek ways."

"And, so I do," Nadab said, never taking his eyes from Ephraim's face. "But that does not mean that I have forsaken who and what I am. Will you dine? Tonight, at sundown?"

Ephraim's face was full of quandary. Nadab watched it play out on his features as he sat quietly and waited. He almost chuckled as he imagined what must be in the Jew's mind: should I connect myself to this creature of Menelaus? Is it safe to work with the

Greeks? I know I have to ally with them, but must I dine with them to get at the Maccabee? What would my poor, dead father say?

At last, Ephraim nodded and said, "At sundown, then." He stood, bowed and left Nadab's office.

Barbatus' chair tilted against the wall where the assassin had his head back in an attitude of slumber. "I do not trust him," he said without a sign of sleep in his voice. "He could very well be a double agent for the Maccabee—it is a very dangerous game you are playing here."

"There is no danger to me," Nadab scoffed. "The only one who will be in danger will be Ephraim if we catch him in a lie," Nadab said. "I am cultivating other contacts up north who in the future will be able to help us learn more of the Maccabee's mind and strategy. For now, however, Ephraim Bar Naphtali is our best hope. That does not mean that I do not want you to monitor his movements. Do so and do so diligently." Nadab idly stared out of the window and said, "I must have intelligence on the rebellion, and I mean to get it, one way or another. Now, Barbatus, I need you to deliver a message for me."

"May I remind you, advisor," Barbatus said, "that I am not a messenger."

"And may I remind you, Barbatus, that I employ you at a good price. I think you can deliver a simple message for me."

"Oh, very well. What and to whom?"

"You are to go to the Greek barracks and tell Apollonius that Menelaus is debriefing an important contact, one that will bring him a wealth of intelligence, but that he will not be able to meet with the general until tomorrow morning."

"General Apollonius will skewer me with one of his pikes if I deliver such a message."

"Nonsense," Nadab said. "You have wiles. Use them. Tell him it will be well worth the wait."

As Barbatus mumbled out of his office, Nadab sat back in his chair with a great sigh of relief. He and Menelaus would debrief Ephraim first thing tomorrow morning then would deliver the intelligence straight to Apollonius. This time, Menelaus would be sure to accompany Nadab since there was actually some intelligence to report. Perhaps they would keep their heads for at least another day. That is, if Ephraim's report were copious and plausible.

Nadab stood, straightened his desk and headed for his quarters. He only had a few hours to prepare his house for his dinner guests. And if things went right with one particular guest tonight, tomorrow could yield great things for Nadab's career.

Nadab made sure that the repast and the dinner guests were sedate. He wanted Ephraim to settle into the idea that the people who surrounded him now were not so different from the Jews he had just left in the Gophna hills. Milk and meat were kept meticulously separate, and no pork adorned the table as it was forbidden by the law. Ephraim seemed at ease and was engaged in conversation with Marcus, a Jew who was thoroughly Hellenized as far as his belief in the beauty of Greek philosophy, yet was Hebrew in his observance and attire. Nadab listened intently and noted with satisfaction that according to his instructions, Marcus kept his remarks entirely Hebraic, expounding on the new scriptures of Daniel, and did not venture into the tenets of Plato, Socrates or Aristotle.

The dinner was cleared away and as per Nadab's prior instructions to his guests, the topic turned to anti-Greek politics. As all the diners were astute lackeys of the Greek empire, but also members of the ruling Jewish class, they were adept at subterfuge in their leanings. Whereas, they clove more to the Greeks, they had been raised as Jews and appeared thus in their demeanor and dress. They were able to hold forth on subjects such as the orthodoxies of prayer, temple worship and sacrifice and talked of Greek rule as if they themselves were not the beneficiaries. As collaborators connected to Menelaus, they enjoyed almost as many perks as did the Greeks in their midst.

Ephraim seemed relaxed as he discussed pacifism and resistance. He held forth on possible methods of peaceful engagement with the Greeks. The talk of resistance led to the rebellion, and that led to a discussion of the Maccabee. Nadab, who had been silent during the discussion, interjected the fact of Ephraim's acquaintance with the Maccabee, then sat back and watched.

Ephraim seemed hesitant at first to discuss his connection to the rebellion, but gradually warmed to the topic when he was urged to relate his account of that first day in Modiin. His retelling of the event of his father's death at the hands of Mattathias had his listeners rapt. They watched with great concern as he broke down at the memory, then fled the room. Nadab followed him into the atrium outside the dining room.

"I am sorry," Ephraim sobbed, embarrassed. "I have ruined the gathering."

"Think nothing of it," Nadab soothed. "After all, he was your father. There is no shame in this."

"I must make him pay," Ephraim murmured.

"Make who pay?"

"Judah. His father is dead and beyond my reach now, but as I told you before, Judah is the heart of the rebellion. He and all his clan."

"We will speak more of this tomorrow," Nadab said, patting Ephraim's back to comfort him. "No more politics tonight. Now, return with me and we will partake of a rare dessert." He steered Ephraim back into the banquet and said, "I tell you, this will make you feel better. I brought the last of the fresh snow from Mount Hermon so my cook could make a delectable treat—he will not tell me what is in it, but if a nectar of the gods truly does exist, this is it. It tastes like frozen cream, sweetened with honey."

* * * * *

As Ephraim lounged back on the fine cushions and partook of the strange dessert, he looked about him at his new associates. Nadab had left his side and was engaged in deep conversation with an official from the temple. Mingling with the men were women, their tittering laughs adding a gaiety to the rumbling male discussion. Although this mixing of genders was foreign to Ephraim's sensibilities as an orthodox Jew, there was something agreeable about having females about in such close proximity. He glanced about, guilty, doubtful, expecting someone to remonstrate with him for enjoying the female company. Then Deborah drifted across his mind and he started to shake. He moved away from the center of the room to a corner, the arboretum of the house. He sat on a bench and gripped its edge, the cool marble calming him. He sat there for many minutes, then ventured out of the foliage. He found where he had left his iced goblet and picked it up, happy to have something to do with his hands. The low murmur of the men and the tinkling laughter of the women merged, calming Ephraim further, the lilting cacophony making him feel less alien in these new surroundings. He caught the eye of Nadab who was engaged in deep conversation with one of the women. Nadab smiled and raised his small goblet of the iced sweet in a silent toast. Ephraim returned the gesture and nodded.

Chapter Thirty

Jerusalem, Judaea   The 4th day of *Iyar* 3594 (April 29th166 B.C.E.)

Apollonius said, "I am to return to Samaria within the week, High Priest. I was expecting this report yesterday, and I do not like to be kept waiting. You had better hope that the information was worth the wait. I have some intelligence on the Maccabee and his forces, but I can always use more." He leaned back, his face stern as he appraised the two Jews.

Menelaus glanced over at Nadab and said, "Yes, your honor. We have some rather useful information. It is said that many are gathering themselves to the Maccabee in the hills of Gophna—"

"High priest," Apollonius said wearily, "if you are going to spend this debriefing telling me everything I already know, then it is not much of a debriefing, now is it?" His look was affable, but irritation tinged his smile.

Menelaus licked his lips. "Of course not, general. I was just going to say that the Maccabee is planning to stay atop the hills of Gophna and worry your troops with barrages of arrows and rocks."

"That Jew did not go to all the trouble of forming a rebellion just to sit in the hills and throw rocks at us. I do not believe it. You had better come up with something else."

Apollonius watched as Menelaus leaned toward Nadab and listened to a whisper from the advisor. "Well?" Apollonius thundered.

"We, ah, also understand that the Maccabee is attempting to train skirmishers. However, our source says it is not going well. The Jews do not seem to have the ability to adapt to new tactics. He apparently is on the verge of abandoning the training."

"So, he does understand something of Greek warfare," Apollonius murmured. "Skirmishers. What else?"

"It is also said that the Maccabee has spent a great deal of time mapping out the great valleys and flat places round about Gophna. He had shown a particular interest in the field of Armageddon."

"So, perhaps the Jew will meet us in battle. Does he have armaments?"

"Very crude ones, from what our source is saying. It seems that the Maccabee was a blacksmith in the days of peace and that he is skilled, after a barbarian fashion, in forging swords, shields and even pikes."

"Pikes." Apollonius said. He called, "Syrus!"

The two Jews jumped at the bellow and Syrus came running into the office. He planted himself in front of Philo's desk where Apollonius was beginning to shuffle the ever-present parchments and tablets.

"Syrus, I want you to gather the commanders at the pavilion in the exercise yard. I want them there in a half-hour."

"Yes, General. One-half hour." Syrus saluted and left.

"You also might be interested to know that he has not sent his non-combatants away," Menelaus went on. "The women and children remain in the hills—"

"And I will sell every one of them as slaves when this is all through," Apollonius grumbled. "I intend to obliterate the national and religious consciousness that has fueled this ridiculous insurrection; death will teach most of them, slavery the rest. Is there anything else?"

"Only this, your honor: the Maccabee seems to be planning for a clandestine war. Everything our source says indicates that they are training for guerilla strikes and not for open warfare. They have tried training for battle, but do not have the bent for it. That does not mean the Maccabee does not want battle with a Greek force. I believe that his interest in the field of Armageddon flies upon a wish. But all indications are that they will not be at home on a battlefield."

"Who is this source?" Apollonius asked.

"He grew up with the Maccabee," Menelaus said. "He became disaffected after his father died at rebel hands. Now he is working for us."

"I will have his head on a spit if this intelligence is not correct. You may tell him that for me. Now I must go." Apollonius stood and with greater courtesy than he felt, bowed and said, "I thank you for your service to the emperor. Your cooperation will be duly noted and will ensure your safety under the Greek banner."

"Under your command, I have no doubt that Gophna and the Maccabee will soon be nothing but a distant memory," Menelaus said, returning the bow.

Chapter Thirty-one

A s Nadab followed the high priest out of the Greek barracks, he clasped his hands behind his back. Deep in thought, he barely heard the high priest. Something was not right about this intelligence. Everything the Maccabee had undertaken thus far in the rebellion had been genius in execution. He seemed to anticipate every Greek move and had been successful in thwarting his enemy's efforts to gain control of Judaea. The rebel leader had, in essence, confined the Greek presence to Jerusalem so that their patrols no longer ventured far from the city walls. Nadab had chosen to believe Ephraim's reports of what he had seen in the Maccabee camp, but wondered if the Jews really were as inept in training as he said. He hoped they were, but if Apollonius met with a different scenario up north, it would not only mean Ephraim's head, but perhaps his and Menelaus' as well. As much as he dreaded interacting with Barbatus, he decided that he needed more of the assassin's advice on the matter. Nadab knew that Barbatus had a deep mistrust of Ephraim. Barbatus' very existence depended upon his prickly assessment of the human psyche. It was likely that his mistrust was not misplaced.

"High priest," Nadab said as soon as they reached the doors of the palace. "I have some business to conduct in the city. May I take my leave?"

Menelaus waved him off and Nadab hurried away toward the Greek quarter of the city. The fleshpots of Jerusalem were not places he liked to frequent, but that was where he would find the assassin, Barbatus.

"Advisor Nadab, how interesting to find a man of your persuasion in a place like this," Barbatus said into the rude wooden cup of ale. "I do not think this place follows your—what shall we call them?—oh, your dietary restraints."

Nadab stood regally over the agent and waited for him to disengage from the harlot lounging on his lap. Only then did he sit down. "I need to know what you think of Ephraim."

"Oh, he is a good enough sort," Barbatus slurred into the cup. "I think he is a fine, upstanding Jew."

"But," Nadab pressed, "what of his intelligence? Do you trust it?"

"I trust no intelligence," Barbatus said sharply, still slurring, but more coherent in his vehemence. "No spy does. An agent trusts only his own instincts, and even those can betray him."

"What can you mean?" Nadab asked impatiently. "How does one operate like that? No certainty? No trust? It is a wonder that you are still alive in this line of work."

"That is precisely why I am still alive," Barbatus said. "A spy is only as good as his own wits. He cannot depend upon anyone for his continued existence." He grabbed another harlot who was balancing two goblets of rough ale and said, "That is why I rely upon these for my companionship and entertainment." He patted her buttocks playfully and went on, squinting at Nadab, "No connections make for a long life in my business."

Nadab forced the disgust out of his voice. His successes depended largely upon the assassin's good will. He said, "I understand, but what of Ephraim? You do not trust his intelligence, but does he at least think he is telling the truth?"

Suddenly, Barbatus took a profound interest in his cup, surveying its contents, the rough workmanship of its line, the color of its ragged wood grain. He then said, "Let me put it this way. I would be very surprised if he is telling the truth in these matters. His reports on the Maccabee do not make sense to me. It surpasses all credible thought that the rebel leader is making no plans for battle. Now, it could be as he says, that they are planning on continuing the guerilla war; after all, it has been quite effective. It also does not hurt the Jews that the Greeks are conducting their confused campaign as if they were drunken followers of Dionysus. But, I maintain that something is not quite right."

"I agree," Nadab said, scratching his beard. "I want you to shadow Ephraim. I need to know where he goes and whom he sees. Does he have contact with any truly orthodox Jews? Does he have contact with any of the insurrectionists here in the city? All these are questions to which I need answers."

"It shall be as you say," Barbatus said with disinterest. "But if he leads me out of the city during this chase, your fee will increase as well as my expenses."

"Yes, yes, of course," said Nadab impatiently. "It will be well worth it if we find that our Ephraim is not all he seems. It may well save our heads."

"Speak for yourself, counselor. My head is quite safe. I made no guarantee to Apollonius for the veracity of your Jew's word. If need be, by the time the general returns from his little campaign up north, I will have disappeared down a dark alley in a wisp of vapor."

Nadab stepped out into the fetid street, delicately lifting his robes out of the open sewer that ran in front of the establishment. He sniffed in distaste, and avoiding two poxed whores who clutched at his finery, hurried back to the palace.

Chapter Thirty-two

Gophna, Judaea   The 4th day of *Iyar* 3594 (April 29th 166 B.C.E.)

Aulus muttered, "Why you waste time with those slings, I will never know." He picked up a bucket of water while taking a break from training the new recruits that Judah had brought in from Beit Horon the week before. After pouring the bucket of water over his head, he tousled his short, bristled hair dry. Although it was early spring, the sun at mid-day was an annoyance. "There is no way these scrawny strips of leather will help against the royal phalanx and the skirmishers, not to mention the elephants. Instead of sling training, you should spend more time immersing them in the art of hand-to-hand combat."

"Aulus, look at them," Judah said. "Watch Gad—that is Ephraim's younger brother, you know—watch, watch. There! With all your Roman *catapultae* and *ballistae*, you could not achieve better accuracy than that young boy with his sling. You'll see. You will be thanking your god, Mars, for those slingmen one day."

"When we finally do meet the Greeks in battle, I'll be lucky if I am not slain with a stray rock from one of your lads, your young David's," Aulus said sourly. "I will be just like your—what was his name—oh, yes, Goliath the Philistine."

"One of your ancestors," Judah said, laughing, then he turned serious. "Aulus, we must study our maps and figure out where to draw out the Greeks to battle. Eleazar and I scouted as far north as the Jezreel Valley a moon ago—what a battlefield that would make! It is too bad it is so far away. Some of our most famous heroes fought there: Deborah, Barak, Jehu."

"Yes," Aulus said. "It would be a fine battlefield for the Greeks to make mincemeat of the Men of Modiin. Judah, you must not entertain thoughts of meeting the Greeks on a plain like that. You are not Romans, trained for deploying huge blocks of manpower in elaborate battle formations. Now, do not look at me like that. We have been at this business for hundreds of years. You are newcomers to the science of war strategy. You will learn quickly, but if Apollonius marches on us in the next few weeks, you must make use of your strengths."

"And what are those?" Judah asked, not without some bitterness. "I wonder that you think we have any strengths whatsoever."

"Your knowledge of these hills," Aulus said resolutely. "Your ability to move quickly in and to strike quietly, and, more importantly, the Greeks underestimation of that ability. Later, you will meet the Greeks on the field of battle, and you may be victorious. Now, however, you must drive the Greeks into unfamiliar venues for their pikemen: ravines, wadis, narrow gorges and canyons. That is where you will find victory. Hear me, brother."

Judah was touched by Aulus' earnest face and clapped him on the bicep. "All right, all right. I trust you, old friend. Let us scout your ravines, wadis, narrow gorges and canyons. Do not roll your eyes. I would like to wait until I have word from Ephraim, but I do not think I have enough time."

"Ephraim?" Aulus asked in surprise. "But I thought you two had quarreled—you dog!" His face lit up. "Now I see what you are up to. You have turned him into a spy." At Judah's embarrassed smile, Aulus shook his head. "Well, I hope he is a good one, we are going to need the intelligence. He is not your only one, is he?"

"No," said Judah. "I am cultivating others, but no one is as valuable as Ephraim with his connection to the high priest in Jerusalem. He will be very important to us, if he can stay alive in that Greek nest of cockatrices."

Aulus nodded and then said to the newcomer in the tent, "Ah, Brita. You are a dear. We needed a more refined drink than just water for me and the commander here." He held up the goblet and peered at it. "Are you sure it is clean?"

"You were ever a fop," Judah said in disgust, taking the goblet from Brita. "We have been eating sand and drinking mud for the past months, and you wonder if your little goblet is clean?"

Brita's laugh was a musical cymbal and the two men looked at her with appreciation, Aulus more openly than Judah. "Master," she said, "I assure you that I washed it thoroughly, just as I do all your personal items. And, Master Judah, the drink in your cup is clean according to your law. I keep a little of it in our stores in case—" Brita did not finish but put her head down. It was not in the attitude of a slave, but rather that of an embarrassed woman.

Since fleeing Aulus' Roman estate in Modiin all those months ago, Brita rarely crossed paths with the Jews on Gophna as Aulus' bivouac was separate from the rest of the camp. Slavery, although not unknown among the Hebrews, was generally frowned upon; therefore, Brita kept solitary her comings and goings and made herself content with tending her master and his tent. Judah and she met occasionally only because of his extended dealings with the Roman.

Aulus harrumphed and drank from the goblet and Judah followed his example, never taking his eyes from the tawny slave. She returned his gaze for a moment, then stepped back, head down, and waited as she had been trained in the Auli Roman household.

Judah was glad she stepped away, for he was getting that uncomfortable stirring in his loins he experienced whenever he encountered Brita. He was always surprised by this weakness. After his wedding he had thought that his marriage bed would banish those improper yearnings for the slave.

Judah excused himself and strode to the tent he shared with his wife. He pounded aside the flap. She was not there. He stood at the front threshold for a moment, kicking aside some errant pebbles that were scattered on the entry rug and glanced down. That entry rug had graced the front atrium of his estate in Modiin. He wondered where Miriam had found it as he did not even know it had made the journey with them to the hills. His father, he remembered, had bought it from a Persian merchant who had passed through Modiin years ago. His mother had always hated the rug, saying that it made her think of heathen gods with its vulgar colors and intricate weavings. She would hide the rug, but Father would always find it, returning it to his favorite spot, the entry of the atrium. Judah smiled at the memory and thought for a moment about his father.

Mattathias had been dead for nearly a month and Judah missed him. During command meetings, a question for Mattathias would form on Judah's lips, then die away when he recalled that his father was gone. In his mind, however, he would always imagine how Mattathias would respond to a particularly knotty problem. He would listen until he felt he could almost hear his father's voice speak the answer, then he would make his decision. He never shared this strange phenomenon with anybody, fearing his men would think him unhinged or downright crazy, but so far, his decisions had been sound. At least none in his command circle had complained.

"Judah, what are you doing here? I thought you had a meeting with your commanders." Miriam was shaking out the wash that she had just taken down from the line behind their tent. She smiled at her husband. "Now, here I find you loitering in front of our tent as if you had nothing to do. Perhaps the great warrior would like to help me get more wash from the line."

In answer, Judah grabbed her waist and swung her around. A shriek started from her throat but was reduced to a hiss as he dragged her into the tent.

"What! Are you crazy? In the middle of the day? Judah," she giggled, "stop! The neighbors will hear!"

"Not if you keep your caterwauling to a minimum, they will not!"

* * * * *

Judah napped, but sleep fled Miriam. After all, it was mid-afternoon, and she had many chores. The tent was getting hot, but she did not want to wake her dozing husband. They had such little time together that even watching him sleep was a welcome pastime. She rolled over on her back, stared at the faint outline of the rough tent seams above her head, her mind reverting to its familiar worry.

She and Judah had been married for three months and Miriam had yet to experience the signs of a child within her womb. Shoshanna had confided in Miriam

119

that very day that her womb was thickening with Eleazar's child. Miriam had outwardly rejoiced with her sister-in-law but felt as if ice had spread through her vitals at the news. Was she barren? Would she have to live her life without issue? These were questions that had plagued her mind for many months and as she watched the other women's bellies swell and the midwives called to their tents, she wondered when the same would ever happen to her. Surely, the wife of the great rebel leader, Judah the Maccabee, was destined to bear his child. Surely, the people needed to see his seed continue through the generations of their tribe. She sighed.

"Wife," Judah murmured, stupid with slumber, "you are waking me with your sighs. What is amiss?"

"Nothing, husband," she whispered. "I am sorry I awakened you. I must return to my chores anyway."

"No." Judah reached for her. "You will stay here by me." He buried his head in her neck and pulled her closer to his chest.

"What is next?" Miriam asked.

"What, wife? You will wear me out with your cupidity. What could be next? Did we not just. . ."

"I mean the war, *teepaysh!*" She knuckled him lightly on the chest. "What are the Greeks going to do next?"

"I do not know, but I hope to soon find out."

"How? How will you find out?" Miriam asked, interest consuming her. "We women need to know so we can plan. A fight? A migration?"

"Be quiet, woman," Judah sighed, burrowing deeper into her body. "The commander needs to finish his nap."

"No, you need to tell me how you will. . ." She paused to allow her intellect to solve the question. It did not take long for the truth to dawn upon her and even in the dark tent, Judah could see her eyes alight with excitement. "You and Ephraim did not quarrel, did you? It was all planned, was it not?"

"I do not know what you are talking about," Judah tried to sound nonchalant. "You should have heard the foul things Ephraim said about me and the rebellion and even about my father, may his soul rest."

"Judah, I know about Ephraim's meeting with the advisor to Menelaus. Was not Nadab his name?"

"You know about that? When did he tell you?" Judah sat up and looked at her.

"He did not tell me, I overheard one day as you and he were conversing in the command tent." Miriam said. She had also sat up and was staring at him warily. "I did not mean to eavesdrop, but, well, I could not help it. He is your spy," she said with conviction. "He will notify you of the Greeks' movements. Good work, husband."

Judah enforced his nonchalance and leaned back on their bed of skins. He said, "You have a fertile imagination, wife. I wonder that you do not join the troupes of storytellers that wander the Greek towns acting out their heresies." But knowing that his face was hidden against the skins, he smiled.

Miriam smiled, too, but her smile faded when she remembered that it seemed only her imagination was fertile. This time she was the one who reached out and sought comfort in the body of her husband. Finally, both of them found sleep together.

Judah and Miriam emerged from the tent an hour later. Miriam set to finishing sorting the laundered robes, and Judah sped off to the command meeting for which he was now late.

"Do not tell them why you were late!" Miriam called, the timbre of her voice as subdued as possible. "I will never be able to show my face to them again!"

The Maccabee paused at the entrance to the command tent, and mentally pulled the foolish smile from his features. It would never do for him to enter the meeting with the moony visage of a schoolboy. He opened the tent flap.

Aulus' and Asher's faces were not five inches from each other. Like game cocks, their chests were thrust out, fists clenched like talons, and Judah swore later that he could see the hair on their necks bristling in anger. All faces turned to Judah upon his entrance, and both men upon seeing the commander, backed away from each other and struggled to gain control of themselves.

"It seems," Schmuel said, his smile grim, "That we have a differing of opinions on further training of the slingmen."

"Yes," Judah said, sitting and gazing up at the Roman. "I understand that Aulus would like us to concentrate our efforts elsewhere."

"Well, it only makes sense," Aulus said defiantly. "If we are going up against pikes and superior armor and even elephants, as we discussed before, Judah," Aulus paused and looked meaningfully at him, "We must concentrate on increasing our prowess at swordplay. Not only that, but we have not even begun to set up a defense for the Greek Phalanx. We must even learn to create our own phalanx. We are not ready!"

Judah stood and put his arm around Aulus, "You are right, of course," he said into Aulus ear, but loud enough that everyone else could hear. To the group, he said in a raised voice, "This Roman understands Greek warfare. We must listen to him. I want you to think what he has given up to be with us here. He is indeed a stranger in a strange land as Moshe was, but he has stayed among us to add his strength to our impossible conflict. We are to treat him with all deference and courtesy." Judah grabbed Aulus on both sides of his bristled haircut and tapped his forehead against his own. "I honor you, friend."

"But, Judah!" Asher protested. "Our armies have thriven on our slingmen. It is an ancient art that we should not forsake. And it *is* effective!" This last he directed at Aulus and the two glared at each other for a moment.

Judah put up his hands. "When I said that Aulus is right, I meant it. We do need to better train in swordplay. We do need to set up a defense for the phalanx. But we also need our slingmen." Among the murmurs of approval, he spoke to Aulus. "We Jews must keep a semblance of our ancient art of war. The slingmen will continue to train, but," he raised his voice to the entire tent, "they and the rest of you will train to be at least as good with your swords as you are with your slings. We will also start forging more pikes so that we can train with them and prepare to face the enemy phalanx. We must be ready when we are forced into combat on an open battlefield. I fear that time will soon come. But for now," he said as he glanced over at Aulus, "we will forsake the idea of fighting on open battlefields until we are ready with our swords and pikes." He nodded at Asher, saying, "But we will not abandon the slings as per our traditions. But we will strive to push the Greeks into a venue of fighting that is more strategically sound for us: ravines, wadis, narrow gorges and canyons."

He did not turn to see them, but he could sense Aulus' and Asher's smiles.

Chapter Thirty-three

E phraim lounged in the palace atrium as he waited for Nadab. Having been summoned for a meeting with the high priest's advisor, he now idly lunched upon some items slaves had arranged on a large banquet table under the canopy of citrus and eucalyptus trees. In deference to Ephraim's dietetic sensibilities, as always, Nadab had made sure that all the items were prepared in accordance with Jewish law. As Ephraim ate the fruits, bread delicacies and succulent kosher flesh, he decided that he was beginning to appreciate at least some of the Greek way of living. It seemed more refined, gentler, at least when one was part of the inner circle of Greek rule.

Ephraim hung around the palace as much as possible in the days since he had first met Barbatus in Beeroth, the Place of Wells, north of Jerusalem. He could see why it had been so popular a stopping place for caravans all these centuries. It seemed to cater to all nationalities and peoples in their thirsts and travel-weary senses. Therefore, it did not seem odd when the clean-shaven Barbatus, so obviously a heathen, for all that he was disguised in Jewish attire, approached Ephraim. When Barbatus had indicated that he was an agent of Nadab, Ephraim had secretly rejoiced and inwardly intoned with gratitude the watchword of the rebellion, "The Lord of Hosts With Us."

Now waiting in the atrium, Ephraim hoped that Nadab would bring him news that would help Judah and wondered how he would get word up north. Because it seemed a shame to end his valuable relationship with Nadab by fleeing up north, he also hoped that leaving would not be necessary. Nadab was a prolific mine for intelligence, but Ephraim could see no alternative to leaving if he were presented information that would benefit the rebellion. Stupidly, he had not thought to recruit anyone to help him extend his contacts here in Jerusalem. He had also felt that he could not take responsibility for another's death should things go wrong in the espionage. Now he rued his weakness.

All of his previous pacifist friends had perished in the butchery of the caves, and it was too late to cultivate anyone now. That meant that if and when the time came, he would likely have to make the dangerous journey back to the hills of Gophna himself to warn Judah. He was not frightened for himself, his life since the death of Deborah had not much meaning, but he did not want his intelligence to die along with him. Perhaps he could send a letter with a caravan. At least if he met his death on the journey, there would be a chance that Judah would still get his message, whatever it happened to be. He searched the table for another piece of sweetened chicken and spun around when he heard footsteps entering the room. It seemed he would soon find out what message he could take to Judah, for Nadab was sweeping into the atrium at that very moment.

"I am sorry I am late," the advisor panted. "I had some urgent business with Menelaus."

"You always have urgent business with Menelaus," Ephraim observed, sucking chicken juice from his fingers. "And it nearly always involves your cleaning up some political mess he has gotten himself into."

"That is enough out of you," Nadab said, but without any real malice, for he had shared with Ephraim many of the peccadilloes involved in serving the disorganized high priest. "I have news. You will find this very interesting. It seems that the days of Judah the Maccabee are coming to a close."

Ephraim, who had been lounging on a couch and was now using a lemon-watered cloth to clean his fingers, sat up with real interest and said, "Truly? What has happened?"

"Nothing yet," Nadab said, drawing a ripe apricot from a bed of lettuce. "But I can assure you that Apollonius will see to it that the Maccabee and his cohorts will plague the Greek empire no more."

"Is he marching?" Ephraim asked, trying to sound eager for the correct reason.

"Not only is he marching, but he is going to surprise the Maccabee and his forces in Gophna by marching from the west and not from the more popular southern approach direct from Jerusalem."

"G-d is great," Ephraim chanted gently. "When does he march?"

"Upon the morrow," Nadab said, finishing the apricot, carefully wiping his manicured beard. "At sunrise Apollonius will depart for Samaria. He is taking two cohorts from his Samarian *kotaikai* to march on Gophna."

"The Samarian cohorts?" Ephraim asked, attempting nonchalance. He knew full well that this would be very frightening news for those at Gophna, for all that it had been expected for some time.

"Yes. They are Apollonius' hand-picked cohorts from the only Macedonian *kotaikai* maintained since Alexander's time. They are the most fearsome troops in this quarter of Antiochus' empire, and certainly in Judaea. As I said, Apollonius will make short work of your rebels." Nadab bit into a honeyed date. "Now, *that* is a date. Our Jericho dates ever surpass those of Egypt, Especially this season." Devouring it, he went on, "If Antiochus is thrifty—a doubtful proposition—the revenues from the date groves of Jericho alone would satisfy the tribute to Rome and fill the emperor's coffers."

Ephraim nodded in agreement, but not in contemplating the date harvest. He must leave Jerusalem by nightfall to get to Gophna in time to warn Judah. His only advantage was that he could travel much more swiftly than Apollonius' two cohorts with their baggage train and animals. He could be in Gophna by tomorrow if he traveled all night. The cohorts would take at least two days, and their need for stealth would rob them of a quick march. It seemed he would have to jeopardize this hard-won liaison with Nadab after all.

"The march is good news, indeed," said Ephraim, rising. He yawned. "Well, I am weary. I think I will retire, but I will sleep better tonight than I have since my dear father's death. His blood perhaps will be silent tonight. It has often cried up to me from the ground in my dreams. The death of the Maccabee may assuage his spirit."

"You have been through much, my friend," Nadab said, his eyes soft with sympathy. "You have earned a rest. I feel that vengeance will be yours in not more than a few days."

Ephraim bowed and asked, "Will there be anything else, advisor?"

"No, you may go."

Ephraim nodded and exited the Atrium, his robes jerking behind him in his haste.

*   *   *   *   *

Nadab sat down on the same bench where he had lamented his missed chance for intelligence from Ephraim almost a week ago. He sat, chuckling with satisfaction until he was interrupted by the nasal voice that came from behind a tree back in the thicker foliage of the atrium.

"So, you think he is leaving to go take a nap?" Barbatus emerged from behind the tree where he had concealed himself during Ephraim's and Nadab's exchange. "He had a rather quick gallop for one who supposedly is about to seek Somnus' mace."

"I do not believe that he is on his way to inform the Maccabee of Apollonius' movements," Nadab said lazily, "if that is what you mean. But, in case I am wrong, you will act as the failsafe to my plan. You will follow Ephraim as we agreed earlier to make sure that I am right."

"It will not look very good for you if I catch him trying to make his way to Gophna."

"Nonsense," Nadab said, scooping up a couple of olives to eat on the way back to his office. "The fact that I am engaging you indicates that I have covered both of the possibilities, either his fidelity or his flight."

"Experience in this business has taught me," said Barbatus, "that there are seldom only two possibilities. A third, fourth or even fifth often rears its head."

"In which case, I have every confidence that you will dispatch all of them with a swift swipe of your sword. Just like Hercules dispatched the Hydra of its nine heads," Nadab added cleverly.

"Yes, but you might recall that each head of Hercules' hydra sprouted three heads for every one he cut," Barbatus pointed out. "One must always be ready for a myriad of—heads."

"I will leave those 'heads' in your capable hands," Nadab said irritably, eager for the exchange with the assassin to end. "You may go now."

Barbatus shrugged, filled his pockets with an assortment of fruit from the banquet table and took his leave.

As Nadab watched Barbatus disappear into the copse of Eucalyptus trees at the edge of the atrium, he hoped that Ephraim was not on the way to the Maccabee as Barbatus suspected. Not only would he lose a budding friend, but also an excellent informant on the doings of the rebellion. But he could not suppress a shiver as he remembered Barbatus' feral expression of a moment before.

Chapter Thirty-four

Jerusalem, Judaea   The 5th day of *Iyar* 3594 (April 30th166 B.C.E.)

Ephraim knew he had to travel unencumbered, but how? The heavy cloak was still necessary as the spring nights were chill. The mezuzah from his old dwelling in Modiin, his father's tefillin, his mother's necklace: none of these was he willing to leave behind. And food, he would need some for the long journey. Comfort, that was something else. He put aside the sturdy sandals he had just bought in the marketplace, donning his feet instead with an older, shabby, yet more comfortable pair.

He sat down on the bed and studied the sandals. They were the ones he had worn all during the cave habitation. They were the ones he had worn during the slaughter. He had had to scrub and scrub to destroy the sheen of blood that had molded itself against the leather. Now, instead of the earthen brown of cattle hide, they shone with a strange crimson hue that bespoke of the horrors through which they had trod. At first, he had peeled them off his feet in disgust when he reached the Gehonna well after the butchery. He had almost left them at the foot of the well's worn brick, but something made him keep them. In fact, he had torn a rag from the hem of his robe, doused it in the bucket of well water, and proceeded to start scrubbing right at that moment. He was mindful of little else as he had sat there, weary, shock-worn and shaking, rubbing the ridiculous rag over the sandals, dipping it again and again in the well bucket in an effort to clean them. They did not come clean. Even the tears he shed over them, over Deborah, as he sat there scouring, did nothing to lessen the hold of blood on the leather.

He slipped them on his feet, surprised that he was weeping again. He had not wept for Deborah the many weeks since the slaughter and that the tears came so easily now worried him. He was a spy about to embark on a dangerous enterprise. If Nadab or any of his minions knew he was attempting to flee to Gophna to warn Judah of the impending assault by Apollonius, he would die a very unpleasant death. More importantly, if Ephraim were to die, Judah would not know of Apollonius' coming from the west. He wiped his tears on the sleeve of his robe, folded his cloak over the few belongings and slipped out of his room.

The corridor was dark with only one torch mottling the walls with flame. Ephraim glided along the darker wall away from the torch until he found one of the doors that led out to the palace courtyard. His footfalls were surprisingly silent, and he looked down at the sandals with gratitude. Apparently, his emotional decision to keep the bloodied sandals turned out to be pragmatic. The stone beneath him gave no hint of the movement of leather over its surface.

*   *   *   *   *

But Barbatus needed no hint to follow. The assassin emerged from a shadow and followed Ephraim through the dim hall. It did not matter that the stone did not speak of movement, he had no trouble keeping up with Ephraim regardless of the corridor length he kept between him and his quarry. Instinct alone told him of Ephraim's direction, and he knew he had to be heading for the courtyard. That it proved to be so did not inspire Barbatus to congratulate himself on his heightened senses. He simply drew himself along the same walls and down the alleys where Ephraim now skulked. It seemed that Barbatus had been right all along—that the Jew was indeed intending to flee Jerusalem for Gophna to warn the Maccabee.

Barbatus gritted his teeth. He was unusually weary today and did not relish hunting this night. As he followed Ephraim, he determined that he would end this chase quickly with a stealthy garrote to the Jew's neck. Nadab may not approve, but Barbatus never did intend to follow Ephraim all the way to Gophna. It was obvious that Ephraim was about to betray the Greeks and killing him would invite no recriminations from his employer. That meant, however, that he needed to eat up some distance between himself and his prey. He escalated his gait to a trot, and after a few minutes he paused. Up ahead, he saw an increase of torches, their fires moving up and down in the hands of men who were shouting drunken epithets. Barbatus could not discern the language as the words bounced incoherently off the stone of the alley, creating a reverberation that assaulted his ears. He edged up to the scene. The torches belonged to a battalion of Greek soldiers that had just emerged from one of the brothels marking the entrance to the Greek quarter of the city. Ephraim was nowhere in sight.

Barbatus knew that Greeks had no real love for Romans. The Roman victory over the Greeks at Magnesia and subsequent extraction of tribute from Antiochus had tainted relations between the two nations for the past thirty years. He had no wish to encounter these Greeks in this questionable neighborhood, but Ephraim had passed that way. He had no choice. He decided that bravado was the best way to handle the situation, so he steeled himself and walked boldly toward the group.

As nonchalantly as possible, and doing his best to cover his Latin accent, Barbatus addressed the soldiers in Greek, "So, my Greek brothers, how goes it for you, tonight? I know this place well; I trust Sappho treated you well?"

The Greeks stopped, eyeing the intruder.

Barbatus shrugged and made as if to hurry through the soldiers. One soldier stopped him, grabbing him roughly by the shoulder.

"Why are you about so late, citizen?" The soldier asked.

Barbatus tried a new tack: aggression. "Do not detain me, scrub," Barbatus said, putting derision into his tone. "I am on garrison business for General Apollonius." He would have said 'high priest's business' but he did not feel that would hold much weight with this group.

"What is it?" Another soldier asked, thrusting his drunken face into Barbatus' and laughing. "It is not Jew. Nor is it Arab."

"No," another said, pulling off Barbatus' cow and rubbing his bristled head. "Look! A Roman haircut!"

A few others began manhandling the assassin now as he had started to struggle away from the one who now said,"I *thought* he was a Roman. See?" He had ripped Barbatus' robe off his shoulder and was displaying the "SPQR" that every Roman legionnaire had tattooed to his shoulder.

"A Roman? In these parts?" The Greek seemed to be the leader and at his chuckle the rest of the soldiers dissolved into drunken gabbles of laughter. "The last time I saw a Roman was outside Alexandria, when Laenas derided and humiliated our emperor."

The laughter subsided into a hostile silence. Barbatus cursed inwardly. He should have never tried to plough through these soldiers. He could have let Ephraim go and caught up with him on the road to Gophna. Now that extreme lack of judgement could well cost him his life. He, Barbatus, one of the most successful assassins in the civilized world, was caught. It would not have been so bad if he had been bested by a worthy adversary, but to be apprehended by a cadre of drunken Greek soldiers was humiliating, indeed. Barbatus attempted to reach the shank that he kept in a sheath at his calf, but the soldiers' grips had closed as tight as nooses and there was no opportunity for movement.

"Oh, yes," the officer went on, "You Romans are forever taking what is ours: our dignity, our money, our lands. And now you feel as though you can walk our streets as if you own them? No, Roman. We own these streets, and you are not welcome here."

By now, the Greeks had wrapped a long leather strap around Barbatus' face, gagging his mouth so that he could utter nothing but incoherent burbles and screeches. They enjoyed the great sport of shoving him against each other, the hard stone of the alley walls and the cobbles in the street. Their drunkenness heightened the humor of every thud and crash, and they did not tire for a long time. At last, they noticed that the Roman was not resisting them any longer and that his face and head were very bloody. After one last head-catapult into the wall, they let the Roman bleed where he lay, against an anonymous alley wall just outside the Greek Quarter of the city.

Chapter Thirty-five

Antioch, Syria   The 5th day of *Iyar* 3594 (April 30th 166 B.C.E.)

As Nicanor looked out on the Orontes from the palace balcony, he decided that he missed his elephants. A wife could be a comfort, it was true, but it was the giant greys that gave him true pleasure, of a military sort, that is. His wife was an understanding creature who had lived with the vagaries of having a husband in army life for thirty years. He did appreciate her and the comfort she offered in his bed, but he did not crave her as he did the daily business of rearing, feeding and training of his beloved animals.

He wondered how they were faring in Judaea. Were they being fed the right combination of mash and straw? Were the handlers keeping to their strict training regimen? Was Apollonius visiting them as he promised? Elephant worries, however, were one thing; the beasts were so far away. There were other worries here in the palace of Antioch, closer at hand and of a more sinister character.

General Seron had not returned to his governorship in Gaza, opting instead, Nicanor guessed, to stay here among the intrigues of the palace to gain more of a foothold in the intricate power plays choreographed by the emperor. Antiochus delighted in pitting the members of his court against each other. Lysias the chancellor and Philippus the regent vied for control of young Eupator, Antiochus' son; Antiochus' mistress and Teman, competed for the ear and general attentions of the emperor; and now, Nicanor found himself in a contest with his colleague, General Seron, regarding his rival's misplaced notions of the military governance of Judaea.

After hearing about the Jews' rout of Timotheus in Gophna, over the past few weeks Antiochus had been summoning Generals Nicanor and Seron to his dinner table, his bath and even his bed in the middle of the night to confer about his Judaean subjects. The meetings were all the same: Antiochus would ask about his children the Jews, Seron would pontificate on the ease of subduing them, and Nicanor would wearily point out that the reason the Hebrew rebellion was alive and well in Judaea was Greek arrogance. This underestimation of the Jews was the reason the rebellion had become a conflagration that defied all means of extinguishing.

But it seemed that neither Seron nor Antiochus listened to anybody but themselves during these redundant meetings, and Nicanor was tiring quickly of the incessant summons he received to attend the emperor. Seron was always there, and so were the same old discussions and arguments.

This day, Nicanor and Seron arrived at the meeting place, the atrium of Antiochus' calisthenic chamber, at the same time. After exchanging a mutual look that said, "Well, this is new at least," they wandered around each other in little claustrophobic circles as they waited for the guard to admit them to the emperor's training venue. Finally, the ponderous doors swung slowly inward to reveal Teman, Antiochus' advisor. Agitation jerked in Teman's features, and without a word, he lifted a beckoning hand, turned from them and stalked off toward the sounds of the clatterings of sword, shield, javelin interspersed with the grunts of an emperor in training.

In training for what? Nicanor wondered as he followed the eager Seron and the lurching Teman.

He ambled along slowly, determined to put off the boring exchange for as long as humanly possible, and stopped to inspect the artistry of the mosaic that graced the atrium of the calisthenic yard. He had beheld these murals many times before, always a dangerous endeavor, because every time he looked at the art depicted in the scatterings of ceramic, he had to use every shred of soldierly mien he possessed to keep from laughing. The mosaics were unparalleled in their workmanship, the shards of ceramic blended and shaded just so to imitate the human form in the beauty of competition: two wrestlers entwined in the contortions of an athletic hand-to-hand contest, a javelin hurler poised at the ready with his missile, a hoplite with his lithesome shield and short sword, and even a phalangite wielding the three-cubit-long pike in the attitude of battle. Nicanor tried not to snort. Beautiful mosaics all, but their artistry a bit fraught as all the faces were faces inlaid with a likeness of Antiochus.

It was as if the palace art commissioners had hired a seasoned and talented artisan to sculpt the bodies depicted in the mosaic and an inept hack to fashion the likeness of the emperor. The result was a grotesque mixture of art and propaganda that would assault the aesthetic sensibilities of anyone except the lowest cretin.

Nicanor moved away from the mosaic and stood in a corner until his jocular heavings ceased. He had just achieved a measure of control when he thought of his old friend Apollonius and how he would respond to the ludicrous scenes of the emperor's athleticism. He choked again in a paroxysm of deep giggles.

"Oh, how I miss you, Apollonius," Nicanor sighed as he moved into the exercise yard. "I wish The Divine One would let me return to Judaea so we could work together and solve this Jewish problem once and for all. Zeus!"

Nicanor uttered the epithet when he walked onto the imperial training field, for both Teman and Seron had stripped to their undercloths and were engaging each other in swordplay. He turned his head until he could control the wide smile threatening his new, tenuous attempt at control. When he was finally able to turn his attention to the field, Seron was the only one looking, or rather, glaring at him, as Teman was doing his best to stay alive under Seron's experienced slashings. Antiochus' eyes were riveted on the one-sided contest before him.

At last, the emperor seemed to sense Nicanor's presence, for, without even turning his head away from the spectacle, he said loudly, "General Nicanor, come and help me judge these athletes. They are well-matched, no?"

"Very well-matched, Sire." Nicanor allowed himself a grin which he directed pointedly at Seron. "I have never seen two opponents better matched, no, not in all the training fields in the empire."

"It is a good contest," Antiochus said, nodding resolutely. "See how Seron wields the shield to slough off Teman's thrusts. And Teman! Advisor! You have a very strong sword arm. Thrust, Teman, thrust!"

Nicanor had to turn away again. Even the humorless Seron retreated from Teman until he could gain control of himself.

"Come on, men!" Antiochus continued cheerfully. "Engage! Engage! Engage!"

A slave brought chairs for the emperor and Nicanor and the two sat down to watch Seron's half-hearted parryings and Teman's fight for what looked like his very survival.

"Nicanor, are you ready to return to Judaea to help your friend Apollonius? There are still too few Jews to greet me in the afterworld."

The general turned to the emperor and said in surprise, "With all my heart, Divine One. Should I leave today?"

Nicanor's eagerness seemed to amuse Antiochus. "Patience, patience, my good general. You will leave in very good time. I know that you have sent Apollonius my directive about having my Jewish children sent to me. Seron does well with a sword, does he not?"

"None surpasses him in the art of the sword, unless of course, it is Apollonius," Nicanor said, his wits a little off center at the allusion to his letter to Apollonius. Of course, he knew that Antiochus would have access to all his missives, but he was furiously trying to remember if he had written anything seditious in that particular one. It must not have been too bad if he was still alive.

"That is enough," Antiochus said. He nodded at the attending slaves who hurried over to Seron and Teman with towels and drink. Other slaves brought out chairs that they placed opposite Antiochus and Nicanor. Antiochus nodded first at Seron and Teman, then at the chairs indicating that they should sit.

"That was well fought, well fought," Antiochus enthused. "Teman, I would not have thought you could keep up with Seron, but you did very well." Antiochus leaned conspiratorially toward Seron. "And you, I hear, are second only to Apollonius with your skill with a sword. Nicanor has a very good opinion of you."

Nicanor's back became even more rigid. He did not know why the emperor enjoyed creating rivalries among his sycophants, but it was a reality of court life under which one either flourished or was handily demoted or even executed. "I honor Seron and his skill," he said simply.

Antiochus chuckled and sat back, sipping his drink. His eyes darted back and forth between the three men and he waited.

"So," said Seron, "I understand that Apollonius is preparing a march to quell the rebellion in northern Judaea."

"He has been authorized to proceed. I would be surprised if he is not already on the move with his Samarian cohorts." Nicanor said, hooding his eyes with careful indifference.

"How many cohorts is he taking?" Seron asked.

"Two."

"That surprises me."

"What is surprising about it?" Nicanor asked. He became aware of the hair on the back of his neck.

"I would have thought," Seron said as he studied his goblet," that he could easily dispatch the Jews with one."

Not again. Nicanor did not feel like engaging Seron on the subject of the idiot commanders in Jerusalem and their ridiculous arrogance. Paulus, Timotheus, Philo, Seron, all were of the same ilk in that they disdained this contest of the Jews as being beneath them. But, since Antiochus' eyes were upon him, he felt he had to say something, even if it was the same old argument.

"That," said Nicanor, "is the attitude causing the debacle in Judaea this very moment. It is because of the failures of Paulus, Timotheus and Philo that Apollonius has had to uproot his Samarians and march them up north. They all failed because they underestimated the foe." Even as the words left his lips, he felt oppressed with an almost unsupportable boredom.

"Can the Jews even be called a foe, I wonder?" Seron asked. "I would think that they are mere slaves."

"Call them what you will," Nicanor said. "But they are creating a great expense for our beloved emperor." He nodded deeply at Antiochus and continued, "They are responsible for the great isolation of our cohort in Jerusalem. Our stone fortress, the Akra, is now finished, Oh, and Great One, I wish you could see it. It is a marvel. I regret to say, however, that instead of serving as a strategic lookout for our forces as was intended, it may very well be reduced to a mere enclave to protect us against the eventual invasion of the Jews. And although it is rather old history, Apollonius is the only general who has experienced success with the Jews. His ingenious parade quelled them for quite a while. But he will thoroughly subdue them in the campaign upon which he is embarking now."

Antiochus leaned forward eagerly, "Was that not the parade when he fooled the Jews into coming out of their houses to watch our troops in full regalia, then turned the pikemen on the spectators?"

"Yes, Sire," Nicanor said.

"Apollonius," Antiochus pronounced happily, "is a true genius."

Seron nodded politely but Nicanor could see brimstone in his eye.

Nicanor was well aware that Apollonius and Seron had crossed paths many times during their respective services in Judaea, and the encounters had been anything but pleasant. Like Achilles and Agamemnon, they had once fought over a slave they had taken during one of their campaigns. Apollonius outbid Seron for the woman during the auction for the Thracian camp followers and Seron had never forgotten the slight. Then there was the time that Apollonius had actually saved Seron's cohort from a Bedouin ambush during a routine march to Egypt years before to check on empire holdings. That was something Seron could not countenance: beholden for his very life and the lives of his men to Apollonius, a man that he hated.

Now Nicanor was truly enjoying himself. He tried to keep the gloat off his face at Antiochus' praise of Apollonius but found it extremely difficult in the flare of Seron's jealousy. Seron's transparent attempt to wedge himself into the emperor's favor appeared to have run afoul of Antiochus' trust in Apollonius.

Good work, old friend, Nicanor said in his mind to Apollonius. Even in your absence from court you are more of a presence than this slight, little Seron.

"Enough drink for you two," bellowed Antiochus. "It is back to the training field. Seron, you need work on your backward thrust, and Teman, you need, well you just need work. You, Nicanor, sit here by me and we shall speak more of Jerusalem. I cannot wait to hear how Apollonius fares in his march on the Jews. When will we hear, do you think?"

"I would think the results will find their way to us in about a fortnight, Sire," Nicanor said, trying not to laugh at the irritated resignation in Seron's face. Smiling, he watched Seron take a sword from the rack and wield it, juggling it loosely in his right hand as he glared at Nicanor.

Chapter Thirty-six

Pulling at the corner of his beard, Judah said, "So Ephraim reported that Apollonius is marching from the west," During moments of intense consideration over a knotty issue, he had taken to worrying his beard. "That could either mean that he is following the Ridge Trade Route all the way up, or perhaps the Way of the Sea closer to the coast."

"I think we can eliminate the possibility that he is taking the coastal route," Eleazar said while tracing the map with his finger. "That would take him too far out of his way. He would not feel the need—"

"Unless this whole report is a plant," Asher said. "I expected Apollonius to draw us out to a wider plain so he could put his pikemen and skirmishers to good use. Ephraim, are you sure that Nadab did not suspect your loyalties? Could he have fed you false information? I cannot believe that he would lead the assault from the west. That is our hill country."

"Believe me, I have been turning over that possibility again and again in my head," said Ephraim. "I wish I could say definitively that the information is without taint, but I cannot."

Judah looked at the crude map and leaned over it, resting on his elbows so he could look closer at the spidery lines of blacking that indicated ridges and hills. His eyes fell on Lebonah. "Look at this."

The commanders, Asher, Eleazar, Aulus and Avram, leaned over Judah's shoulder and peered at the parchment.

"The best approach to our position in Gophna would be here at the Lebonah pass," Judah said with some excitement. "If you look at all the other approaches from the west, there is no other that would make sense. Lebonah would offer them a healthy ridge over which to bring their troops."

"That ridge is wide enough," Asher agreed. "But I agree with you. Why would they not try to draw us out to a flatter area? That is where their pikemen and skirmishers would have a better crack at our fighters."

"Their intention, according to Nadab," Ephraim said, "was to use their mountain fighters to hit us where we live in the hills. They want to destroy our camp. But Nadab mentioned to me once that the Greeks may lay siege to some of the towns round about and start slaughtering civilians to draw out your fighters."

The men looked at each other grimly and down at the map once again. They knew they must steel themselves for more Jewish bloodshed, but they wanted it to be their own blood and not that of their defenseless countrymen and women. More and more Jews were joining them in the hills and their encampment was becoming vast, indeed. But there were many more who were left in the cities, towns and villages along the principal trade routes, who had shunned flight and were still trying to eke out an existence as if there were no rebellion. They would be the most vulnerable in their unfortified houses and farms. It made sense that the Greeks would prey upon them to get the rebels out of the hills to engage them on a true battlefield where the Greeks would have the advantage.

"It is all a gamble," Judah said. "Aulus, do you remember anything that your father told you about the battle of Magnesia that would help us determine where the Greek forces would be most likely to hit us? After all, Scipio fought Antiochus III, Epiphanes' father. Perhaps the father and son think alike when it comes to military strategy."

Aulus thought for a moment. "Magnesia was a fairly open coastal plain. I do not think that battle has much application here. We Romans and the Greeks met in a straight-forward battle, although it was pitched in our favor. I do not believe the Greeks intend such a battle, now. I feel that they will operate by stealth to get up into our stronghold. I do not think they are planning an honest meeting of arms as at Magnesia."

"Also," broke in Eleazar, "we must remember that this Apollonius is the same butcher of the Parade of Death where thousands of our people died. That monster had no reservations about loosing his phalangites on unsuspecting spectators. He has a reputation for utter ruthlessness."

"That is right," Ephraim said. "It seems that Apollonius argues with the other generals because they underestimate the Jews. I overheard Nadab talking to High Priest Menelaus about the disagreement before I left. It seems that Apollonius regards Judah as a competent opponent. His colleagues say that Judah has just been lucky. Except Nicanor, that is. He agrees with Apollonius."

The commanders chuckled over the map. "I would say," said Avram, "that the Greeks are lucky when they go against defenseless Jewish civilians, and we are lucky when the Greeks go against us." The chuckles ended in assenting grunts.

"They will have no more luck against civilians if I have anything to say about it," Judah said. "I have heard of no more Greek patrols venturing north of Jerusalem. I would like to think that we had something to do with that. And, there have been no more ridiculous edicts from Antioch. I have reports of many villages tearing down the heathen altars as we did in Lydda and resuming orthodox observance. In fact, I have it on good authority that a rebel cell not connected to us cleared out the village of Shechem, forcing its Greek contingent to flee to Jerusalem."

"Your messages to those villages indicating your willingness to ride down on them in force if they did not return to the old ways probably had something to do with that," Asher pointed out. "It is not as if they were free to make a choice."

All the men in the tent conscientiously studied the map, and without even looking up, they seemed to sense the hostile stare between Judah and Asher. A sudden wind pounded the north side of the tent and the men noted the undulating wall, grateful for anything to dispel the tense exchange.

"I tire of your constant harpings on this issue," Judah said, keeping his head to the map. "I have given the apostates ample warning. They are free to go over to the Greeks in Jerusalem if they do not want to honor our Law."

"Yes, and uproot everything they have built over the years and have to move to an unfamiliar community," Asher said. "Many of them are old and will now have to start over."

"Like we had to start over?" Eleazar said to Asher, his voice rising. "Like we were uprooted and forced out of Modiin, Beit Ur and all the other villages who have rallied to our post here in Gophna? You could spend less time crying over the Greek sympathizers and more crying for your own people."

"*My* people have never been the aggressors, Eleazar," Asher retorted. "*My* people have always had righteousness on our side, until now."

The men in the tent hissed in surprise.

"What about Yehoshua? Deborah? Barak? King David? They did the same thing we are doing now," sputtered Eleazar. "Do you think them unrighteous?"

"That was long ago, and those tales have been obscured with the dust of years." Asher rolled up the tattered parchment he used for command notes. "Who knows if the scribes wrote about true events or embellished the telling?"

After Asher uttered the words, the men erupted in horror at the blasphemies. "Who can fault the *Tanakh*?" They asked. "The written word is holy!" "The Lord G-d is a merciful G-d!" and "You are as bad as the Greeks!"

Asher shrugged and stood before Judah who had remained silent. "I am still loyal to you, Judah," he said, "but some of your ideas about the purity of worship go against my very grain. When Jew and Greek lived together in Lydda, it was not so bad. We got along, and people, while they had their disagreements, were able to carry on their business and lives. It was a thriving community. Yes, yes," he said, raising his voice at the crescendo of protest in the tent, "I know that the Greeks were killing us and attempting force upon us, too. But, are our methods any different? In Gezer you killed thirty Jews who would not abandon their Greek gods. Well, Antiochus has killed thousands of Jews because they would not abandon Jehovah. Now we are all killing Jews. Does it matter why?"

After another hard look at Judah, Asher disappeared through the tent flap amid yells of "Blasphemer!" and "Apostate!"

Judah let the vehement discussion against Asher continue for only a few moments until he finally said, "Enough!" The noise ceased. Judah said, "Asher is entitled to his opinion. I do not want to hear any of you impugning him again with catcalls and insults. He is with me." He turned to the Roman. "Aulus, I think we should start moving our fighters to the western hills of Gophna. We will keep scouts out in force along all the routes, but I think I will commit most of us to the pass above Lebonah. Ephraim, what do you think?"

Ephraim, who was inspecting some of the documents gathered by other spies, jumped in surprise at the question and was quiet for many moments. Finally, he ventured, protesting slightly, "I see myself more as a messenger than a military strategist, but Nadab *was* adamant about the western approach. But, in case he fed me false intelligence, as long as you have a back-up plan that will allow you to move swiftly to wherever your scouts report movement, I believe we can go forward with our plan based on the intelligence. But you must move quickly. They are on the march even now."

Eleazar said, "What of those in Lebonah? Should we not warn them?"

The men looked uneasily at each other, knowing the answer but unwilling to voice the horror. Ephraim finally said, "If we warn those at Lebonah, we also warn the Greeks."

"I agree," Judah said reluctantly. "Despite what I said before about keeping civilians safe from Greeks, as repugnant as it is, we must leave the village of Lebonah to itself to preserve our surprise. The Greeks must have no inkling that we know anything about their approach. And refugees pouring out of Lebonah would have that very effect."

A few in the company opened their mouths to disagree, but closed them again, knowing that Ephraim and Judah were right.

"Avram, Eleazar," Judah said, "Report to the commanders of all the camps and tell them we move tonight. Aulus, send out the scouts and tell them to take the fleetest horses in camp. I need to hear of any deviations in the Greeks' stirrings. We have been lucky so far in our contests with the Greeks. We must not rely on luck again."

Chapter Thirty-seven

Samaria, Judaea   The 7th day of *Iyar* 3594 (May 2nd 166 B.C.E.)

A pollonius said, "Oh, to be out of Jerusalem!". He urged his horse into a jaunty canter when he saw the familiar tree line that abutted the Samarian outpost.

"Sir!" Syrus called. When Apollonius did not respond, Syrus urged his horse ahead so the general would at least have one bodyguard, not that it would do any good if they came up against a Jewish patrol. For all the closeness of the Samarian fort, he did not want to take any chances.

Apollonius had honored Syrus when he allowed him to exercise his new promotion by bringing one of the Jerusalem cohorts to Samaria. He knew the new colonel was anxious to polish his cohort's rough edges against these rebel Jews. Almost the entire march, Syrus had ridden alongside of Apollonius, exchanging strategies, small talk and some gossip here and there. Apollonius found that he enjoyed the young colonel's company and was happy that he had relegated Timotheus and his Jerusalem cohorts to the rear. He was also sure that Syrus was glad that he and his old commander did not occupy the same marching space on the way to the Samarian *kotaikai*. He had heard rumbling rumors that Timotheus was extremely unhappy with Syrus' promotion and especially his new closeness to Apollonius.

Now Apollonius was in full gallop, as the gates of the Samarian outpost had been flung open and soldiers were filing out to welcome their long-absent commander. The welcome was warm, but hardly raucous. The Samarian *kotaikai* was too disciplined for that.

Syrus finally caught up with the General who had already dismounted and was thumping his second in command, Castor, on the back.

"I regret that I have not been here to help you oversee the preparation for the march on Gophna," Apollonius said. "I tell you, I would rather have been here, arranging baggage and shoeing horses than dealing with the politics of Jerusalem."

"General!" Castor stepped out of the embrace and saluted. "All is ready. We are waiting only for your order, which, I am sure, depends upon the politics of Jerusalem."

"'My politics' as you so cheerily put it, are ripe," Apollonius said. "Nicanor has given us the authorization to move, and I finally received the intelligence from the high priest about the disposition of the Gophna Jews."

"Intelligence and Jews," Castor said as he followed Apollonius to the gates of the fort so he could be received by his troops. "I am surprised that you use the two words in the same sentence."

"That is the very thinking that we must avoid," Apollonius said harshly, "and is why the Jerusalem cohorts have failed so far. They underestimate the Jews. I am sure you are aware of the thrashing we have received at Jew hands. As we speak, I still have ten patrols that are unaccounted for."

"Ten patrols missing. I admit that is problematic, but none of these 'thrashings' of which you speak were pitched battles," Castor protested, but added, "Sir," at Apollonius' glare. Apollonius was a commander given to fair treatment of his subordinates, but he demanded a certain deference all the same. "Once we force them out in the open," Castor went on carefully, "our phalangites will make short work of them. These Jews have no notion of battle tactics and strategies. They are conducting an underground war."

"And, that is precisely the problem," Apollonius said, "The Jews are not conducting the war on our terms, and that is what must change. We must force them to meet us in a venue where we are superior."

"Yes, sir. As I was saying, out on the field of battle. There they will not stand," Castor insisted.

"Whether we meet them on an open field of battle or engage them in Gophna, itself," Apollonius said, drawing himself to full height, "this is an order: you and the rest of the Samarian cohort are to think of the Jews as formidable a foe as the Romans. Do not snicker," he said, his face stern. "I am completely serious. And I will bear out that seriousness with twenty stripes for every man who makes light of our impending action against the Jews. If I have to start by making an example of you, Castor, I will. Do not think that our friendship will preclude your punishment. I assure you, it will not."

"Yes, General," Castor said with appropriate gravity. "It shall be as you say."

"We will have a meeting of all the commanders and lieutenants of our Samarian *kotaikai* when the shadows indicate late afternoon. At that time, you will gather your men at the pavilion outside the command hut."

"Sir," Castor ventured into a different subject.' "Tell me of the Akra. I hear it is completed. I haven't heard of its like in all of Seleucia."

"Nor will you, especially after you are privy to its inner mazes and spacious quarters. My engineer is on loan from Antiochus himself, and it shows. King Minos and Daedalus himself could not have done better."

"I have heard that it is indeed Labyrinthine in its architecture," Castor said. "My men have been aching to see it."

"We have plenty of tenants already, for the bottom floors are a prison. They are those of our men who also underestimated the Jews. Fifty lashes were theirs for deserting their posts at our holding at Lydda. They are serving out their sentences while they heal. Their commanders were beheaded."

"So I understand," said Castor soberly, obviously having lost all desire to cast aspersions on the Jews and their military capabilities. "But, General, you need your rest. I will tell the men of the meeting, and I will see to it that they assign the proper sobriety to the planning of the mission."

"I have full faith in your abilities, commander," Apollonius said. "I know you will not fail me. And you are right, I am tired, and hungry. I have missed Adras. Have him cook me up some lamb. No one in Jerusalem is able to spice it just so."

The pavilion was well-aired in the late afternoon and Apollonius gratefully eased himself on to one of the benches buttressed against its railings. It was good to sit and feel the breezes from the hills play about his face. It was also good to see the leathered features of his commanders nodding and opening in expressions of soldierly camaraderie as they sat down discussing training, women and their latest gambling ventures, losses more prevalent than wins.

Castor stood while the commanders commiserated good naturedly for a few moments and said, "Let us proceed. First, I would like to welcome the general back after so many months away. See, after only a few hours, he is losing the pallor he sported while living in that cesspool of Jerusalem." The laughter ruled for a time, then Castor, speaking as an opening for Apollonius, said, "The intelligence the general gleaned in Jerusalem indicated that the Jews are ensconced up in the hills of Gophna. General?" He sat down.

Apollonius rose. "I need to discuss all possible strategies with you, my Samarian brothers. Such incompetence in Jerusalem! It makes me glad to be back in your midst. But, we have a decision to make. Should we engage the Jews in full battle, where we may use our skirmishers and phalangites to full advantage? Or, should we march on their stronghold in the hills, giving our mountain fighters a crack at them? We would take our entire cohort, of course, but simply deploy them for the ridges rather than the battlefield. Athos?"

"Sir." A formidable man, young for a commander, with strange yellow hair like that rumored of Alexander, stood and loudly clasped his hands together. "Let me at them, General. It does not matter where. On bluff or field, the Jews, for all their wiles (Castor had made it clear to the troops that afternoon that no disparagement of the Jews was allowed) cannot stand against us. Oh, I have heard they are valiant, it is true. But we will hone our strategies so that courage or no, wiles or no, they will fall under our shields."

"A fine, patriotic speech, Athos. But not very specific. The question before you commanders," Castor said, addressing the others, "is where to take the battle? I, for one, would like to take the fight to them and wipe out their camps once and for all."

Apollonius smiled at Athos, a son of one of his distant kinsmen in Apamea, and said, "But what of a nice, wide field? There is much to be said for drawing the Jews down from their stronghold. We can easily do this by cleansing the villages round about Gophna. We would start with Beit Horon and move from there."

"But Commander, have not many of the villages been razed already?" An older, grizzled veteran pointed out in query. "That is what started the trouble in the first place. Modiin, was it not? That is where Apelles forced the Jews into the hills."

"Stratos, it was not a matter of Apelles forcing them anywhere," Syrus broke in. "The Jews killed Apelles, then fled."

"A small technicality," said Stratos. "I wonder that more of the same may not widen the anarchy of rebellion."

"Our patrols cannot venture far from Jerusalem as it is, now," noted Castor. "General?"

"Yes, I am still awaiting the return of ten patrols that have disappeared from Jerusalem," Apollonius said, scratching at his neglected beard. It had not been oiled for days. "Thank you for pointing that out, Castor."

The men coughed, but Apollonius' smile toward Castor was benign. "That is why I am asking my trusted commanders of the Samarian *kotaikai*. "We are trained for both field and mountain fighting."

"There is the issue of time," said Stratos. The other commanders must have agreed with this for they nodded vigorously. "It will take time to fan out and rid the countryside of the rest of the Jews. It will also take time for the word to get up to Gophna."

"That would not take much time," said Castor. "These Jews are able to send messages with fires and couriers who are savvier with the land than we. And, it will feel good to slaughter a few Jews and have their women."

"Not Jewish women," said Andros. "I would not touch one with a four-cubit pike."

The men roared, then sobered at Apollonius' serious face. "This campaign is firmly in our hands," he said. "The Jerusalem cohorts have tried and failed to overcome these Jews. It is now up to us. I hear there are thousands up in the hills of Gophna with this Judah the Maccabee. If we could hit them there, in their supposed territory, it may speak louder than decimating useless villages in our frontier. And, there is a chance that for all our killing and rapine, they will not come out of the hills. If we drag this out for months or even a year, our emperor will not be happy."

The men were silent for many moments, and Apollonius sat down to let them think. He had already made his decision but wanted the men to feel as if they were part of a concord.

The discussion did not take long to begin, the men feeling free under Apollonius to vent their opinions, and many spoke into the verbal fray. "I, for one, do not want to waste my time on Jewish villages. Let me at the rebels themselves!" and "Oh, but for a good battle! My pikemen are tiring of drills. Let them meet Jew flesh rather than wood and air!" and "Ares have your pikes! My mountain fighters already have an assault plan. We are ready for Gophna!" and, finally "Apollonius is right! Time is our enemy. We must on to the Gophna Hills and speedily dispatch the Jews while they cower in their camps!"

More and more of the talk gravitated toward that of marching directly on Gophna. After dissent dwindled and the views seemed to converge, Castor stood and said, "We are in agreement, then? All for marching on Gophna?" He watched the nodding faces, and said, "General, we only need your final word." At the slight incline of Apollonius' head, Castor said, "We must now plan the deployment of our infantry, skirmishers and phalangites for a mountain assault. Hail, Antiochus!"

"Hail, Antiochus!" The commanders chanted.

Apollonius left the commanders to their planning. The desire to wander through the barracks, stables and huts of his Samarian *kotaikai* had been burning in him for all those months in Jerusalem. Now that he was here, he decided to indulge in an absence in the strategy session; his commanders were more than capable of putting together a mountain assault. His would not be an aimless wander, however; he also needed to converse with the commanders of the Jerusalem cohorts. Especially Syrus. He was hoping to use that young man to be his eyes and ears amongst those of the Jerusalem cohort. Apollonius wanted to know if his strict treatment of them—their march in the rear, his seeming disregard for their very presence—was turning them mutinous. A commander had to know such things so he could temper his discipline to the best effect. So far, Syrus had indicated that all was still well, that the Jerusalem troops still were displaying a certain sheepishness at their rout by the Jews during the Gophna campaign under Timotheus five months before.

"Hercules! It has been too long!" Apollonius had arrived at the stables and was rubbing his cheek against the formidable jaw of his favorite warhorse. He fed a carrot proffered by his stable master into the eager maw of the stallion and patted the black forelock. "Chiron, has he been well? Any problems?"

"Master, his only problem is that he has been pining for you."

Hercules' resounding snort made them both laugh.

"And I have been pining for you, as well," Apollonius said into Hercules' ear, kneading it until the horse jerked his head away and snorted again. "I have forgotten what a beauty you are. That roan color—how do the breeders get that color? It looks like you were dipped in the clay of Idumea. Chiron, here is a gold piece. You have tended him well during my absence. He looks fine and healthy." Apollonius nuzzled the horse's jaw again. "Ready him for our march. We leave the day after tomorrow."

Apollonius hung around the stables as long as possible, but it was clear that the stablers were attending too much to his presence rather than their work readying the horses for the march. It was with real regret that Apollonius ambled his way over to where the Jerusalem contingent was encamped.

Timotheus, as ever, was lounging in front of his staff tent with a goblet in his hand. He had always liked his wine, but ever since the Gophna debacle, he had taken even more to drink, and in a big way. By this time every afternoon he was on his way to a quiet, sullen inebriation that must have deadened his sense of failure. Today seemed no different until Apollonius approached, then it looked like Timotheus was doing everything he could to appear sober, casting the goblet from him, snapping to attention—though the snap was more of a wobble—and saluting, but looking much more like he wanted to vomit.

"General Apollonius," Timotheus tried not to slur. "It is a great honor to have you in our camp. When do we march?"

Apollonius steadied the old man and sat him back down. "The day after tomorrow. Are your men ready?"

"Ready as always, General! They are eager to help themselves to Gophna loot. They feel as if they have earned it. I understand that the Jews have taken everything to the hills—golden religious vessels for their ridiculous practices, their women's jewelry. There were many rich landowners among those who fled. My men are hankering for all that gold."

"The loot is secondary, Commander," Apollonius snapped. "If all your men think about is Hebrew plunder, you have failed in your commission." He had not planned to be a disciplinarian during this conversation, but Timotheus always made the rebukes necessary with his silly, shallow greed. Now, it appeared to have rubbed off on his men. "There is a people to conquer, and a unified people at that," Apollonius pointed out, "and it is you, General Timotheus, who have unified them."

Apollonius could not tell if Timotheus' ruddy face was a result of his chronic drunkenness or sudden rage, but his anger seemed to banish the effects of the wine. "How so?" He sputtered, although Apollonius was sure the idiot knew the answer.

"You handed the Jews many great victories with your botched handling of Gophna. Your incompetence was what infused the rebellion with a new life." Apollonius strode over to the discarded goblet and picked it up. He waggled it at Timotheus. He had not even planned on mentioning the drinking, but the rebuke was taking on a life of its own. "And if I find you drunk at mid-day again, I swear to Ares that I will string you up myself and bid the birds tear at your carcass. You should be out drilling your men instead of sitting here besotting yourself. You are a disgrace to the empire. Now go sober up, or by all the gods, I will dunk you in one of the horse troughs up yonder."

As Apollonius stalked away, he realized that he had not briefed the general on his plans. Uttering an epithet, he stopped. Seeing that Timotheus had retreated into his personal tent, Apollonius decided to visit the Jerusalem command tent not fifty paces away. The guards, having heard the rebuke to their general, snapped to even more rigid attention than usual. They nodded at the general as he passed between them and then knowingly at each other. They did not dare smile although they felt like it. Not many of Timotheus subordinates liked or even respected him. And, for all that Apollonius had delivered a stinging rebuke to the Jerusalem cohorts after their miserable failure in Gophna all those months ago, those who received the rebuke appreciated the truth behind it and even more the man who delivered it.

"Attention!"

Syrus' lieutenant was the first to see General Apollonius and barked the order too loudly. The men seated at the command table almost swore in surprise, but luckily, their training took over and they simply rose and saluted.

"Sit, sit!" Apollonius motioned to the men.

"General! We are honored!" Syrus bowed. "Here is my chair. Please sit down."

"Thank you, Commander Syrus. I must brief you on how we plan to proceed against the Jews. I would have sent one of my commanders, but they are busy planning the assault."

"Again, we are honored, General." Syrus motioned to a slave. "Please, refresh yourself."

As the slave poured the drink, Apollonius sat back and surveyed the men. At that moment, he decided that he would see to it that Timotheus met his death on this campaign. The faces of these Jerusalem commanders were honest. And their faces told Apollonius that they were eager. These men needed a new commander who would not squander their eagerness. They were good soldiers.

After Apollonius told the men of the mountain assault, Syrus said, "It seems a stout plan, General. Where do you want us deployed?"

Apollonius was sorry to disappoint the men with a rear position again, but there was no help for it. Timotheus' punishment must also be borne by his men; such was the way of it. "I will have you at the rear of the march." The men, of course, knew the reason for the dishonor, and notwithstanding their disappointment, bore it with grace. Apollonius softened the blow by saying, "You will provide a good ballast for the skirmishers. We will need heavies like yourselves to complete the assault. There is no dishonor." And he meant it. Again, he vowed to himself that these men would not have to suffer under Timotheus after this campaign. He wasn't sure how, but he would see to it.

Chapter Thirty-eight

Samaria, Judaea   The 9th day of *Iyar* 3594 (May 4th 166 B.C.E.)

A s he watched his slave hoist the last of his gear on the baggage cart, Apollonius said, "Syrus, I want you to keep an eye on Timotheus."

"Yes, General," Syrus said as he helped Apollonius arrange his ebony chest against the tent poles propped in their pegs. "I will report to you daily on his demeanor and actions."

"Daily will not be necessary," Apollonius said. "If he deviates from my orders at all, that is when I want to hear from you."

"It shall be as you say," said Syrus. "Will there be anything else, sir?"

"No, you may go. I shall see you on the march."

"Yes, sir."

Apollonius made one more cursory walk through the camp, manned now by only a few men from the *kotaikai*, the rest in march formation outside the gates. Long fingers of shadow mirrored the lateness of the day and the dusky reds, yellows and oranges of sunset crept across the compound. A few pieces of lumber disturbed the amber glow that spread over the ground. "Lieutenant! Clean up this detritus. Just because we are leaving for a few days does not mean we want to come back to a pig sty."

As Apollonius watched the harried lieutenant pick up the errant staves of a crate broken during the muster, he felt great relief that the ridiculous saga of the Maccabee would soon be at an end. He did not feel he was being overconfident in the thought that the force at his hand was more than enough to deal with the Jewish rebel. His Samarian cohort, the reduced Jerusalem cohort and his Mysian mercenaries combined gave him a fine army of three-thousand strong that he believed would overwhelm the Jewish commander, despite his obvious gift of strategy. He was reasonably certain that their sheer numerical strength would be enough to counteract Judah the Maccabee's military wiles. Both Philo and Timotheus thought that Apollonius was lending too much dignity to the rebel by deploying such a large and unnecessary force, and that morning Timotheus had told him so again, but Apollonius had been immovable. "We have had enough defeats going up against this Jew," he said. "It is time we had a victory; it is time we foisted a pitched battle upon the enemy. Timotheus, you are adept at the butchery of civilians. Now it is time for you to see the butchery of war. Foe against foe, bronze against bronze. It will be a good lesson for you to see my Samarians at work. Now it is time you see what a trained army can do."

He chuckled at the memory of the red bulbous veins throbbing in Timotheus' angry face. "It served the old bastard right," he said to himself as he stooped to pick up one of the staves the lieutenant had juggled unsuccessfully in his last armful to the fire pits. In fact, as Apollonius thought back on Timotheus' incompetent handling of the earlier Gophna campaign where he had lost hundreds of Greek troops, he wished he had been even more vitriolic in his criticism. He grasped the stave in his hand, wishing the old fool were at hand so he could give him a good thrashing. Not that protocol would allow that, general to general, but it was a nice fantasy.

Apollonius discarded the stave in the fire pile and headed out to the main road where a dusty and fetid swell of men, horses, wagons and families rose in a dry mire of dust. At his approach, men stopped what they were doing and stood erect to attention until he passed, then resumed their preparatory duties. Those who had drawn positions in the front of the march were already armored, ordered in rank and had their personal equipment slung aback. These soldiers were his beloved Samarians. Apollonius wandered among them, patting his many favorites on the shoulders and issuing words of confidence. His occasional inspection of accoutrement was cursory and playful as he buoyed their already formidable courage. Their faces remained stolid under the general's condescension, but a close look at their eyes revealed their fierce pleasure. After passing through the ranks, he greeted his commanders and lieutenants, and, ascending his horse at last, raised his hand, a sign that he wanted to address the cohorts before they set out. Those who were further down the marching order put aside their various tasks and listened.

"My beloved *kotaikai*! We are about to engage the enemy. They are a guerilla force, underground fighters, but if you will follow me up to the hills of Gophna, we will force them to face us in a true battle. There is an expanse in those hills that my scouts tell me is ideal for our phalangites and skirmishers. It is there where we will meet the foe and we will put this destructive Jewish rebellion to rest at last."

As Apollonius waited for the obligatory cheers to diminish, he looked out over his Samarians who were at the front of the train, his Mysian mercenaries who were horsed in a sturdy group up a sloping hillock opposite the barracks, and the reduced cohort from Jerusalem who lingered near the back. A wave of confidence rushed through his vitals, spurring him on.

"There are many who say that the Jews are pressing upon our Jerusalem cohorts by not allowing patrols to venture up North. There are many who say that the day of

Antiochus is finished and that our great empire is fading into the dust of this desert of Judaea. Will we allow our Great God to go unworshipped?"

"No! No!" Thundered the ranks.

"Will we allow the Jews and their desert god to dictate the terms of our demise?"

"No! By Zeus. No!"

"Then wield your weapons and shields and march with me!" Apollonius roared. "And we will enrich the Jews' sterile, fallow land with their blood and take it for our own. We will sow their accursed hills with their teeth. But, unlike our forbearer, Deucalion, those teeth will not people their land. Those teeth will rot in the soil as will their paltry rebellion!"

The Greeks beat their shields, whistled, yelled, and brandished their pikes, swords and helmets in a great expression of filial and military love for their commander. Apollonius allowed the tumult to expend itself, then said sternly to his officers, "Mount up and form the tail ranks. We march!"

Apollonius slowed his horse and fell back into the thick of his Samarian cohort, his grim men happy to be on the advance with their general once again. It had been much too long.

As the three-thousand ponderously flowed away from Samaria, they soon filled the entire breadth and length of road from Hazor to Beit Shean on their steady way to the Hills of Gophna.

Chapter Thirty-nine

The Hills above Lebonah, Judaea   The 9th day of *Iyar* 3594 (May 4th 166 B.C.E.)

J ohn adjusted his body over the uncomfortable perch "It seems like we are always and forever watching," He said. "I'm getting sick of having my backside crammed into a ridge, waiting and waiting."

"These ridges have kept your backside in one piece," Shimon said. "I thank the Lord of Hosts for these ridges."

"Yes, but when are we going to be in a real fight? I want to kill Greeks. I want to butcher them. I want to pay them back for what they have done to us and our people," John retorted.

Shimon watched his brother John settle his rump again into the small indentation of granite. Their elder brother, Judah, had assigned them to lookout duty again after he relocated the assault force to the hills over the Lebonah Pass. The thousand men, fighters from the various villages who had sought refuge with the Maccabee, had scattered themselves after nightfall over the tufts of scrub and cedar that grew in the sedimentary mortar in these hills.

On their tedious march that day, Shimon had overheard Judah and Eleazar talking. Judah said he wished he had a greater force with which to meet the Greeks but that only one-thousand were trained and ready. Even Shimon and John had had to do some pretty strident persuading to get Judah to allow them to accompany the fighters, whining that they were the Maccabee's brothers who had been with Judah from the start. John had always been stouter and stronger than Shimon who was two years younger, but Shimon's wits and cunning more than made up for his lack of years and brawn. Shimon and John had left Modiin as gawky adolescents, intent only on mischief. Now, their journey through puberty and living in the wilds had equipped their bodies with rangy sinew and muscle. Up in the hills, Judah had immediately assigned his two younger brothers to a strict training regimen so that their skill with sword and shield was mounting, but they were still too small to be matched with a full-grown man in their sparring.

However, they were excellent lookouts with their young eyes and swift feet. Many times when Timotheus had attempted to mount assaults against them during the Greeks' first campaign in Gophna, the two 'grubs,' as they were cheerfully nicknamed in the camp, had delivered warnings about the Greek movements in a very timely manner. The two boys were treated as mascots throughout the camp, often having to dodge good-natured cuffs and chokeholds from the fighters as they wandered about performing errands for Judah and his commanders.

John sat up. "Look! I think it is one of the scouts." He stood and Shimon scrambled up beside him.

The horse pounded up the pass and Shimon said, "John, go and tell Judah."

"No, you go tell Judah! It is your turn!"

This was the one problem that the two excellent lookouts occasionally did have: a tendency to argue. Judah had quelled that bent somewhat by beating the two whenever he caught them at it, but they still often gave over to the urge. This time, Shimon finally relented, likely remembering the last beating, and ended the argument by loping away from the ridge to fetch Judah who would want to meet the scout as soon as he arrived in camp.

* * * * *

Judah and a few of his men were sitting among some rocks, trying to keep warm without a campfire. Judah had not allowed any fire in their new camp so as to be invisible to Greek scouts in their perch above Lebonah. They were discussing, of all things, business. Judah and Eleazar were quietly talking about starting up the farm and renewing their other enterprises in Modiin. When they kicked the Greeks out of Judaea, they often said during these fanciful sessions, the farm would be more than ready to support the grain harvest, having lain fallow for all these rebellion years. Eleazar was extolling the possibilities of a new irrigation system he had in mind for the farm when Shimon arrived with his message of warning. As always, normal talk and, indeed, life had to be put aside for the war.

"Judah, it is a scout," Shimon panted. "I think it is Schmuel."

"Where?" Judah stood and walked toward his brother.

Shimon said nothing but beckoned Judah with an arm and ran back toward the overlook.

As they rounded the path, Judah's horse, *Tiklit*, Schmuel's mount for the scouting expedition, appeared in a rush of hooves and almost trampled Judah and John. Judah pressed John against the shallow outcropping to keep him out of the way as Schmuel yelled in surprise and sawed at Tiklit's bit to rear him away from the two brothers.

Finally, he maneuvered Tiklit down the path, dismounted and tied the horse to a dead cedar tree.

"They have not wandered from our expectations," Schmuel said as he walked up to Judah and Shimon. "They left Samaria four hours ago as soon as the sun set and are staying to the ridge route just as Ephraim said they would."

"The Lord of Hosts with us," Judah breathed. "Bring *Tiklit*. I want you to tell the other commanders what you have told me. I also want to know of their numbers, weapons, and siege engines or artillery if any."

Upon entering the command circle Schmuel gratefully accepted a crust of bread from Avram and gnawed at it for a moment before he began. The others waited politely, knowing he had been out since they had left the main camp eight hours before. "It looks like they are planning to sleep during the day and march by night to hide their movements and numbers," Schmuel finally said, dusting the crumbs of bread from his hands. "However, you will be hearing from many other scouts along the way in the increments that we discussed. In fact, Malachai will be arriving very soon, I think. He can tell us where the Greeks stop to rest, if that is their intention, which I think it is."

"How many are deployed?" Aulus asked. "And what is their weaponry?"

"I counted approximately 3,000 troops: mostly infantry, but it looks like they have at least one cohort of light skirmishers and one of phalangites. Those are an awesome sight," he said. "Their pikes are twice as high as they are and they wield them as one, never one out of line, never one too high or too low."

"They must have taken lessons from your grain furrows," Eleazar said, laughing, for Schmuel had been their overseer on their farm and was well-known for having the straightest grain rows of all the farms in Modiin.

"The pikes, again," Judah said wearily. "Always the pikes! I tell you, as awesome as they look, those phalangites will be sorry they tried to use their silly pikes against us." He looked around at the men. "What? You are afraid after all our training? *Mehercle!*" He said, his voice rising in frustration. Ignoring the shock on the men's faces at his Latin epithet, he went on, "Do not let the size and number of those stupid pikes frighten you! Did we not teach you to go at them from the side? I cannot believe that Alexander had so much success with them! The Romans finally discovered that once you got into a Greek phalanx from the side, it toppled like so many loose fence posts after the first one falls. We have taught you the technique! Do not let the sight of those ridiculous spears marching along scare you. Remember too, that those pikes weigh at least half a talent. You can use that weight against the enemy and knock their arses to the ground."

The men were quiet for a moment, then Avram began a low chuckle. He was followed by Eleazar's creaking laugh, then Shimon's and John's immature cackles. Soon all the men were laughing, or rather stifling their croaks and guttural rumbles as Judah had imposed silence on the camp from the moment they had bivouacked here hours ago.

Judah did not join in right away and the laughter surprised him for a moment. Finally, he saw what was funny and chortled softly for a moment before raising his hands to quiet the men.

"I tell you," he whispered into the men, "that as fearsome as the Greeks seem as they march along, no one is as fearsome as the G-d of our Fathers. The Lord of Hosts with us."

The men were solemn once again and as one, they saluted Judah the Maccabee. "The Lord of Hosts with us," they whispered back and sat down in the dark to wait for the Greeks.

Chapter Forty

Jerusalem, Judaea   The 9th day of *Iyar* 3594 (May 4th 166 B.C.E.)

N adab had to look very closely at the face to identify it. The features were so distorted from what must have been a horrific beating that they were difficult to make out. Finally, he pulled delicately at the bloodied robe and inspected its brocade closely. It was Greek-made, but it was definitely the one Barbatus had often donned to disguise himself during missions. For further identification, he looked at the bloody crown of the head for help. Not many wore their hair shorn as closely as a Roman did. Nadab had once commented on its short length and the wisdom of Barbatus wearing it in the Roman style on his missions. Barbatus had been rather imperious in his reply. "I would rather wear a hood for disguise than have head lice!" As Nadab looked down at the body, he addressed it, saying, "Well, I see only one louse, so well done!"

After shooting Nadab a puzzled look, the lieutenant said, "We found him outside Sappho's brothel. The poor bastard never had a chance, the way they worked him over. The Romans are pigs, yes, but even a Roman doesn't deserve to have every rib broken and every bone in his face shattered. What a mess—"

"Yes. Thank you, lieutenant," Nadab interrupted, a green tinge creeping over his face. "I appreciate your commander referring this matter to my attention. You may dispose of the body as you see fit."

"There's not much of him left, really," The lieutenant observed. "Well, at least of his head. And see how gray his skin is? That means that most of the blood—"

"Thank you, thank you, Lieutenant," Nadab said, hastily backing out of the barracks stall where they had placed Barbatus' corpse. "I will relay the information to the high priest."

"The Great Assassin," Nadab harrumphed, outside of the Greek barracks yard at last. "Great at getting himself killed on his most important assignment!"

Nadab started walking, not in the direction of the high priest's palace, but south toward the Jewish quarter and the marketplace. He badly needed a calm diversion, and he could think of a place no more appropriate for this than Shem's establishment. He wanted to sit and think, preferably while nursing a rude wooden cup of Ruth's nice, honeyed mead.

Fresh thatches of roof over the market booths and stalls gave off the smell of date palms in the spring. It was a smell that Nadab remembered well from his childhood in Beit Horon and he breathed in the nostalgic fragrance as he walked along the familiar market street.

As was his custom, Nadab had his ears open, nearly straining the sides of his skull to hear what people were saying as they milled along the curbs where the merchants were set up.

"The butcher is marching up north, did you hear?"

"Yes, and with the dreaded Samarians!"

"Perhaps he will stage another Parade of Death."

"What? In the hills of Gophna? Not if the Maccabee has anything to say about it."

"No, I mean in the villages round about Gophna."

"Only Jerusalemites are stupid enough to stand around and watch Greeks march with their pikes." Grim laughter. "Those up north hide, then kill Greeks when they're not looking." More laughter.

So much for the secrecy of Apollonius' march, Nadab thought ruefully as he passed the patch of mirth. "The gossips of Jerusalem have punctured our stealth yet again." It seemed that even if Ephraim were a spy, having eluded Barbatus to go to the Maccabee, the Maccabee did not need him. Probably no less than a score of Jerusalem Jews was headed up north to warn the rebels. Nadab listened to the next discussion as he passed another group of Jews.

"My son fled Jerusalem. The last I heard, he was in Gophna aiding the Maccabee and the Faithful."

"Do you not fear for him? They say that Apollonius has ten thousand against the Maccabee's five-hundred."

"It is no matter; the Maccabee will crush them as he did Timotheus. Especially if all the other warriors are like my son; he is a stout fellow. He can take care of himself."

These people, Nadab thought, glaring at the gossiping huddle of Jews as he passed. Their rumors always increase the numbers of the enemy and diminish their own. Ephraim had said that they had at least 2,000 warriors trained. But then, all of Ephraim's reports were now suspect.

"The Maccabee will soon rid us of these dirty Greeks. Then we can crown our own king."

"I wonder if a descendant of King David's line can be found?"

"Or perhaps Hezekiah's."

"Or Nehemiah or Ezra."

"Why not the Maccabee, himself? Let us crown him!"

By the time Nadab reached Shem's booth, he was sick of hearing about the Maccabee. He said as much to Shem.

Shem was silent for a moment, then said carefully, "It is true that the people overestimate the Maccabee's power. The Greek host under Apollonius is no paltry force. Still," he went on as he poured Nadab's drink, "he has had many successes against the Greeks. They say that he is a great strategist to use his small numbers to such great effect."

"Beginner's luck," Nadab muttered into his drink as Shem wandered away to attend to his other customers. He wondered how he was going to broach the subject of Barbatus' death with the high priest. Menelaus was a buffoon, it was true, but this buffoon still had more than enough power to crush Nadab's career aspirations. He would not be happy that Nadab had lost his spy—if Ephraim had ever been a spy, that is. Nadab was seriously beginning to doubt that Ephraim ever had any intention of turning on the Maccabee.

More patrons of Shem's establishment converged upon the small booth with its fresh smell of palm fronds. The spring sun was quite strong now and the happy customers shunned the canopy for its warm rays. To Nadab's dismay, the talk all around the café burgeoned into a new discussion of the Maccabee and his strength, his strategies and, above all, his bravery.

In weary disgust, Nadab took a coin from his purse and was about to slap it down on the table. If he had to hear one more thing about the Maccabee, his head would burst. The advisor in him restrained his exit, for the talk was swiftly devolving into that of serious treason, if one was allied with the Greeks, that is. Since Nadab's fortunes depended entirely upon that of the Greeks, he listened carefully. He only had to listen for a few minutes to realize that, although the talk was deeply seditious, it was far from dangerous. Most of the men in the café were ancient blowhards, too old to do anything about the Greek occupation, even if they wanted to. Jews liked to talk and gesticulate, and it seemed that the Maccabee gave them something to talk and gesticulate about, but that was all. This time he did slap his coin down on the table and took his leave of Shem.

"Next time, Silvanus, do not stay away so long," the friendly voice of Shem boomed down the street after Nadab, the advisor to the High Priest Menelaus.

It is likely that I shall never come again, Nadab thought sadly. For, if I start to see young men congregating here, I shall have to report it to the commander of the Greek palace cohort. Then my lovely haunt will be no more.

Nadab meandered toward the palace. He walked slowly so as to give himself time to think of a good way to break the bad news of Barbatus' failure to High Priest Menelaus.

Chapter Forty-one

C astor sat up in his saddle. "There it is."

Apollonius, who had been dozing in his saddle, snorted himself awake. "What? What."

"I say, Commander," Castor repeated. "There is the ridge. And, that is the village Lebonah." Castor unsheathed his sword, using it as a pointer. "Do you see where the rolling slope climbs toward the east? That is where we should begin our ascent. The ridge will accommodate us easily."

Apollonius yawned. A mound of light was growing in the east, and the silhouette of the hill became stark against the dawn. "Are you sure?" The swirling ridge did not look very accommodating to him and he turned around and surveyed his 3,000 with uncertainty.

"Not only that," Castor went on. "This village of Lebonah is very small. It should be a paltry matter to silence its residents and preserve the surprise of our attack."

Apollonius considered this, then nodded. "Make it so. It is still dark enough to preserve the secrecy of our attack, but you must kill them quickly. Soon the town will be awake, and their panic will be noisy. After you dispatch the village, move the troops into and around these huts. Drive the livestock out of their enclosures and get as many of our horses behind fences as possible. Then we will bed down for the day. Impose silence upon the troops. I do not want to hear a sound: not the clang of a sword or an outcry from the village. We will sleep the sun out and begin our assault two hours after nightfall."

The silence that stretched into the dawn hours was remarkable given all the horrors that grew out of Apollonius' commands. Their senses dulled by the atrophy of recent sleep, every man, woman and child fell quickly beneath the swords and daggers of the Samarian cohort. Apollonius did not allow the Jerusalem troops to enter the village until his Samarians had done their bloody work. He did not trust the palace cohorts to perform such a command as effectively as he did his Samarians.

After the village was silent, a gesture of Castor's arm dismounted the cohorts. The Samarians moved away to attend to their horses and the Jerusalem troops silently filed amid the huts, booths and stalls into the village. It was they who were assigned the harsh duty of removing the corpses from the huts of the village so that the Samarians could have a place to sleep that night. The Jerusalem troops would only be housed after the Samarians had had their pick of shelter. Steam from the running torrents of blood rose and mingled with the morning mist that stood at the base of the ridge. Soon the blood became a congealed mud beneath their boots as they dragged the bodies out of the confines of the village and discarded them at the bottom of a nearby ravine. There were more villagers than expected and the shallow ravine was now brimming with the dead. The soldiers finally were reduced to discarding many of the corpses under the shallow brush just beyond the village border as the ravine would receive no more of the gruesome refuse.

* * * * *

Syrus, being a colonel, thankfully did not have to handle any of the bodies, but supervising his men in the distasteful task was almost as bad. These were hardened troops, and most had had their share of killing Jews during their duty in Jerusalem, but Syrus could tell by their faces that it was difficult for them to not think of their own children as they carried out the small corpses from the houses.

Timotheus stayed aloof of the duty, having his adjutants set up his camp well away from the ravine. Even he was not to have one of the shelters until all the Samarians had one, so he opted to avoid the indignity of waiting by setting up his opulent tent far from the carnage. Apollonius had decreed that any tents had to be well out of sight of the main road, so Timotheus chose a spot that was concealed among a copse of trees, again, with the village between his camp and the ravine of the dead.

Finally, the last corpse had been located and discarded, and Syrus saw that the men were settled either in the more squalid huts that the Samarians had not taken or in tents behind the various structures of the village. His next task was to deliver his official report to Timotheus, the task after that an unofficial report to Apollonius on Timotheus.

He located Timotheus' camp by asking his way through the ranks and approached the copse of trees hoping that no further orders awaited him. The night march, not to mention directing the macabre disposal, had depleted him. He needed to rest.

"General?" Syrus entered the tent after being nodded in by one of the guards. "We have completed the task."

Timotheus looked up from the missive he was writing and said, "Very good, Syrus. You have done well. Are the men situated?"

"Yes, sir. They are resting. Some are in huts; some are in tents behind the huts."

"So, there were some huts left? That is good. It is a disgrace how Apollonius is treating our fine Jerusalem cohorts. Well, you need rest too. You are dismissed. I shall see you in the morning."

Syrus exited the tent and headed for the center of the village where he heard Apollonius had bedded down in the largest dwelling there. He found Castor outside what must have been a high priest's house. It was larger than the other buildings and had plaster rather than mud walls.

"Is this where the general's quarters are, Lieutenant?" Syrus asked. "I thought I had better deliver my report before he takes his rest."

"Go on in," Castor said. "He is expecting you." Castor cupped a large cloth in his left hand and with his right was picking through various pieces of gold, assessing their value. "These Jews have interesting jewelry, not exactly my taste, but it is gold, nonetheless." He looked up at Syrus. "It must be difficult for you."

Syrus stopped at the door. "What must be difficult?"

Castor smiled as he put the gold in a sack at his feet. "This running back and forth between Timotheus and Apollonius. It must get confusing at times."

Syrus set his face, not willing to concede any truth to the Samarian. "I obey rank. That is all. I simply do my job."

Castor hooted an odd laugh. "Well said, Colonel Syrus. The prerogatives of command and duty are sometimes at odds with one another. You seem to be one who has reconciled himself to that fact very well. We, all of us, have to be two-faced at one time or another."

Syrus resented the implication and it must have shown on his face, for Castor hooted again. Ignoring the laugh, Syrus entered Apollonius quarters.

He found the general inspecting the food stores of the former occupants of the house. He noted Syrus' entry with a nod and said, "The food is rustic, but good enough. We will have no want on the rest of our march. How goes it, Syrus? What news have you of your commander?"

"He is behaving himself. He grouses at the treatment of our Jerusalem cohorts, but made sure that the corpse detail was carried out."

"You are too charitable in your assessment, Colonel," Apollonius said, sitting down in one of the chairs by the hearth. "My people tell me that Timotheus retired to his camp and had you carry out my order."

Syrus decided to be diplomatic and said with a shrug, "I did what I was told, General."

Apollonius chuckled and said, "Well, Syrus, there is much in store for you after we finish this business with the rebels. How would you like to come back to Antioch with me when I report our victory to Antiochus, himself?"

Syrus did his best to stifle his inhaled gasp with a cough. "I would like that very much indeed, General," he said.

"Well," said Apollonius, "I will remember you when we adjust ranks after this affair. You have proven yourself very useful. You are dismissed."

158

* * * * *

After Syrus left, Apollonius unrolled his cloak and lay it across one of the straw ticks in the largest hut. He cursed when he saw he had trod through some of the blood of the hut's former residents.

"Castor!"

His adjutant immediately appeared. "Yes, sir?"

"Spread some straw in here to soak up that mess. That blood will stink up the room as soon as it warms up in here."

"At once, sir."

Apollonius lay back down and did not acknowledge the private who entered with an armful of straw. He closed his eyes to the gentle sound of straw tufts glancing against the dirt floor and was soon asleep.

Sitting up abruptly, Apollonius peered groggily about. The night march must have wearied him more than he thought, for outside he saw that the winnowing sunset had sapped the village landscape of light. He had slept all day. Usually, he would have to arise at least once to relieve his aged bladder; after all, he was nearing 45. He chuckled when he attempted to rise from the mean bed and his sword and buckler clanked against his shield. He had not even removed his weapon and shield from the bed. Of course, he always slept in his armor on a march such as this and kept the hilt of his dagger close at hand, but he was more careful to keep the sword safely away from his thrashing sleep. Especially this sword.

He unbuckled the weapon, unsheathed the blade and held it up to the window so he could inspect the metal better in the waning rays of the sun. Apollonius smiled at the memory of Nicanor's frequent jokes about this sword. During a visit to Damascus long ago, he and Nicanor had been wandering that city's opulent bazaar when Apollonius happened upon this sword. Its price was exorbitant, but Apollonius bought it anyway. He was not even deterred by Nicanor's jibes that the younger man was using the purchase to assuage his ego after an unsatisfactory encounter with a whore the previous night.

He sheathed it and peered at the elegant scabbard. The cured and hardened leather was almost like wood and was inlaid with artistic swirls of metallurgy. He favored this *kopis*, a single-edged sword, over the *gladius*, the short thrusting sword of Roman design. He liked its sleek lines and swift sweep of motion. As he looked over the elegant hilt, leaves entwined with motifs of various flora and fauna, his name cunningly engraved so that the Greek runes were one with the aesthetic of the sword, he decided it was worth the five talents he had paid for it in Damascus, ego assuaged or not.

He rebuckled the sword, grabbed his shield and stooped as he exited the hut. Outside, the only sound from the men milling about came from the thick slosh of their boots in the mud. Observing the command of silence, they readied their weapons and packed their gear on the horses they had retrieved from the various enclosures and hiding places throughout the village.

Apollonius found Castor caressing and patting his horse, already having strapped on the saddle. Hailing him with a wave, he said quietly, "You should have awakened me. I slept like a dead man. Where is my horse?"

Castor gave his horse one last pat and moved to a nearby pen. "Here he is, General. I took the liberty of preparing him myself." He handed the reins to Apollonius.

Apollonius grunted his thanks and mounted his horse. He inhaled and coughed, attempting to mute the explosion of stench with his mailed sleeve. "It is fitting that we leave this place. That smell!"

"The sun was strong today," Castor said. "The carcasses of the villagers did not hold up very well, I am afraid."

"Well, the stench will render this area impassable for many weeks. I am not sure how that helps us, but well, there it is."

"The smell will mingle with that of the rebels we kill up in that ridge." Castor said. "It is a good smell. The smell of rotting Jew flesh."

"From your mouth to Ares' ears," Apollonius said, urging his horse toward the ridge. "Reduce the marching breadth of the phalangites to that of the ridge access. Send the Mysian skirmishers ahead of them. Have the Jerusalem infantry under Timotheus bring up the rear of the ascent.

"Where did the scouts say the meadow was?" Apollonius asked.

"About twenty furlongs up the ridge. It is not far from the rebel's main camp."

Apollonius gazed at the gentle slope that led up to the ridge. "Again," he said to Castor, "make sure that silence rules our ascent. I do not want to lose any more men than is needful for defeating these rebels. We have had enough waste in this ridiculous war."

"It shall be as you say, General Apollonius."

"Go form up the march," Apollonius said softly. "Long live our divine emperor, Antiochus. May he thrive!"

"May we, also," He heard Castor breathe into his horse's mane as he cantered away to arrange the men for the ascent up the ridge of Lebonah.

Chapter Forty-two

The Gorge West of Lebonah, Judaea   The 10th day of *Iyar* 3594 (May 5th 166 B.C.E.)

For the thousandth time, Aulus muttered to himself,"Those damn slings," He did not like the prime position Judah was giving the slingers above the gorge. "Those spots should be taken up by archers, not slingmen," he said, again to himself because the only person who could reposition the slingers was Judah, and he and Aulus had had this argument many times before. Judah had been adamant: the slingmen would stay where they were despite Aulus' misgivings. Judah would not give in to Aulus' desire to get rid of "those silly leather devices that looked like a child's loincloth," maintaining that the sling was a tried and effective weapon for his people. As far as Aulus was concerned, those "weapons" belonged in the museum of Alexandria where other obsolete arms of the ages were on display.

Still muttering, Aulus tore his gaze away from the heights and adjusted the saddle strap under his Arabian. Judah had given him the job of orchestrating the assault of the *alae*, or cavalry. The Latin word for wings was an apt label for the hooved contingent of their force, for they were indeed swift. As he stroked the neck of the big mare, Aulus decided that he was grateful for Judah's appreciation for good horseflesh. It had been an expensive proposition to acquire the best horses from the traders who defied the Greek embargo by passing through Gophna. Not only did Judah have to pay for the horses, but also had to add extra coins to the transaction to counteract the Greek sentence of death imposed on all merchants caught dealing with the rebels.

How long Judah's wealth would hold out, Aulus had no idea. Luckily there were plenty of traders who were willing to ignore the embargo and engage in commerce with the rebels. Moreover, the house of Mattathias had a great store of gold that the family had brought to Gophna in their exile, but the coin could not last forever. Aulus just hoped that the triumphs against the Greeks would continue and a suitable resolution to the conflict presented itself before the money ran out.

At least the money appeared well-spent, and Aulus doubted the Greeks had a better herd of mounts. As Aulus had trained the riders over the weeks since the purchase, it was clear that the horses knew more about a cavalry charge than the inexpert Jews on their backs. The animals were as experienced as they were stunning. Aulus guessed that they had been stolen from the Babylonians, Parthians or even the Greeks themselves. War horses such as these were not bred in Judaea.

Aulus decided to have one more word with the commander before they settled into their positions for the ambush. One of his men reported a scout's visit to the Maccabee in the early watch of the day and Aulus was curious for the latest intelligence about Apollonius' movements.

He mounted and spurred his horse to the command fire, doing his best to memorize every line of ridge and scrub along the walls of the gorge. Although he had never been blooded in battle, he remembered the words of his father, Aulus *Maior*, a seasoned Roman legionnaire, that a soldier must know every mound, ravine, tree and cliff of his surroundings when preparing for combat. His father had stressed that a thorough knowledge of the terrain could often be used against the enemy. As he approached the command fire, he whistled to himself at the irony of his first battle not being among Romans, but Jews fighting for an insignificant scrub of earth

Pulling up and dismounting, he joined Judah and Asher who both were hunkered down by the fire. All exchanged companionable grunts and soon the three of them were flexing their hands carefully over the fire, attempting to warm them in the waning dusk.

"I heard there was a scout," Asher said easily. "What is the word? Is Apollonius still on the move?"

"It is as we thought," Judah said, shaking his head. "After the butchery, the Greeks slept all day in Lebonah and are likely moving against us tonight."

"When will they reach us?" Aulus asked.

Asher took some bread from Avram who had joined them at the fire, broke it and tossed the pieces to Aulus and Judah. "That is why Judah placed the camp this far into the ridge," he said, "It will take the Greeks all of tonight and part of tomorrow to reach us."

"That is a good strategy," Aulus said. "They will be frustrated and exhausted when they finally get here. But, I am not sure that late sun will afford our archers a good target after the Greeks enter the defile. It will be late in the day when they come under our archers and slingmen."

Judah easy face showed that he ignored the scorn that Aulus poured on the last word and dusted his hands into the fire after eating his bread. "I am not worried about our men's ability to hit a target in shadow," he said. "But I am worried about the Greek numbers. If our ambush fails and the battle goes against us, I want to preserve as many of our fighters as possible. I want them to be able to flee into the hills under nightfall."

Aulus said, "It seems a sorry strategy to plan the timing of a battle to accommodate a retreat. You would have done better to plan the timing to ensure a victory."

Judah smiled and said, "Your Roman commanders did not have to worry about numbers at Rafia, Zama and Magnesia the way I do. Until we have more fighters trained, I do not have the luxury of squandering my men. I have a rebellion to feed, and it is hungry for numbers, trained numbers."

"No able commander squanders men," Asher agreed. "But perhaps Aulus has a point. We need more than a few hours of light to defeat a Greek army."

"My father often said that the butchery of battle was long, hard work," Aulus said. "Cutting through dirt and foliage as one does in farming is one thing, cutting through human flesh, that is quite another."

"I do not doubt it," said Judah. "But I will stand firm on this. I do not want to lose my entire force of trained men in case. . ." he trailed off.

Aulus and Asher were silent. Over the months of the rebellion, Judah's strategy had been that of strike and hide. He had always chosen the timing and the method whenever he came against the Greeks. Whether it was slicing their sleeping throats, obliterating their small patrols deployed out of Jerusalem, or dropping rocks on an ascending assault force in the Southern Gophna ridge, Judah had always used guile and stealth to best the Greeks. This would be the first time that Jew would meet Greek, hand-to-hand, in open battle. True, he was using this gorge ambush to level out the Greek's three-thousand advantage against his one-thousand, but it was still a frightening proposition to pit his men against the seasoned Samarian cohorts of Apollonius.

The three men watched the fire pitch to and fro in the blustering wind until Judah stood and said, "Our scout indicated that the Greeks will march all night to preserve their 'secrecy,' and that they will reach this place on the morrow. There must be no sign of our presence. I want every man in position and all signs of our having been in the gorge erased. The Greeks must feel utterly alone as they meander through this defile—our lives depend on it. I shall notify the rest of the commanders. You two see to your men. Asher, are all the infantry armored? Were we able to outfit every man?"

"They are well-covered," Aulus said. "And what we could not supply, their wives and mothers saw to it."

Judah said, "Yes, our women are becoming quite adept at leatherworking. I've seen quite a few stitching together cuirasses with sheep gut, and their work is quite good. The seams are tight—nary an arrow will get through those. And, Aulus, how does your horse, or your *alae*, as you call it?"

"I do not know if this defile will allow for a good cavalry assault," Aulus replied. "I may have to order them to dismount and fight with the infantry if it gets too close for our horses."

"I will leave that to your capable judgment," Judah said. "Perhaps you will want to join our slingmen in the assault."

"And risk hitting an insect or a snake with one of the mighty rocks of your slingmen?" Aulus said, eying his horse that was dancing around waiting for the human. "No, Commander, I will take my chances with *Ignis*, there, or with the infantry here on the floor of the gorge."

Judah laughed. "It shall be as you wish, Roman." Then he became solemn. "Both of you. Do not be careless with your lives."

The three embraced and let their friendship speak for them. Judah released them and Aulus saw the worry to wash over him for just a moment. He said, "You, too, Commander!" Then he warmed his hands over the fire one more time before attending to the final check and preparation for the arrival of the Greeks.

Aulus followed Asher to his horse. Waiting until Asher was mounted, he stepped up to his mount. "Are you frightened?" He asked his old boyhood friend.

"No more frightened than when your father caught us stealing grapes from his vineyard when we were eleven," Asher said. "As I recall, his bark was worse than his bite."

"Yes, but for all his bark, my father did not really want to kill us," Aulus said, stepping back slightly to accommodate the horse's impatient prance. "The Greeks not only want to kill us, but they would also like to chop us up into little pieces."

Asher laughed and said, "Then let the Greeks do their worst. I, for one, trust that Judah's strategy will make the Greeks sorry that they came against us."

Aulus shook his head and said, "I, for one, am going to turn aside and make sacrifice to Mars for victory. I fear we will need it."

Asher became solemn. "Do not let Judah or the others see you perform a heathen sacrifice," he warned. "I had a suspicion why I saw your slave carrying those cages of doves."

"You worry about the strangest things," Aulus observed. "Three-thousand Greeks are but a passing thought to you, yet you fret about my insignificant homage to Mars."

"For all I care, you can sacrifice to your entire pantheon of gods if it will bring you comfort. But then, I am a liberal Jew. The others are not so tolerant."

"Never fear. I will take great care in my observance. No one will be the wiser."

Asher looked around for a moment, then leaned down, his saddle creaking with the movement. He cleared his throat with embarrassment. "Uh, Aulus."

Aulus had been about to go after his horse, but Asher's conspiratorial whisper stopped him. "What?"

"Sacrifice one of your doves for me, will you?"

If they survived the battle, the sheepish look on Asher's face could be the butt of a thousand future jokes between the two, but as much as Aulus wanted to roar his laugh, all he did was grin for a moment then mount his horse and ride away.

Chapter Forty-three

Gophna, Judaea   The 10th day of *Iyar* 3594 (May 5th 166 B.C.E.)

J udah's mother braided the leavened dollops of dough into the challah bread that would be the main staple of the Shabbat feast. As she flattened out the mound on the crude breadboard that Eleazar had fashioned for her before the men's departure for the ambush, she felt the familiar trembling assault her hands. She pushed away the board and sat back. Eleazar had been dissatisfied with the crudeness of the breadboard and had not wanted to give it to her.

"Wait until I come back, and I will have time to make you a proper one," he had said as he mounted his horse the day before.

Hannah had not verbalized her real fear, but only said, "This one is wonderful. I will not have you taking back your gift. Besides, my other board is broken. The time for making Shabbat is upon us; I cannot do without a breadboard." She did not want to tempt the evil eye so had stifled the thought: In case you do not return, my son.

Looking down the row of tents from her own canvas threshold, she saw that the other women in the camp were busy with their morning tasks. The frenetic flashes of labor, sweeping, churning, bread making and washing, could be construed as hectic preparation for the Queen of the Week, but Hannah knew better. Like her, the other mothers, wives, daughters and sisters were using chores to assuage their worries about Judah and the thousand he had taken against Apollonius.

"*Eemah,* Hannah."

Hannah turned and dusted her hands of flour so she could pinch Shoshanna's cheek. "Such a girl! What? Have you no chores? How do you have time to visit an old woman on the eve of the Shabbat?"

Shoshanna smiled and Hannah quelled the urge to pinch her cheek again. The dimple had reappeared. The sight of that lovely crease outlawed the worry for a moment. The gaunt woman who had escaped the Greeks all those months ago was gone, and Hannah was enjoying bonding with her new daughter-in-law. Of course, she had known Shoshanna for years, watching her grow from an elvin-like child into a lovely young woman, but this was different—she had not been blessed with daughters and relished this relationship where she could discuss domestic arts rather than listen to tales and strategies of war from sons all day.

I cleaned yesterday and made my challah loaves this morning. I have time." She sat next to Hannah, reached for the breadboard and started kneading. As Hannah looked on, the young girl deftly patted out the little bread cakes into respectable mounds that would be blessed by the high priest later that day. The girl's repetitive motion kept Hannah's mind busy for many grateful moments. Then she noticed that Shoshanna's face had disappeared into her head covering and the girl was trembling.

"*Nu*," Hannah murmured against Shoshanna's head as the girl sought out her lap so that she muffled the sounds of her sobs in her mother-in-law's robes. "There is nothing to fear. The Lord G-d is with us. I promise you, our boys will return in safety."

Shoshanna raised her face, tears and anguish twisting the usually benign features. "My faith is gone, *Eemah*," she said dully, wiping her face with the corners of her sleeves. "Eleazar is not coming back."

"Oh, my girl," Hannah said, resuming their embrace and now rocking Shoshanna. "He most certainly will come back. The Lord of Hosts knows that Judah needs his brother, just as the Lord of Hosts knew that Eleazar needed you. Do you not remember how G-d raised you from the dead? I am sure that when you were away, held by the Greeks, you thought you would never be among your people again. But, here you are. Eleazar, too, will be with us again."

This seemed to make sense to Shoshanna, and she calmed down, but then, those who sought out Hannah, now the matriarch of the village, found calm not only in her placid demeanor, but also in her wise advice. That she was the mother of the Maccabee only added to her aura of wisdom. In fact, the death of her husband Mattathias elevated her even higher in the people's esteem as they saw in her a continuation of at least a semblance the Hasmonean patriarchy, for all that she was female.

In companionable silence they arranged the cakes on the baking paddle, covering them with a cloth so flies or dust would not sully the fresh dough.

"When is Miriam coming?" Shoshanna asked as Hannah rose to sit at her loom. She assisted the old woman by gathering the skeins of wool that had spilled from one of her baskets.

"Miriam had to milk her goats. She said she would come for the paddles after that."

Shoshanna felt so much better that she actually laughed. "Miriam of the venerable Moshe clan milking goats! If nothing else spoke of our changed lives here, that certainly would."

"Many things change," a voice said cheerily. "And who would have thought I would be married to the greatest Hebrew warrior since King David, washing out his loin cloths and tunics bloodied from battle?   Where are—oh, I see them."   Miriam hefted the huge paddle atop her shoulder, balancing the load with great skill.

Shoshanna reached up and rearranged a couple of cakes.

"Thank you so much, daughter," Hannah said, rising from her loom.   "Are your goats well? Some on the other side of camp have taken with a strange ague."

"Yes, I heard.   Mine still seem fine.   I have been feeding them a poultice that Avram's Anna recommended. I have some here, in fact, that I am taking to the worst cases."   She untied a bag from her belt.   "It is foul smelling stuff.   Here, Shoshanna, smell it!"

"I can smell it from here, thank you, sister."

"Suit yourself," Miriam said, retying the bag.   "I made it from cedar bark, juniper berry and sour milk. Anna said that it clears up the ague very well."

Shoshanna cleared her throat, "Miriam, about what I said—"

"Shoshanna," Miriam said, shrugging.   "I did not think I would be milking goats either. Do not trouble yourself. I find it quite funny, really."

"Well, you are remarkable," said Shoshanna, relieved.   "That is what I meant.   And now, taking poultice to ailing goats on the other side of camp. You are a healer, too."

"Do not be ridiculous," Miriam said. "Anna helped me, and her goats are all right. Now I need to pass the cure on."

"Have you heard any word from the couriers?" Hannah asked.

"No," Miriam said. "Judah told me that they would send one when the battle was underway. Intermittent messengers will be sent throughout to alert us."

The women fell silent. They knew that when the messages started to arrive, they would have to be in a high state of readiness in case the Greeks overran the fighters and advanced on the Gophna camp. There were even some who balked at presenting the Shabbat feast, saying that it would be an unnecessary intrusion on their plans, even their very survival, but Hannah would not hear of it. "Let us observe the tradition so that the Lord G-d will smile kindly on us in our travail," she had said. "There will be plenty of time for observance and readiness, too."

"Well, I had better be off." Miriam announced. "The high priest said he would perform the blessing on the bread in late afternoon. He said he almost wished it were still Passover so he could say a special prayer to ward off the angel of death."

She had quoted the high priest as a dark little joke, referring to the arrival of Passover and Moshe's destroying angel. As soon as the words were out of her mouth, she seemed to realize how sinister and in poor taste they were. "Sorry," she murmured. "That was the wrong thing to say."

Mother Hannah smiled and put her arm around the embarrassed girl, careful not to disrupt the balanced paddle on her shoulder. She put out her other arm, beckoning Shoshanna into the embrace and said, "We shall indeed have another Passover this night, girls. The destroyer will again pass over our people." Hannah released them and returned to her loom. As she threaded the shuttle through the woof of wool strands, she said in a businesslike tone, "The angel of death will not trouble a Jew this night."

Chapter Forty-four

The Gorge West of Lebonah, Judaea   The 10th day of *Iyar* 3594 (May 5th 166 B.C.E.)

A pollonius said to Castor, "I do not like hiking through this ravine," He craned his neck and gazed at the higher ground with yearning."Back at the last ridge saddle, we should have kept atop the crest of this canyon rather than descend into its wash."

"We had no choice, General," Castor said. "The crest would not support our numbers, unless we proceeded single file. Not only that, but the enemy would be able to see us from miles away if we exposed our march like that. Besides," Castor said as he reached down to pat his horse, skittish at some unseen wild thing, "our scouts will pick up any signs of the rebels, wherever they are hiding."

"I just hope they are not hiding above us at this very moment," Apollonius said, looking up at the clumps of rock and trees that canopied above them. "If they are, I guess I will have to execute our scouts for incompetence."

"The Jews will have done that for you, sir, if they are hiding in these hills."

Grim military humor always did much to dispel a gloom such as Apollonius felt at that moment and after he joined Castor in a quiet laugh, he felt quite light as he said to himself, "No harm done. We will just climb out of this ravine at the next opportunity." However, he alerted his archers and reconfigured the ranks so that they were interspersed along both flanks of the march. "Just a precaution," he said to Castor, "in case it rains Jews."

"If it rains Jews," Castor chuckled, "our phalangites will skewer them like lamb shanks."

This time, the men around the General and his second showed their appreciation but had to be roundly shushed as the march was committed to silence.

* * * * * *

If Shimon's Greek had been better and the enemy had not been so deep in the gorge, he probably would have enjoyed the grim joke. As it was, however, the shock of seeing the Greek skirmishers filing into the gorge caused a head rush that made it difficult for him to speak the whispered word along: "Greeks!" As always, because of his prodigious eyesight, he was the watchman stationed farthest out on the ridge. The vantage was excellent, although the tramping soldiers looked more like ants than men. Judah had warned them that Greek scouts would make an appearance first, which they did. Shimon had spotted them first and John issued a prearranged series of waves to the archers who reduced the scouts to worm's meat. The scouts' arrival ensured that the rebels would have had ample time to ready themselves against the cliffs and other attack positions, even though they had not already been in place for hours. At word of the Greeks' imminent approach, anticipation fueled their atrophied limbs, pumping readiness into their vitals until the men in their various niches and ledges finally caught their first glimpse of the massive Greek force.

John, as always, accompanied Shimon as a lookout and John, as always, peppered Shimon with questions.

"What are they, and why are they not on horseback?" John whispered.

"They are the skirmishers," Shimon whispered back. "And sometimes they are horsed if on an open field. Do you not listen to the reports?"

"I am too busy to listen to all the reports," John said. "As chief courier—"

"Chief courier," Shimon scoffed. "You are only one of many command couriers. I am going to tell *Eemah* that you are giving yourself airs."

"Listen, Shimon, I am your older brother, and you are not to talk to me that way. Now, I know what those are! Those with the huge spears are the Phalangites. And—"

"Oh, so you do listen to Asher once in a while," Shimon interrupted softly. "Look, the sun is low in the sky. It is exactly as Judah planned. If it goes ill against us, we will have no trouble getting away. The Greeks do not know these hills like we do."

Four abreast, the Greek ants picked their way along, tentatively at first, then more swiftly as confidence sturdied their march. Down and into the gorge, deeper and deeper they filed, until the entire floor was teeming with silent, determined movement.

"Where are they all from?" John whispered, as he watched the onslaught of Greeks slowly filling the defile. "Are not the yellow and red the Jerusalem cohort?"

"Yes," said Shimon impatiently. "They are bringing up the rear. Apollonius has his beloved Samarians up front. Do you see their blue and green jerkins? That is their color. Judah will make mincemeat of them. Now, shut up. If the Greeks hear us, Judah will kill us."

"If the Greeks hear us," John retorted, "The Greeks will kill us."

Shimon made a mouth at his brother and turned away from the flow of Greeks on the canyon floor. He fixed his eye upon the walls of the gorge. A slight ripple here and there as the fighters shifted in their rocky nooks was the only evidence of life in the cliffs. Unless one were privy to their presence, they would be all but invisible. Shimon strained to see the faces of those nearest him, but since the fighters had obscured themselves using charcoal blacking from the dead fires of the most recent camp, he could not make out any of their features. He wondered if they were afraid.

The silence from below and above was strange. He found that if he closed his eyes, he could easily imagine that the Greeks had not entered the gorge except for the far away muffle of their footfalls against the damp earth. With the Jerusalem light infantry at the rear of his march, it looked like the middle phalangite formation was made up of both Samarians and Jerusalemites, the Samarians in front and the Jerusalemites behind them. He wondered idly why Apollonius did not like the Jerusalem cohorts. He had obviously placed them in positions of dishonor in the column. Shimon had learned enough about the Greeks to know that the commanders had their favorites, and it was obvious that Apollonius favored the Samarians.

Now, all Shimon could see were the red and yellow of the Jerusalem cohort below. The blue and green of the Samarians had all disappeared from his view. They were farther up in the gorge. Now that the thrill of being the first to see the Greeks come into the defile had passed, he wished he were on the other end of the gorge to see what Judah would do.

* * * * * *

The Maccabee had pressed himself and his men into invisibility against the ground and base of the next cove ahead of the defile into which the Greeks were marching. He had split his force of one-thousand into three groups. One group of one-hundred and fifty slingmen and archers he had situated on the north wall of the gorge. Another group of one-hundred and fifty were perched in like manner on the south wall. The remaining seven-hundred crouched hidden with him here at the exit of the gorge that was now filled with Greeks. In fact, he and his men could hear the trampings of Greek boots, an occasional clank of weapons and even slight coughs from the head column of light skirmishers that now was almost upon them.

The seven-hundred tensed almost as one being as they awaited the signal. Coil upon coil of joint and sinew ratcheted against the sheer will of discipline as some watched the throat of the Maccabee for the rumbling sign that it was time to kill Greeks in open battle at last.

The essence of the moment seemed to suspend itself, and the fighters were caught in its lapse until Judah roared, "The Lord of Hosts with us!" His warriors sprang, and the Greeks hesitated. All happened in a space frozen by the timeless gravity of life and death. The Maccabee's roar was as a hundred lions, the fighters swore in the tellings later, and his men followed him, severe pleasure on their faces as some ended quickly, impaled on surprised Greeks' swords, but more, many more found their marks against Greek flesh, and the skirmishers, disabled by the confusion of the Maccabee's attack, fell back, back and back some more. The seven hundred, feeling the advantage and the retreating bodies beneath their swords, drove the Greeks into their own numbers as they killed each other in the chaos of lost ground.

* * * * * *

Apollonius did not hear the sound at first, but he noticed the men around him pause and cock their heads as they strained to make sense of the clangings and grunts that drifted toward them from the way ahead. Their progress slowed, then stopped altogether resulting in a stifling crush as the soldiers behind them continued the march.

Apollonius twisted wildly in his saddle, this way and that, as he sought clarity in the confused scene about him. His blood spiked when the realization came. "Ares damn them all! It is an ambush! Fall back!" He cried. "Fall back!"

As he was the only one yelling in that transfixed sea of men, Apollonius had no trouble being heard and his men did their best to obey. The only trouble was that their own mass penned them from every side and there was nowhere to go. Then it started to rain, not a fresh fall of water, but a wicked, pouring deluge of rocks and arrows.

Apollonius' horse reared, dashing the brains out of one of his phalangites when its hooves stamped back into the earth. The creature snorted and screamed in terror yet continued its mindless rearing and plunging, disabling many of the men around it. Apollonius had a ridiculous thought: Thank Zeus there are no elephants on our march today. How Nicanor would have laughed.

Finally, he and some of his men had enough of a reflex left to lift their shields above their heads to deflect some of the deadly downpour. But it was too late. The initial torrent of missiles had taken too many and it was not stopping. The sheer volume of rock soon shredded the shields and more Greeks died as they attempted to stave off the blows with their bare hands. Apollonius felt his horse sinking beneath him, its forelock a bloody crater from one of the obscene rocks. He was just barely able to leap free of the animal's crushing weight when the beast pitched over in its rictus. His beautiful warhorse now part of the offal of dead steeping the ground around him, Apollonius crawled over the quagmire of flesh in an attempt to get to the relative safety of the base of the gorge wall.

Then the Jews came. Leaping and flailing over Greek bodies, they swiped wildly with their swords at everything that moved, horses, men and even the bushes that rustled in the evening wind.

Apollonius drew his sword, again admiring it, not pausing in the killing of Jews as he did so. The blade flashed only for a moment as its sheen soon dulled with the blood of those he sent to Hades. Two, three, four—the count climbed—five, six, seven. He was able to kill many, as the Jews did not have the skill to stop him. Eight, nine, and his blade stopped, grinding and sawing against another sword that allowed no more practiced sweeps against Jew flesh. A scruffy Jew held the opposing weapon. Burning eyes above an unkempt beard, an artless, silly helmet perched over a threadbare head covering. The strength of the arm belied the mangy appearance. At last, a contest!

"Judah! Shall I give the order for the slingmen and archers to descend?"

Another disheveled Jew was addressing his opponent. Apollonius looked from the Jew who had spoken to the swordsman with whom he was bladelocked and an exciting realization gripped him. His opponent was the author of the rebellion, the man who had attempted to stand against the divine Antiochus. This was Judah the Maccabee.

The Jew's eyes indicated an understanding of Apollonius' identity at almost the same moment and the two looked at each other, studying and studying. Both pulled away and the Maccabee, never taking his eyes from Apollonius, said to the other, "Yes, brother. Give the command."

Apollonius held up his sword, shook it gently and nodded. He then crouched into an attack stance and waited. But not for long. Arcing his sword in a wheel over his head and down, he held his eye to Judah's neck seeking to sink his blade there. Satisfaction filled him at the sight of Judah's artless scramble. The blade fell short, slicing at the air to the right, but Apollonius pressed further, sweeping the blade to and fro.

The rebel was having great difficulty as he, Apollonius, clearly had the offensive advantage. Backing away, the Jew stumbled over the bodies of Greeks, some of which were only wounded, and they plucked at his feet to trip him, pride in their commander's sword imbuing them with a brief stay of death. The Maccabee's fighters did what they could to stifle that behavior, running the wounded through, but they had to stay clear of both combatants' swords to avoid death or injury themselves.

Apollonius knew he had to take full advantage of Judah's flailing scuttle across the corpses. His first contact with Judah's strength a moment before told of a formidable opponent, and the Greek became relentless in his lunges, grimly looking for an opening so he could finish the Jew and possibly even the rebellion. The dead Greeks around him spelled his own defeat of course, for even if he killed the Maccabee, he would not last a moment under the vengeful swords of the rebels who surrounded them, urging on their leader. But perhaps if he killed him here, the rebels may be as the hydra without its immortal head and die easily under future Greek swords.

Sweep and Swipe—the Maccabee parried every one, and Apollonius was starting to weary. The Jew must have sensed his weakness, and although he had not fully regained his footing, the strength of his arm absorbed Apollonius' blows until he was finally able to stand, clawing his way up from the ground using an errant stump of a dead tree that stood amid the carnage

"See, General. You have lost. Do you understand me?" The Jew rasped, but at last he was standing, and the contest existed once again. He advanced away from the stump and pointed his sword at Apollonius. "Even if you kill me, you and your Greek empire are all done."

Apollonius understood enough of the bastard language to reply, "It is not 'done,' as you say, Jew," he said in a halting attempt at the tongue. "You and your paltry band cannot withstand the divine Antiochus and his forces."

The Maccabee then did a surprising thing. He laughed. The raucous sound of it bounded back and forth between the walls of the gorge. "The 'divine' Antiochus! I know enough about you, Apollonius, that you do not think Antiochus is divine any more than you think our G-d is divine. Antiochus is *Epimanes*, the crazy one, and you know it as well as I. Our nation will replace your misbegotten empire!"

"There is no 'Jewish nation,'" Apollonius breathed. "And I—"

Judah's sudden sword at his throat made him realize his mistake and his mind uttered an inward curse. The old trick, the distraction of speech, had confused the warrior in him, words replacing what should have been unrelenting action. He did not even have time to steel himself for the carving of his neck. Judah did not hesitate long enough.

The Greek general died wordlessly, as I should have fought, his mind said as it folded in upon itself in death.

* * * * *

"Get him to talk" the old Roman had said. Judah remembered old Aulus and his training long ago in Modiin as he was scrambling away from imminent death under Apollonius' stunning sword. Judah had hoped the Greek general knew Aramaic, because he knew little or no Greek, but decided to try Aulus' strategy and engage his foe in conversation. He had little to lose, he thought as he figured out what to say amid the bone-jarring sword clashes. It worked better than he could have imagined, and he was glad he had enlisted Aulus *Maior's* help back when Judah had begun to see the need for a Jew to learn the sword.

Judah's men looked on and when they saw Apollonius' headless torso fall, the cheer that rose from their throats was checked by the Maccabee's cry, "Fight on! Fight on! It is not finished. We must fight to the edges of the gorge!"

By then the slingmen and the archers were on the ground of the defile, fighting alongside the seven-hundred, now reduced to five-hundred. However, the Greeks were in full retreat, fleeing the swords of the ragtag Jews.

* * * * *

Syrus was one. He had been fighting alongside the Samarians with Apollonius. The horror of the ambush and the general's death had completely vanquished their resolve, and he ran with what was left of Apollonius' warriors, the cream of the Seleucid empire.

The Jerusalem cohort under General Timotheus was far enough to the rear of the action that some of the soldiers were able to see the debacle happening and fled also. The general had been miffed at Apollonius' dismissive treatment of him throughout the march and was not loath to share those feelings with Syrus at regular intervals during the march. In fact, Syrus had resolved to share Timotheus' every word with Apollonius as was his mandate from the general. That mandate had expired with Apollonius' fall, and Syrus was reasonably certain that Timotheus was now mighty in his appreciation at being the tail-end of the march into these wretched hills.

"General!" Syrus now addressed Timotheus, as he, a Samarian lieutenant and a few of the men from the Samarian cohort had found their way to the general through the carnage by keeping to the walls of the gorge. "Apollonius is dead, and the rest of the Samarians lie dead in the bottom of this accursed canyon. What should we do?"

The most profound failure Timotheus had ever given voice to was uttered at that moment in answer to Syrus. "Retreat!" the general said, and he and what remained of the Jerusalem and Samarian cohort ran—some mounted and some on foot—like wild men toward the rear of the defile.

"But General," Syrus panted as he urged on his horse to keep up with the retreating Timotheus. "We should go back and help those left in the defile."

"There is no one left to help," Timotheus said with scorn. "You yourself gave the report. They are all dead."

Syrus opened his mouth to protest, then kept silent. The colonel and the other twenty-one Samarians who had made it out of the debacle alive did not look so fearsome and proud now. Although Syrus had found a niche in the Samarian cohort because of Apollonius' favor, he knew that the rest of the Jerusalem cohort had suffered much ridicule at the hands of the Samarians; therefore, he allowed himself to enjoy, however unseemly, the sight of the hand-picked cohort of the great Apollonius breathless and on the run from a gaggle of Jews. As phalangites, they had not been mounted so had commandeered the surviving horses to escape the onslaught of Jews. Leaving their terrible pikes behind, they now were forced to join the Jerusalem cohorts in their careening exit out of this wretched chain of ravines. No skirmishers joined them in retreat, however. Having been at the head of the march, they bore the first crush of the ambush. All of them were as dead as the rest of the Samarians.

They trudged as quickly as their spent legs allowed through the now seeming countless defiles until they found the friendly ridge to climb. As is always the case, the ascent was more troubling than the descent had been, and to a man, they were not sure they would make it. Finally, the last man had clambered to the blessed aerie, and it was not long before the stench of dead Lebonah assailed them. The smell of decay was as a wall and many of them stumbled to a halt with an involuntary gasp, covering their faces with their mailed jerkins. The mail did nothing to keep the smell at bay. They had to stop their flight until they could rip enough cloth from their tunics to wrap around their faces. Still, it did little to stanch the flow of rot into their nostrils.

Conversation was slight as they passed over the ravine. The smell was simply too overpowering for them to open their mouths to breathe.

The main road seemed to dwarf their numbers even further, and now that they were out of danger, the magnitude of the defeat settled over them like the rot of Lebonah. Most of their force had been annihilated.

"Count us, Syrus," General Timotheus said, holding up his hand to halt the flight. "I need an accounting of our number."

Syrus wearily sat up and turned about until he could survey all the survivors. Some were in quite bad shape, but these were the ones who could still sit a horse. Some had severe facial trauma, and quite a few had lost eyes from the destructive hail of arrows and rocks. Some even had arrows protruding from their bodies and their comrades used the blessed pause to attempt extractions. Syrus shuddered from the screams. If these were the ones who were well enough to come down with them, he did not like to think about the ones still left in the gorge. At the same time, he envied their oblivion. He wondered if the Jews took prisoners. All during these thoughts he counted until he had a reckoning of all the men.

"Seventy-six," Syrus said with as much aplomb as he could muster. He did not have the stomach to number those among them that were wounded. He guessed that number would also approach seventy-six. "That is not including the twenty-two Samarians. Ninety-eight," he amended.

Syrus watched Timotheus' face drain of pigment. He knew what was going through the general's mind. That Timotheus survived a defeat after all his other failures with the Jews would not sit well with Philo, the ranking commander of the Jerusalem barracks. And Syrus was certain that the news would be even less happily received in Antioch.

"Are we returning to Samaria?" The lieutenant of the Samarian cohort asked. "My duties require me to make a report to the office—"

"I care more about a tick on your horse's arse than I do about your report," Timotheus snapped. "Get back to your fine rank of Samarians. You will return with us to Jerusalem. Apollonius' death puts you under my command."

The lieutenant returned to his men, but their surly faces worried Syrus. The Samarian cohort was greatly honored in the empire, and if word of their treatment under Timotheus got back to Antioch, Syrus decided it might not go well with the general, and by extension, him.

Well, he thought. That may not turn out to be my problem. If anything, it could mean a promotion for me if I ally myself with the right story. He wondered what that story would be. It depended upon what tale Timotheus would use to explain his survival. He was surprised when Timotheus' next words answered his question.

"I wish Apollonius would have taken my advice about entering that defile," Timotheus said airily, glancing over at Syrus. "I told him that this was exactly the kind of place where these Jews like to hide."

Syrus had to gulp heavily to hide his astonishment. He had reported to Apollonius on a daily basis about Timotheus' commands and demeanor. Since Syrus was the liaison between the two generals, he knew that Timotheus had never once communicated face to face with General Apollonius, so this lie was even more audacious than he expected. He decided to probe the commander a little, but cautiously. "I did not know you had a conversation with Apollonius," Syrus said innocently. "I thought I saw him at the front of the march the entire campaign, and we, well—we were at the rear."

Apollonius' death now gave Timotheus massive rank over Syrus, a mere colonel. A colonel, he thought ruefully, that had been on his way up the ranks until Apollonius' death. After Syrus' patrol had been only one of ten that had escaped the Maccabee's decimation last season, Apollonius had favored him. That favor was worthless, now. He now depended upon Timotheus favor.

Timotheus lifted his hand and pointed forward to get the march going again. After the clatter of horse hooves resumed, muffled though they were by the dust of the trail, he leaned toward Syrus and said, his eyes hard and bitter, "I know what you were about on the march, Syrus. Apollonius was not the only one who had spies. Reporting on my doings to Apollonius may have seemed like a savvy political move, and perhaps it was at the time. But your benefactor is dead, and I am alive. Your fortunes now seem allied with my own." He sat up easily and looked around to make sure the men's attentions were engaged elsewhere. When he saw that their vacant gazes were attuned to the dreary Judaean landscape, he went on, "You will accede to my version of events, whatever form it takes. If you do not, I will take special care that you and your career become as dust."

As the general, signifying an end to the conversation, cantered up to take his place at the head of the tiny column, Syrus thought, So, that is why he is a general and I am a colonel. Blackmail, politics and now, in Timotheus' case, luck that he survived when Apollonius did not, would continue to keep the incompetent general wedged in the tower of command. It looked like Timotheus was right, at least for the moment. Syrus' fortunes did indeed seem one with Timotheus'.

Chapter Forty-five

The Gorge West of Lebonah, Judaea   The 10th day of *Iyar* 3594 (May 5th 166 B.C.E.)

J udah held up the head of Apollonius. The men who had been the immediate spectators of their contest were the first to cheer, and this time, Judah let them. That cheer spread like a desert wildfire to the very walls of the gorge, causing an earthquake of sound so that a few boulders became dislodged from the rock walls and hit some of the men. One was killed and many were injured by the avalanche, and the sound died among that number, but the cheer took no heed and continued to roll through the defile.

Avram took the head from Judah and skewered it onto one of the phalangites' pikes and raised the gruesome trophy even higher to the absolute delight of those farther away up and down the gorge.

Judah's body failed him, then. The weariness and stress of the long campaign assailed him all at once, and he sat abruptly. Carnage filled his gaze, Apollonius' headless corpse foremost. As Judah looked at the Greek general's gilded armor, now running with blood, he wondered how many battles it had seen. It was not as pocked and marred as that of the regular soldiers that lay nearby, but then Apollonius must have been in command for many years, aloof from the battle, directing his men. The famous general Apollonius, along with these of his men, would soon be part of the earth at the bottom of a nameless gorge. Judah felt the familiar blackness assail him.

He watched the men celebrate for a moment, but when they started to take disrespectful liberties with Apollonius' head, he wearily stopped them. He shook himself to banish the blackness so he could once again attend to his command duties. Surveying the field of dead uneasily, he did not know what to do next. Should they bury the Greeks? Perhaps they should burn the bodies. Then, the beautiful *kopis* of Apollonius caught his eye. Gripped in the Greek general's hand, still proud and defiant even in its rigor, the single-edged sword lay at an odd angle, propped up by the chest armor of a dead Greek near the general. Judah stooped and gently pulled away Apollonius' dead fingers from the hilt. He held aloft the sword. As he eyed its workmanship with appreciation, all the ennui of the previous moment faded, and he became the hard soldier once again.

Tearing his gaze from the sword, he surveyed the ground of bodies and suddenly became avaricious for the accoutrements of the corpses lying about. One of his main worries about his men had been their shabby armor. Many of the swords, shields and armor that his fighters used were some of the very weapons that he himself had forged long ago under Avram's apprenticeship in Modiin. He had been very proud of those weapons and the forges in Gophna were now ablaze with copies of those early endeavors. Next to the fine Greek implements, however, they looked ridiculously primitive. He decided that weapons retrieval was more important than attending to the Greek dead: the enemies would lie where they fell. Even Apollonius.

He held up his hands to quiet the cheers that were edging on annoyance. "Every man is to strip the Greek bodies of their armor, shields, cuirasses, swords, indeed, everything that is of value to us in our fight."

"Infidel arms?" Eleazar, who had already begun directing the mournful task of extricating the Jew dead from the bloody marsh of bodies, looked up in surprise. "Judah! We do not want to wear unclean armor."

"Then we will clean it, Eleazar," Judah said. Having pulled the breastplate from Apollonius' body, he grasped the fine cloak from the general's torso and cheerfully rubbed the blood from the gilded metal. "See? It polishes up nicely." To the rest of the men he thundered, in case any others sought to protest, "We will use their own arms to defeat them. No longer will we go into battle unprotected. After every contest with the Greeks, I want you to return to your wives and children. If I have to use Greek armor to accomplish that, then so be it!"

Any protest that was on the lips of the other men was stilled in the face of this pragmatic pronouncement. They fell to the grim task of denuding the Greek bodies of their battle wear. However, as they handled the armor for themselves and saw the richness of the workmanship and the intricacies of the protective flaps designed to protect every vital of a warrior imaginable, the task became more palatable. They even were able to joke callously among themselves.

"This armor is too big for you anyway, you Greek dog. You did not fill it out very well," one said. He modeled it for his mates, "See, it fits me better."

"If you were Goliath, perhaps," a comrade said, holding up a helmet and admiring the blue plume that fountained from the crown of metal. "Now, this is something! Come to me, my beautiful bird. Fly away from this heathen and grace the head of one of the chosen."

Judah enjoyed the men's buffoonery for a moment. The blackness was completely gone. The carnage no longer upset him. The Greeks had brought this upon themselves. The butchery they had fomented against his people more than justified this slaughter.

Sighing, he found that his face was wet. The tears, however, were not a signatory of the death around him, but rather tears of relief at the victory.

"Eleazar!" Judah called.

"Yes, brother," Eleazar said, looking at Judah carefully. "What is it? Are you all right?"

Judah dashed the tears from his face, only a little embarrassed. "Yes, of course." He paused, almost hating to ask the next question. "How many lost?"

Eleazar looked around and said, "Well, we do not have the final count, but some families will suffer losses from this day. But, not many." Eleazar smiled and put his arm around Judah, jostling him, "Not many!"

"The Lord of Host with us," Judah breathed.

He looked up and saw two riders attempting an approach to his position, but their horses were not cooperating. The mass of dead bodies was too much for the psyches of the beasts to overcome and they reared and protested despite the curses of their masters. Judah smiled when he saw Asher and Aulus dismount, and he plunged through the kills to greet them. "You are alive!" he said when he at last reached them and grasped both of them in a warm headlock.

"Ow! You would do Eupolemus to shame!" Aulus said, pounding Judah's helmet until Judah released the headlock. The Roman glanced over at Asher and said, "I bet your arm was never that strong even when you were the Great Eupolemus of Greek fame!"

"Then, I was never allied with the famous Maccabee of Gophna fame. Judah!" Asher said, "The victory was complete. There is not a Greek alive from the point of the defile to the rear. Many of the slingmen and archers reported, however, that a small group of Samarians joined some of the rear Jerusalem guard and fled down the ravine to Lebonah. Should I assign a group to pursue them?"

"No, said Judah. "Let them go." He squinted. "Not only that, but the sun has gone down, and we only have a few more moments of light. We have much to do. Those Greeks that flee can serve as our messengers, for they will surely report our victory to their superiors in Jerusalem."

"Or twist it into propaganda," Aulus said. "Is that Apollonius?"

Avram had relinquished the head of the Greek general and its pike when he joined his fellows to gather the Greek weaponry. He had planted it in the ground so that it stood upright, a macabre standard of their rout.

"Yes," Judah said.

"Well, I hope Timotheus' head will grace a pike as well," Aulus said. "He is a jackal. If he survived, no doubt he will be the one to describe this defeat as his victory for the Greeks. My father had some dealings with him. He always maintained that the main reason for Timotheus' height in the Greek ranks was his ability to lie."

"Do you know what he looks like, Aulus?" Judah asked.

"As a youth, I met him a couple of times when my father brought me to Jerusalem with him. I think I would recognize him."

"If you would, accompany our burial detail as they extract the Hebrew dead, and see if you can identify Timotheus among the bodies."

"Yes, Commander," Aulus said and made his way toward the Jewish death detail that was plying their gruesome work a little ways to the rear of the gorge.

"Oh, and Commander Aulus," Judah said, interrupting the Roman's departure.

"Yes, Judah?"

"The Greek bodies at your feet are the handiwork of those 'leather loincloths' as you called them."

"And of our archers," Aulus grumbled, then added in a deprecating tone, "You and your slingmen." As Aulus watched where he stepped, though, Judah could see him looking at each Greek body inventorying the wounds: those caused by arrows versus rocks.

"What is that you have there?" Asher asked. "A sword?"

"Apollonius' sword," Judah said, handing it over to Asher by the gilded hilt. "What do you think?"

Asher turned the weapon over and over in his hands and crooned his admiration. "It is a fitting weapon for the commander of the rebel forces. It will serve you well." He gave the sword back to Judah who grasped it in his fighting hand once again. Asher then took Judah's hand by the wrist and held it and the sword over their heads. "The Sword of the Lord!" He thundered. "Let it be known that the Greeks now have to face Judah the Maccabee and the Sword of the Lord!"

Although battle weariness had begun to press down upon the fighters, the sight of the Maccabee with the enemy's sword revived their throats. The raucous cheer soon organized itself into the shouted chant, "The Sword of the Lord!"

Chapter Forty-six

Gophna, Judaea   The 12th day of *Iyar* 3594 (May 7th 166 B.C.E.)

Miriam was the lookout this time. Shimon and John, the regular watchers, were with the attack party, but other boys were slated to fill in for them. Miriam would have none of that, however, and she sent them flying away with a harsh wave of the hand and an epithet. She simply did not have the patience to wait calmly in camp for word of the men. She felt she had to see their arrival, herself. She had to be first to tell the others, "The Maccabee and the Faithful have returned!"

But the hours passed, and fear replaced the impatience. The couriers did not even appear.

"How do they expect us to know what is going on?" Miriam said aloud, her only audience the void of the ravine. "That is irresponsible. Judah will hear about that from me." She drummed her fingers against the peeling bark of a juniper bush, then gripped the scrawny plant with more and more ferocity as her own fear escalated. More hours crawled by.

When she opened her eyes, she was staring into a star-encrusted vault. She must have dozed. Night had fallen. She pulled away from the bush and cried out. Her head covering had pulled away from her head while she was asleep, and her hair was caught in the thicket of juniper.

"Damn," Miriam said, and as she reached for the offending tendril of hair, she looked around to make sure no one had heard her swear. Judah was standing over her.

* * * * *

The scream was involuntary, and Judah did not shush her. He was no longer stalking Greeks under a silent march and the unrestrained yell was a welcome sound. He simply smiled, then stooped to assist her in freeing her hair.

"You are as Absalom! Mind your hair, woman! You are lucky the Greeks did not prevail against us and march up here. You would have been easy prey for them, as Absalom was for Joab. Not only that, but sleeping sentries do not fare well in most armies."

"Well, I am not a sentry, I am the Maccabee's wife, and—comparing me to the traitor Absalom! Husband, for shame! When I have been waiting here for an entire day, no couriers, no word on—What did you say? The Greeks did not prevail against us?" The cadence of her voice rose with each word until, again, she was shrieking. The shrieks were not of fear, however.

"I am here, am I not?" Judah said, smoothing his wife's hair and murmuring into her ear. "Yes, the Greeks fled." Then he grasped her arms and lifted her off the ground. It was his turn to yell. "We were victorious! The Lord G-d was truly with us!"

The two shunned propriety and returned to the main camp arm-in-arm, but no one seemed to mind as the other warriors were milling about with their families, great joy on most of the faces. Some of the men were bloodied, but most were whole.

Not every expression was that of joy, however, and many wails and other sounds of grief cut wide gashes into the general celebration. Judah quieted the crowd and bowed his head for many moments.

"Yes, it was a great victory. But we lost many." As Judah intoned the names of the dead, murmurs of sadness accompanied each utterance. Schmuel the overseer, Malachai, Judah's old Yeshiva mate, in fact, a quarter of his class—all had been lost. The crowd was chastened even in victory.

Judah had made sure every corpse had been borne back, and they were laid out with great tenderness by the fighters. As the families wept over the dead and bedecked themselves with ash from the firepits, the rest of the village stood back and respectfully observed the terrible, age-old rituals of grief.

Ephraim had been one of the first to embrace Judah as he walked into camp with Miriam. And, even with the word of his friend Malachai's death, his old rancor about the death of his father Naphtali did not return. Allowing the comforting hands of those around him to assuage his grief, he reached into the ashes of the fire where he had kept his vigil waiting for the fighters for the past day and a half. Quietly weeping after hearing the names of the dead, he shrouded his forehead with the charcoal and left to keep vigil of another kind.

As night descended further and the mourners drifted away to their tasks of preparing their dead for burial, the victory celebration resumed, although subdued. There was no dancing and there were no songs of triumph, only soft words over campfires, the pall of death having sapped some of the happiness.

But not all. After winding down, the warriors retreated at last into their families. They put aside their new swords and shields, spoils of the Greek dead, and rested. And, as they lay next to their wives and watched their children sigh in their sleep, their brows deepened and they slept the untroubled sleep of those under peace, infant and untried though it was.

Chapter Forty-seven

Antioch, Syria   The 19th day of *Iyar* 3594 (May 14th 166 B.C.E.)

Nicanor hollered, "Coriolus!"

When the slave gave no answer, the general rose from his bed and walked to the balcony that overlooked the Orontes River. "I am tired of this accursed city," he grumbled. "Apamea is where I belong." He rubbed his eyes and blearily assessed the river.

It was muddy today; its depths still mesmerized Nicanor with their murky swirls and eddies. Hearing a sound behind him, he said without turning around, "There you are. Where have you been?"

"I am sorry, master! The door is almost kindled with knocking this morning. There are many messages. The most important is from the Divine One, himself. He is calling for a meeting of all the high generals. I believe that includes you, although Seron would not have it so."

"Mind your tongue, slave," Nicanor said as he pulled his sleeping tunic off over his head. He muttered unintelligibly as Coriolus' assisted him. "You are not fit to even utter the name of my colleague."

"Hmmm. Seron a colleague," Coriolus said. "So, all rivalries are forgotten? All battles have become a truce?"

Nicanor impatiently strode to his bath. He descended quickly into the tepid water but did not linger. He rose almost as soon as the water had surrounded his body.

"That is not much of a bath," Coriolus clucked. "The advisor will not even have to announce your arrival, they will smell you long before you enter the room."

"At least it will be the smell of a man. The insipid fragrances that these court fops use—well, it makes them smell like a Cappadocian brothel. Disgusting, really. How I long for the old days when we warriors decided all state matters. I have had enough of diplomacy and meetings."

"Well," Coriolus said, his eyes askance. "From the rumors that arrived with the couriers from Jerusalem, it seems that a warrior did decide at least one state matter."

"What do you mean? Have you heard news of Apollonius?" Nicanor's faculties sharpened. He knew that the slave network often trumped the official palace couriers in the latest news from abroad. Apparently, this time was no different.

But Coriolus was fussing at the elegant chest that held Nicanor's tunics, slyly avoiding comment. Nicanor knew that slaves felt important at such times when they had information, especially that of a dire nature, to tell their masters, and Coriolus was no different. He held up two of Nicanor's best tunics. "Do you like this one, Master?" He asked coyly. "Or perhaps this blue would be better."

"What have you heard?" Nicanor barked. And at Coriolus' simpering, he advanced on the slave, one fist up. "Tell me, you fool!"

Nicanor shook as he dressed himself that morning, having waved Coriolus away. It could not be true. His old friend. It was impossible.

The fierce stone griffins stared down at him as he passed through the entry of the throne room; he had no trouble ignoring them, but he found he could not will away the stone in his gut that told him that the slave's terrible news was true.

Teman's face spoke all. The advisor's customary sourness was replaced by the blanch of fear that accompanied negative reports from abroad to the King. Any hope that Coriolus' gossip was mere rumor dissipated when he saw Teman's ashen face.

So, it is true, Nicanor thought and the stone sank deeper into his vitals, leaching away all desire, happiness and strength. He said nothing to Teman but forced his shaking legs to convey him to his regular seat.

The other commanders drifted in, their laughter and carefree features telling of their ignorance regarding the terrible debacle. Nicanor hoped that none of them approached him to make small talk. He simply was not capable of speech at that moment.

Horns signaled the imminent entrance of Antiochus Epiphanes and the generals who were not situated near a seat hurried to their places. Epiphanes apparently had not heard the news either, for the last time Nicanor had seen such opulence was when the emperor had entered a victory banquet commemorating a triumph over the Thracians. He was dressed all in gold, borne in a golden litter carried by gold-painted slaves. That is how he entered now, bedecked in aureal splendor.

After the emperor settled himself in his throne and Teman gave the nod to sit, Nicanor tried not to slump in his seat, but it was very difficult to stay upright. Apollonius. His friend was dead, but how? An assassin? An altercation with a rival? Apollonius had made many enemies only because he was more competent than everyone else with whom he had served. Perhaps Timotheus had hired a thug. That general had suffered greatly during a humiliating parade orchestrated by Apollonius after being chased out of Gophna by the Maccabee. It could have even been a bad night at a brothel, given Apollonius proclivities for sexual extremes. Nicanor straightened his back and gave his attention to the emperor, certain that the Divine One would soon ask for the courier's report. Curiosity lifted his depression a little. At last, he would find out the particulars of Apollonius' death.

"Our Emperor, the Divine One, Antiochus Epiphanes, Beloved Son of Zeus will hold forth!" Teman announced in his most somber, yet sonorous voice.

Strangely, Nicanor's mood rose further at the sight of the emperor all in gold. For all the idiosyncrasies of the ruler and his disinterest regarding Judaea that most likely led to the demise of Apollonius, Nicanor's patriotism still allowed him to deify Antiochus. The golden spectacle was still somewhat revolting, but he found himself leaning forward in his chair.

Antiochus sat still for many moments. The gold that encased him sheened his being in an aura that seemed otherworldly.

"Teman," Antiochus said formally. "I need a drink of water. This golden monstrosity is giving me hives." As Teman hurried off, Antiochus took off his cloak and his breastplate. He sat for a moment, then started peeling off his cuirass, belt, greaves, arm bands. Confused slaves hurried to attend him and with their help, Antiochus soon had stripped himself of every piece of clothing and royal accoutrement that had hung on his person. The only accessories that he kept were his crown and his silk loincloth.

His audience knew better than to react to this display. They sat, not turning, not pursing their lips or rolling their eyes, as they were used to this type of behavior from their emperor. Not that they had ever seen the emperor strip in the throne room in this manner, but such was his unpredictability.

It was at this moment that Nicanor missed Apollonius the most, and the wave of grief that assailed him almost made him slump again. How he missed that wonderful askance glance that Apollonius would direct at him during these strange exhibitions of their emperor. Then after, they would discuss what they had seen over a goblet of excellent wine and discuss all the political ramifications of having a crazy monarch. He urged himself to breathe deeply in an effort to banish the debilitating grief.

Antiochus sat, gold paint covering his arms and legs, but ending where the under-tunic had covered him. Slaves moved in with wet cloths to remove the paint, but he shrieked them away. Looking out at the crowd once again, the Emperor nodded.

"Our dear Apollonius is dead!" Antiochus intoned. "What shall we do? It is not as if he went into the battle unprepared. He had his Royal Samarians with him, after all. Who is this person, this Jew that I hear about? The Maccabee? What kind of heathen name is it? Nicanor."

So, the emperor did know of his death. Wrenched out of his torpor, Nicanor rose. "Yes, sire?" he managed to croak.

"You have heard of this Maccabee?"

"Only in a fleeting fashion, Your Majesty."

"What is your assessment?"

Nicanor paused. Suddenly, the grief that bore down on him flamed into extreme anger and he did not dare continue or his voice would betray him. All patriotism vanquished, he became enraged that Antiochus would enter the room as the ridiculous golden god to deliver the news of the demise of one of the greatest generals in the realm. A younger, more inexperienced man would have blurted a response not caring whether the emperor heard the venom in it or not. But Nicanor was versed in palace politics—that was why he was still alive. So, he waited until the rage cooled. It took an eternity of seconds.

"I have not heard the full report, sire, so I am ill-equipped to be of service in this matter." He sat down.

"Teman!" Antiochus barked. "Deliver the missive."

"Timotheus to the Great Antiochus. If it is well with you, I so wish. This is a report of the ambush of Gophna. Apollonius took a contingent of three-thousand into the hills of Gophna to apprehend the rebellion of one Judah the Maccabee, a Jew flouting the laws of our Divine emperor, Antiochus the Just. I urged Apollonius to keep to the heights and not descend into the gorges that populated these hills. Against my advice, Apollonius led his valiant Samarians, with a reduced palace cohort from Jerusalem, into a defile, twenty furlongs east of the village of Lebonah. It was here that Apollonius suffered under a cowardly ambush from the Jew rebels. Only one-hundred of our troops emerged alive. Apollonius was not among them. I, Timotheus led the survivors out and now write this report to the glory of our Lord Antiochus."

Silence lingered in the hall for many moments until the legs of Nicanor's chair rattled over the floor as he stood up again.

"And how is it that Timotheus survived to write this letter?" Nicanor ventured, his face dangerously still. "And how is it that he did not accompany the letter to speak for himself, as is the custom?"

Antiochus acknowledged Nicanor's gaze by standing up, a gesture that made the emperor look even more ridiculous as slaves reached to keep the cloth from sliding off the royal loins. "An excellent question, but one I shall leave for a later time. It is time that I attend to the Jews myself. I will take Nicanor and as many troops as Antioch can spare to Jerusalem to quell this nonsense once and for all. We will have a new and spacious land for my subjects in Judaea that will be free from rebellion and strife, for I will purge that golden city of Jews. There will not be a Jew babe squawking for its mother's teat when I am done with Judaea. Lysias, Gorgias, Nicanor, Seron, and Teman, attend me. The rest of you may leave."

As the courtiers withdrew, Nicanor looked about uneasily. The thought of sharing a debriefing about Apollonius' death with these men made him queasy. Now with his friend gone, he was the only real military man among them. These were creatures of Antiochus' court, better equipped for political intrigue than military strategy. He forced himself out of his chair and moved to the enclave of seats that the slaves were arranging closer to the emperor's throne.

After he sat down, he looked at each of those who were easing into their seats beside him. Lysias, of all of them, was probably the most power-mad. Through his service and political acrobatics, he had gained the regency over Antiochus' son, Eupator. It would be he who would gain control of the kingdom after the emperor died, ruling through the young Eupator. Gorgias, although his forte was experiencing the delights of the various vices that were replete in the Greek culture, was also astute enough to keep himself close to Epiphanes through political gamesmanship. Seron—it was difficult to assess why Seron was invited to attend this meeting. He was given to ill-advised bravado in his rule of CoeleSyria and was only in Antioch these last few months to escape a scandal regarding misappropriated funds in his particular satrapy. Perhaps Antiochus enjoyed having someone like the immature general around for ridicule fodder as Seron did not enjoy the gravitas of the other three generals that usually did not have to allow for jibes, even from the emperor. And Teman, well, Teman was there serving as the political purist, totally devoid of military acumen but skilled in the diplomacies inherent in ruling the disparate mob that made up the Greek Seleucid Kingdom.

The men waited for the monarch to speak. Antiochus fussed with his loincloth for a moment, then looked up. "Nicanor, I will take you with me to Jerusalem. I will attend to the rebellion myself, but with your military expertise aiding my decisions."

"Of course, sire," Nicanor said. "I am always at your service."

"But," Antiochus went on, "I want the others to weigh in as to how to proceed."

Seron, even though he was junior in rank, jumped on the opportunity to speak. "Sire, as commander of CoeleSyria, I believe I should accompany you and Nicanor to Judaea. I am due to return anyway, and I would like to be part of the campaign to rid the territory of Jews."

"All in good time," Antiochus said, his condescending tone a verbal pat on the head as one would give a small boy. "You will have your chance to shine for me, General Seron, but not yet. Lysias, as regent, you will stay here and see to Eupator's education and other affairs of state. But you must also keep abreast of the doings in Jerusalem. I may have to call upon you to bring down some of the *kotaikai* from Seleucia."

"Yes, sire," Lysias simpered, bowing. "I doubt you will need them, but as always, they are at the ready."

Nicanor shifted in his seat. "Sire, I believe we should deploy the *kotaikai* and bring them with us now."

Eyeing Nicanor with derision, Seron said, "That should hardly be necessary, Sire. Our *kotaikai* in Judaea should be more than enough."

"We have always underestimated the Jews, Sire," Nicanor said, pointedly ignoring Seron. "That is why Apollonius took all 3,000 of his troops up to Gophna—"

"—and got them all slaughtered," said Seron. "Apollonius is dead and squandered his Samarians because he made an error in judgment. Timotheus said so."

"Timotheus is a liar as well as a coward," Nicanor said easily, still not acknowledging Seron with a glance. "That is the only reason he survived. I do not trust his story and I intend to look into it when I return to Judaea. As for you," at this, Nicanor finally looked at the junior general. "You are not to disparage the name of Apollonius in my hearing again or I swear by Ares I will—"

"Enough!" Antiochus said, but was smiling at the entertaining exchange. "I will not have my generals squabbling like a flock of geese. Gorgias, what say you?"

"Nicanor will carry the day," Gorgias said, arranging his cloak sedately over his knees. "I do not know what happened with Apollonius, but I agree with Nicanor that Timotheus' word is not to be trusted. I would just suggest, Nicanor, that if you do take the *kotaikai* with you, that you take a healthy cohort of phalangites to replace those that were lost at Gophna. I think that most of them would relish a trip to Judaea."

The others looked sharply at Gorgias. The cynical lift of his eyebrow and a slight smile was all that greeted their scrutiny.

In appreciation of Gorgias' sarcasm regarding the phalangites' relish of Judaea, Nicanor almost smiled back in spite of himself. The general disdain for service in Judaea was so entrenched that it was part of the military consciousness among the Seleucid ranks.

Nicanor harrumphed loudly in an effort to squelch the smile. "I think," he nodded toward Antiochus, "that, with your permission, Sire, I will mobilize the palace *hypastists*. After all, with your attendance on this campaign, it would be entirely appropriate for them to accompany you. They are the best phalangites in the kingdom and I can think of no better way to honor Apollonius than to use them to avenge his death."

"A delightful notion," Antiochus agreed. "You are welcome to them. Teman, you have been uncharacteristically quiet during this meeting. What do you have to say?"

Teman cleared his throat. "Sire, it is my duty to remind you that there are other issues besides Judaea and the Jews that demand your attention." He paused, clearly uneasy about continuing.

"Well," Antiochus flapped his hands against his naked legs, "Go on, Teman. I am able to consider more than one thing at a time."

"Sire," Teman quickly said. "We are in dire need of money for the treasury. May I remind you that you were preparing to march east to Parthia to uh," Teman cleared his throat again, attempting to find the right word, "uh, acquire gold for our accounts. I am sure that I do not need to remind you that the Romans' tribute payment is still past due, as it has been many months. Nicanor, here, even planned out a route for you so that you could take advantage of the, ahem, temples and palaces along the way."

"Yes, yes," Antiochus said impatiently. "You will not let me forget it. Well, generals, it seems that the exigencies of revenue are rearing their ugly heads once again, keeping me from serving with my beloved fighting men."

Again, Nicanor missed Apollonius. His old friend would have seen the hilarity in Antiochus' pretense of sadness in aborting his trip to Jerusalem. He knew the avaricious monarch had no intention of missing the march east to Parthia. And Teman was right. Nicanor had plotted a lucrative route where the emperor would pass many temples and holy places—plunder, not worship, being his aim. The emperor's too-quick agreement to stay would have been the subject of many hours of discussion and laughter. He could almost see the twinkle of Apollonius' eye. "Yes, sire," was all he said.

"Nicanor, I still want you to direct the campaign. Do not take the *Hypastists* as they will accompany me on the march to Parthia. However, the Antioch *Argyraspides'* pikes are just as long and sharp and will do well for you in Jerusalem." He nodded toward Seron. "Seron will go with you."

"But, sire," Seron protested, seeming to forget his desire of marching to Jerusalem voiced but a few moments before. "I was planning to march with you to the East. You need my assistance with—"

"Counting and dividing the plunder?" Antiochus chuckled. "No, no, Seron. I need you to learn strategy and cool from General Nicanor." He leaned toward Seron and said, "And, you have much to learn about finesse, Commander."

Nicanor was somewhat gratified at Antiochus' faith in him, but was also chagrined that his traveling partner to Judaea would be the tiresome Seron. Of course, he knew that Seron hated him, but that was only because Seron was an ambitious man and wanted his job. Nicanor never begrudged a man his ambition, so long as it did not interfere with his own service to the empire. Not only that, but Seron was too far beneath him in rank to present much of a threat. But Seron was well versed in the doings of Gaza and Nicanor was always eager to swap stories and debriefings that would help him learn more about the situation in Judaea. Oh well, he thought, maybe Seron can school me in the low arts of politics and diplomacy. He has been enough of a politician to cajole superiors into overlooking his incompetence.

Seron had turned to Gorgias and while the two conversed, Antiochus stood, beckoning Nicanor to walk with him. Nicanor eased out of his seat and accompanied the emperor, trying to hide his embarrassment at walking with the nearly nude monarch.

"I am sorry to have saddled you with Seron," Antiochus said. "But he would have driven me crazy if he had accompanied me to the East. And we could not have that, a crazy emperor, now could we?" Then the emperor did something remarkable: he laughed in self-deprecation.

The old fox, Nicanor thought as the emperor patted him on the shoulder and walked away toward Lysias and Seron, still chuckling. He watched him as he approached the generals, giving them a hearty clap on the back and almost reeled from the realization, He knows everyone thinks he is crazy. He actually is using it as a political strategy to keep everyone around him on edge. Lysias and Seron certainly looked on edge as the emperor's manic chuckles continued, punctuating their discussion. At a particularly shrill cackle of the emperor's that echoed into the vaulted ceiling of the throne room, Nicanor shook his head and said softly, "The old fox."

Chapter Forty-eight

Gophna, Judaea   The 21ˢᵗ day of Sivan 3594 (June 14ᵗʰ 166 B.C.E.)

Judah snapped, "Miriam! Enough! I will not speak of it further!"

The wife of Judah the Maccabee, acquiesced, a stunning anomaly of behavior. She gathered the rags that she had thrown at her husband's face during the argument and shook them free of the dirt, but did it slowly, deliberately. One by one she separated the squares of homespun and flapped them, not always avoiding Judah's direction.

He coughed and considered grabbing his wife and shaking her but thought better of it; the village was coming awake and people were emerging from tents, shrugging into their outer robes. Stirring the dormant coals of the pits until the embers raged enough to bake their morning breadcakes, his neighbors glanced at him and nodded. He watched his brother's wife, Shoshanna, at the next tent over poke at her fire for a moment, and accepted her wave, using it to get away from his tense camp. Why did his wife persist in arguing about matters over which he had no control? He could not help it if the new refugees were disorganized in their Shabbat observance. He had other things on his mind than what the displaced Gezer people considered sacrificial lambs without blemish. And he did not care if the lambs seemed a little undernourished. The people of Gezer had just dragged themselves and their stock up to Gophna, for *Are's* sake, and he told Miriam so. All of them, including their lambs, looked bedraggled.

"Welcome, brother. Eleazar is in bed," Shoshanna said, shielding her face from the fire with a corner of her head covering."I was about to go screeching in, but perhaps—"

"Say no more," Judah said. "I'll get him up."

Judah entered the tent that smelled of sleep. He kicked his brother's foot, stepped back and grinned.

Eleazar was on his feet in an instant, a warrior now used to such awakenings. When he saw he was in his own tent and not on the march, he frowned meaningfully at Judah and collapsed back to the skins. "Let me sleep. My wife kept me awake into the third watch."

Judah squatted and poked Eleazar roughly in the ribs. "Your wife is no worse for the wear," he pointed out, "and is already up, cooking to feed your sorry belly. She wants you up, and I need to speak with you before she enslaves you for the day. And, for shame, that stool Shoshanna is using needs repair—and you call yourself a carpenter." He kicked Eleazar again. "One of our merchants had news from Antioch."

At this, Eleazar sat up but still attempted nonchalance, though Judah could tell he was very interested. "What did he say?" He mumbled, scratching at his beard. "What general is the Crazy One going to send against us, now?"

"I keep hearing the names Gorgias, Seron and Lysias," Judah said, smiling at Eleazar's reference to the Greek emperor, Antiochus IV. He was also known as Antiochus *Epiphanes,* meaning "the enlightened," but most, including his Greek subjects, called him *Epimanes*, meaning "the crazy." It was a convenient pun.

Eleazar struggled into his robes and said, "I have not heard of any of them. What does Aulus say? Does he know them?"

"I'm on my way to Aulus, now. Will you accompany? We shall ask him."

"Anything to get out of—how did you say?—being enslaved by my wife," Eleazar grumbled.

"Come along then, Brita will feed us. She keeps food acceptable to the law in their camp."

Eleazar and Judah exited the tent and camp before Shoshanna could stop them. All they heard was a faint, "But, Eleazar! I wanted you to . . ." The rest was lost under the brothers' trotting feet as they made their escape. Passing Judah's camp, they saw no sign of Miriam.

"The high priest tells us that when a man marries, his sins decrease." Eleazar panted.

"The high priest did not have Miriam for a wife," Judah said. "That woman drives me insane." He immediately felt ashamed and amended, "But she is a good sort. She has been a good wife."

Judah felt his brother's gaze. Eleazar simply said, "Yes, Miriam is a good sort."

To get off the subject of wives, Judah said, "I wish I understood politics as well as Aulus!"

"A Jew can never understand politics as a Roman does," Eleazar said, batting at a swarm of gnats, "They have been a nation for many centuries, and we have been subject to the whims of foreign kings since the Assyrian invasion. We have no experience."

"One could argue that we are even more politically astute than the Romans," Judah retorted. "Otherwise, we would not have survived as a people. But maybe when we become a nation, we can use politics to further our interests rather than just survive. In either case, allies like Aulus can help."

The brothers walked along in companionable silence toward the outer edge of the Gophna encampment. Although the Roman had been helpful beyond measure in their fight against the Greeks, most of the Jews did not trust him being in their midst. Aulus was good-natured about this Hebrew xenophobia. He was used to it after living among the Jews in Modiin for most of his life and had taken it upon himself to make his camp as far away from the others as possible.

Eleazar broke the silence. "I wonder. Why does Brita keep food to our liking in Aulus' camp?"

"Why, for our visits, of course," Judah said. He stopped and tousled the hair of twin boys who had been following the two commanders.

"Are those not Avram's?" Eleazar asked. "They grow even as we watch. See, they have grown nearly a hand-span since I last noticed. Amazing. And, we do not visit Aulus' camp that often. He attends meetings at our command tent. In fact, this is the first time we have been to his camp for a number of months. So, why would they keep food for us?"

"I do not know, Eleazar," Judah said wearily. "What does it matter? He and Brita are just trying to be hospitable."

"I think Brita is trying to be more than just 'hospitable.'"

"Now, what is that supposed to mean?" At Eleazar's knowing look, Judah scoffed. "Do not be ridiculous. She is a slave. I am married. And if you bring up the subject again, I will pound you into the ground—and then I will tell *Eemah*."

Although it was a joke, and Eleazar knew it, Judah also knew the mention of their mother would induce Eleazar to keep future comments on the matter to himself. Elizabeth was becoming a formidable matriarch and Judah was sure that Eleazar would rather face an entire phalanx of Greek spears than go up against their mother.

"Judah! Eleazar!" Aulus boomed. "Welcome to my camp!"

Judah gratefully grasped Aulus' hand. The Roman, for all his heathen proclivities, never failed to hearten Judah with his confidence. Aulus had been a boyhood friend of Judah's in the village of Modiin. Although Judah's father had not liked the idea of a Roman associating with his family, Judah and Aulus' friendship thrived anyway. Now, Judah was glad for Aulus' presence in his camp. He was also touched that the Roman had stayed this long with the rebellion. It was not his fight.

Aulus had just returned from a visit with his family. He had taken advantage of the spies' reports of a lull in Greek activity and made the journey to Tarsus, where his mother Julia and his father Aulus *Maior* were luxuriating in their winter home. He wanted to make sure they were safe. Although the province of Cilicia was a Greek holding, its capital city, Tarsus, was diverse enough to easily hide an elderly Roman couple.

"And how is your father, Aulus *Maior*?" Judah asked with real interest. Having known his friend for years, he no longer thought twice about the strange custom Romans had of naming all their heirs after themselves. His friend was known as Aulus *Minor*.

"He and Mother are healthy and are keeping well away from Greek concerns. Luckily, Tarsus is such an amalgamation of trade that no one notices an old Roman warhorse and his wife. Even if it did not escape the Greeks' notice that they sired a son who is fighting with a Jew against their divine emperor, they will never find them there. Brita! These men need food! They are wasting as we stand here! And, make sure it is according to their law."

The diminutive Nordic beauty emerged from the makeshift camp kitchen and brought the men a platter of bread with meat sop in little bowls. Judah and Eleazar took the stools offered them by the Roman and eagerly dipped their bread and started to eat.

They ate too greedily for talk and no questions entered the sounds of tearing bread and sloshing sop until the men had washed their hands with cloths proffered by Brita.

"So, Judah," Aulus said. "I understand that we have news. I only heard smatterings as I was training new recruits for our cavalry, the *Alae*."

"What do the names, Lysias, Gorgias and Seron mean to you?" Judah asked. "Have you heard of them before?"

"Lysias and Gorgias I know. Seron? Hmm." Aulus fisted his chin and considered for a moment. "Oh, yes. He is the governor of the region north of Judaea. CoeleSyria. Not much of a military man, I hear. He achieved his post through nepotism. His family is quite well-placed in the empire. Lysias and Gorgias, though: they are quite formidable. Why?"

"It is being noised about that these could be the generals that we face next."

"Not Seron, surely," Aulus said almost to himself. "He is regarded as Antiochus' pet—having earned his proximity to the emperor by charisma rather than deeds. I cannot believe that he is being considered to lead the next campaign against us. Gorgias, perhaps. Lysias is the regent to the prince, Eupator. I would not think that he is available. What about Nicanor? Was he mentioned at all?"

Judah looked at Eleazar who shook his head. "No, but was not Nicanor close to Apollonius?" Judah asked. "I would think he would be the one to come and avenge his friend." He put his hand to the hilt of his sword. "Perhaps to retrieve his sword?"

The men laughed. After beheading Apollonius, Judah had taken the general's elegant sword and now wore it as his own. The *kopis*, in fact, was responsible for a new battle cry that the rebels were beginning to use in training: "The Sword of the Lord."

The irony of an enemy sword being used as a focus for the rebellion was not lost on the men.

"All those swords I forged for our ungrateful men," Judah said, clucking. "And they choose a heathen *kopis* to rally around."

"Well," said Aulus. "You were the one who yelled out the ridiculous cry after slaying Apollonius."

"The heat of battle and the glare of the sword made me lose my wits." Judah said. "I lost my head."

"No, it was Apollonius who lost his head." Aulus said, his face a deadpan for a moment until it erupted in laughter.

Eleazar and Judah stoically watched Aulus double over at his banal pun. The Roman enjoyed his hilarity for quite a few moments. Finally, he wiped his eyes, still chuckling.

"Are you finished?" Judah asked. "Then, tell me more about Gorgias."

"That one is a very able general." Aulus said, sobering. "Not as well reputed as Apollonius was, but he is known as a solid field commander. I imagine he is working with Nicanor. Nicanor, as you probably remember, had many doings with Apollonius in Jerusalem. In fact, both of them were present at your 'abomination of desolation,' where they defiled the temple at Jerusalem. If I were a religious man, I would say that at least one of them paid the ultimate debt to your Hebrew god. *Caput!*" Aulus dissolved into laughter again.

"*Mehercle,* Aulus!" Judah said. "It is not that funny." He turned to Eleazar and said, "'Caput' is the Latin word for 'head.' I give up. Aulus, we would rather face our wives than listen to any more of your bad punning."

"Speak for yourself," Eleazar said.

Brita approached the men, smiling slightly at the giggling Aulus, and said, "May I serve you anything else?"

Judah and Eleazar had been drawn, in spite of themselves, into Aulus' laughter, and they had trouble keeping their faces straight as they watched their Roman friend. Judah, however, lost his humor and became nervous. Sweat stood on his forehead and he did not know what to do with his hands. They flapped uselessly at his sides, ventured up to his face, and finally, settled into an awkward fold at his chest. He felt Eleazar watching him with intense satisfaction.

"Master!" Brita's tone was rather sharp for that of a slave. "I think these men deserve more than silly laughter from you. Judah the Maccabee and his brother are important warriors, now. You must treat them so."

Judah turned toward the slave in surprise. As always, when Brita's true persona emerged from that of a slave, he thought uncomfortably about his wife and realized the stirrings he now felt should be reserved for Miriam. He stammered, "Thank you for the hospitality of your camp. We must leave."

"Not I," Eleazar said, settling himself on a stool, and accepting an excellent joint of lamb from Brita. "I want to stay for a while."

"No, Eleazar," Judah said through gritted teeth. "Now!"

"Oh, very well. May I take this?" Eleazar held up the lamb.

Brita's bow and smile indicated, Of course!

As Judah retreated, he heard Aulus say as he tore at his joint of lamb, "That boy needs a break from his wife. You really do bring out the worst in him!"

"Master, I do not know what you mean. Bring out the worst in whom?"

Judah turned around to grab Eleazar by the bicep to hurry him along, and as he did so, he saw Brita smile.

Chapter Forty-nine

Antioch, Syria   The 8th day of *Tammuz* 3594 (June 31st 166 B.C.E.)

G orgias' tone indicated it was more of a statement than a question. "So, you did not accompany Seron to Judaea?"

General Nicanor decided he could answer Gorgias' question. Nicanor's dislike of Seron was no mystery to those of Antiochus' court. Nevertheless, the question bored him, almost as much as the banquet itself. The night lamps and braziers had been lit and even stoked once. He looked in real earnest at the gilded door that led out to the street.

"No, I was able to make excuse to go later, thank all the gods at once," Nicanor said. He tried to make himself comfortable but found it rather difficult, given all the erotic activity in the dining area. A slave helped him to plump up the pillows to ease his back, but he waved her away when she deliberately dangled her breasts in his face.

General Nicanor found the forays into Gorgias' estate more and more tiresome. These events were nothing short of rampant orgies, thinly disguised as banquets. Gorgias was always sly when he invited Nicanor to one of his so-called "strategy meetings." He would couch the invitation as "talk, with a little dinner on the side." Nicanor was sure that Gorgias enjoyed watching him squirm when the courtesans and prostitutes invariably entered the dining hall and began their lewd gyrations. And, Nicanor could not help but feel that his dignity diminished with each new ruse that Gorgias used to get him to attend these "meetings."

"Well, it will not happen, again," Nicanor mumbled at the leg of mutton that he held poised at his mouth. At least the food was unsurpassed. Perhaps that was why he allowed himself to be tricked again and again. It certainly was not the whores and their activities. Nicanor never had enjoyed the distasteful oriental proclivity for mixing sex and food. And he happened to follow the old values of morality, out-of-date though they seemed during the reign of Antiochus IV. The honor of staying true to one woman appealed to him. He did not care that Diana was aging. Having only one consort kept things uncomplicated. Not only that, but he was aging as well. Watching all the prurient exertions around him did not arouse him, it only made him feel tired and old.

"I am sure that he has arrived by now," Gorgias said as he watched a lithesome dancer.

"Who?" Nicanor asked, disinterested.

"Seron. General Seron." Gorgias said.

"Why your sudden interest in that little pomegranate in Judaea?" Nicanor asked. "He has gone back to CoeleSyria where he belongs, for all that he wanted to go east with the emperor looking for treasure in the temples of Parthia. Actually, I was getting to the point of feeling sorry for him—he was the butt of virtually every joke of our divine emperor while he was here in the palace."

"Well," Gorgias said, "Seron has a new plan to attract the attention of our divine emperor."

"What 'new' plan could he have?" Nicanor asked. "He does not rely on strategy. He relies upon his looks and gift of banter. He could give the god Hermes a run for his money with that glib tongue of his. That is the only reason he has found a spot close to the emperor. He is a good conversationalist."

"I and others actually heard him say that he is planning to engage the Maccabee," Gorgias said and waited for Nicanor's reaction.

"That fruit? Engage the Maccabee?" Nicanor snorted. "Where Apollonius failed, Seron certainly would not succeed." He said into his goblet, snorting again, "Engage the Maccabee, indeed."

"The irony of it all," Gorgias said, "is that all Seron was worried about was Antiochus' opinion of him. It made me weary to watch him, as he bowed and dipped to every whim of the emperor's. And, he exhausted me with all his questions about Antiochus' likes, dislikes, history, family—both legitimate and illegitimate. He had a singular interest in Antiochis, the emperor's mistress."

"He had better stay away from her," Nicanor said, eyeing his slave, Coriolus, who was skulking in the shadows with the rest of the help. "She does not endure sycophants well, for all that she is one herself."

"What satrapy did our emperor just give her?" Gorgias asked, the gossip seeming to intrigue him almost as much as the lascivious conduct around him. "I heard it was Thapsacus."

"I do not know, but for his safety, it was just as well that Seron departed Antioch. He would not live long if our emperor got wind of his interest in her. Not only that, but if he tries to bring his troops against the rebel in Judaea. . ." Nicanor drained his cup and did not even know how to finish the sentence. He caught the eye of Coriolus again. He inclined his head toward the door. He turned to Gorgias and said, "Well, general, I must away." He rose, easing himself out of the entwining arms of a number of slaves about him. "I have dispatches that I must finish tonight. The courier is due to leave for Parthia at moonrise. And if what you say about Seron is true, I must send a message to Tyre. If that inexperienced lunkhead blunders into another debacle against the rebel, our satrapy in Judaea may not survive."

"Ah, yes," Gorgias said. "And all our planning would be as naught. You may sign my name to the missive, if you wish." He yawned. "I have some reports for the emperor, myself. Thank you for reminding me. But, surely you can stay longer? Have your accountant write the dispatches."

"I thank you for your hospitality, but I must write these missives myself."

"To be sure, to be sure. Well, stay safe in the streets and keep away from the banks of the river. It is running high tonight."

"Long live Antiochus!" Nicanor said and saluted.

"Hail the divine Antiochus," Gorgias returned. "I do not envy Seron, the letter you are about to write," he chuckled and turned to focus on the impossible contortions of two courtesans vying for his attention.

Out on the street, Nicanor waved aside his litter bearers and grumbled, "No, I will walk. I need the fresh air in my face. Coriolus!"

His slave bowed and pointed to two of the largest bearers. Relinquishing the litter to their comrades, they moved to either side of Nicanor to serve as his bodyguard. They had to trot as Nicanor was already on his way to his temporary quarters in Antiochus' palace.

"If I do not get away from here," Nicanor muttered aloud, picking up his skirt to avoid a mound of dung, "I will go as insane as the Emperor. It is time that I return to Apamea."

He thought of his home with its lovely columns and gardens. His wife keeping order, her strident yelling at the slaves, and his heart relaxed. Ever since hearing of the death of his best friend, Apollonius, his chest had felt too tight, as if he were wearing armor forged for one of his sons. He had even consulted with one of the court physicians. The bleedings and incantations had not helped, however, and he found that he was becoming more and more wistful and depressed as his stay in Antioch matured. It was definitely time to leave.

"Apollonius," he said, addressing his dead friend as he often did these days. "I had not realized how important our friendship was until you very selfishly got yourself killed. Was that the office of a friend?" He gently shook his fist at the sky. "And, now you have me talking to myself. I can almost hear your laughter." He sighed. "And killed at the hand of a Jew. What in *Hades'* name were you thinking? Well, old friend, as soon as Gorgias and I have worked out a plan and Antiochus authorizes it, I will on to Judaea to avenge you. I assure you, it will not be that pomegranate Seron who gives you back your honor."

He sighed again. Now would not be a good time to return to Apamea after all. He felt his chest tighten.

Chapter Fifty

Jerusalem, Judaea   The 22nd day of *Tammuz* 3594 (July 15th 166 B.C.E.)

Syrus cursed himself. He should never have tried to negotiate the winding tunnels of the Akra by himself. Now he was lost. The Greek colonel wound around in the maze of limestone, and became dizzy as he passed an annoying infinity of cubicles. A gaudy splash of color assailed him, and the tapestries helped him retrieve his bearings. The anomaly of décor in this labyrinth told him that he was on the third floor of the fortress, the future apartments of Menelaus, the high priest of Jerusalem.

Although the mound of stone had been designed as a fortress, every day it was looking more and more like an opulent palace. Menelaus had stocked much of the third floor with his favorite hangings, couches and sculptures in an attempt to make the Akra as livable as possible. He and the other Jewish collaborators were anticipating the time when they would have to flee to the Greek tower to escape the rebels. The threat of the Maccabee was becoming more palpable, given his victory over Apollonius and the fact that virtually no Greek patrols ventured out of Jerusalem to the North anymore. Menelaus, Nadab and the rest of the Hellenized Jews fully expected Judah and his men to storm Jerusalem at any moment.

Two months before, Syrus had been part of the expedition that Apollonius had taken up north to root out the Maccabee and his rebels. The campaign had not ended well, the rebels having virtually butchered the entire Greek force after ambushing them at the bottom of a defile. Apollonius himself had not survived.

During the campaign, General Timotheus, a subcommander under Apollonius, had been relegated to the rear of the march because of his incompetence in previous dealings with the Maccabee, and that was the only reason he survived. The general, along with Syrus and about ninety others, fled the defile back to Jerusalem. There, Timotheus spun lies about Apollonius' handling of the affairs and succeeded in vaunting himself to his superiors, saying that he had tried to temper Apollonius' commands that had led to the massacre.

Although Syrus knew the truth about the debacle, that it was an honest mistake of Apollonius' that led the troops into the defile and that Timotheus had not uttered a word of suggestion about it to Apollonius, he was ordered by Timotheus to go along with his lies or suffer the consequences of demotion, or worse.

Syrus picked up a little statue of Ashtaroth, the fertility goddess. Her grotesque anatomy was comforting somehow, and it was not difficult for Syrus to understand why Menelaus, a Jew, had brought her along to these Spartan quarters. He still shrugged at the high priest's notion that the Greek compound was in danger. Syrus and the other Greeks of the palace guard did not share the collaborator's terror of the Maccabee. Although they had seen the massacre firsthand, the they still thought Judah's victory was a matter of luck.

Anyone can be ambushed, Syrus thought as he approached one of the tapestries and inspected it with the tips of his fingers. Its fine, deep nap spoke of the fabric's expense, but its subject matter did not speak to the religion of its owner, the high priest. Syrus laughed when he stepped back to pull in the full story of the tapestry: the image was a familiar one, Hercules subduing the Caledonian Boar. It was hardly a Jewish theme, especially given the Jews' revulsion at any depiction of human or animal form in art, not to mention their strictures against swine's flesh. At times, he forgot that Menelaus was a Jew, so steeped in Greek ways was the high priest.

"Exquisite, is it not?"

Syrus nodded, recognizing the voice of Nadab, Menelaus' advisor. "It is, indeed. An interesting choice for Menelaus' new quarters. Whom does the boar and Hercules represent?"

Nadab harrumphed and coughed. "Ah, Colonel. I leave such matters of symbology to my superiors. I really have no opinion. My heritage does not allow for artistic criticism."

"Oh, I think you Jews know more about artistic criticism than you let on," Syrus said, still looking up at the tapestry. "I have studied your *Tanakh* enough to see that your Hebrew god is extremely interested in the arts."

Nadab sat on one of the couches and said, "Enlighten me, please. *Tanakh* from a Greek point of view. How droll."

"There is no need for sarcasm, advisor," Syrus said. "Your story of David, for instance. Your greatest king is depicted as a fine musician who strummed his lyre to calm his flock of sheep, goats, and, not to mention his predecessor, Saul. Not only that, but he was a gifted dancer as well. In fact, he danced with such wild abandon that his wife upbraided him for his exhibitionism. No, you Jews are well steeped in the arts. Then there is. . ."

"Yes, yes, Colonel. I am sure you could quote my scriptures to me all day," Nadab said impatiently. "Answer your own question. Whom do you see in that tapestry?"

"I think Hercules has a noble face—the resemblance to our divine emperor is uncanny," Syrus said thoughtfully. "And that boar has the snout of a Jew: an obvious representation of the rebel, Judah the Maccabee."

"An interesting observation," Nadab said, slight irritation in his voice.

Syrus knew the Jew felt little affinity for his natal race as he claimed to be more Greek than Jew, but decided to goad him anyway. "I think the symbolism of our great conflict with the Jews is apt," Syrus went on. "Hercules thoroughly subdued the boar."

Nadab rose from the couch and said, "If I remember the story correctly, Colonel, Hercules eventually let the boar go. But, come! Enough of symbols. Let me show you the rest of the Akra."

"I really must be going, advisor," Syrus said, attempting to skulk back the way he had come. I have a meeting with Timotheus."

"Nonsense." Nadab had Syrus by the elbow and was guiding him toward the outside turret. "You must see the view of the city from the tower. Come on, then—up these stairs."

Nadab's push could just as well have been the emptying of a water gourd over Syrus head. Sweat cascaded from the Greek's brow as Nadab led him up the stairs and teetered him near the edge of one of the stone parapets of the Akra.

"Is not that vista incredible?" Nadab asked the dripping Nadab. "I swear there is not a view like it in all Judaea."

By now Syrus' phobia had drained all the blood from his head. His mouth was dry, and he could not feel his feet. "Yes," he whispered. "It is a veritable feast for the eyes." He reeled slightly. "May we descend, now?"

"Why, of course, Colonel." Nadab seemed to be enjoying himself.

The look of enjoyment on the advisor's face was not lost on Syrus, for all his weakness, and he hoped that if the Maccabee did storm Jerusalem, Nadab would be the first collaborator fed to the rebel leader.

Nadab led Syrus down the turret stairs, through the interior maze, and down the three flights from Menelaus' new quarters to ground level. When they emerged at the base of the tower, Nadab struck up an amiable conversation about future Greek doings in an obvious ploy to get Syrus' mind away from his phobia. Syrus hated that Nadab had seen his weakness of heights. He was sure that the advisor had tricked Syrus up the turret to gather information about him. A sycophant's business is to know the weaknesses of his associates, friend and enemy alike.

"Word is Governor Seron returned from Antioch last week," Nadab said innocently, but Syrus could see him straining to hear what tone Syrus' reply would take.

Syrus made him wait, staying silent for many moments.

"Yes, that is right. The governor has returned," Syrus said carefully.

Nadab asked, "Should we expect a visit from him?"

Syrus could not restrain himself from peering at Nadab. "Why do you ask?" He was indeed aware that Seron was planning a visit to Jerusalem, but how did this Jew know?

Nadab answered, "Oh, I just heard that the governor wanted to come to Jerusalem. Did I hear that he was bringing fresh troops? Perhaps his Thracian mercenaries," he said, almost to himself in an obvious attempt to achieve more nonchalance in the face of Syrus' increasing agitation. "I wonder how his semi-heavies will perform against the Maccabee?"

Now, Syrus could not keep from sputtering. "How can you know this? That is highly classified information!"

"Commander Syrus," Nadab said patiently. "I am simply doing my job. It is in my interest to know what the Greeks are doing so I can tell my superior, Menelaus. I would rather get all my information from you and your other commanders, but I cannot always rely on your—shall we say—cooperation? Now please do not be coy. If the governor is coming, we must prepare. The logistics of housing the governor of CoeleSyria and his troops can be somewhat daunting if we are not ready for them."

Nadab stopped walking, for he was a few cubits ahead of Syrus, whose astonishment left him standing in the middle of the exercise yard. Just the day before, Syrus had been in a meeting where Timotheus and Philo engaged in an hour-long rant about Seron's designs on their command and territory. They called Seron an upstart and a bloody neophyte, among other things, saying that someone of his inexperience was fit to do nothing but kiss Antiochus' arse, which had been exactly what he had been doing up in Antioch for so long.

"Well, Colonel?" Nadab said politely. "What can you tell me?"

"Oh, all right," Syrus snapped. "He is coming."

"I would think that you would be happy for the help. Perhaps more numbers would be efficient against the Maccabee."

"Seron has made it clear that he does not want any of our troops helping him. He wants to use only his Thracians."

"I see, I see," muttered Nadab. "Come in out of the sun. We must talk."

Nadab guided Syrus up through the corridors of Menelaus' palace to his own office, seating Syrus well away from the window and balcony that looked over the barracks.

"Janus!" Bring some cold honeyed mead for the colonel. Now, commander Syrus, why are you and your superiors so upset at this Seron's encroachment?"

"How would you like it if someone moved in on your territory, advisor?"

"Indeed," Nadab said, "I would not like it much, but if this someone were my intellectual or, in your case, military inferior, as this Seron seems to be, I would not worry."

"Why, in the names of the gods?" Syrus asked, taking a goblet from Janus.

Nadab accepted his goblet and looked thoughtful. "I remember once, one of my assistants tried to depose me by sidling up to Menelaus. I saw his intentions from a furlong off. So, I stepped aside."

"You stepped aside?" Syrus said, incredulous. "I would not step aside. I would break his head. Anyway," he said after draining his cup. "Why are you telling me all this? I am less than interested in your little court intrigues."

"Hear me out, Colonel Syrus. This assistant had certain foibles that I knew would be his undoing. Specifically, he was given to interrupting in conversations and was also arrogant. Yes, I know everyone in a political or even a command position needs a certain amount of arrogance, but this chap's arrogance would not allow him to follow instructions or even listen to them. And, I was right, I had to do nothing to undo him." He turned thoughtful. "Well, almost nothing. He undid himself. Menelaus eventually not only fired him but exiled him as well."

Syrus considered this but said nothing.

Nadab went on. "So, what if this Seron comes down from his satrapy and engages the Maccabee? That will save your Jerusalem troops for a future sortie and will likely be his undoing. And, Antiochus will blame him, not the Jerusalem garrison. He is no Apollonius, and we know how Apollonius fared against the rebels." At Syrus' glare, he amended, "Fluke that it was."

After leaving Nadab's office, Syrus stood out in the barracks yard and took a moment to survey the Akra from a safe distance. The tower that had been commissioned by Nicanor and Apollonius to give the Greeks a healthy vantage from which to observe the Jews overlooked the temple and the Jewish quarter. Although it was built as a monument to the Greek superiority over the Jews, Menelaus, acting like a scared chicken, was adopting a siege mentality by moving all his belongings into the fortress. And now, that he, Syrus, a commander of a Greek cohort was taking advice from a Jew about handling a Greek governor was not a good sign.

"And my wishing for Seron's failure is not a good sign, either," Syrus said as he trudged off to his barracks.

Chapter Fifty-one

Tyre, Capital of Coelesyria/Phoenicia   The 22nd day of *Tammuz* 3594 (July 15th 166 B.C.E.)

G eneral Seron shook his head with relief. "Thank the gods, the old warhorse did not accompany me home," Governor Seron said aloud. The gulls overhead screeched as if affirming his relief, and he smiled. He did not know how he would have survived Nicanor's sullen company and his occasional and unwelcome advice on the Jews. When Nicanor had begged off Antiochus' command that he return to Judaea with Seron, saying that his and Gorgias' time could be better spent planning their own campaign against the Jews, Seron's feeling were not hurt. This way, the glory of a victory against the Jew rebel would be all his.

He had big plans for this Maccabee. It was true that he did not have a mandate from the emperor to act against the Jews, but he was sure that Antiochus would not mind if he brought his Thracians against the rebel—that is, if he won. He planned to sail with his troops within the week. Timotheus and Philo, the commanders of the Jerusalem cohorts, had been notified and would be expecting them.

A wind drove a blast of spray up over the barnacled dock and pilings, and Seron and his men moved away from the explosion of water. As they walked toward the fish market, a vendor approached the governor and his men. He was brutally pushed aside by Seron's adjutants.

"No, no," Seron admonished his men. "I like those little cakes. Give me a few, Seller.

The vendor happily complied, and Seron and his men moved on. As he ate the cakes, the governor marveled at the smells of the wharf. He could not say that the fresh smells of the ocean conquered the obscene wafts of rot and disease that lingered on and around this pier, but his senses still reveled in the wisps of ocean air that trailed in from the sea.

Antioch had its pleasures, but was an inland city, unlike his beloved Tyre. Seron was a creature of the ocean. The striped sails of the Phoenician schooners billowed with the wind and when he stopped as one sailed out of the harbor, his heart was one with its canvas—even more so when he recognized it as one of his own trade fleet. He tried to remember which cargo was on that ship. He liked to keep an accounting of all the comings and goings of his ships and their cargoes in his head, but now there were too many of them. In fact, the prodigious number of his fleet had gotten him in trouble with the emperor.

It seemed that a number of his business rivals had not felt the need to kowtow to Governor Seron and complained to Antiochus about Seron's monopoly on the trade out of this harbor. His recent trip to Antioch had been one of damage control, smoothing the matter over with the emperor. In concert with his thoughts, he and his men happened upon a burned-out skeleton of a ship bumping precariously against the dock and tied apart from its whole companions. He kicked at one of its jutting charcoaled boards. That was how he had taken care of at least one of the complainers. Others had been subjected to a brutal interview and had been rather glad that Seron had given them the option to turn their ships over to him in exchange for their lives and that of their families. Seron's heart became a full sail: his fleet was bigger and more lucrative than ever. And, the merchants would not complain to Antiochus again.

Now that he thought of it, the ship that he had just seen out to sea would likely be the last to sail as a merchant for a while. He had had to decommission his merchant ships for a few weeks so he could use them to carry his Thracians down to Jaffa. He was looking forward to the trip, not only for the sea voyage, but also in anticipation of the fight. His men were itching to get at the Jews, and most were already packed, their armor and weapons primed and polished for the trip.

The Jews had encountered a number of his troops before. Apollonius, during his many subjugations of Jerusalem, had requested that Seron send some of his Thracians down to deal with the insurgent riots that culminated with his notorious and effective Parade of Death, where Apollonius' phalangites skewered thousands of Jews with their pikes. With their broad, honed *rhomphaia*, the long sword that the Thracians favored, they were a great help to Apollonius in clearing the streets of rabble during those difficult months. Jerusalem itself was quiet at the moment, but Seron had heard that the collaborator populace was becoming extremely nervous at the Maccabee's activities north of Jerusalem. Word was that Philo was sending no more patrols out of Jerusalem, because none came back. It was believed that the Maccabee had such great control of the roads and villages north of the metropolis that no Greek soldier was safe there.

Seron chuckled to himself. A greater opportunity to extol his military acumen had not presented itself in many years since he became governor. His obscurity rankled him, and he was determined to put his name forth so that Antiochus would hold him in the same esteem as Gorgias, Nicanor and even the dead Apollonius. His vanquishing of the Maccabee and his rebels would certainly ensure respect for his name and that of his heirs.

Perhaps he did not have as much experience in battle strategy as Nicanor and the others, but his campaign against the rebel would remedy that.

"Commander Seron."

"Yes, Lieutenant Nilos, what is it?"

"General, there is word of a missive awaiting you at the palace. Shall I send a slave to retrieve it?"

"No, I was about to order us back. Get my horse!"

Seron and his men clattered through the nether streets of Tyre. The port was so central to the empire and indeed, of all nations roundabout that it was almost impossible to distinguish the different cultures that massed in its streets. The city was a shriek of business, hawkers, masons, artisans, prostitutes and clothiers all yelling their wares and bullying their customers until a transaction consummated a deal. It was a difficult city to rule, but lucrative nonetheless, since all these individuals paid a heavy tax to the governor.

Crime was also a huge issue here, especially down by the docks. Piracy, both on the seas and piers, was rampant, and that alone would have kept Seron busy beyond the hours in the day. He was ruthless in the extreme in dealing with these criminals, but wherever he stamped out one felonious dynasty, another three would rise up in its place, just like the Lernaean Hydra.

Before he knew it, a palace slave had his horse by its bridle. His circulating thoughts had carried him home. He walked up the massive steps where another slave took his helmet and cloak. Followed by a cadre a body and house slaves, he found his way to his quarters where his second was waiting.

"Well, we were expecting this, governor," Leonidas said. "I do not even have to read it. Nicanor has gotten wind of our plans."

"Zeus," Seron said wearily and sat down. He allowed his slaves to remove his accoutrements until he was clad only in his tunic then gestured, sending them away. "How could he have found out?

"Well, sir, you were not exactly clandestine in your remarks about the Maccabee while in Antioch," Leonidas said, aiding the governor with removing his wrist bands. "I think you were rather open with Gorgias, in fact, about your intentions to take your Thracians to deal with the rebellion."

"Damn him to Hades! I did not think he would noise it about and tell Nicanor."

Leonidas' silence indicated that, for all that he was Seron's brother-in-law, he knew better than to point out his obvious foolishness. He simply smiled.

"All right, wipe that smile off your face," Seron snapped, "and let me read the letter."

"Very well. Here it is."

General Nicanor to His Most Excellent Governor Seron

Hail to Our Divine Antiochus Epiphanes, beloved of Zeus.Greetings.If it is well with you, so we wish.Regarding the Jewish rebellion in northern Judaea, you are to take no action.

Hail to Antiochus.

"Concise old brute, is he not? Not even an expression of his tender regard." Leonidas said, picking the note up from the ground from where Seron had tossed it after crumpling the parchment. He smoothed it out, laughing. "He knew your exact plan. What are you going to do?"

Seron stood up and wandered to a window. He pounded the stone lintel once and let his hand rest against its cool surface. "Disregard the message, of course," he said.

"You cannot! It came by special courier from the Royal Court of Antioch, itself. You dare not disregard it."

"I have come too far to let an old, tired infantryman like Nicanor tell me what to do. We shall sail for Judaea with the first tide. A victory," he said as he tore up the missive, "will keep me out of trouble."

"Then you had better make daily sacrifice to Ares, for I hear that the Jews are a hard lot."

"Not against my Thracians. The *rhomphaia* of my Thracians will cut them to ribbons."

"I am sure that Apollonius said something like that before he went against the Maccabee,"

Ignoring him, Seron opened a small teak box inlaid with gold that one of his slaves had placed on his desk "What is this? Ah, it is from Menelaus."

"The high priest of Jerusalem?" Leonidas asked.

"The very same. Ah, an alabaster urn." He uncorked the stopper and smelled the contents. "Frankincense from South Arabia."

"That is expensive stuff!" Leonidas said, carefully taking the urn from Seron and sniffing it. "Whew, but why?" He made a face and gave it back to his brother-in-law.

"There is more where that came from, dear brother, especially if I can defeat the Maccabee," Seron said, placing the urn on his desk. "I hear Menelaus is especially keen to keep him at bay. He is truly frightened of him. Collaborators are often the first to feel the steel of those against whom they collaborated. Did you know that the Maccabee and his rebels are actually usurping our trade commerce in northern Judaea? If I can gain those trade routes back, the gratitude of the powers, both commercial and political, will be immense."

"Well, when the gratitude starts rolling in, ask for something besides Arabian Frankincense. That is a nasty smell."

"Perhaps you should cultivate your tastes. You are in the minority as to your dislike of the fragrance of frankincense."

"As you are in the minority about your favorable chances with the Maccabee—"

"Keep talking if you want a demotion."

Leonidas kept silent.

Chapter Fifty-two

A ulus said, "Again I say, Brita. Judah needs you. His wife is becoming ever more shrewish."

"Master, Jews do not think that way. They are true to their wives. Or they are stoned by their village."

"Nonsense. I know of quite a few, even up here, who are getting away with it," Aulus said. "Here, help me with these greaves. I have got to get this strap repaired."

As Brita helped Aulus with the strap, she said, "I wonder that she is not with child, yet."

"Oh, so the stoic little German *is* thinking about the Maccabee." Aulus pulled at her braid and laughed. "I knew it."

"I was not thinking about Judah. I was thinking about his wife," Brita said and added under her breath, "If you would listen."

"I heard that," Aulus said good-naturedly. "And, the talk around camp is that she is barren. Perhaps you could provide him with a child. Some sturdy, good German stock is just what this race of Jews needs. Your child would rule Judaea, you know. Ouch!"

Brita said, "There, master. The greave is snug, but I do not know if it will hold. If you can leave it here for the day, I can repair it or even have the tanner look at it."

"Not today," Aulus said, patting the greave against his shin. "I am sparring with Judah and he is becoming too formidable, even with the *rudis,* for any part of me to go unarmored against him."

"If he hits that greave, even with a wooden sparring sword, it may fall off," Brita persisted.

Aulus took her chin in his hand and said, "Let me worry about that, little German. You just worry about my dinner. I will take lunch at Judah's fire. Make a stew of that venison Judah brought us last night. Have you finished dressing it? I have not had your stew for a long time."

"No one has brought me a deer for a long time."

"Yes, I must thank Judah for that. I wonder why he brought that deer to our camp?"

Brita folded her arms and shrugged slightly. "Because he knows you like venison, master." But she smiled.

Aulus bellowed his huge laugh. "You know what you are about, my girl. Keep it up and you will mother an heir to the throne of David."

"I do not know much about Jewish observance, master, but I do know they would call that blasphemy. And, I know Judah looks at me, sometimes, but I also know that Judah would never be untrue to Miriam."

Aulus scoffed. "How do you know that?"

Brita said, simply, "Because he is the Maccabee."

Aulus patted Brita, grabbed his *rudis* and trotted off toward the command tent. She watched him go and set about to gutting the deer. Expertly she skinned and quartered the animal, stoking the fire while she did so to make ready for the stew. She was surprised that all these rustic duties such as preparing a deer came so easily to her. Perhaps the collective knowledge of her ancestors to the north was responsible. She had always been a house slave for the Auli Roman family, but she had never felt so in her element as here in this camp. She was also surprised that she had to interrupt her gory task of cutting up the deer by intermittent weeping.

She sat back on her haunches and tried to control herself. Why weep? There was no help for her feelings about Judah. When Aulus took her in the night, it was always Judah's face that she saw, his arms that she felt. Her love for Judah was as her servitude to Aulus, something that had to be borne, a reality that had to be endured.

She turned to the flank of the deer, and peeled and cut until she had a number of long filets. She carefully hung them over the wooden rack so they would dry into the thin dry strips that the men liked to devour on the march. They would not take long to dry as the sun was an excellent oven this time of year.

It took her the entire day to shred and prepare the deer, quarter by quarter and as the sun waned, deer meat was arrayed in an orderly scatter around the camp. A shank boiled in one pot, stew in the next, and as she packed the dried meat away in folded layers of homespun, she heard, "I wanted you to see what my little German can do with a deer. She really is astounding."

Turning, Brita saw Aulus approaching the camp with Judah the Maccabee. She looked down at her shift. Blood from the deer covered her arms, legs and her tunic was besotted with gore. She patted at the sides of her scalp and groaned, realizing she had forgotten that her hands were red with blood. Now the hair at her temples was streaked with bloody clots.

Faster than thought, she scooped her hands through the water of the cleaning bucket outside their tent and scrubbed her arms, legs and face and now the side strands of hair hanging over her ears. Brita's escape into the tent was so quick, it was as if the spirit of the deer had entered her body.

* * * * *

"Ah, the stew," Aulus said, sniffing in appreciation. He picked up the ladle that was bobbing with the motion of the water in the pot and suckled a taste. "Try this, you Hebrew lout, and see what you are missing by not having a German wench in your camp.

When Judah saw Brita duck into the tent, he had experienced a mixture of relief and ennui. Perhaps she would remain in the tent to clean up; part of him hoped not. He had seen that she was awash in blood. It made him think of the time that he and his men had slaughtered Timotheus' 200 Greeks in a night ambush. They too, had been drenched so.

He took the ladle from Aulus, tasted and exhaled in appreciation. "How does she do that? I have never tasted its like."

"She is a witch. I have always thought she was of Druid stock," Aulus said, helping himself to one of the wooden bowls that were stacked next to the stew pot.

Judah cocked his head. "What is that? Druid—is that a race of people? I have never heard of it." He held the spoon away from Aulus and retrieved more stew from the pot.

"The northern countries are still a mystery to our republic," Aulus replied, taking another ladle that rested on the fire grate. He shoveled more stew into his mouth. He chewed mightily for a moment, swallowed and said, "However, my father spoke of some scouts who told of seeing strange rituals during a reconnaissance into the northern countries. It seems that those barbarians worship their heathen gods by dancing and copulating among oak trees. They also perform human sacrifice. Something about burning their prisoners alive in huge straw totems."

"It sounds like Judaea under the Canaanites," Judah observed. "Except that they also sacrificed the innocent: they would fry babies in the bronze arms of a burning statue of Moloch."

He and Aulus both shuddered and Aulus said, "It is one thing to punish the criminal and even an enemy, but babies?"

"Leave that stew alone, you two. Let me serve it to you properly. Aulus, for shame! What would your mother say? And, yours, Judah!"

The two men stopped mid-chew and stared at Brita. She had not only cleaned up, but had put on one of her most fetching dresses—a blue *palla* that Aulus had brought her during their recent visit to his parents in Cilicia.

"Not only that, but I am not a Witch. I just know how to cook. Druid, indeed," she scoffed. "Now, sit down and let me serve you properly. I have some bread left over from this morning."

Judah and Aulus obediently sat down on the elegant camp stools that Aulus had rescued from his estate in Modiin before the Greeks ransacked it. Brita gave them clean bowls which they proffered like two chidden little boys. Although they were still squirming under her rebuke, they grinned mischievously at each other from behind the bowls.

"Now, eat like gentlemen," Brita said after carefully ladling the stew into their bowls. "You need to learn decent manners. After all this is over, you will likely be dining with kings, emissaries of kings, and even a queen or two."

At that, Judah and Aulus spewed the contents of their mouths, letting go of their laughter.

Brita stood, arms folded and said, "It is true. You must stop eating like hooligans around a campfire and learn to be more refined." When their laughter escalated, she unfolded her arms and walked over to the entrance to the tent.

Judah and Aulus, having sparred and trained all day, were happy for the mindless relief of laughter. Interspersed with their shouts of mirth, they joked with each other.

"You are going to be dining with a King!" Aulus said, pushing Judah.

"And, you will be consorting with a queen!" Judah retorted, slapping Aulus on the side of his head.

They carried on thus for a moment or two, but soon realized that they were hot, sweaty and ravenously hungry, so they soon returned to their bowls of stew, still chuckling into the broth.

They were unprepared for the onslaught of water that cascaded over their heads the very next moment. Since the contents came from the bucket in which Brita had washed herself, the water was very bloody.

As one they came up, sputtering and choking. Brita had disappeared into the tent. When she emerged a few seconds later, the blue *palla* was gone and she was again clad in one of her rough tunics that she usually wore around camp. Her hair, which had been smoothed and coifed into a braid, was still in the braid, but loose in flighty tendrils about her scalp from yanking the *palla* over her head. The men, wet and chastened, dropped their eyes under her stony stare that preceded her stalk out of the camp.

Judah and Aulus watched the jerking gait of the offended young woman for a moment as she disappeared into the scrub. After noting each others appearance, they collapsed again, and their laughter filled the camp. The battle-hardened lion of the rebellion, however, did not roar as loud as the Roman.

213

Chapter Fifty-three

Jerusalem, Judaea   The 4th day of *Av* 3594 (July 26th 166 B.C.E.)

P hilo confirmed, "So, you have been commissioned to march against the Maccabee?" As he sat next to Seron, as he nodded at the Thracian color guard parading past the dais upon which the generals sat. The rest of the Thracians, a magnificent force with their *rhomphaia* held aloft in salute, followed the color guard in impressive precision.

Seron stood when his Thracians marched past and held his arm in a high salute. "Yes, Commander Nicanor commissioned me, himself," he lied.

"Hmmm, interesting," Philo looked thoughtful. "I thought he and Gorgias were putting together a battle plan for the Maccabee, themselves." He looked askance at Seron. "But Nicanor's commission is a coup for you, Seron. Congratulations."

His dubious look was not lost on Seron and he worried, but only for a moment. The lie would not matter if he were triumphant over the Jewish rebels. And, he had no intention of failing.

After the parade, Seron and Philo lounged under a canopy in the barracks yard. It had been beautifully stocked with Greek delicacies of all kinds. Cunning little pastries with a million layers of crust, skewers of lamb, pork pies, dates, olive paté, and countless exotic fruits and vegetables, in or out of season, it did not matter. The disruption of the trade routes up north had made it difficult to manipulate the seasons, but not impossible.

As the command elite mingled around the banquet tables, a herald announced the arrival of the high priest of Jerusalem. Menelaus and his entourage entered the shade with great pomp and he at once bustled up to Seron and bowed.

"I am greatly honored to have the great Seron here at last. I trust you received my gift?"

Seron looked at the Jew with great amusement. "Yes, Excellency. It was an exquisite offering." He turned to Philo and said, "A box of Arabian Frankincense. Very fragrant. A fine gift."

"Nothing is too good for the man who will finally rid us of the Maccabee."

"Word certainly travels quickly," said Philo. "I wonder how it is the high priest knows of your plan. Will that not diminish the surprise of your attack?"

Seron watched confusion fill Menelaus's face as he turned to his advisor, a foppish Jew who took great care to look Greek from the toes of his expensive shoes to his carefully coifed beard.

"I believe what the high priest is trying to say," The fop said carefully, "is why else would the great General Seron grace Jerusalem with a visit, if it were not to engage the Maccabee? I assure you that we have not heard any concrete plans to that effect."

Menelaus seemed to see the route, circuitous though it was, that his advisor was attempting to navigate to cover up his faux pas and said, "Well, of course not. What can we Jews know of Greek battle strategy? If I misspoke, please forgive me."

Seron saw that Philo did not look convinced, but he said only, "Yes, of course. It must have been a lucky guess." He held up a goblet. "Well, success to our noble Governor Seron. May he enjoy total victory over the Maccabee." His voice rose. "An end to rebellion!"

The tent echoed his toast, and the celebrants drank to the words in real earnest, and Seron, imbued with the warmth of his cup, happily offered another toast. "To Antioch and Antiochus!"

The room drank again, the enthusiasm dimmed somewhat.

Chapter Fifty-four

T he gatherings were a sad affair, now. Where Ephraim's aunt and uncle's house once had teemed with friends, good food and banter, now it was only a faded notion of that happy time.

That Aunt Magda and Uncle Avram were still alive was simply a matter of kismet. When it had come time those months ago for them to leave for the caves with Ephraim, his friend Hezekiah and his family and the others, Uncle Avram had taken ill and could not travel. Although he had almost died with the flux that worried his body for nigh to six weeks, the fact that he was not in the Kidron caves when the Greeks launched their bloody massacre enabled him now to sit with Ephraim and their few remaining wisps of friends.

They were mostly old. Ephraim was the youngest by far. All those who had been near his age and younger had been butchered by the Greeks that day.

Deborah. Ephraim's betrothed had also died in horrible manner at his own hand. He shook himself to banish the unspeakable image and attended to his uncle who was speaking.

". . .to the north, the Maccabee is gathering more and more to his army. It is said that of fighting men, he has almost 5,000 trained and ready to engage the Greeks."

"And, I have heard that it is but 1,000 that are of any use in the fight," his neighbor Yitzhak said. "Most of the refugees are only good with a plough or a scythe."

"A scythe will cut down a Greek as well as any sword." His Uncle Avram retorted.

As the old men argued back and forth, Ephraim found his mind wandering back to the cave. He had found such happiness there. And, untold horror. Deborah. He groaned within himself and struggled to his feet.

"Uncle."

The old men's discussion parted for Ephraim and he said, "I am sorry to have to leave so abruptly, but I have an errand to perform before nightfall."

Avram said gently, "What is so important that you must brave the streets? There has been a new crackdown with all the insurgent activity." He turned to Yitzhak, and said, "The rebels have emboldened our insurgents. They grow more courageous with tales of the Maccabee's victories."

This started a new discussion and Ephraim, rather than interrupting again, slipped out of the house.

It was a little more difficult for Ephraim to gather information for Judah nowadays. He no longer had access to Nadab, the advisor to High Priest Menelaus, and therefore lacked the wonderful conduit of information of he had enjoyed in previous months. In fact, he had to make sure he avoided Nadab. His unceremonious disappearance before Apollonius' assault on Gophna had undoubtedly confirmed Ephraim's leanings. Nadab's suspicion would have been well-placed since Ephraim had indeed fled north to warn Judah about that very assault. And, since that battle ended with the routing of Apollonius' Greek army, he supposed that his name must be rather infamous within the hierarchy of the Greeks and their collaborators. His uncle Avram's worry about the danger for Jews in the streets was an understatement as far as Ephraim was concerned. He was sure that any Greek patrol that caught him and confirmed his identity as a spy would be greatly rewarded. And, his death would not be a quick one.

Ephraim shivered though the night was warm. He still had to gather information, and the best reservoir for hearsay about Greek movement was located in one of the grossest nether regions of Jerusalem: Brothel Row. But first, he must change.

If Uncle Avram knew how deeply embedded Ephraim was in insurgent circles, he would be shocked. Ephraim appeared to him as sedate as ever; however, his nephew was famous among the Jerusalem rebels. Their furor was being suckled on Ephraim's tales of the Maccabee. It was at one of their safe houses that he knocked now.

A thin, pinched face appeared from behind a cracked door.

"Eleventh Horn," Ephraim whispered, and the door opened.

A candle on the verge of a death gutter did not offer much light to the room, and Ephraim squinted. An empty chair had been pulled back from a rough-hewn table. Upon the table was a ratty scroll. The man who had opened the door for Ephraim sat down and peered at the parchment.

"Where is everybody?" Ephraim asked.

Issachar shrugged his thin frame and said, "Jeremiah said something about a raid, but I did not pay attention. Have you learned anything?"

"There are rumblings about a Greek general arriving in the city, but that is all I know. I need my Greek clothing."

"You are going there, again? I wonder if the danger of frequenting that place is worth the little information you glean?"

"Izzy, do not worry. I am careful—oh, you are talking about spiritual danger." Ephraim smiled. He enjoyed ribbing the conservative Issachar, a scholar who reminded him very much of Judah's brother, Yehonatan. This was why Issachar did not go out often on raids, opting rather to man this hideout. He was not given to physical pursuits and his brawnier comrades often joked that the clumsy Issachar on a raid was more valuable to the Greeks than to the great Maccabee.

"Well, those women are a temptation!" Issachar warned, his face twisted in earnest revulsion.

Ephraim laughed. "Not those women, I can assure you. They are not like the beautiful temple whores—oh, really, Issachar!"

Ephraim marveled that Issachar could still put up his hand to ward off the evil eye at the mention of whores. The young scholar had seen his sister raped, his mother and little brother hurled off the walls of Jerusalem and his father impaled during Apollonius' parade of death. Even after all that, he seemed to clutch at the Law, finding comfort in its yods and tittles and expressing his righteous indignation at foul language and other what Ephraim thought were minor infractions of the law. But then, Issachar was of the tribe of Levi, the keepers of the law and the administrators of the temple compound. Not that Issachar and his male relatives who were alive frequented the temple anymore. After the defilement, no observant member of Levi would step foot upon the holy ground of the mount.

"It is not necessary for you to speak thus," Issachar said, his tone still admonitory as he helped Ephraim into the fine Greek robes. "I understand what you are doing and that spies are necessary—our history is full of spies—but you can still show a little decorum."

"Decorum is at a high premium when the Greeks are trying to wipe us out as a race. Counting one's footfalls on the Shabbat does not seem so important, anymore."

"Oh, be serious, will you? You are descending into Satan's maw, soon. You should be frightened."

Ephraim put his hand on Issachar's arm. "I am sorry if I am distressing you. Yes, I am worried. I worry whenever I have to go among the collaborators. If anyone from Menelaus' court recognizes this face, it will not go well for me. I will become Greek fodder, as so many of us before have done. But, I must find out what form the next assault will take, and this is the only way. I thank you for your concern—now help me with this accursed diadem."

Ephraim had let his hair grow out and clipped his beard as closely to the Greek style as he dared. He and Issachar arranged his hair about the golden circlet in the trend that was now the rage among the Hellenized youth.

"Very fetching, if I may say," Issachar said.

"Thank you. A joke. Izzy, there is hope for you, yet," Ephraim said. "I will probably not be back until dawn."

"Please be careful," Issachar said. "We do not have enough spies to spare you."

"*You* can replace me," Ephraim said, enjoying the shock, then churlish recovery on Issachar's face as Ephraim and his robes flowed out into the street.

Dusk was deepening and as he rounded through the Jerusalem maze toward Brothel Row, more people and torches lighted the way, for this was a nocturnal haunt. Ephraim felt he should have dreaded his visits here, but he found that impossible. It was the same sensation he felt when he had earlier inculcated himself into Nadab's Greek world. Exotic food, fine wine and opulent clothing suited him more than he like to admit, and he had to consciously revive the image of the bloody aftermath of the caves to stay focused on his mission to defeat the very people with whom now liked to consort. Deborah.

"Saul! I have not seen you for so long!" The young Jew who addressed Ephraim was dressed in like style. He was a thoroughly Hellenized youth, but his build was not that of Ephraim's. His was the body of an athlete who trained regularly in the gymnasium, a gift to the Hellenized Jews of Jerusalem from the high priest Menelaus.

"Hermes! It is good to see you! What is happening tonight at our tavern?" Ephraim did not have to playact. He really was happy to see Hermes.

"We are to be gifted with a musician from Athens. He is supposed to be famous, although I have never heard of him."

"Hermes," Ephraim patted his friend on the shoulder. "You were ever gullible. A famous musician, here? In this backwater? It is not likely."

"Well," Hermes scowled, "he is better than nothing, eh? Come, Lyria asks after you often."

"Lyria?" Ephraim asked uneasily. "Lyria—I don't remember—"

"Sure you do, Saul," Hermes reminded him. "She is the whore who participated in the gala at the temple—now, that is a fine claim to fame. You should be honored at her interest."

Ephraim felt the hair prickle on his neck. She had actually been a part of the "Abomination of Desolation" that was quoted in the new book of Daniel. Various rabbis identified the "abomination" as the temple desecration which Hermes had described as the "gala." The prophecy that had just come to light was a source of great discussion in scholarly circles and yeshivot throughout Judaea.

"Come on!" Hermes led Ephraim into the dank tavern whose entrance was lit by a couple of guttering torches that barely kept their flame as the two men passed.

Ephraim circulated among the patrons of the tavern until late in the morning. Unfortunately, no one was interested in talking political or military gossip. A lewd contest between two of the whores held everyone captive and their minds had no room for any other considerations.

The hour became late enough so that all but the most devoted of revelers went home. The hearth that had been kindled more for ambience than heat—as it was mid-summer—pulsed with a foundering glow that barely made itself known in the dark room. Hermes' cheek lay in what may have been a nice plate of hummus once, but was now a mere crumble on the youth's face as he slumped, doubled over in sleep on the table. Ephraim lay his head down. He was much too tired to try to get back to the safehouse right now. Perhaps he could sleep for just a moment to take the edge off his weariness. He drifted away.

Of a sudden, he was with Deborah in the cave. The wedding *chuppah* domed the two of them and Ephraim heard the wedding blessings being read. Deborah he could see, but no one else. And she was strange. She was not the way he remembered her. The words of the blessings faded, but the Hebrew characters of the blessings hovered before the wedding couple. Ephraim was not part of the couple anymore, but an observer watching apart. *Aleph, Beit, Gimel, Daleth*: the letters flamed into blades that found the bride. Writhing, she sank to the ground. The groom was untouched, but her blood soaked the hem of his garment.

Ephraim felt the blood under his face and his body jerked, but he did not sit up. As he came awake, he discovered that he had fallen asleep on the table and that the moist warmth under his cheek was not blood, but saliva.

He sat up and wiped the drool off, disgusted with himself. All night, as he hobnobbed with these Greeks, he had settled into a mien of superiority. He watched how they consorted with the whores, drank themselves into oblivion and became violent over the most paltry offenses. He had told himself again and again that at least he was of the chosen race with the one true G-d. The dream from which he had just awakened, though, reminded him that he was more human, more debauched than they: he had murdered his beloved. It did not matter that he did it to interrupt her rape, redeem her honor and save her from torture. The fact remained that he had cleaved Deborah almost in two.

Ephraim struggled off the table and almost vomited when he stood. Hermes, who had awakened from his dish of hummus was been having a quiet conversation with the proprietor. In a drunken glide, he hurried to Ephraim's side to support him.

"Oy, Saul! Too much to drink, again? And, you ignored Lyria, again? Saul, Saul. What am I going to do with you? No satisfaction, only a hangover."

Ephraim felt foolish. He had wasted an entire night and had procured no information that would help Judah. He had learned about the best ales and meads from the Sinai to Dalmatia, and now knew which whores on Brothel Row were the most limber, but still had learned nothing about the Greeks and the general who had just come to town.

Hermes grabbed Ephraim's arm and strung it around his own neck and supported his back with his other arm. "Pollux!" He said to the man who had shared his conversation during Ephraim's nap. We must away. My friend, here, needs to find a bed, and quick. You must tell me more about the gossip over at the barracks. General Seron sounds like he might just rid us of the Maccabee."

Ephraim's mind perked up immediately, but he forced his body to stay slack in Hermes' arms. Here he had wallowed with these Greeks all night to learn something—anything—about the enemy, only to find that Hermes and the proprietor had discussed it in some detail. All while he slept like a drunkard.

Luckily, he was not too drunk to slur, "Seron? Who is this Seron?"

Luckily, Hermes had not tired of the topic.

Chapter Fifty-five

A ulus squinted into the dusty canyon. "Well, you may thank your g-d of no name that Seron is the general that the Greeks chose to send against us, for look!" Judah had been dozing under a cedar tree atop the lookout, but leapt up at Aulus' words and peered at the distant twinkles of Greek shields and pikes. He exhaled in disbelief. "It is Apollonius all over again. They are marching up the pass. They have committed themselves to the defile. Ephraim said that this Seron was ill-esteemed among the Greeks and I can see that is with good reason. The man is an idiot! The Lord of Hosts With Us!"

"Yes," said Aulus. "But our men have been marching all day. They have not eaten."

"What of it?" Judah said, squinting against the haze of the Aijalon valley. "This is the time for battle, not for stuffing their bellies."

After Aulus left, Judah forced himself not to caper with glee. The Lord had burdened these Greeks with a stupidity that he had not heard in all the war stories with which the Auli had schooled him. Even at Thermopylae, Xerxes had used the guile of his spies to find a back way, thus defeating the valiant 300 Spartans from behind. But this Seron seemed to have no plan but a dogged ascent up the most difficult part of the climb.

Asher came puffing up the steep lookout. "Judah. The men are complaining. They want to rest and eat."

"Again with the food," Judah said in exasperation. "The enemy is upon us. There is no time—Oh, never mind. *Ares*, I'll talk to them."

Judah sped to the clearing where the men were sprawled in various poses of rest, taking advantage of every pool of shade they could find. A few rose to their feet at his approach, but most kept to their lounging.

"Get up! Get up, fighters!" Judah shouted. "Ephraim's report was correct! It is as we hoped! Seron, the idiot general, is advancing up the pass, but we must get in position now."

"But, we are tired," One of those from the village of Gezer whined. "And we have not eaten."

"How can we, just a few, fight against so many Greeks?" Another from Beit Ur asked.

Judah seized the first man by the neck of the tunic and raised him up so that his feet dangled. He shook him a few times, clubbed him once across the face and threw him aside. Judah stepped forward and drew his sword. "I will do the same to each one of you if I have to. If that does not work," he brandished the sword, "then I am ready to use this! I am your commander and the time for a fight is upon us. We will not wait for full bellies and a nap."

The fighters scrambled to their feet, never taking their eyes off Judah. The young man from Gezer did the same. One of his friends helped him wipe the blood from his nose and cheek.

"It is easy to deliver many into the hands of few, and there is no difference before Heaven to save us with many or few. For not in a great army is victory in war, but from the Heavens come valor. They come to us full of pride and evil to destroy us and our wives and our children to despoil us. And we fight for our lives and our Law. And He will smite them from before us, and you need not fear them."

"As for their numbers, Ephraim told us that this Seron has brought 6,000 with him. But the Lord of Hosts cares not whether the enemy brings six or 6,000: our victory will come from Him. The Greeks come to us full of pride and evil to destroy us and our wives and our children. We fight for our lives and our Law. The Lord who gave us that Law will smite the enemy from before us! You need not fear them."

The men listened intently to Judah's speech and were silent for many moments. Far at the back, one throat began, then more and more added their voices. Soon, all were as one in their repeated murmur "The Sword of the Lord!"

Judah almost lifted the sword until he remembered the need for silence. He immediately sheathed the weapon and held his arms out, palms down, a desperate signal for quiet. The men understood and their voices ceased at once. Their eyes fixed on something behind Judah. When he turned, he saw that Asher and Aulus had come running, waving their arms, their eyes wild at the intrusive sound of the men's cheers. There were a few chuckles from the warriors at the comical halt of Judah's two commanders when they saw that the unwelcome shouting had stopped.

Judah smiled and said, "Quiet must rule us from now on. I and the faithful will show ourselves at the top of the ridge. The rest of you, archers and slingmen, will hide yourselves in the walls of the ridges and rain upon the enemy on my command. The enemy will be ignorant as to our full complement; that will be their undoing. How convenient of Seron to allow us to use some of the same strategies that we used against Apollonius. The Lord of Hosts With Us!"

The men raised their swords and held them aloft, a silent cheer, until Judah sheathed his *kopis*. As he did so, he patted the scabbard and said, "Perhaps Seron will make a gift to me of his sword as well. I can start a collection."

Stifling their laughs, the men followed Judah, Aulus and Asher, the great bulk of them taking a dry wadi into the larger canyon so their numbers would be hidden from the Greeks.

Chapter Fifty-six

Lower Beit Horon, Judaea   The 9th day of *Av* 3594 (July 31st 166 B.C.E.)

S yrus looked up, his eyes raking the rock face as he and the Thracians approached the steep cleft of Beit Horon. Seron's question interrupted his apprehensive study of the cliff.

"Colonel, what was the scouts' report?"

"General Seron, sir, they report enemy activity at the top of Beit Horon ridge." Syrus was not happy that Philo attached him to Seron's Thracians, but he tried to keep the pique out of his voice. "Sir, I was a survivor of the Jew's ridge assault on Apollonius, and we are walking into the same situation."

Seron was not listening. He was too busy ordering his commanders to halt the march, so he could speak. "Thracians! It is time now to don our armor and hold to our battle formation. I know it is hot and the climb is hard, but you must be protected. That was Apollonius' mistake. He was not ready for the Jews and he paid dearly for that miscalculation." Seron removed his helmet and tousled his neckerchief through his curly hair. "I have twice as many in my assault force as he did, and it looks like the Maccabee is operating with reduced numbers. Perhaps his people tire of the fight, I do not know. But, it looks like we shall overwhelm him with sheer numbers. Not only that, but I doubt the Jews even know we are coming."

Although Syrus was alarmed at the general's complacent assessment, he waited until the speech was finished to address Seron. Syrus said, amazed, "Oh, sir, they know we are here. Their network of scouts is a phenomenal set of eyes and ears for the Maccabee." He looked up the ridge. "Yes, they know."

"Well, no matter," Seron said. "The result will be the same. His annihilation."

"Yes, sir," Syrus said with a dubious look up the climb.

Chapter Fifty-seven

A ntiochus, amazed, asked, "My children killed Seron? How is that possible? It grieves me when my children quarrel."

Teman stood in the entrance of the opulent tent and waited. The take on this movement east for plunder had been very lucrative for the emperor's coffers. Just as he had raided all the golden vessels and fixtures of the Jerusalem temple, he was now stripping every tomb, temple and estate of all that was of value. With the magnificent Seleucid army of Antioch behind him, the local feudal lords and even the king of Parthia were loath to send their men against them.

The statuary that Antiochus and his troops had procured was probably the most impressive of his acquisitions. The Parthian motifs of bulls and lions were well represented here, as well as the god, Ahura, of the Mithraic and Anahita cults. The more familiar pagan gods, Dagon, Baal, Astaroth and even the gods of the Olympic panoply also filled Antiochus' tent. Most were marble, some were alabaster, almost all were inlaid with gems and precious metals. As big as the emperor's tent was, the booty was so tall, wide and deep, that beside it, Antiochus was rendered dwarflike.

The emperor would have cut a comical figure if all of the labor of dragging all these artifacts in and out of the tent at each pause in the march could be forgotten. There was nothing funny about the manpower it took to haul the stuff, then arrange it to the emperor's liking. And Teman had to oversee it. If only he had not murdered Karpos to get his position. Teman wished the old advisor were here at such times to relieve him of this onerous subservience to Antiochus.

At last, the emperor beckoned him in. "So, Teman. Tell me what is afoot in Jerusalem."

The advisor took the proffered seat, an exquisite chair that looked like it came from the mysterious East, where it was said people had freakish eyes. Strange dragons swirled around the enameled legs, the weird combination of red and black creating a stark effect. "Sire, it is the Maccabee. It is all the Maccabee."

"What is 'Maccabee'? A disease? What must we do to rid ourselves of it?"

Teman paused for a moment, weary that he was about to embark on a redundant conversation about the rebel's name. "It is a man, sire. A Jew. He is leading the rebellion against you. He was responsible for defeating Apollonius and now, Seron."

Antiochus held up a parchment. Teman knew what was coming and he steeled himself. It was the missive from Nicanor.

"How is it that an order given by my favorite general is disregarded?" With his finger, Antiochus traced the elegant lines of a dragon embedded in the arm of the chair. "Nicanor reports here that he had sent Seron an order not to engage the rebels. And Seron went ahead? On his own authority? Of which he had none?"

Teman nodded uncomfortably. Although he had nothing whatsoever to do with this failure of command, it was always dangerous to be the bearer of such a debacle to the emperor.

"It would seem so, sire." Teman said, keeping his voice neutral. He did not want the emperor to sense that he was fearful. "However, Seron did pay for his insubordination with his life. Perhaps your brother gods punished him for his insolence. He is in their realm, now."

Antiochus seemed to consider this. He called for a slave. "I hunger. Bring us something to eat. Teman, will you take some food?"

"Thank you, sire. I have not eaten since the dispatches went out this morning."

The slave brought in some of the local Parthian fare: rustic breads, grapes and some strange vegetables he had not seen before. As Antiochus ate, Teman stayed quiet while the emperor held forth on various topics concerning his rule: collecting the tributum for the Romans, keeping various holdings in check and, of course, the Jews, always the Jews.

"So, what does our intelligence tell us about this Maccabee?" Antiochus asked as he tore at the bread. "Why have I not heard of him before?"

"To tell the truth, sire," his name has not come to the forefront until just recently—after Apollonius' defeat," Teman said, watching him eat. Although he had been asked to dine with the emperor, he knew better than to really take him up on the gracious invitation. Antiochus did not like anyone dining with him except for his family, consorts, or chosen individuals like Nicanor or Gorgias. Teman knew he did not fit in this category. "It seems that this Jew rebel is somewhat of a strategist. Seron walked straight into a trap, not unlike Apollonius."

"Tell me about the battle."

"Well, it seems that Seron and his troops misjudged the rebels' numbers," Teman said, doing his best to remember all the details of the courier's report. "Whereas Apollonius was totally blindsided by the Maccabee in Gophna campaign, Seron at least knew the Jew and his men were in the pass waiting for them. What they did not know is that the Maccabee had his primitive slingmen and archers hidden up on either side of the Beit Horon pass. All Seron could see were the Maccabee and his men taunting him at the very top of Upper Beit Horon. Five-hundred of our men were slaughtered in the canyon and the rest when they fled back to their camp that they had established in the Aijalon Valley. Some survived when they were able to get away from the camp, but eight-hundred of Seron's Thracians died."

The emperor sat very still and regarded the skeleton of twigs that had been full of grapes just a moment before. The bread was nothing but a few crumbs on the plate and the vegetables were all but devoured. Teman gazed at the food with disappointment. He had been hoping for a few leavings of the meal after Antiochus had left, but there was not enough left to feed even a mouse.

Antiochus' chin dropped to his chest. All pretence of madness, all pretence of grand nobility stripped from his demeanor. Teman saw with surprise that among the statuary and artifacts sat only a tired, old man. "My kingdom in Judaea is spent. I feel it. My kingdom is spent. And, I—I am spent."

Teman, for the first time, was truly worried. He had never seen Antiochus thus: bereft of virility and hope. At the same time, Antiochus had never seemed more normal and human than at that moment. Teman said, "Sire, the Jews are but a small part of the great kingdom of Seleucia. And, Nicanor and Gorgias will see to their downfall, never fear."

Antiochus turned to Teman. The eyes of the emperor shone with a strange clarity and Teman shrank back. The emperor said with great but quiet force, "No, my great generals will fail in their enterprise against the Jews." He stood and leaned against a particularly garish statue of Zeus, patted its cheek and whispered, "We shall all fail."

The emperor sat down again in the elegant chair and patted the arms, caressing the dragons again. He seemed to recover and some of the old madness and arrogance crept back into his features. "Did any of the Thracians survive?" He asked.

"Some did."

"Send an order back that I want the survivors put to the sword. You say they fled? That is unacceptable behavior when they are up against Jews, for Zeus' sake. I want no more of our forces running away from the Hebrews. You will put that in a missive putting the greatest possible force into your words. Is that clear? Was it one of the Thracians who brought this report back to Jerusalem?"

"No, sire. It was a special attaché who was assigned to the Thracians from the Jerusalem guard. Philo assigned this Colonel Syrus to serve as a liaison between himself and Seron."

"Well, have him put to death, too. One of my royal guard in Jerusalem, fleeing the Jews? I will not have it."

"Yes, Sire. I will see to it."

Teman bowed out of the room, but looked up one more time at the emperor. Again, all he saw was a tired, old man. His neck hair prickling, he scraped his way backward out of the emperor's presence.

The hindquarters of the immense Arabian muscled down the path that led to the well-worn trade route; the courier did not look back at the advisor. Teman marveled that a piece of paper could have the power of death for so many soldiers, soldiers who had spent their lives shedding blood for the empire and in some cases having their blood shed. He wondered if they would mind death any less if it came by the direct command of their emperor, himself. Perhaps they would look at it as the highest honor; perhaps they would feel betrayed. He shrugged and started back to the emperor's tent. He wanted to see if the emperor's needs had been met for the evening, for night was beginning to descend on the camp. He reeled suddenly, and ran back down the path that had been dusted by the courier just a few moments before.

"Zeus, Diana and Hera!" he exclaimed, his harried wave having no effect on the dot that was now merging with the caravan traffic on the road. "I forgot to add the colonel to the order." He chewed his lip for a moment, then shrugged. Commander Syrus, it seemed, would live until Teman could send word with the next courier from Antioch.

Chapter Fifty-eight

N adab said, "Yes, I am sure it was horrible." He was not refilling Syrus' goblet again and again to be polite. The Greek would not have noticed anyway, as he was already starting to slur his words. Keeping one's head free from wine was advisable in most situations, but was not always possible, given the nature of Greek banquet practices. Syrus' unusual drunken ramble was a welcome digression as Nadab had had a long day and did not have the energy to employ his usual art of information gathering. It would be nice for a change to have the intelligence spew forth, even if it was from a drunk.

"Horrible ish not the word," Syrus gabbled. "Beit Horon ish a precipish. A precipish, I tell you." His hands started shaking and he dropped the goblet. A slave stooped to pick it up. Nadab gave a significant nod to the slave, who refilled the cup and guided it back into Syrus' hands. "I am sorry. 'Sank you."

Syrus stared sullenly at his cup for a while. When he did not resume his narrative on the battle, Nadab said, "I hear that Seron did not die well."

Syrus came awake. "No, the fool ran shcreaming down the pash. Rather than drive our fight up to the Jewsh at the top of the pash, he went into full retreat. It was horrible. And I was shtuck up ahead of everyone at the very top of the ridge with the Jewsh shooting arrowsh all around me." The memory was too much and Syrus doubled over and vomited loudly into one of the many buckets that the slaves kept handy for Nadab's banquets. After a slave toweled off Syrus' face, he stared blearily at Nadab and said, "By the time I shtumbled down the path with this—" he raised his slinged arm, "—I came across Seron's body—so many arrows in his back. It was horrible. Horrible."

"Yes, I gather that it was horrible. Well, at least you survived, my friend. Surely that is something."

"Yesh, it is something," Syrus said. "I have survived two notable battles in which most of our forces were deshtroyed. That does not bode well for a promotion, I can tell you."

Syrus struggled up from the couch, reaching for one of Nadab's slaves who helped him to his feet. Another slave came on the other side of the young Greek and supported him while he said his blunt goodbye. They swayed with him to the door where other slaves aided him into a litter.

Nadab followed Syrus and the slaves to the door, pulled one of them aside and said, "Make sure he gets to his bed and that his manservant attends him. I do not want him demoted. He is in enough danger of that already and I need him to stay as high in the Greek ranks as possible."

Nadab clasped his hands and wandered to his sleeping quarters where his wife lounged. Newly arrived from Idumea, Arinya looked up and yawned. "Did the drunk Greek tell you anything? Husband, I did not come back to stay cloistered while you entertain your Greek contacts."

"I am sorry, love," Nadab said. He was happy that his wife had decided on a visit, although this was not the best time for it. He had encouraged her to stay down south with her family because of the danger in the city, and Jerusalem was taking on a siege mentality, many Jerusalemites fleeing its walls. Some were fleeing back to the orthodoxies of their youths, fearing the Maccabee's reprisals against collaborators. Others were crowding into Greek satrapies of the north, much to the dismay of the Macedonians residing there who looked upon the Hellenized Jews as refuse, for all that they had adopted Greek ways.

His wife, although from red Idumea in the south, was well received in the familial hierarchies of Jerusalem Jewry. Her father was a wealthy tradesman whose monies had done much to prop Menelaus into his present situation, and Nadab had counted himself lucky to get a wife so entrenched in the high priest's esteem. Her beauty was unsurpassed as well, her hair as red as the crimson cliffs of her homeland.

"Do you think it is as everyone says?" Arinya asked. "Is the Maccabee really a danger?"

Before Seron's defeat, Nadab would have gainsaid such a notion. Now, however, he was not so confident of the Greeks' ability to stand against the rebel. He did not want to alarm his wife, so he said in a reassuring growl, "No, of course not. Seron was an idiot. Nicanor and Gorgias are not, and they will be the next to engage the Maccabee. The rebel is only good at ambush and surprise. He and his ruffians cannot withstand our phalanx and skirmishers in open battle."

"Yet, he has defeated everything your Greeks have sent against him," Arinya said, pulling her hair away from her face and adjusting it under her veil. "I would like to meet this Maccabee. Word has even reached Idumea of his exploits. He must be quite a man."

"If he does storm Jerusalem, you may have your wish to meet him, but it may not be an agreeable proposition. Remember that the orthodox Jews despise you Idumeans almost more than they do us collaborators and the Greeks themselves. All your wars with them, you know."

"Nonsense," Arinya said. "It is said that the son of one of their great prophets, Yitzhak, founded our nation."

"Yes, but his son Esau, the father of your race, was an outcast in Israel. He did not receive his birthright from Yitzhak. Yacob tricked him out of it with a mess of pottage, if I remember the story correctly."

"We are still blood relations," Arinya persisted. "And I would like to meet him."

"Well, let us hope that you do not get the chance," Nadab said, caressing her. "I would not like to see you dragged out into the streets, hair shorn because you are Idumean and killed because you are married a collaborator. If the Maccabee takes Jerusalem, he will cleanse it of anyone he deems a gentile."

"That will never happen," Arinya said. "The Greeks prize Jerusalem too much to leave it to rebels. Antiochus will send huge reinforcements under Nicanor and Gorgias. I do not know why everyone is so worried."

"Our one chance is Nicanor. The Maccabee, for all his wiles, will not be able to withstand a Greek army under him. The General will also deploy his elephants that he left here. He may even bring more from his farms in Apamea. I have never seen a battle with elephants, but I have read accounts." Nadab's face turned grim. "The Jews will not stand under an onslaught of elephants."

"Not to mention the Greek army in, as you say, 'open battle.'" Arinya said. She put her arms around Nadab's neck. "My husband, you have ever been the pragmatist. You do have an alternative plan, do you not? I mean, in case the rebels do attack Jerusalem."

"My dear," Nadab said, smiling. "Have you ever known me to be without an alternative plan, whatever my circumstances?"

"My little scorpion," Arinya said. "May I know your plan?"

"Why," said Nadab, "to join you in Idumea!"

"Even with my mother there?"

Nadab did not want to get in trouble with a hesitant answer so plunged ahead, "Of course with your mother there. She has ever been good to me. Did she not give me you?"

As Arinya nestled against him, he sighed and thought, General Nicanor, save me from the Maccabee—and more importantly, from my mother-in-law.

Chapter Fifty-nine

Gophna, Judaea   The 12th day of *Elul* 3594 (September 2nd 166 B.C.E.)

B rita liked to sit on the high bluff behind Aulus' camp, where she could safely observe the growing community of Jews. Since Judah's defeat of Seron, more and more refugees added themselves to the congregation of the rebel leader and his faithful. She especially enjoyed watching their more mundane activities. A young mother feeding her child, an old woman milking her scraggly goat, errant boys stoning a pigeon and getting in trouble from the priest, all these small scenes and more entertained her every day when she finished her camp chores.

Most of her time was solitary, except when Aulus was there. He was not a brutal master, but of course was indifferent to her emotions and needs. After all, she was only a slave. Luckily, she was used to emotional solitude and found that her loneliness was comforting in a strange way. She supposed she could allow herself to get with child, but did not feel that it was her right to bring another slave into the world. Her lot was not intolerable, for she had met many slaves with lives more dire than hers. That did not mean she wanted to watch a son or daughter live in servitude. Not only that, she was not sure how Aulus would feel about offspring. If he did not like the idea of siring a possible heir by her, he could force her to expose the child, an easy thing in this wilderness. No, it was better to keep chewing the herbs that kept her from conceiving.

As she watched the camps, it was the collective activity that interested her, not that of individuals, since she liked the idea of watching them in their anonymity. There was one exception: Judah and his wife, Miriam. It was a special day when her voyeurism allowed her a glimpse into their married life. When they wandered into her realm, they showed her a mixture of joy with each other, boredom with their marriage, and on some days, a real, mutual hatred.

Brita, of course, had never been married. Her consorting with Aulus may have been a marriage of sorts, since in many ways wives were no better in their status than slaves, anyway. But, she was mystified by the idea that a man and woman were supposed to be joined to each other and no one else. Not only that, but the union was supposed to last for their entire lives. This mystique was one reason that she enjoyed watching Judah and Miriam so much. The other reason was that she was in love with Judah the Maccabee.

Since she had already come to the conclusion that hers was an impossible love, watching him with Miriam was not as painful as perhaps it should have been. As a result, she started to feel a special kinship with the woman who was Judah's wife. A few months before, she had idly wondered to Aulus why Miriam was not yet with child. After all, she and Judah had been married for eight months. Aulus, of course, had deemed her interest an exhibition of her interest in Judah and had teased her unmercifully. After observing Judah and Miriam from her perch, however, she decided that nothing could be further from the truth. She wanted to help Miriam. This was a marriage into which children should be born. If there were to be a kingdom where the Jews governed themselves, everything could depend on an heir to the Maccabee.

The village had settled into late afternoon, and it was almost time for Aulus to return. She had found some edible roots that she planned to pulse into a mash, and she needed to get them on the boil. She slid down the steep incline of the bluff supporting herself with her strong hands and graduated her descent into a swift run.

Putting the roots into the pot, she went to her tent and out of her pouch pulled out the pocketed leather belt that was filled with her herb collection. Thank the gods she had thought to collect the nettle leaves in early spring. If she had waited until now, when they were dry and brittle, their fertility properties would have been lost. She started another small pot of water and upon its boil, carefully laid the leaves in. She would create a tea for Miriam to drink.

She sat back on her heels. How on earth would she get the tea to Miriam? She was so immersed in her thoughts that she forgot that she had never spoken to the Jewess. Indeed, she did not know if Miriam even knew of her existence. Brita had never ventured into the Jewish camp, keeping herself carefully away. She circulated among the pots, one containing the tea and the other, Aulus' dinner, and stirred them as she thought. She decided she would prepare the tea, and think further about how she would approach Miriam. The tea would still be good tomorrow. She would think on the problem; perhaps something would come to her.

A hand cradled her shoulder and she jumped and swore in the guttural language of her childhood.

"Ha, Brita! It is not often that I can get a rise out of that icy Nordic blood!" Like a boy, Aulus exulted over his feat for a few moments, high-stepping a little jig. He embraced her and asked, peering into one of the kettles, "What is in the pot?" Oh no, not the mash again!"

"Master, it is good for you. You cannot live on meat alone. You must vary your food."

"It is too much trouble in these conditions," Aulus grumbled. "I would rather just grab a piece of dried meat."

"That is why I am here," Brita said. "You would die of starvation if it were up to you to take care of yourself. Now, wash up. It is almost ready."

"What's in this one?" Aulus had moved to the other pot boiling on the fire. He lifted its lid and sniffed, making a face. "Whew! I'm not drinking that! What is it? Tea?"

"Yes," Brita said, bracing herself for a stout lie, but he simply put the lid back on it and looked sadly around camp.

"Is there any beer left?"

"Master, the beer has been gone a long time. You know that."

"A man can dream," Aulus said, wistful.

Yes, one can dream, Brita thought.

Chapter Sixty

Antioch, Syria   The 12th day of *Tishri* 3595 (October 1st 166 B.C.E.)

G orgias asked, "How many elephants do you have in Jerusalem?"
Nicanor did a mental count. "Let me see. Trained and ready?" At Gorgias' nod, he continued, "I have thirty corralled outside the western gate. Under heavy guard," he added. The rebels are putting the squeeze on Jerusalem and I want my children safe. Twenty-five of them are ready to take into battle."

The two generals had hiked to the pinnacle of the stone wall that guarded the southern approach to Antioch. There they could assess the numbers for the march and make sure all the baggage train had been assembled.

Gorgias squinted at the thousands of troops that were bivouacked in the plain below them. "And Apamea?" He asked.

"Apamea counts a herd of fifty-six. Only thirty are fighting males. My roustabouts left a week ago to drive them down to Jerusalem. They will be integrated into the Judaean herd and their training coordinated."

"Why so sad, old friend?" Gorgias asked. "You will see your 'children' as you call them, very soon."

"I would rather drive elephants than these beasts." Nicanor said, gesturing vaguely at the troops and rubbing his beard. "The elephants are smarter and easier to train."

Gorgias laughed. "I knew you were pining for your Jerusalem elephants. You have not seen them for—how long has it been since you were last in Jerusalem?"

"Eight months." Nicanor said. "The last time I saw Apollonius. Oh, you are counting. I will be silent!"

Gorgias grunted, "Oh do not worry! Just let me finish with the flags."

Nicanor watched as Gorgias pointed at each flag as he took inventory of the cohorts.

"All accounted for," he finally said and turned to Nicanor. "We are a little short with our beloved emperor taking so many of the royal cohorts east to Parthia. I hope the treasure hunting is going well," he mumbled, "because we may lose Jerusalem, indeed, all of Judaea, because of Antiochus' privateering."

"What? What was that?" Nicanor said, who had sunk back into reverie, this time thinking about Apollonius. "Oh yes, I was worried about the limited manpower, too. But if you consider our resources, I believe it will be enough."

"Have not you been trumpeting your horn about how we underestimate the Jews and need plenty of troops to subdue the rebels?" Gorgias asked in exasperation. "Well, I agree with you. This Maccabee has almost all of northern Judaea under his control. Very dangerous! I hear that our Jerusalem garrison is beginning to move into the Akra."

Well, they had better hurry," Nicanor said, "or there will not be any room left in that monstrosity. From what I hear, the Jew collaborators are taking up all the space." Nicanor allowed himself a chuckle, then sobered at Gorgias' dour expression. Oh, how he missed Apollonius. "As to our numbers, you must remember that our plan this time is to draw the Maccabee away from his strength: the hills of Gophna. I want him nowhere near those hills. Also, we will add the Jerusalem garrison to our force. That will give us more than enough even for that scoundrel of a Jew. We will keep away from the gorges and defiles as they seem to be our weakness. No longer will we squander our centuries of training under Alexander's legacy by playing to the Jews' guerilla strengths. Our phalanx and skirmishers are meant for an open plain of battle. And, do not forget about my elephants. The Jews have never seen the slash of my elephants' tusks. I assure you, my beloved creatures will be the last thing these upstart rebels will ever see."

"Gorgias put his hand on Nicanor's shoulder and said, "Old friend, undoubtedly it is as you say—troop strength is sufficient for our aims in Judaea. Do not fret."

"I am not fretting," Nicanor said impatiently, easing out from under Gorgias' hand. Apollonius used to call him 'old friend,' too, and it cut him to the heart whenever someone else used that term to address him. "We will subdue the accursed Maccabee, his men and all who follow them. There will not be a dog to wag its tail when we are finished with Judaea."

Gorgias nodded and they descended the lookout. Nicanor looked out over the expanse of troops once again and said quietly, "And, I will avenge you, Apollonius, my old friend, or join you in Elysium in the attempt. By Ares, I swear it."

Chapter Sixty-one

Gophna, Judaea   The 20th day of *Tevet* 3595 (January 7th 165 B.C.E.)

Mother Elizabeth called to Judah. "Son! Come here. I am good with the loom, but not with fitting armor. John! Hold still."

Judah had been honing his *kopis* on the grindstone that he kept in back of the forge. Mother, Simon and John had come to the forge to visit Judah and to make adjustments on the armor that had been scavenged from the Greeks at Beit Horon.

"I thought this armor would be too big for you John, but see?" Mother said. "It fits almost perfectly. Judah, what do you think?"

"Ah, the young warrior. Simon, where is your armor? Oh, yes."

Judah took the armor from his youngest brother and admired it. The intricate workings of leather against metal were something his armorers were trying to perfect. At least after the latest Greek defeat, they had plenty from which to make forms for new armor patterns. For now, however, the rebels had just enough to outfit their five-thousand fighters who were trained for actual battle. Apollonius' and Seron's fallen and all the patrols that they had killed over the past few months provided enough armor that Judah' men were beginning to look more like an army instead of ragamuffin farmers with pruning hooks.

John had always been bigger than Simon even though the latter was two years older. But now that they were seventeen and nineteen, Simon was beginning to catch up with John, although more in height than breadth. Judah had stepped up their training so they could be promoted into command positions. It was not that they had any more aptitude than the rest of Judah's camp, but the men of Modiin were anxious to be commanded by all of the brothers of Mattathias' family. In fact, Judah had resisted the idea of their promotion, but his commanders had insisted. They wanted to be led by the blood relatives of Mattathias, the true author of the rebellion. If it were up to Judah, the boys would still be serving as lookouts, but much to their delight, he had allowed them to join in the ranks against Seron and they had done very well. As Judah listened to his men tell of his brothers' prowess in their hand-to-hand contests with the Greeks, he grudgingly realized that they had been ready to fight for a while. The training over the past two years was certainly telling on their young bodies. That, combined with the austere living conditions atop Gophna, was transforming them into young warriors, as competent as any of the older men. After all, old and young, the men of Modiin had been in the fight for the same amount of time. And, all of them had started out as mere farmers and tradesmen.

"Judah," John said, his voice now a full baritone, "Who are the Greeks sending against us, now?"

"Aulus thinks it will be Nicanor or Gorgias, or maybe both."

"It does not matter," John said, swelling his chest. "We will rout them as we did Seron."

"You have a lot to learn about command," Judah growled. "One of the first rules is not to underestimate your opponents. Seron was one thing; Nicanor and Gorgias are quite another. They are to be feared."

"I do not fear them," John said. "And I do not think you should either."

"That is something else about being commander," Judah said, smiling. "I do not have to listen to anyone's advice. Especially a grub's."

"A-hem," Elizabeth cleared her throat.

"Er, that is, except *Eemah's* advice, that is, Judah amended. "Now, you two, have you studied the battles of Rafia and Magnesia? I told you to place yourself under the tutelage of Aulus." At the boys' emphatic nods, he said, "Then, I want a report. Tell me what you know."

As Judah listened to the rather copious details of the two battles, his brothers handing the narrative and strategies back and forth in their impromptu recitation, he stole a look now and then at his mother's face. A mixture of pride and worry was fixed in her features. When she became aware of his scrutiny, she bowed her head once again to the armor.

"Well," Judah exhaled when they were finished. "It is too bad you are so young— all that military learning probably is lost on you. I do not know if you will ever be ready to lead an army—you are such little grubs. . ." He looked at the disappointed faces of his two brothers and went on, ". . .But, I think you *are* ready to lead a division in an assault."

John and Simon's crestfallen faces turned to that of joy when they realized what Judah had said. Judah did not dare look at his mother, but reveled in the exultation of his two younger brothers.

"Did you hear that? The Lord of Hosts With Us!" John yelled.

"The Sword of the Lord!" Simon answered.

Judah cuffed them both across their heads. "Those are holy war cries, and you are not to use them thus. That is the same as blaspheming the name of the Lord! And do not get too puffed up. You will act under the direction of one of the older commanders. John, you will be a lieutenant to Aulus, and you, Simon, to Asher. It will happen thus in the next battle. So, listen, watch and learn. Also, say nothing of this until I speak to the commanders."

The boys backed away from Judah. "Yes, Commander," they chorused and attempted to act ashamed at their previous blasphemy, but their pretended looks of shame turned to joy again as soon as they were a safe distance from Judah, and he heard them say, "We are going to lead an assault! At last! The commander thinks we are ready!"

Judah's smile disappeared when his eyes met those of his mother's. He busied himself with a length of strop he had carried from the forge, pretending to use it to sharpen his dagger. Turning the blade this way and that, he eyed its edge and hummed to himself.

"You have no business sending them into battle," Elizabeth said, attempting to turn Simon's armor inside out to learn its design, "let alone lead an assault. They are only boys. Not only that, but the next battle will be far more dangerous than the last."

"Mother, that is what we have been saying every single time we have gone up against the Greeks. The next battle, the next battle, the next battle will be the real thing. Well, we have been triumphant against them in every contest. Where is your faith?"

"Do not question my faith, boy! I raised you and did my best to keep you from harm—it did not always work, however," she said with a smile.

"Yes, where were you when I jumped off the roof of the stable? I almost impaled myself on the stave I was using as a sword." Judah patted his mother's cheek. "And you also were not around when Eleazar beat me within an inch of my life when we were boys."

"That turned out not to matter because you soon became bigger and meaner than he," Mother said as she threaded a leather strip through an eyelet on the armor's shoulder. "It was nice Eleazar at least had one chance to beat you up."

Judah was surprised at this newer, darker aspect of his gentle mother's humor. The men were not the only ones who had become harder and more callous; their women were changing, too. In Lydda, he had had to kill a Greek in his Aunt Anna's yard. He and Eleazar had almost fainted at his aunt's nonchalance in suggesting a place to hide the body. He also remembered her feral eyes.

Elizabeth took Judah's hand and stroked it. "I am sorry, Judah. I know I am being inappropriate, but you must remember how difficult you were as a child. *Nu*, you were a crazy little goat! Always into everything! And now you are the commander of Israel."

They sat silently for a while watching Avram as he worked efficiently in the forge pounding out yet another sword. Avram had been Judah's boss at the forge when Judah had been assigned as his apprentice and now served the Maccabee as a lieutenant commander. He had returned to the forge to help Judah with the supply of weapons and as ever, in any task he put his hand to in the forge, the results were stunning pieces of weaponry, rivaling even those scavenged from the battlefield.

"Avram!" Judah asked. "How many swords today?"

"I would say ten, commander. Those swords we have forged here, added to our Greek acquisitions, give us quite a hefty inventory of weapons."

"As always, Good work, Avram." To his mother Judah said, "I am not the commander of Israel." He inclined his head at his erstwhile overseer. "He is. And, Reuven, Ephraim, Asher, Dan, Yitzhak, and all the others, and now John and Shimon. And even *you*, mother. We are all of the army of Israel. I misspoke when I told John that I did not have to do what anybody says. I am bound to listen to every idea, every strategy and every complaint. Everyone is *my* commander."

"You have learned much, my son. Your father would be proud."

Judah blinked rapidly and looked away. His mother put her head down out of delicacy and resumed her fiddling with Simon's armor.

"Judah!"

He did not turn toward the voice. "Yes, wife."

Miriam paused at the gate of the forge to catch her breath. "Aulus would like to speak to you. He asked you to meet him at his camp. He also said that I should come."

"You?" Judah said. "Why does he want you there?"

"I do not know, but I do not want to go."

Judah did not want to fight, especially in front of his mother, so he simply kissed his mother, opened the gate and left the forge.

As he passed, Miriam glanced at Elizabeth, then followed him.

"I do not want to come. He is an infidel who keeps a slave."

"Then do not come. I will give them an excuse," Judah said.

"I wonder that you even keep him in the rebellion. We do not need him."

At this Judah stopped, turned and looked at Miriam. She stopped also and watched his fists, obviously waiting for them to unclench.

"You are never to speak that way of Aulus again," Judah said quietly. "I will not have it."

To Judah's surprise, Miriam kept quiet, for a few moments, that is. As she followed him to Aulus' camp, she kept a little distance between them so she could mutter to herself, but loud enough for Judah to hear.

"Keeping an infidel in our affairs—it makes our camp unclean—The Lord of Hosts will not suffer an infidel in our camp—the slave is golden and beautiful—she lusts after you—everybody can see—"

"*Valete*, you two! *Amici!*" Aulus came out of his camp to greet Judah and Miriam, though he smiled at Judah when he saw how far behind him his wife was. Judah knew the Roman was aware of Miriam's antipathy toward him since she had never been anything but cold to his greetings. "Miriam, you are more beautiful every day! This wild life agrees with you," Aulus said. "And, Judah! How goes it at the forge? I hear Avram is pounding out new swords every day."

"We will be ready, soon—for whatever the Greeks have in store for us," Judah answered, gazing uneasily at Miriam, who had enveloped herself in an unpleasant fog of silence. "I await intelligence from the north. There are rumblings that another force is coming against us."

"Is that where Ephraim is?"

"Let us just say that Ephraim is in a prime location for gathering intelligence. I have not told anyone where or how. I do not want you or anyone else spilling any of our secrets if captured and tortured, my friend."

"That is wise," Aulus said. "Not many can withstand Macedonian torture practices, it is true. The Greeks are almost as brutal as we Romans in extracting information."

* * * * *

Miriam moved a little way off and looked about the camp, trying to be disapproving. She was unsuccessful, because the camp *was* well organized. All was clean and symmetrical as if someone took great pride in appearances, and she was sure that someone was not Aulus. The Roman was not known for his fastidiousness, except in his weaponry. Miriam had not had enough contact with him to know this firsthand, but she had heard enough stories from the men about his slothful behavior to know he would not keep a camp such as this. She jumped when she noticed the white creature, her manner deferential, standing behind some lashed shelving. Her head was down, so Miriam could not stare at the strange eyes that had been the subject of camp gossip. Blue eyes were uncommon among her people, but the slave's eyes were said to be as the devil's. The blue was suffused with an outline of translucent white around the edge of the eye. Some of the women said that when they had unwittingly looked in the slave's eyes, they had not been able to talk or even move for a moment or two. Miriam did not believe such nonsense, but wanted a look at the eyes, anyway. Since the slave's head was bowed, she had to content herself with a long look at the hair.

Its yellow was startling enough, but the fact that she wore it uncovered tempted indignation and even a little envy. The braid was plaited into a single thick rope down the slave's back and its length was astonishing. The women of the village tried to keep their hair as short as decorum allowed for comfort under their head coverings. Unconsciously, Miriam's hand strayed under her veil to her own hair and found only dull bristles that felt like the brush she used to clean her rugs. She had the feeling that if she were to touch the slave's hair that it would be as flowing water.

Brita lifted her head at Miriam's stare, then dropped her gaze when their eyes met. Miriam studied her husband's back as he conversed with Aulus and noticed that Brita did not move. The slave seemed to be waiting for Miriam to speak, which Miriam had no intention of doing.

The men left the camp abruptly in the direction of the overlook that was near the Roman's camp, Judah obviously forgetting that Miriam was there. She did not know what to do since she did not dare interrupt her husband's intensive conversation with the Roman.

Brita seemed to understand Miriam's discomfiture and brought one of the stools from behind the tent. She put it near Miriam and indicated that she should sit down.

Miriam sat down in surprise and watched Brita crouch near a pot, ladle a liquid into a wooden cup and hold it out.

"It is clean according to your law, "Brita assured her.

"You know our language?" Miriam asked, in spite of herself. "Your accent is ugly, but I understand you."

Brita simply bowed, smiled and sat on a low log near the fire. "I learned it from doing trade in your village before the rebellion."

"I never saw you in the village," Miriam said.

"Not all would trade with me, and I was very discreet as to the hours of my marketing. I would only venture there when most escaped to their houses for the rest watch."

Miriam nodded her head, astounded that this conversation was taking place. Although she had not planned to speak to this woman, she found that curiosity would not allow her to observe the mores of shunning. And, now she could stare at those eyes. She saw that what everyone had said was true: they were the eyes of the devil—that strange blue, with white around the pupils. The face and demeanor of the girl, however, were so kind, that Miriam did not have it in her to be as harsh as she should be.

"You are very strange in your looks. Where are you from?"

"Germania. I was taken as a slave when I was very little. I do not remember my family."

"Are you not angry? You could kill Aulus in the night, you know. Then you would not be a slave anymore," Miriam said. Her tone was matter-of-fact. "You could go home where you belong."

Brita simply stirred the mead and said nothing for a moment. Then, "I have something for you."

The slave disappeared inside the camp tent and Miriam sat, wondering. She was just about to ask the slave why she was here. But what on earth could the slave have for her? She decided that she was angry at Judah for putting her in this situation. It was all so strange and disconcerting, and she did not like being here in the first place. Now she was going to have to accept a strange gift from a woman she did not know and should not even be talking to and she did not know how to get out of it. I could just run back to my camp, she thought. But she was sure that she would get in trouble with Judah. Not that she was frightened of getting in trouble, but she and her husband had been fighting so much lately that she did not want another topic for argument. So, she sat and waited, feeling rather stupid for sitting and waiting.

Brita finally emerged from the tent, looking somewhat flustered and holding something cupped in her hands. She stooped in front of Miriam and opened her palms.

Without thinking, Miriam took the small earthen jar and peered into it. All she saw was a sickly green paste. Her head jerked up when she heard men's voices. Judah and Aulus were returning.

Brita looked in the men's direction and said quickly, "Make a thin tea of this pulse and drink it hot as you are able." She lowered her voice to a whisper, "If you do this, you will bring forth a child from your and your husband's loins. Drink it one week after your monthly issue, then lie with your husband as often as possible. She stood and retreated to where Miriam had first seen her, behind the lashed shelving.

"So, when I told him to duck the sword thrust," Judah was saying, "what do you think he did? Just the opposite! That is when I was able to beat him down, I knew his stubbornness would be his undoing."

Aulus rewarded Judah's story with a laugh and glanced at Brita. The exchange was noted by Miriam and in her bewilderment, all she could do was stash the jar in her robe and follow Judah after his farewell to Aulus. Did the Roman know of her shame? And why was Brita interested? She had no answers to these frightening questions. It would be indelicate to discuss such a subject with Judah, but there was a question she *could* ask.

"Why did Aulus say I was supposed to come to camp with you?" Miriam asked as they walked away from the Roman's camp. "You never told me."

Judah stopped and looked at her. "He did not say. Maybe Brita wanted to talk to you."

"Why would a Roman's slave wish to speak with the wife of the commander of Israel? Anyway, she said nothing," Miriam lied. She was not about to embarrass herself by revealing that she conversed with an infidel slave, let alone the topic.

"She did not?" Judah said, acting perplexed for a second just to be polite, in Miriam's view. "Well, we have a mystery, wife."

"Yes, we do," Miriam said, and followed her husband back to the main camp.

Chapter Sixty-two

The last time Nicanor had been here in Jerusalem, it was with Apollonius. Everywhere he looked, old reminders of his close friend assaulted him. The barracks yard where they would often watch the soldiers train, the wall overlooking the western approach to the city upon which they would perch and discuss politics, and even the elephant enclosure where Apollonius had been an unwilling passenger on one of Nicanor's beloved elephants. This was the place he visited now that he had seen to his troops' quarters and rest, and as he stroked Deucalis, his favorite bull, he remembered Apollonius' wild ride on the elephant and the strange, whispered agreement between his friend and the beast. After that, Apollonius had not complained about his elephants again.

"Oh, Apollonius," Nicanor said, rubbing his bearded cheek against the elephant's musky chin. "It is ridiculous that I think of you so often. It makes me realize how valued friendship should be in this life. Not only that, I found it easier to plan strategy when you were around. Your mind worked such that your words fed into my thoughts and made me think of maneuvers and attacks that I otherwise would not consider. And, if I could not think my way through a problem, you always could."

Deucalis murmured loudly, seeming to sense the human's mood, then backed away to join the other beasts that were feeding on a great mound of hay in the middle of the pen. Nicanor watched him go and jumped off the fence. His knees protested at his heedless treatment, the leap having reminded them of their age, and Nicanor groaned. He hobbled over to his horse. One of the slaves gave him a boot up and he mounted.

Working with Gorgias on this campaign made him miss Apollonius even more. Gorgias was a flibbertigibbet whose mind could not stay with one focus at a time, and Nicanor was weary at having to keep the general's mind on task. They would be talking about the arrangement of the pikemen, and Gorgias would be on to the deployment of the elephants. Before that strategy was placed, the fool would want to talk about the skirmishers, then on to the terrain.

As Nicanor galloped through the streets back to the barracks yard, he worried about the Jews. He did not feel he had a plan that was stout enough to defeat the rebels. Perhaps if he sat down with one of the subcommanders whom he could trust, he could route out a cohesive scheme that would satisfy his unease. He would ask Philo.

His mind was so busy, he almost forgot that he had his bodyguard of lieutenants with him. They had insisted upon accompanying him to the elephant enclosure because of the unrest in the streets. It seemed, one of them had said, that the Jerusalem insurgents had become emboldened with the successes of the Maccabee. Now the guard clattered around him as he dismounted at the gate of the barracks office. He jumped in surprise when one of them addressed him.

"Will that be all, general? Would you like us to wait?"

"Wait?" Nicanor tried to cover his confusion, then realized that the lieutenant wondered if they were dismissed. "No. You are dismissed, all of you." Nicanor saluted, waited for their return salutes, and mounted the steps of the barracks headquarters.

Philo rose when Nicanor entered his office. "I have already received Gorgias, your honor. Do you need my office to direct your operation? You may sit here if you wish. Apollonius used this very desk for many weeks before he was. . . er. . . ."

Nicanor bowed and sat down, not at the desk but in a stool opposite as he knew he had interrupted Philo. "That will not be necessary, Commander. There is an office in the Akra that is suitable for my headquarters. Gorgias and I will work from there. Sit down, sit down."

Philo sat down very uneasily, his face a twist of chagrin, likely at having mentioned Apollonius. He cleared his throat and asked, "Would you like the latest intelligence on the Maccabee?"

"Yes, of course, thank you, general Philo," Nicanor said, taking off his helmet. Where are the Jews encamped?"

"They are coming farther and farther south. Whereas before they largely kept to the area up north around Gophna (the Jewish refugees have made their camp there, along with the women and children of the fighters), now they are making incursions into the areas south of this stronghold. Even more troubling is their ability to use the local populations as an intelligence network. We cannot sneeze or relieve ourselves without the Maccabee's knowing about it."

Nicanor considered this for a few moments. "We must make an example of those local populations. When Apollonius was here under the emperor's order, he kept the population under control by torture and executions. Why have you not done the same?

The rabble here is running wild. I actually had to have my bodyguard with me in our emperor's city. Our emperor's city!"

"We are pinned down here," Philo sputtered. "We do not even send patrols out anymore because none of them come back. The Maccabee has control of everything north of Jerusalem. He has effected a take-over of all our Greek cities."

"While you cower here in the accursed Akra!" Nicanor said. He was becoming agitated and angry. "His voice rose, "Apollonius and I would not have commissioned that monstrous tower to be built if we thought you were going to use it as a hiding place. And then you let that idiot Seron waste eight-hundred of our troops on that ridiculous sortie up Beit Horon." Now Nicanor was shouting. "We are losing control of this satrapy and the responsibility is largely yours!"

Philo's look of confusion did not stop Nicanor. He fumed and raged for a few more moments. Finally, his curiosity at the other general's blank look made him stop. He snapped, "Well, what do you have to say for yourself?"

"But, sir. Seron said he had your commission to act on the Maccabee. That you had ordered him to root out his forces and solve the problem once and for all."

"I did no such thing. It was well known among all of command that Gorgias and I were planning our own assault. Why would I send an inexperienced court fop like Seron to do my job?"

"That is why I was surprised when he informed me of your commission. I knew of your and Gorgias' plan, and I told him as much." Philo put his hand up to his mouth as he tried to recall the memory. "I do not remember what he said next."

"Did you ask for the commission or proof of my command?" Nicanor thundered. "Did you follow protocol and inspect his orders?"

"I did not think it appropriate, General. Seron was a provincial governor and outranked me. It was not my place to review his commission."

Nicanor wished Seron were still alive so he could take out his rage by punishing him. His lie and misplaced ambition had cost the empire not only eight-hundred valuable Thracians but also the esteem of the realm. The propaganda that these victories provided was an incalculable detriment to the morale of the Greek troops stationed here, just as it was an asset to that of the Jews. Nicanor was not sure that it would be physically possible to reverse the damage of Seron's stupid and unnecessary failure.

"I would like you and your commanders to meet with me and Gorgias tonight. I need the latest intelligence on the Maccabee and his movements. See to it, Commander."

"Yes, sir," Philo said and saluted. "Glory to the Divine Antiochus and his Empire."

Nicanor's return salute was curt as he left the office.

Chapter Sixty-three

Gophna, Judaea   The 17th day of *Adar* 3595 (March 4th 165 B.C.E.)

Miriam did the best she could to avoid Shoshanna, but it was not easy. The families ate together, did chores together and sat together at the campfire outside Judah's tent where they conversed. Village gossip, war strategy or Greek movements were some of the topics at the fire, but no matter the topic, Shoshanna was always there. It seemed that Miriam could not get away from her.

It was another early evening at the campfire and now, as always, Miriam could not help but stare at her sister-in-law's growing belly and all the activity that encircled Shoshanna. Judah's mother chucked her under the chin. Eleazar's hand was invariably drawn to the belly holding the unborn child. Even Judah would joke with Shoshanna about the coming infant; he would joke, that is, until he caught his wife's eye, then would abruptly cough and withdraw to another cluster of family and talk about something else.

The hideous encounter with the German slave four months before told Miriam that her barrenness must be a lively subject for camp talk. She heard none of it, of course, but she saw of late that people were not a garrulous around her as they had been in the past. Their guarded remarks and stiffness were painful to her and she wondered what the specific gossip was. She imagined that they blamed the lack of a child on her temperament. She was aware that everyone thought her a shrew. That was not to say that she regarded that perception was fair. She had never thought of herself as shrewish, but rather as outspoken and smart.

Whenever she came across the little jar with the tea concoction, she considered making the tea and following the directions Brita had whispered to her in Aulus' camp.

But, reflecting on the talk around camp that Brita was a witch, she would always put the stuff back where it was hidden in her personal basket.

"Are you warm enough, wife?" Judah's arm found its way around her shoulders as he settled next to her. This night, Ephraim was regaling them with the latest reports he had gleaned from his safehouse in Jerusalem. It seemed that he was not alone in his spying activities anymore. He had quite a few enthusiastic recruits from his new acquaintances in Jerusalem and they were bringing in much information about that city's Greeks and collaborators.

Miriam watched Judah's face because she knew he was a little uncomfortable at Ephraim's debriefings at the family fire. He often said that he should confine this type of information to the command tent with his inner circle. Finally, Miriam had pointed out that the only ones here who did not attend the regular command meetings were the women, and they had every right to hear these reports. After all, their privations were even stiffer than those of the men. The men were engaged in training and strategizing and didn't have to worry about the actual domestic running of the camp. That was left to the women and it was very heavy work. It was work that Miriam knew Judah would have liked to spare her, but he was simply too busy, and as they listened to Ephraim, she realized that soon the women would have to be left entirely to themselves, perhaps for months.

"General Nicanor, it is believed," Ephraim said, "is planning to bring the fight to an open plain south of where Seron engaged us."

"Or where Seron attempted to engage us!" Eleazar said.

"Sh!" Judah hissed at the laughter. "Which plain?" Judah asked, his arm around Miriam tightening. "Not the plain above Lydda, surely."

"No, I said south, Judah. Near Aiyalon."

"The lower Beit Horon, again?" Judah asked. "That does not make sense. Why would they choose the very place where we defeated Seron?"

"I think they will camp near Emmaus," Ephraim said. "There is an open plain that is more suitable to the deployment of their phalanx and elephants."

"Elephants?" Shoshanna shivered. "I saw them down in Jerusalem. They are frightening beasts. Apelles said. . ."

At the mention of the Greek who had raped and imprisoned Shoshanna, dead silence seemed to subdue the very campfire. No one dared look at each other, but John and Simon, who were sitting near Eleazar, swore later to Miriam that their older brother became so upset that he had to grip his hands together to control their shaking.

Shoshanna seemed to sense the unease and said nothing else. Mercifully, after the obvious discomfiture of the group, Ephraim continued as if Shoshanna had said nothing. "The Greeks will not attempt to fight us in the ridges again, I think. And, Nicanor is too crafty to make the same mistakes his two predecessors did. We have always thought that they would have been wise all along to attempt to draw us out onto an open plain like that at Emmaus. We have just been surprised, to say the least, that the only thing that matches their predictability is their stupidity."

This laughter Judah did not shush because his face with tight with thought. Finally, he said into the dying mirth, "We must be careful not to get caught in a trap. Did you or any of your agents feel that this information was fed to you?"

"There is always that possibility. I cannot say one way or another," Ephraim said, tossing kindling into the campfire. "You have ever been wise to consider that as a reality of intelligence. But I would doubt that you are planning to march headlong upon Emmaus. . ."

Judah smiled. "Who knows what I will do? I do not know myself. There are many things to consider. Are we ready to fight the Greeks on their terms? Do we have enough armor? Do we have enough men?"

"Well," Ephraim said. "I am off to Jerusalem to see if I can get the answers to some of those questions for you. I may be able to glean more information from our agents in the streets of Jerusalem."

"Be careful, friend," Judah said. "I wonder if it is too dangerous for you to venture too much into the city. Surely the Greeks suspect that our victories come from the intelligence you collect."

"They may," Ephraim said, smiling. "But they do not know who is collecting that intelligence. I am too crafty!"

"I hope so," Judah said, "but use extra caution in your 'collecting.' *Nu.* I must think on what to do. Eleazar, Shimon and John, we will meet on the morrow to plan. I need your opinions of our strengths, and a plan for scouting the terrain round about Emmaus. Eleazar, would you notify the other commanders of a meeting at the very end of the morning watch? I am thinking that we shall have to move soon. There is much to do."

The family understood the signal and began various stages of withdrawal from Judah's campfire. Shoshanna lingered until only Judah and Miriam were left and said, with some embarrassment, "I am sorry that I mentioned Apelles. I did not mean to be so awkward. I fear facing Eleazar tonight."

"Do not think on it, dear sister," Judah said. "And if you have any trouble whatsoever with Ephraim, holler for Shimon to come and get me."

After Shoshanna had gone, Miriam leaned against Judah and stared at the fire. It was true that Shoshanna was with child and she was barren. But Judah had never raised a hand against her and there was some talk about Eleazar's treatment of Shoshanna, that his rebukes sometimes were too physical in nature.

"Husband?"

"Yes, love."

"I am sorry that I have been short with you, lately. I do not mean to be."

"You are under a lot of pressure, Little Mare. I understand. I wish our lives were as before. I am sorry that I make you work so hard." Judah increased his embrace. "You should be the great lady of my father's Modiin estate. Your biggest worry should be that of yelling at the servants and worry about which stallion to breed with which mare. Things like that."

Judah's remark about breeding was unfortunate, but Miriam bore it with good grace, even bussing her husband's bearded cheek. At that moment, she did not grieve for her own lack of a child, but rather Judah's lack of an heir. He should have many sons as his father did. And his particular lineage should go on and on. She looked at his noble profile, the defined cheekbones, nose and brow and decided that she would use the slave's green powder as soon as she visited the stream for her ritual cleanse after her monthly issue. But if the tea were to have a chance she would have to hurry as Judah and his Faithful would soon march south to meet Nicanor and his Greek army.

Judah seemed to read her mind, for he became amorous. As his hands became more and more provocative, Miriam had to murmur, "Husband. I am yet unclean. Tomorrow, however, I bathe. We must wait."

"As always, wife," Judah murmured into her hair, for he had pulled off her head covering, "I am at your bidding."

Aloud she said, "Yes, husband," and suddenly became imbued with ridiculous hope. To herself, she said, "The Lord of Hosts with Us."

Chapter Sixty-four

Menelaus was incredulous. "Nicanor is not staying to defend Jerusalem?" .
"No, Excellency," Nadab sighed. "He came from Antioch to attack the Maccabee, not to defend us."

Menelaus' voice became more shrill. "But, Jerusalem is important to the emperor, is it not? Surely, Nicanor must protect Antiochus' interests here!"

Nadab arranged the piles on Menelaus' desk so they were more chronologically accurate. Menelaus' desk was ever disorganized. He wished it were as easy to arrange Menelaus' mind so that the high priest understood the workings of politics better. "Excellency, there is really nothing to worry about. Your quarters in the Akra are almost complete and there you will be well protected. Even if the Maccabee does attack Jerusalem, which I assure you, he will not (Nicanor is leaving much of the Jerusalem royal guard behind), no one can penetrate the Akra."

Menelaus muttered his way about his desk, pushing the piles of parchment around to no effect. The high priest had been in a constant state of angst as the Maccabee's hold on northern Judaea became more intrusive. Unlike Menelaus, who fluttered about complaining about the rebel's incursion into Greek territory, Nadab was doing something about it. For quite a few months an escape plan had been forming in his mind as the rebels claimed more and more land around Jerusalem. Of course, Nadab had not shared his plan with his superior, and he was audacious enough to believe that he could easily flee to his home in Idumea if things became too hot in Jerusalem for collaborators like him. But, if Nadab kept his political options open, there may be a place for him in the new government. Many conquering nations often kept the local hierarchy in place to foster stability in a new occupation. He was not sure if the Jews' hatred for anything or anybody associated with the Greeks would preclude that possibility, but it was worth a try. A careful try. Let Menelaus stay holed up in the Akra like a lowly roach. Nadab had no intention of doing the same. But, in no way was he counting on a position in the Maccabee's impending government, as he had already arranged a caravan berth on a friend's next trade excursion down to Idumea.

"Your Excellency?"

Menelaus stopped his muttering and stared at Nadab.

"I have something to deliver to the Greek barracks. Will you give me leave to go for a time?"

Menelaus gave a distracted nod and resumed his muttering, sitting down in an attempt to peruse the documents on the desk.

Nadab bowed and hurried out of the palace. He barely glanced at the increasing Spartan lack of fine furnishings, Menelaus having moved virtually everything to the Akra. The activity of slaves, however, did attract his attention. They were frantically washing the limestone walls and mopping the tile of the corridors as if they were preparing for guests. He wondered if Menelaus were planning to banquet tonight. The high priest probably decided that he needed a diversion from his anxiety about the possible attack on Jerusalem. Or maybe he was even preparing the palace for the possible turnover to the Maccabee and his forces, thinking a clean building might induce clemency.

I doubt the Maccabee will care about the state of this palace if and when he does enter Jerusalem, Nadab idly thought and stopped before exiting the palace. Another destination entered his head, and instead of heading for the Greek barracks, he moved back into the stone bowels of their headquarters toward the courtyard. He pushed the arched wooden gate that led out into the gardens and stared at the massive wall that surrounded the temple.

No, the Maccabee would not concern himself with the cleanliness of any building except the one that stood beyond that wall. The advisor looked at the chinked limestone uneasily. Nadab had not ventured into the temple since what the local population was calling the "abomination of desolation." The desecration of the holy building ordered by Antiochus almost two years before had been complete. Pigs had been slaughtered on the sanctified altars. Prostitutes had romped with patrons in the Holy of Holies. A statue of Zeus with the face of Antiochus had been erected to the left of the altar. It was a glorious statue, to be sure, with its gold leaf and inlaid precious stones, but Nadab knew that the Jewish population did not appreciate the virtues of such a piece of art. In fact, they would loathe it.

The main gate through the wall to the temple was manned by two of Menelaus' guards. They simply nodded at the advisor as he lifted the heavy iron bolt, one of the guards even pushed on the gate to aid Nadab's passage onto the temple grounds.

Since the slaughter at the caves of Kidron, where the temple high priest and his family had been massacred with a thousand others of Jerusalem Jewry, no others of the covenant had been interested in keeping the grounds. Keeping themselves alive and out of Greek prisons had taken precedence over tending a sullied temple.

Even so, he was unprepared for the shocking state of the courtyard of the temple. Weeds had choked their way into almost every stone crevice of the pavement, and even the lower blocks that formed the foundation of the edifice were shabby with thistle and noxious vines that invaded the ground if not controlled.

After seeing the terrible state of the grounds, Nadab was almost afraid to enter the temple itself. As he approached the great doors, he saw that one was ajar. He pushed on it and when it creaked open, he warily eased through. If he had not known that the veil of the Holy of Holies had been torn down by Greek soldiers, he would have sworn that he just passed through it, the cool interior of the temple was so like a curtain that banished the heat of *Elul* outside.

Even before the "desolation" the temple had been stripped of all its gold. None of the gilded paneling was left on the walls, making them appear ragged and bereft. The great marble tables had been stolen long ago, their silver and gold ritual vessels, too. It was said that Antiochus had taken some, his generals had sold the rest for the tribute to the Romans and even the high priest Menelaus had some of the artifacts squirreled away in secret recesses of the palace. Nadab thought back to the marble table that Menelaus had kept in his office in better days. He wasn't sure where it was now— Menelaus probably had it well hidden in case the Maccabee took Jerusalem, not wanting to be caught with the ritual bullion.

Nadab walked toward what had been the Holy of Holies, but it was anything but that, now. Wild, red desert dust covered every surface; Nadab's feet created eerie steppingstones of displaced sand that followed his winding progression through the edifice. When he reached the stone dais that preceded the Holy of Holies, he allowed himself a look at the statue of Antiochus. Given Nadab's agnostic leanings, he was surprised at the brazen statue's effect on him. Although it was gold, its essence seemed black to the advisor. Its looming presence amid the spiritual carnage here almost made him a believer in the Dark One. He shook himself. At this point, it was too late for him to assume religion. It was politics that kept him alive with a flourish all these years, not religion.

He entered the Holy of Holies and stopped. He looked up and could see remnants of the veil hanging from the brass rings that had once borne it in its fluttering pomp. Suddenly putting his hand to his head, he withdrew from the place, descended the steps down to the main hall and lounged against the altar. Its stone girth was the only reason it was not languishing in Antioch storage. He put his hand to his head again and rubbed his forehead. He felt sick.

"Ah, there you are!"

Nadab turned. "Commander Syrus. It is indeed a pleasure. I apologize, but I cannot offer you a chair. In fact, as you can see, I cannot offer you much of anything here. It has been, shall we say, thoroughly denuded."

Syrus looked around and laughed in appreciation. "I was here that night of the gala and the building was not the only thing that was denuded. Ah, but you were not here, as I remember. The prostitutes were indeed, er, talented."

Nadab, as always, felt more and more Jewish during such conversations. After all his time embracing Greek ways, he was always surprised when Greek callousness offended. "Yes, I heard. Well, you are off to the North, I understand."

"Yes, we leave tomorrow. The previous debacles will soon be forgotten when we bring the heads of the Maccabee and his brothers back."

"No doubt. No doubt," Nadab said, doubting all the same. "I am sure you will be victorious at last."

"The reason I am here," Syrus said, drawing his hand across the altar and wincing at the dust on his fingers, "—Zeus, this place is dusty—is that my barracks chief has brought some spies to the Akra for interrogation. I thought you might want to be present for their questioning."

"You mean, for their torture. I know all about your Greek 'questioning.'" And, I did not think there was any room left in the Akra for prisoners, commander," Nadab said sardonically, "what with all the Greeks and us collaborators rooming there, now."

"Oh, there is plenty of room for prisoners," Syrus said cheerfully. "In fact, I have one who has been asking particularly for you."

"Oh?" Nadab's tone was that of disinterest. Prisoners asked for his intercession all the time. This was nothing new. "Did he say his name?"

"Yes, he said he was a friend of yours. One Ephraim of Modiin."

Chapter Sixty-five

Jerusalem, Judaea   The 7th day of *Elul* 3595 (August 18th 165 B.C.E.)

E phraim shivered against the rough stone beneath him. "So, this is the famed Akra," He muttered to himself after the guards dumped him on his head inside the cell. "Not that I wanted this close a look. How could I have been so stupid?" He felt like cursing.

He had just arrived at the Jerusalem safehouse when word of a Greek raid reached Issachar and the other insurgents. It seemed that either through informants or torture of a captive, the Greeks had been able to ascertain the location of many rebel nests. The announcement brought by one of the youthful runners was so urgent that Ephraim did not even have time to remove his traveling pack before Issachar had him and the other Jerusalem rebels racing through the dank alleys of the Jewish quarter to another safehouse located on the edge of the Greek quarter. Just before reaching their new hole, they had run headlong into a Greek patrol. In the confusion, Issachar was able to escape, but Ephraim and the other six who had fled with him were caught. Now he lay in shackles amid a paltry scattering of straw in the most feared fortress in all Judaea. Some spy he was.

Those afternoon and evening watches of that first day of captivity were the longest he had ever known. If someone had told him in his youth that time could pass more slowly than those hours in yeshiva with *Adohni* Nahor, he would not have believed him. Now, however, the sun stood as still as it must have under Yehoshua's hand in the Valley of Ashkelon and when night finally fell, the moon moved not at all.

"Get up, Jew!"

Ephraim awoke and rose unsteadily to his feet. He weaved a bit as the guard opened the heavy barred door and beckoned him out.

Two other Greek jailors stood out in the corridor and formed a tight escort as the guard led them through interminable passages until they came to a widening in the corridor. The guard shoved Ephraim through an opening in the corridor wall and left. The two jailors stood outside the opening.

Ephraim found himself in a large room. At a table, a Greek commander was seated next to a Hellenized Jew. A cold hand gripped his heart when he saw that the Jew was Nadab.

"God be with you, Ephraim of Modiin," Nadab said easily. "I wonder, how have you been?"

"Advisor Nadab. It is good to see you. Is your family well?"

The Greek commander rolled his eyes. "Enough niceties!" He snapped. "Nadab, so you do know this Jew?"

"We are well acquainted, Commander Syrus," Nadab said. "He is an old friend. An old friend who once gave me the slip."

"That was a misunderstanding, advisor," Ephraim said, smiling. "I was sure I told you I was taking a trip up north. I know I told you. Did you not hear me?"

Nadab folded his hands on the table. "I must have been a little deaf that day, my friend. What you told me is that you were going to take a nap. But the news that Apollonius was marching on Gophna must have preyed upon your sleep, for immediately you rushed up to Gophna to warn the Maccabee and his rebels."

Syrus stood, his eyes wild. "This was their spy? He is the one who took the surprise away from Apollonius? This is the man who was responsible for the decimation of an entire cohort of Greeks and Samarians?"

"I think you give me too much credit," Ephraim said, his smile wider. "But did not Apollonius also have his Mysians with him? Do not leave them out. I think the Maccabee decimated them, too."

Syrus' voice rose, and his hand curled around the hilt of his sword. "Do not banter with me, you rebel filth. I will not have you speak the name of Apollonius let alone make sport of it."

Nadab said, "Please, please. Syrus."

"So, Ephraim. Shall we have a little talk?" Nadab turned to Syrus and said, "I think I can handle it from here, Commander. But I will be sure to call you if I need you."

Syrus glared in response to Nadab's meaningful look, but left the room, nevertheless.

Nadab watched him leave then turned back to Ephraim. "Old friend, you played me false. We had an agreement."

"Please, advisor," Ephraim said, "We both know the stakes here. We are in the same business. Politics and subterfuge. Do not take it personally, not that I really think you did. You are a creature of guile, not emotion. Let us at least speak plainly, you and I."

"Very well. But I could have made you a very comfortable man. If you had thrown your lot in with the Greeks, who knows how high you could have risen—"

"In a collaborator's government?" Ephraim scoffed. "A puppet government? And, if I had come over to your side, I would be fearing the Maccabee right now. When he cleans the countryside of Greeks and their collaborators, he will march on Jerusalem, and he will not be merciful to the likes of you."

"He has only faced local militias," Nadab warned. "Antiochus will be sending his seasoned troops against you. You have not seen their like, I can tell you."

Ephraim stayed silent. He knew that Nadab had tried to trick him into a slip by mentioning the seasoned troops marching on the rebels. He wondered if Nadab was aware of his knowledge that such troops were readying themselves under Gorgias and Nicanor to march on the morrow. Of course, Ephraim had no intention of exposing his intelligence. He simply sat and smiled at the advisor.

"Ephraim," Nadab's voice took on a kinder tone. "I can help you. You think that I am totally against the rebels? I am not unfeeling to their concerns. Am I not a Jew also? Sometimes even I chafe under the Greeks and their practices. And, they *are* arrogant. I am in a position to let you return to your Gophna hills." He leaned forward. "But I need certain assurances."

"What kind of assurances?" Ephraim acted interested so Nadab would press on in his attempt to win him over.

"Assurances that you will act as my agent as you agreed before. That you will give me information on the Maccabee that is helpful to the Greek cause. I will have other agents follow you to ensure your fidelity. If you agree to all this, I can let you go. I have no desire to see you tortured. But once you are in Syrus' hands, there will be little I can do to save you."

Ephraim pretended to consider these words by saying nothing, knowing that Nadab would use the silence to further his case.

"You must understand that in the real world, allegiance to a person or idea is a luxury that one who wants to survive an occupation cannot afford. And you are choosing to ally yourself with a family who was responsible for your father's death. Not only that, but I know that you lost your betrothed in the Kidron massacre."

Nadab must have seen the look of surprise in Ephraim's face, for he said, "It is my business to know many things, Ephraim. I understand now why you left for Gophna back then. You blamed me and the Greeks for the death of Deborah. Is that not her name?"

"Yes," Ephraim whispered. "Yes, that was her name."

"Well, then," Nadab said eagerly, "consider this. Instead of blaming her death on the Greeks, you should blame those fools who would not allow you to defend your lovely girl simply because it was the Shabbat. Chances are that if you Jews in the cave had worked together to defend yourselves, Deborah would still be alive and the two of you would be raising fat babies at this moment."

Ephraim was very quiet. He was so quiet, in fact, that Nadab must have taken the silence for assent. "You know that I am right. Join me and live. Let us work together to make Judaea great again as in the days of King David. The Greek empire is strong, but Antiochus will not live forever. The next emperor will likely have a more benign attitude toward the Jews as Antiochus' father did. This war is becoming destructive. If the unrest in Jerusalem and the rest of the country persists, there will not be a kingdom for anyone to rule."

Ephraim whispered something.

"What? What was that you said?" Nadab said.

Ephraim forced defiance into his voice. "I said, I cannot live as a collaborator. I would rather die than further the Greek cause in any way. The Greeks murdered Deborah and you were agreeable to her death, just as you have been in the other thousands who have died under the murderer Antiochus. I will not help you, even under the pain of a thousand hot irons."

"Oh, my friend," Nadab said sadly, shaking his head. "If only your death were going to be that pleasant. You will be pleading for the mercy of a thousand hot irons by the time Syrus is finished with you."

Chapter Sixty-six

Jerusalem, Judaea   The 7th day of *Elul* 3595 (August 18th 165 B.C.E.)

Issachar was no warrior, and he did not possess stealth in any fiber of his body. But even he knew that the only way he was going to get out of Jerusalem was to get out of his clothing. Being a Levite, his robe was the most conspicuous of any of the tribes of Israel. The black and white stripe woven into the field of red would not allow him to blend into the mass of travelers that fed in and out of the city day to day. He needed a Hellenic look. As he was the treasurer of the safehouse, he always had his purse next to his heart. The purse was fat with talents and it was with one of these that he paid for a new Greek robe. He also bought an exquisite turban that was now the rage of those in Jerusalem with any kind of a Greek bent. He hated spending so much on this ridiculous costume, but there was no help for it. He had to pass for a collaborator or even a Greek. He bought a few more robes so he could pose as a clothing merchant and stopped at another shop so he could buy a big traders' satchel in which to put his "inventory."

A Bedouin horse trader had set up a stall on the outskirts of the market. Issachar bought as sleek an Arab mount as his thrift would allow and although he was no horseman, he did his best to look competent as he ascended the animal. He took the most ignominious exit he could find out of Jerusalem and thought, I hope Judah the Maccabee is in Gophna. He will want to know that his premiere spy is in Greek hands.

Chapter Sixty-seven

Gophna, Judaea   The 11th day of *Elul* 3595 (August 22nd 165 B.C.E.)

T he Roman's tone was impatient. "Judah, I know he is a valuable spy, but we cannot mount a rescue. This is different from the time you took the anonymous 'Men of Modiin' into Jerusalem to rescue Shoshanna. You are not anonymous anymore. Every Greek is looking for you." At Judah stoic face, he shouted, "We cannot afford to put you in harm's way!"

Issachar stood by, uncomfortable at being part of this exchange. He had delivered his message and wanted to leave and get some food, but did not feel as if he had been dismissed by Judah. Although the Maccabee and the Roman knew he was there, he still felt like he was eavesdropping. He waited.

"Aulus, I thank you for your input. But I am not planning to ride down to Jerusalem and all the way back to Gophna. If you will remember, we were planning to leave for Mizpah within the week anyway. We will just leave a little sooner. From Mizpah, we can stage the rescue."

The Roman asked, "What is the importance of Mizpah? I heard your scouts say that it has some religious significance. However, I also heard that it is atop a significant hill near Jerusalem. Will the Jerusalem garrison not be able to observe our movements?"

"It is a ritual gathering place for our people," Judah said. "During the time of the judges, it was where the tribes of Israel would gather to do battle against the Philistines. It was also where Samuel anointed Saul king. And I do not care if every Greek in Judaea knows where we are. I will explain later."

"I do not approve, and it is crazy to let the Greeks have any knowledge of our whereabouts, but I know it is ever useless to argue with a Jew about anything having to do with religion. Very well, then. When do you propose to leave?"

"Tomorrow."

The Roman erupted again. "Tomorrow! Judah, have you lost your mind? We cannot have our store and provender ready by tomorrow. The grain is not even harvested. The women were going to reap the fields the day after tomorrow."

"Then we will have to rely upon what we can gather along the way. Miriam says that we have plenty of bread and dried meat and there are many of our people who will give us what we need as we march." He put his hand on the Roman's shoulder. "I never like to disregard your advice, because it is always good advice. But we need Ephraim. It may be too late already. Tell the commanders that I need to meet with them."

As he walked away, the Roman said over his shoulder, "Well, at least it will be you and not I telling them of the change in plans. You had better put on your armor and helmet before you address them. They are not going to be happy at rushing around at the last minute."

Issachar stood, fumbling with the reins of his horse. He cleared his throat to remind Judah he was still there.

Judah extended his hand to Issachar and pulled him along to the center of camp. "You have done us a great service. We have much to talk about, but first you must get something to eat. Ask the way to my command tent after you have sated yourself and I will have you brief us on the doings of your insurgent activities in Jerusalem."

"I? Address the Faithful?"

Judah said, "And who else is as qualified as you? Next to Ephraim, you are probably the most valuable agent we have. Gather your thoughts as you eat and then report to the tent."

"Yes, Commander," Issachar said unhappily. "I will do my best." He felt the bile rise in his throat at the thought of addressing a tentful of warriors.

"That is all any of us can do," Judah replied.

* * * * *

Judah accompanied Issachar to the mess area then hurried to his tent. He wanted to get what he knew was going to be an unpleasant exchange with Miriam over with as soon as possible. She would not be happy about having to gather supplies so quickly for the march. Also, his wife had been demanding the conjugal duty more and more lately. Not that he minded, but he was beginning to feel more like a randy coney than a human being. It was likely that after his and Miriam's argument about the stepped-up departure date was over, that she would demand him in bed yet again. It was often so after they argued. He squared his shoulders before entering the tent.

As matters stood, he saw that Miriam was indeed ready for him to join with her. She had disrobed and was lying provocatively on their bedding skins. Sighing, he went to her and decided that he did not mind putting the argument off for a while.

After, while they lay entwined, as much as Judah hated to broach the subject, he finally did announce the change of departure to Miriam. The argument turned out to be as passionate as the lovemaking had been, and Miriam stormed about the tent, throwing baskets and whipping robes and skins about as if she were a desert wind dervish.

"How can you ask this of me? Of the rest of the women? Not to mention your men! Husband, we cannot be ready! A commander asks for that which is do-able and possible. He does not put forward crazy demands!"

Judah donned his loincloth and robe. "Everything I ask for is crazy. It was crazy and impossible to rebel against the Greek empire. But we did it. It is crazy for us to live up here like mountain sheep. But we do it." He wrapped his head covering about his neck. "Wife, you may yell all you want in here. Go ahead and throw things if you feel the need. Hit me if you must. But once we step outside this tent, you are to act as if we are one in our expectations for this departure."

Judah's eyes forced Miriam to calm. They were no longer the eyes of her husband, but the eyes of the commander of Israel. And they demanded obedience. She had a pot in her hands ready to throw, but she put it carefully down and moved toward her husband.

Judah flinched and backed away, expecting a fist to the side of the head. Instead, Miriam put her arms around his neck and put her cheek to his. He completed the embrace as she said, "I will do as you ask, husband. I am sorry for my untoward behavior. "Now, let me go so I can make preparations. I will tell the women that we must work into the early morning watch if necessary, to gather everything for the march."

Judah watched her dress, then leave, reeling as if she indeed had clouted him in the side of the head. As always, after experiencing her unpredictability, he rolled his eyes and exhaled.

"That woman has done more to prepare me for Greek warfare than any training exercise Aulus has cooked up," he muttered to himself as he pounded through the tent flap and headed to the command meeting.

Chapter Sixty-eight

Jerusalem, Judaea   The 14th day of *Elul* 3595 (August 25th 165 B.C.E.)

Nicanor asked, "Is he still alive?" He pressed his face against the wax tablet so he could see the figures etched there. "Damn my failing sight." He looked up at Syrus and rubbed his eyes. "Well?"

"Yes, sir," Syrus said. "We were extremely lucky to have caught this one. We think he is the spy who was responsible for the Maccabee's knowledge of Apollonius approach to Gophna. His name is Ephraim Bar Naphtali."

Squinting at the colonel, Nicanor lost interest in the tablet. He would make sure that *he* had the satisfaction of dispatching this prisoner after all possible intelligence had been extracted. Apollonius. "Has he given up any information that could help us on our march? We leave within the week."

"He is proving rather formidable in his silence. Almost all the bones in his hands are broken and his feet are burned almost to the bone, but he has not given much up."

"Would that we had the Bull these days," Nicanor said wistfully. He was sure that roasting the Jew inside a brass bull as in the days of Phalaris would have borne fruit. As it was, they had to resort to more primitive methods. "Maybe we should crucify him in the barracks yard." Nicanor was thoughtful.

"I do not think that he would last very long, and I fear that anything of worth would die with him. I said he was alive, but just barely so."

"I will attend the next session. When is it scheduled?"

"I was going to resume after I reported to you, sir."

"I will accompany you back to the barracks," Nicanor said, putting the wooden lid on the wax tablet to save the figures from the heat. "I would like to speak to this Jew myself." And, he thought, if I cannot get knowledge, perhaps I can get a measure of revenge. For you, Apollonius, old friend.

"As you wish, General," Syrus saluted and stood back to allow General Nicanor to precede him out of the Akra office.

Activity was strong in the barracks yard with soldiers milling, carrying, loading, polishing and sharpening. Excitement had replaced the pervasive boredom that usually reigned, and it showed in the rugged faces of both the Jerusalem cohorts and the troops from Antioch that had accompanied Nicanor and Gorgias to Judaea. The men hailed Nicanor with happy shouts and rallying cries. "Death to the Jews! Death to the Maccabee!"

Nicanor acknowledged their greetings and enthusiasm, feeling imbued with confidence. "We will not fail again," he said to Syrus. "These men will see to that! 'Death to the Maccabee,'" he chuckled. "I like that!"

"Yes, General," Syrus agreed. "The men are indeed ready."

Into the foundation of the old stone barracks, the two descended. The prison was quiet at this time of day. No screams rattled the mortar as the jailors were at their midday meal. Only a few moans punctuated the stillness, but as all who frequented this place were inured to screams, they heard the moans not at all.

Syrus approached the prison guard who was sitting at the table at the entrance to the Jew's cell. He was an important prisoner; therefore, Syrus had instructed the guard to make notations of any delirium. "Do you have anything to report, lieutenant?"

The lieutenant stood and saluted, his eyes round at General Nicanor's attendance. "Nothing, sir. A few unintelligible cries, but that's all."

"Open it."

The guard opened the door then moved back.

Nicanor stepped inside the cell and resisted the urge to put his cape over his mouth and nose. He had forgotten how foul a prison cell could smell. The prisoner was curled about his leg shackle, his breath coming in shallow rasps.

The prisoner stirred, inadvertently touching one of his feet against the other leg. A howl rose from his throat. He obviously had forgotten about his charred feet. Looking up blearily, he attempted to sit up. But Nicanor could see it was very difficult. The prisoner's hands were useless, the digits now misshapen caricatures of his fingers. He rolled to his side, cradling the claws against his chest and struggled to a sitting position. He could barely speak, and Nicanor had to stoop to hear.

"Welcome, gentlemen. I am afraid I cannot rise to greet you." The Jew's voice trailed off, the flippant tone lost in his ragged breathing.

Nicanor reached down and lifted the prisoner by the neck of his tunic and pushed him against the wall of the cell. The screams were deafening as the general forced the prisoner to stand on the ruined feet and even grabbed one of the broken hands and crushed it anew.

"You will tell me what you know, when you knew it, and how you know it. And, you will tell me what the Maccabee's plans are. Is he marching upon us? Is he planning an assault on Jerusalem?" He shook him. "You will tell me, Jew, or I will break the remaining bones in your body, one by one."

Ephraim's screams increased at the shaking and crescendoed when the general, enraged by the prisoner's response, took the other hand and closed his fist over the broken flesh.

Syrus looked on with alarm. Nicanor was not schooled in torture and this rough treatment would not result in anything except for more screams and perhaps a premature death. He lightly put his hand on the general's shoulder. "Uh, sir, if I may?" He pushed the general slightly until Nicanor released his grip on Ephraim's hands. Syrus caught the prisoner and eased him to the floor. The screams had ceased, a merciful faint had taken the Jew away.

Nicanor stiffened. "I am sorry. I forget myself. But when I think that this scum was partly responsible for Apollonius' death and defeat. . .again, I am sorry."

"He will revive." Syrus tried to sound cheerful. "I will just wait until he comes to and start again. No harm done. But, perhaps—"

"Yes, of course," Nicanor interrupted. "I believe I should stay away and let you do your work."

"As you wish, general. However, as soon as we are finished here, you will have the final say on what to do with him. "Perhaps a crucifixion upon your departure for the north. That would buoy the men's spirits."

"Yes, it would. Not to mention my own." Nicanor made for the door, paused and looked with distaste at the prisoner. "Hades take you, Jew scum."

* * * * *

Syrus lingered in the cell for a moment after Nicanor exited and stooped next to the prisoner. He leaned his ear down toward Ephraim's face. Good, breath was still coming. It was faint, but the prisoner was still alive.

"Commander." The jailor leaned into the fetid cell. "The collaborator is here as you ordered."

"Good, bring him in." Syrus stood up and beckoned to the figure at the cell door. "Come in, come in, Advisor Nadab! It is good to see you. I thought you would like to see your friend before—well, anyway, if you like, you may speak with him. He has not been very forthcoming."

Nadab stepped into the cell opening, but stayed there. In a voice as strained as his face, he said, "No, that is quite all right, Commander. I really must be going."

"No, no, advisor," Syrus said. "It is good for you to see that your decisions keep you whole. You have chosen the right side. Why not relish your choice to work with our empire? It was entirely correct."

Ephraim moaned and his eyes fluttered, but did not open. Nadab backed out of the cell and Syrus heard a weak, "No, I really must go."

"Oh, very well," Syrus said, following him out. "But there is another matter that I must discuss with you. Come, friend. Let us leave this place."

Nadab ascended the stairs as quickly as his woozy head would allow and tried to listen to the Greek whose cheer was a dreadful sham in these surroundings.

"You were raised in Beit Horon, I understand, Advisor," Syrus said.

"Yes," Nadab managed to breathe.

"So, you are well acquainted with its hills and ridges?"

"Yes, my brothers and I played and hunted there—" Nadab stopped and leaned against the wall. "Oh, no. You cannot mean—"

Syrus passed him on the stairs. "Why yes, you would be a great asset on our march to Mizpah. In fact, I can think of no one better to guide us among the ridges and hills of those parts. I believe we will be using the Beit Horon Pass, itself. I am sure you are very familiar with that route."

"But, Seron," Nadab sputtered. "Seron's force was decimated climbing that pass—"

"That is because they did not have you as a guide," Syrus said, chuckling darkly. Then he became serious. "Nadab, I know you have aspirations. Well, what better way for you to ingratiate yourself to Nicanor and Gorgias, indeed, Antiochus himself, than to help us defeat the Maccabee, once and for all? Your contribution will bring you great rewards." Syrus grasped his bicep. "Take this opportunity, my friend. You deserve it."

Syrus watched the Jew's face, darkened by the bowels of stone around them as her considered the proposition, and could almost see Nadab's thoughts regarding the man they had just left in the cell downstairs in the Akra.

"I'll do it," was all Nadab said.

Chapter Sixty-nine

Mizpah, Judaea   The 21st day of *Elul* 3595 (September 1st 165 B.C.E.)

S oldiers lay in every shallow ravine; every furrow housed a few men. The land seemed to come alive with its renewal of ancient gathering. Not only was it a military muster, but also an assemblage of priests and families. Because of the comprehensive intelligence network that now had spread throughout Judaea, the people believed the great gathering to be as that of old, and they wanted to be part of it.

Judah had been relying on Yehonatan for the scriptural background he needed to conduct a war council that the Lord of Hosts would sanction. The young scholar had set out his many scrolls and pored over them now. Aulus and Asher looked over his shoulder, Aulus with his hands clasped behind his back and Asher tracing some of the writing with his index finger.

Yehonatan, although more interested in scripture and learning, had become a rather formidable warrior. And, because he was a scholar, he was well-versed in command strategy and martial doings. He had been instrumental in working out the attack strategy against Seron, and Judah was beginning to rely upon his judgment as much as he did Aulus' and Asher's.

"It is fitting that we meet here, brother," said Yehonatan. "Our effort to meet at Mizpah will usher in the undoing of the abomination of desolation. One can almost see Jerusalem over yonder."

"That is why I do not like this place," grumbled Aulus. "The Greeks will be able to see everything we do."

"And even if they do not see everything," Asher said, "the civilians gathered here will noise it about. We are very exposed. Judah, are you sure that we need to engage in the rituals? We have other things for the warriors to do. And the civilians are going to get in the way."

"Not only that," Aulus pointed out, "but having the men fast before the battle—well, that is sheer folly. They are going to need every ounce of strength for this contest with the Greeks."

Judah stood up from the scrolls he had been studying with Yehonatan. "I will answer your concerns, and after that, I want to hear no more about it. The Greeks are bringing 20,000 hand-picked troops against us. If our five or six thousand go into this battle alone, they will not come out alive. We need the Lord of Hosts with us. If we attend to His holy rituals and show Him that we are still following the law, then He will stand with us. Let the Lord see us bringing our tithes and first fruits! Let the Lord see us replace food with spirit! And, let the people to see that their soldiers are going into battle under the Law."

Judah stopped for a moment, caught up in the speech. Asher and Aulus said nothing. Judah wondered if they were moved, or just cowed. He went on.

"And, let the Greeks see us assemble! Let them be consumed in confidence that they know where their enemy lies. But, we shall be as the whirlwind. Lo, the Greek will think we are here, but we shall be there." Judah leaned over one of the scrolls that Yehonatan pointed out to him. "'Let not your hearts faint,'" he quoted. "'Fear not, and do not tremble, neither be ye terrified because of them.'"

Judah waited. Asher and Aulus were his two most able commanders, but the least steeped in the Law. Asher had been apostate among the Greeks for many seasons, and Aulus, a Roman, was an infidel and did not understand their ways. Judah looked into their faces and saw acceptance of his words. He ploughed ahead, covering his astonishment with more command protocol. "Asher, have you numbered the men, and do we know who is to return to Gophna?"

"Yes, after the selection, we will be left with four cohorts of 1,500 each," Asher said. "You, Judah, will command the first; Yehonatan, the second; Simon, assisted by Aulus, the third; and I will assist John over the fourth. Now each commander must divide further into hundred, fifties and tens."

"We will do the formal divisions on the day of ritual," Judah said. "But I want everyone to know his division before then, so we do not have chaos on that day. I do not want the civilians to see us in disarray. Also, on that day, we will attend to the selection as it appears in *Tanakh*. All those who must return to Gophna for planting, personal business or urgent construction are to be excused. If we use all of the men who came with us from Gophna, we will have too unwieldy a force. Let the people see the selection as it happened under the Prophet Samuel of old."

Aulus mumbled, "Ye Gods, it seems like a lot of trouble. I never heard of a Roman force making such an oblation to their gods before battle."

"A Roman force would not even know what an oblation is," Asher said, having to duck to avoid Aulus' fist.

"Let us organize, then," Judah said, ignoring the horseplay. Make all speed and meet me back here. I want you each to bring five of your best men for Ephraim's rescue. I will take them to Jerusalem with me."

"Judah," Aulus said. "Do you really think it is wise to mount a rescue for Ephraim this close to battle? He may already be dead."

Judah nodded. "Gorgias and Nicanor have not set out, yet or we would have seen the signal fires. We have time—we will be gone for only twenty-four hours."

"That is some hard riding, down to Jerusalem and back," Asher pointed out.

"That is why I am leaving all the rest of my cohort commanders here, except for you, Asher. I need your clean-shaven face and your Greek to get us into the Akra. As I said, I will organize my cohort before I leave."

"And, what if you do not come back," Aulus asked. "Who will command your cohort? Indeed, who will command the army?"

"I will be back," Judah said.

*   *   *   *   *

As Judah mounted *Tiklit* and galloped off to mind his cohort, Aulus said to Asher, "I cannot doubt him." The Roman shook his head. "His strategy does not always make sense, but somehow, I know he is right."

"Why, Aulus," Asher said, grinning. "I believe we shall make a Jew of you yet." He clapped the Roman on the shoulder. "Shall I summon the priest for your circumcision?"

"Jupiter, Mercury and Hades!" Aulus said, shuddering. "Following Judah into battle is one thing. Surrendering my foreskin is quite another."

"If the Greeks get hold of you," Asher said, winking at Yehonatan, "I am sure they could arrange for both at the same time."

Aulus exhaled a comic whimper as his hands covered his privates.

Chapter Seventy

Unlike Nicanor, Gorgias was schooled in torture and a great aid to Syrus as they worked to get at Ephraim's mind. One of his eyes was already extinguished and they were now threatening the other with a hot iron.

Gorgias seemed to be enjoying himself so much that he chatted with Ephraim about his and Nicanor's plan for the upcoming assault. The conversation, one-sided at best, nevertheless did pass the time, at least for Gorgias. For Ephraim, time did not pass. Pain was the only entity he was aware of.

"Did you know, Jew," said Gorgias, "That we are going to split our force? The Maccabee will be entirely fooled. We have already had reports that he has arrived at Mizpah for some kind of ancient ritual or ceremony. We will entrench ourselves at Emmaus. My soldiers will then use the Beit Horon pass to make their way to Mizpah. Nicanor's force will remain in Emmaus."

Ephraim collected himself enough to utter, "Did you not learn a lesson from Seron? I would think that the Beit Horon pass would pose—" Ephraim's throat was so used up by the torture that he could not continue. His vocal cords had been shredded by his own shrieks, and coughs now hacked through his very frame. "Water."

"No water for you," Gorgias said cheerfully. "At least not until the end of this session. And, you must not worry about the Beit Horon pass. Although this may sound treasonous, Seron was an idiot and no strategist—I do not mind telling you this, for you will be a dead man very soon. The Beit Horon ridge was a problem for him because he cut and ran. I assure you that we will not do that."

Ephraim persisted with another croak. "But morale—Seron's failed campaign—"

"Morale?" Gorgias said, dismissing the idea. "Our men do what they are told. They do not rely on morale to do their duty. They care not a fig about what went before. They are disciplined and immovable."

Ephraim forced himself to stay conscious. His thin grasp of Gorgias' words annoyed him because he knew that he was hearing something very important. What was it? Now he could not remember. The pain. Beit Horon? Splitting forces? A ridge? What was it? If he could only stay awake. But, the pain.

* * * * *

"He has passed out again, General," Syrus said, adding to himself, You are probably boring him to death, you old gasbag. He was not having good luck with this prisoner at all. First, Nicanor almost beat him to death with his ham-handed treatment and now Gorgias was giving information to the prisoner, not the other way around. Ephraim would soon be dead, it was true, but the general's loquacious boasts made him very uncomfortable He sighed. At least, Gorgias was making signs as if to leave.

"Well, I will leave it in your capable hands, Commander Syrus," Gorgias said. "I must make ready, for we leave on the morrow for Emmaus."

Perhaps you would like to announce it to the rest of the prisoners on this cell block, Syrus thought. I think there was one in the furthermost cell that did not hear of your plans to split the forces. Aloud he said, "I will make one more attempt to extract information from the prisoner, then I believe that Nicanor wanted to finish him."

"No doubt, no doubt," chuckled Gorgias. "Nicanor is still pining for Apollonius and needs to take out his grief on someone. But I doubt he will have time to dispatch the prisoner himself. He is too busy readying his troops for departure as well. And you are coming with us as well, as an advisor, are you not? You must have a prodigious knowledge of the terrain here about."

"Only too well," Syrus said, thinking of Nadab's aid, but keeping the credit for himself in his exchange with the General. "I led patrols against the Maccabee in that area, that is, until all the patrols were called in."

"Well," Gorgias said. "After this battle, we will have to renew those patrols so we can mop up any followers of the Maccabee. In fact, after this battle, we have been commissioned to wipe out all the villages that have not retained their Hellenic complexion. But, first, we must attend to the Maccabee. Farewell. I will see you on the march."

"Yes, sir." Syrus watched Gorgias mount the steps that led out of the Akra and turned back to the prisoner. He put his face down to Ephraim's and listened. He heard nothing. He watched the chest. No movement. No, wait. A slight rise and fall was barely perceptible. "Hardly a bellows," Syrus mumbled, "But at least he is still alive. I will let him sleep. He will need his strength for our last session."

* * * * *

But, Ephraim was not asleep. He was attempting to put Gorgias's information into a coherent package in his mind. Unfortunately, he did not know to whom he would report.

Chapter Seventy-one

The road from Mizpah to Jerusalem, Judaea   The 22nd day of *Elul* 3595 (September 2nd 165 B.C.E.)

Judah said,"I have not seen the Akra, The last time I was in Jerusalem, I do not believe they had begun its construction."

"It is an awesome thing, now," said Elijah, a Jerusalemite who had joined the Maccabee only two months before. "I believe the Greeks are not only using it as a prison, but also as a fort to protect themselves and their collaborators."

"I understand that you are familiar with its accesses and layout?"

"I was forced as a slave to carry its stones until I escaped. I am well acquainted with at least its foundation, and that is where the prison is located. Ephraim is probably housed within the very blocks that I and my comrades set."

The force plummeted along, the road giving up its curves and hills to the sureness of the horses. As there had been no Greek patrols north of Jerusalem for quite some time, they flew along with little worry. The rescuers had outfitted themselves with captured Greek armor so they could enter the enemy compound more easily, but they still wanted to avoid Greek contact.

"Let us water our horses. I know a spring up around that cove," Judah said.

Sure enough, the cove opened out of the mountain as he said. The stone mantle that led from the road to the water was so smooth that they were concerned that their horses might slip. Anxiously, they watched the hooves of each others mounts, hoping the beasts had sure feet. Finally, the horses found the water and as they sucked greedily at the churning spring, Judah spoke quietly to the men.

"I am not sure how we are going to get into that massive fortress, let alone find Ephraim within, but I want to tell you that this is an important mission. Ephraim is our brother, yes. He is our friend, yes. But there is something else that makes it crucial that we get him out of there, and I do not know what it is." Judah could think of nothing else to say. Something told him he was supposed to get Ephraim, but he had no idea why.

The men seemed to sense his bewilderment. They looked at each other until Asher said, "Judah, we have followed many of your orders without knowing the reason. You are the commander. That is reason enough."

As the men muttered agreeably, Avram the big smithy said, "Well, Commander, then let us go get him."

Judah nodded with gratitude and wondered at their trust, but said only, "We must be quiet at we enter the city. How many of you were on the rescue mission when we came to fetch Shoshanna?"

About half the men raised their hands and Judah went on, "We will use the same gate, the eastern gate, for our approach. As before, we will dismount and lead our horses through the city. It will take longer, but we cannot afford to engage the Greeks in the closeness of Jerusalem's streets. Let us on."

Their sturdy Arab ponies were up to the ride and it was not long before the domes of Jerusalem rose before them. They turned their horses to the east of the city and rode down the ravine into the Kidron Brook. Taking the opportunity to water their horses for the last time before entering the city, the men noted with satisfaction that the great star was still at its zenith. They had plenty of dark left. They pulled up their mounts and climbed the east approach to the city, dismounting in a copse of cedars outside the gate.

As they pulled their horses along in the silent streets, they frowned at the state of the city. It was not the golden city they had known in their youths, but rather a sloppy metropolis of tawdry brass. Cobbles were missing so that hooves had to be cautious as they clopped over the streets and alleys. Plaster sloughed off stone and the weeds were brazen in their interference of architecture and utility.

The smells were almost as obscene as the rubble and disrepair. The men suffered through a heinously offensive smell for a number of turns until they came upon its source. A rotting mound of dog carcasses forced them to hurry by, the horses almost shying at the stench.

"It is time to take Jerusalem," Judah said under his breath to no one in particular. "I will not live to see the City of David defiled so. We will wrest our city from the Greeks."

Finally, Elijah, who had taken the lead, turned and put his finger to his lips. He pointed down a street and crept away, leading his horse. The men followed him, knowing that they had just entered the Greek quarter of the city. The Akra was not far away.

This street looked familiar to Judah, and it took him only a moment to realize that this was the street where Shoshanna's rescue had failed all those months ago. Back when they were just betrothed, Eleazar's wife, Shoshanna, while visiting family in Jerusalem, had been abducted by a Greek commander. As soon as word of the abduction reached Modiin, Judah and a hand-picked posse rode down to Jerusalem to try to find her. Judah caught a glimpse of her on this very street, but she was spirited away by her captor before her rescuers could catch them. Shoshanna's use by the Greek had been hard, but she had pluck enough to make her way back to Eleazar by joining the Greek force that had been commissioned to travel north to annihilate Judah and the people of Gophna.

As the men rode nonchalantly up to the entrance of the Greek compound, Judah wondered why the streets were not manned. This lack of vigilance on the part the Greeks was incomprehensible. Upon further reflection, he shrugged. Thank the Lord of Hosts for Greek complacency. It was the reason that they were all still alive.

But where to put their horses? Luckily, there was an abandoned house nearby with a large, gated courtyard. After calming their animals and setting them to graze on the copious overgrowth of weeds and vines, the men quietly assembled themselves in the street outside. Judah shaped the rescue force in the formation that he had seen the Greeks use in their patrols up north. In threes he arranged the men, those on the outside with their spears pointed outward toward the direction of the march. He took the head of the column and with smart steps, they headed toward the Akra. They had their bearings now as the tower had spiked into view.

Fear spread through the little column as they were waved through the gate by the sentry. Surely it could not be this easy. As they advanced further into the exercise yard toward the entrance, their step became more sure and they even answered a few hails in Greek, nodding and saluting as they went. Finally, Judah turned around and halted the column, had them stand at ease for a few moments and said, "Disperse and try to look inconspicuous, lounge about, talk in small groups and wait for me. Asher, stay near the door in case I need you."

Taking a long look about him, Judah approached the massive double doors of the Akra. Again, no sentry was posted, so he pushed through, wincing a bit at the loud groan of the massive hinges.

To keep the dawn out, he closed the doors. It was comfortably dark, and he moved about carefully until his eyes adjusted to the muddy light. He hugged the walls of one corridor and moved along until he came to an opening to his right. The jailor sat at the table, writing by the light of a candle. Judah stopped. He felt like an imbecile. He did not know enough Greek to pass, and even if he did, how would he ask where they were torturing Ephraim? "Excuse me, but I do not hear any screams. Could you direct me, please?"

He approached the jailor, and for lack of Greek, drew his sword and struck the man across the throat, killing him instantly. A large wooden door stood behind the desk. It was locked. On the jailor's body, he found a large ring of keys and clinked through them, trying each in the lock until the door clanked open.

He turned back and used the jailor's candle to spear the murky dark of the corridor. The stench told him that the prisoners were nearby.

He called softly, "Ephraim." Then, louder, "Ephraim!"

Pausing, Judah listened then continued to move along the cell block, whispering Ephraim's name. He did resurrect a few moans and vowed to come back and free as many prisoners who could walk on their own. Finally, he heard a rasp from inside one of the doors. It sounded like his name. Fumbling through the keys, he finally found purchase with the door and entered the cell.

Judah brought the candle up to the face and almost swooned. How he knew it was Ephraim, he did not know—the mutilation of features was so complete that the face looked barely human. But somehow, he was able to identify the wasted flesh as his friend. He gathered the body in his arms, doing his best to ignore Ephraim's sobs at being moved, and backed out of the cell.

Stopping at the door where he had heard the heartiest moan, he opened it with one of the keys and threw them into the cell. "Free yourself and as many prisoners as possible," Judah said to the ragged and brutalized figure lying in the filthy straw. He wished he could help all of the captives, but he had to get Ephraim out, and he was unwilling to waste the lives of those waiting outside for him by expanding the mission to free all the prisoners. They would have to help themselves.

He ran through the dark halls, frightened now that he might squander the previous ease of the mission by getting caught. His mind was working furiously. How was he going to get Ephraim out? He looked down at Ephraim's face and saw that it was grey underneath the gore. Perhaps he was already dead. Then an idea came to him.

Coming upon some coarse burlap sacks lying in a corner next to some crates, He lay Ephraim down, tore open the sacks, said, "Forgive me, old friend," and started wrapping Ephraim in the cloth. He then picked him up, marveling at his slight weight, slung him as carefully as possible over his shoulder and ventured out into the barracks yard.

Judah sighed in relief that he was finally out of the Akra's dark corridors, but saw that there were now two sentries stationed at the entrance. He paused, nodded at Ephraim and made as if to pass. The guards stopped him.

In Greek, they said, "What is in there?"

Judah, who knew no Greek, was getting ready to dump Ephraim and solve the problem with his sword. He tensed.

Asher, lounging near the entrance as per Judah's orders, saw the trouble and approached them. In Greek, he addressed Judah. "So, Braxus!" Asher said, gesturing toward Ephraim. "This one did not survive? Probably one of those feeble Jews. They cannot take much of a beating, eh?"

Judah, who had no idea what Asher was saying, simply nodded and smiled.

Asher took Ephraim from Judah and beckoned to Avram to help him. "This one we will take to the refuse heap!"

One of the guards, disarmed by Asher's bravado, laughed and said, "Good! Take the Jew where he belongs! The garbage pile. Ha, ha, ha!"

Judah slunk away, grateful once more for Asher's knowledge of Greek. The rest of his men gathered to him in a nondescript herd and followed Avram and Asher out of the barracks yard. Out on the street, they formed themselves into patrol formation once again and marched to the abandoned house to collect their horses. Unwrapping Ephraim, they laid him out on a bench and did their best to clean and revive him. Pouring some water from one of his skins, Judah washed Ephraim's face and massaged the areas of his body that seemed free of injury. Ephraim groaned and the men gasped in relief. He had been so still and pallid that they were sure he was dead. That groan allowed them to enjoy the victory of their mission at last.

Avram lifted Ephraim up so he was horsed in front of Judah. It was then that the men noticed his misshapen hands and scored feet. Grimly, they listened to Ephraim's stifled sobs when his foot brushed against the saddle, not to mention his moans at sitting a horse. Seeing he could not clutch Judah to hang on during the ride, one of the men lashed Ephraim's body to Judah's with some rope.

All the activity seemed to wake Ephraim, for he said, his voice a mere rasp, "Judah, I have information about Nicanor and Gorgias' battle plan. I must tell you now in case I die along the way."

The men looked at each other. They had been worried at their lack of intelligence on the new Greek assault. This must be the unspoken reason they had braved the Akra this day.

"You will not die," Judah said with finality. "The information can wait. We will hear it after you have rested and eaten. Your wounds also need tending. The Lord did not lead us to you just so we could listen to your death rattle."

"Do not be foolish!" Ephraim whispered. "Gorgias and Nicanor plan to split their force. One detachment will remain in their proposed camp in Emmaus and the other will seek you out at Mizpah."

Judah and Asher stared, each with an intake of breath.

Finally, Judah spoke. "Now you must be silent so you can recover; but this is interesting news, to say the least. I must think on what to do."

Having delivered the main gist of the message, Ephraim seemed to relax somewhat, although often Judah would hear a sigh as if Ephraim wanted to say something. The effort would prove too much, however, and his friend finally sagged against his back. Judah used all the horsemanship he possessed to keep *Tiklit's* gallop smooth to ease Ephraim's travel and he rejoiced, not only at the successful rescue, but also at the intelligence on the upcoming battle. "The Lord of Hosts with us," he once again breathed.

Chapter Seventy-two

Nicanor's tone spiked in surprise."Divine Antiochus! What did you say?"

Syrus shifted from one foot to the other. "General Nicanor, I was not present, but someone slew the jailor and took the prisoner out of the Akra."

Nicanor paced. Obviously distracted, he did not acknowledge Gorgias as he entered their Akra office. He continued in a tense voice, "Did you question the sentries? Did they see anything?"

"They did see two soldiers bring a corpse out early this morning," Syrus said, stopping to think for a moment, then went on, "Upon interview, the guards said that one addressed his partner as Braxus, and the other had a rather scraggly beard."

"A Roman derivative of one of our names, and another with an unkempt beard? Palace cohort guards?" Gorgias asked. "Not likely. Lax sentries."

"I want those two sentries beheaded at once," Nicanor said in disgust. "The intruders must have been rebels. I have heard that Romans are helping the Jews. The Romans would like nothing better than to destabilize our kingdom. Rebels infiltrating our very barracks yard and the Akra! What was the state of the prisoner, Syrus?"

"I was to have one more crack at him then turn him over to you, General," Syrus said. "However, I would be surprised if he survived his own rescue. He was barely alive when I left him."

Syrus watched the two generals converse for a moment. His promotion from lieutenant to colonel enabled him to experience many scenes such as this; he enjoyed knowing the backstories of command. For instance, would Gorgias tell Nicanor that he had bragged to the prisoner about the plan to split the Greek force? He thought not. Politics would not allow a royal general to admit to such stupidity. Syrus knew that if Gorgias did not tell, he himself would have to. He considered the ramifications of that act. He did not like the idea of their attack plan being compromised. If the prisoner retained that information and survived, it could mean another defeat of the Greek forces at the Maccabee's hands.

Syrus thought back to the condition of the prisoner. Ephraim was so near death when he last saw him that it likely rendered Gorgias' boast moot. And if Syrus tattled to Nicanor about Gorgias, it would be Syrus or his career that would eventually end up as dead as Ephraim's corpse. After all, although Syrus was not present when the prisoner was rescued, his head was not safe at the moment as the escape could be laid at his feet as the ranking officer conducting the torture. Not only that, but Gorgias was reputed to have an extensive network of assassins that doled out retribution to political enemies with studied regularity; he was a terrible man to have as an enemy.

Syrus stood at ease, staring straight ahead, but out of the corner of his eye, he could see Gorgias looking at him. It was a quizzical stare, but also pregnant with warning. For now, Syrus decided he would heed that warning. He did not particularly want to pit the two generals one against another. As an adjutant, he was attending them on the march to Emmaus and part of his job was to ensure that the generals' heads were full of strategy against the Maccabee, not each other.

"Syrus. Syrus!"

He came forth from his reverie to the glare, not only of Gorgias but also Nicanor. Rigid at attention, he snapped, "Sir!"

"Pay attention, Commander!" Nicanor barked. "Slave merchants have been arriving in Jerusalem from the various coastal regions for the past week now. I had set Lieutenant Polydorus over organizing them for the march to Emmaus, but I want you to oversee his efforts." To Gorgias he said, "I hope to make a gift of 2,000 talents to our emperor upon his return from Parthia through the sale of Jews after the battle."

"I thought the practice of slave traders following a march was rather outdated," Gorgias said. "That has not been done for decades."

"If we were fighting a recognized nation with sovereignty, I would not engage in the trading of slaves," Nicanor said. "But I would like to help Antiochus by attending to the last tributum payment to the Romans. I understand that our account is still 2,000 talents short. With your help, I believe we will soon have a surplus of slave stock—ready revenue."

"You are a little presumptuous to be inviting slave traders to our battle, are you not?" Gorgias said. "And, you are not heeding your own admonition that we not vaunt ourselves over the Jews? You have always said that we underestimate them. Seron, even Apollonius—"

"We are twenty-thousand against five or ten thousand," Nicanor snapped at Gorgias. To Syrus he said, "Again, Colonel, I say, see to the march. I want all of the cohorts ready an hour before dawn. Also, you need to see to the executions. Dismissed."

"It shall be as you say," Syrus said and saluted.

As Syrus hurried away from the Akra, he realized that he was lucky to have come out of that debriefing with his head atop his shoulders. Nicanor easily could have added him to the execution order, blaming him along with the sentries for the prisoner's escape. Not only the hair at the back of his neck, but also the hairs on his arms prickled at that thought. As weary as he was at going on march after march and getting beaten by the rebel Jews, at least he was still alive. He just hoped he would stay that way. Between the Jews and his own commanders, his odds seemed to be dwindling somewhat.

"Agias!" Syrus came across his second and said, "Detain the two sentries who were manning the Akra entrance this morning and turn them over to the executioner. Then, bring me their heads."

"It shall be as you say, commander."

Chapter Seventy-three

T he firepits of Mizpah were strangely clean.   The charcoal from the logs remained, but all the ash had been swept up and lifted out. Over the plateau, the keening took on as many decibels and tonal variations as there were mourners. Those encamped at Mizpah, soldier and civilian alike wove back and forth, abasing themselves before their G-d.

Issachar, the Levite priest who had spirited the Torah Scrolls from the temple, had his hands clasped in distress over the defiled parchment and watched the community take their hoards of ash and heap the grey dust on their shoulders and heads in the age-old ritual of grief. The keening increased when the priest rolled open the scrolls and pointed at the swine's blood and the graffiti that depicted heathen gods and Greek obscenities on the holy parchment.

The tithes and offerings were collected and borne away. Judah had been entrusted with the shofar, the ram's horn used to signal the beginning of holy days and special rituals, and he held it to his lips and blew.

The people rose at their holy note and shouted, "The Lord of Hosts With Us! The Sword of the Lord! The Lord G-d is Ours! O G-d, be our help!"

After another rolling blast from the Shofar, Judah delineated the troops into their divisions. Because Asher had already created the divisions, the people were able to see an orderly assemblage of soldiers moving with surety among themselves. Judah then permitted the men exempt from the battle because they performed duties essential to the community to separate themselves from the other troops. These uttered the same battle cries of a moment before and in orderly ranks departed from the convocation and began their march toward Gophna. The people cheered them as the excused marched away to the north in orderly columns.

As the gathering broke up, the commanders stayed on the hillside that overlooked the little village of Mizpah. A fall breeze softened the sun's heat, so the men did not have to retire into the shade of their canvas barracks.

"Well, Ephraim was right," Asher said. "We have just had reports from the scouts that Nicanor and Gorgias have indeed begun to set up camp at Emmaus."

"Why did they not engage us, here?" Avram asked. "Why Emmaus? Did they not get enough of a drubbing at Beit Horon to teach them a lesson about those hills?"

"Because the Valley of Aijalon is a good source of water," Aulus pointed out. "It also provides excellent natural fortifications. The Greeks are rather lazy at building defenses for their camps. If I am thinking of the right area, they have camped where they have hills enclosing them on three sides. The only opening to their camp is the coastal plain to the west. And they know that we cannot approach them from that direction. Their visibility is too good."

Eleazar pointed to the civilian camp where all the people who had attended the ritual were now settling down for their evening meal preparations. "I, for one, am glad they are over at Emmaus. I was worried that they would attack our people here if they marched upon Mizpah."

"If we do not engage them soon at Emmaus," Judah said, "that is exactly what they will do. Ephraim said that he overheard some of the jailors bragging that they wished they could be with the marchers to Emmaus, for there would be some very serious plunder, gold and human alike, but they joked that the humans would be scarcer since the orders were to butcher the Jewish populations."

"That is how they plan to disrupt your intelligence network—eliminate your contacts by butchery," Aulus said. "Our spy network is very dangerous to the Greeks, because not only did Ephraim gather intelligence on his own, but he said that he set up intelligence cells in every village he visited. Your name, Judah, was all he had to mention to get their cooperation. And, it was not out of fear," the Roman said, "but rather pride at your exploits. They wanted to be part of your force." Aulus scratched his head. "And it is now likely that they will be butchered for that pride."

"Not if I have anything to say about it," said Eleazar. "I know that as first born, I am to be the *rebbe* of the community and carry on my priestly duties. That does not mean that I am going to let the Greeks slaughter our people."

"You will have your chance, Eleazar," Judah said, putting his hand on his shoulder. "But, now I need one of us, Mattathias' sons, to serve as a Law keeper for the people. You will have your chance," he repeated and patted Eleazar's head covering. But, for now you must stay and attend to rituals rather than fight."

"Does Ephraim yet live?" Asher asked.

"Yes," Judah answered. "My wife is attending to him. If sheer will can keep a man's life blood pumping through his body, then he will live, for Miriam simply will not let him die. Shoshanna is also with him to save him from Miriam's medical violence. I am going to see him, now."

The men's chuckles were half-hearted and mirthless as Judah left them. As they watched him descend the hill into the camp of Mizpah, Asher said, "If we had an army of Miriam's, the Greeks would have given up a long time ago."

This time the laughter had mirth.

The tent Ephraim inhabited during the times he actually lived in Gophna, his intelligence working usually taking him away, did not look like that of a bachelor, but rather that of a man with many wives. So many women were tasking away at chores in and around the tent, shoring up its stakes, tending the fire, sweeping the threshold, that Judah had to remind himself that the practice of taking many wives had died out seasons ago. Miriam was at work mending a tear in the tent's side and only looked up at the gruffness of Judah's voice.

"How is he getting any rest with all you hens cackling around?" Judah asked. "The man needs sleep in order for his body to mend."

"Typical man logic," Miriam breathed. "What good is his rest if he freezes to death with the fall breeze blowing through this hole. He will rest more easily if he has an orderly camp."

"Typical woman logic," Judah retorted. "I tell you that Ephraim does not care."

"Then you do not know Ephraim very well," Miriam said. "He likes order."

"How is he?"

Miriam sat back on her haunches and adjusted her veil. "Avram straightened the fingers. That was unpleasant. I did not know a man could make such as sound." She gritted her teeth. "Husband, you must kill as many Greeks as you can. They are not men, but animals, that they could rend his body like this. Would that I had a sword." She plunged the awl through the canvas and resumed her mending.

"Is he awake?"

"Yes."

At the challenge in her voice, Judah decided to ask, "May I see him?"

"Only for a few minutes. His voice is still raw. I can tell it pains him to talk. I need to dress his feet soon."

Judah parted the flap and entered the tent. There was a strong smell of eucalyptus and myrrh in the tent. He did not know much about healing, but he recognized that smell from the remedies that his mother used to ply on him and his brothers when they suffered childhood cuts and bruises.

"Brother. Ephraim."

The body stirred then quieted as if the exertion of movement was too taxing on its wasted frame.

Judah sat down next to the still form and waited for a few moments. "Ephraim," he said, more loudly this time.

Ephraim opened his remaining eye, its pale gaze finally resting on Judah. "Judah," he whispered.

"How do you feel?"

"Better. Much better."

"You are a liar."

It was more of a grimace than a smile, but Judah was still heartened. "Brother, are you sure about Gorgias splitting his force? Just a 'yes' or 'no' will suffice, or Miriam will have my head."

"Yes, I think so," Ephraim whispered. "But, Judah." His bandaged hand plucked at Judah's sleeve. "It may be a trick—"

"Shhh," Judah hissed, looking behind him. "I will be wary with my men. You are not to think about anything except your health."

Ephraim held up both bandaged hands and shrugged. "I am broken," he rasped. "But you, you—"

"I know, I know," Judah said, seeing the anxiety in Ephraim's remaining eye, the other covered by a merciful square of homespun. "I will be careful." He leaned toward Ephraim and added, "But not too careful."

"That is enough," Miriam said, entering the tent. "I need to dress his wounds."
As she unwrapped Ephraim's poor feet, Judah forced himself to look.

Ephraim did his best not to sob, but his gasps became more piteous as Miriam applied the salve. Judah could actually see bone under the charred flesh, and he had to set his jaw to avoid weeping.

Miriam looked up and said, "You will be surprised, husband, at what these bodies the Lord gave us can do. The pad of the foot will come back, as long as it does not blacken any further. Ephraim," she went on in a matter-of-fact tone. "Did you know that Gad has his eye on little Rebekkah? Esther is thinking about setting the contract next year, that is, if her family is agreeable, which I am sure they will be as his elder brother is the great spy, Ephraim Bar-Naphtali. I was just saying to Elizabeth the other day. . ."

As Judah backed out of the tent to the gossip designed to distract Ephraim, he wished he were facing a legion of Greeks at that moment. Nothing but the blood and broken bodies of a million Greeks under his heel would satisfy him. Then the legion of victims marched before him: Ephraim with his broken body, Hannah and her six sons, Yehoshua, Barak, Caleb, Gabriel, Elijah and Yacob, his friends Malachi and Schmuel, Shoshanna, and so many others. He would avenge all of them and take great pleasure in rending Greek flesh. He entered his tent and laid out his armor, checking it for weakness. After satisfying himself that all was ready, he moved to where he kept his prayer phylacteries. He removed them from a pouch and carefully wrapped one around his right bicep and the other around his head so that the prayer box was centered on his brow. Then blackness overcame him. The familiar dark anxiety overwhelmed him for a moment. How could they hope to engage twenty-thousand Greeks? Over the armor, he bowed low to the ground and prayed.

"Oh, Lord of the Universe, what shall we do with these Greeks and whither shall we carry them away? For thy sanctuary is trodden down and profaned, and thy priests are in heaviness and brought low. And, lo, the heathen are assembled together against us to destroy us: what things they imagine against us, thou knowest. How shall we be able to stand against them, except thou, O G-d, be our help?"

Then a vision entered his mind's eye. He was in his father's house in Modiin. His father was speaking, and his words filled Judah now.

"The Lord G-d of Hosts will grant us victory. If we adhere to the law and the truth, He of No Name will support us in our conflict. We will be victorious, my son."

Mattathias' pronouncement almost two years before was made before the rebellion had even started, before any Jew had dared to stand up to the Greek. Judah smiled when he remembered his reaction to his father's strange vision, a seeming prophecy uttered in the incongruent setting of the dining rug in their Modiin estate. Back then he had been skeptical. Now, Judah simply reached for his armor. His breast was calm. The darkness had passed.

Chapter Seventy-four

Emmaus, Judaea   The 1st day of *Tishri* 3596 (September 10, 165 B.C.E.)

S yrus could not think of a smarmier collection of entrepreneurs than these slave merchants that Nicanor had invited to attend their march to Emmaus. Why did they all look as if dipped in grease? Surely, they made enough money to wash occasionally. Their attire generally was of a fine quality, but it hung on their bodies, whether corpulent or gaunt, as if the clothing had made an uneasy truce in an ongoing battle of taste.

He looked over the trader's camp. The equipment carts for their baggage wound through the camp in an ungainly attempt at order. For all its chaos, however, the slave baggage train was almost as impressive as the military's. Huge amounts of grain and even baked loaves filled wagon after wagon of the slave traders. The only difference was that instead of arms, shields and other military equipment, chains filled the rest of the vehicles. The logistics for the sale of slaves demanded this quantity of goods, he guessed, though he had never thought much about it. He was here to make sure that the military's financial interest in this slave sale was not compromised in any way. The going rate for human stock was one talent per ninety slaves. It was up to Syrus to see that the traders' allotment of slaves was fair and that Nicanor, the face of this military interest, would not be cheated out of his money by miscounts and some of the other chicaneries that occurred on spent battlefields.

"Commander?" The accent of the slave trader lilted with a distinct flavor of Tyre.

"Yes," Syrus said, "what is it?"

Syrus was sitting at a table accompanied by Polydorus, a surly lieutenant who did not relish having an overseer. Syrus knew from gossip that Polydorus had been looking forward to skimming some revenue from the slave sales. That would be impossible now with Syrus, one of Nicanor's adjutants, peering over his shoulder.

"I would like to be first to choose my allotment," The trader said.

"You and the other pieces of filth encamped here," Syrus muttered, "will draw a lot just like everyone else."

The trader looked this way and that, his hand reaching into his robe and drawing out a small pouch. The muffled clinks on the table brought an avaricious smirk to Lieutenant Polydorus' face, full of hope that perhaps this was going to be lucrative enterprise after all.

All hope dwindled out of Polydorus' features when Syrus stood and struck the trader across the face then beaned him with the pouch. "The nature of lots," Syrus said pointedly as he watched the trader skulk away, "is to ensure a fair distribution. Is not that right, Lieutenant?"

"Yes, of course, sir," Polydorus said without much conviction.

"And if I hear that you line your pockets during this assignment," Syrus said, not looking at the lieutenant, "I will personally have you gutted and your living body left to the carrion birds."

Syrus pushed the wax tablets to Polydorus, who had a very disagreeable look, and said, "Each trader has his own tablet. That will keep the transactions separate. And, make no mistake, I back up my threats with concise accounting. Is that clear, lieutenant?" At Polydorus' wan nod, Syrus pushed away from the table and stood. "And now I must report to Gorgias and Nicanor. I will check in on you before the march. I believe I am joining Gorgias on his march to Mizpah."

"Yes, sir."

Syrus heard a little cheer in Polydorus' voice. Perhaps he hoped that Syrus would perish in the battle and he would be left to his graft.

As Syrus distastefully picked his way through the slave trader camp on his way to the command tent, some discomfort rose in his belly about the impending battle with the Jews. He had been part of two failed campaigns already, those of Apollonius and Seron. It was inconceivable that they fail again. This time two of the greatest living generals of the Greek empire, indeed, probably of the world, were directing the onslaught. His soldier's head told him that he was in good hands, and that all would go according to a natural military outcome: intelligence indicated his force had more than double the men as that of the enemy. But his guts told him that Gorgias, with his plan to march on Mizpah and leave Nicanor and the main force behind, was walking into another debacle. And, if the Jewish prisoner Ephraim had not died during his rescue, then that information was in the hands of the enemy because of Gorgias' big mouth.

After the guards standing at the entrance to the generals' canvas headquarters admitted him, he stood before Nicanor and saluted.

"Yes, Syrus. What is it?" Nicanor said.

Nicanor was lounging with a goblet of wine hung loosely in his grasp. Syrus stopped, somewhat uncomfortable. He was unused to seeing the General so at ease. Usually, Nicanor was all business, sitting at a desk directing subordinates, editing maps, ciphering accounts, or waxing out battle plans. It was odd to see the general reclining, his body and features totally relaxed.

"Polydorus has been instructed, General. I have started the accounting procedure for him and have readied the lots. After I leave with General Gorgias, however, I would suggest that you assign another overseer. The lieutenant is a little shifty."

"No doubt, no doubt." Nicanor looked at the goblet with distaste and set it down. "This wine is too warm. So, Commander Syrus," he said, now familiar, now even more relaxed. "What think you of our chances?"

"Our chances, sir?" Syrus asked, confused.

"Yes, our chances." Nicanor stood and wandered around the tent for a moment. He sat on the desk. "How is our readiness?"

Syrus froze. It was almost as if Nicanor knew Syrus had information that he was holding back. But how could he know? He shrugged off the ridiculous thought and answered, "We are more than ready, General. We will march as soon as the sun goes down. The Jews will have no chance against Gorgias. There is a large complement of women and children encamped at Mizpah. We will attack them first and force the rebels to compromise their strategy by defending the civilians. It is unlikely that they will do the smart thing—watch their women and children die and save their energy for the battle. It is a brilliant plan."

"I wonder," said Nicanor. "This Maccabee is a crafty devil." He stood, picked up the goblet and dashed its contents out the tent flap. "I do not trust him." He looked thoughtful. "Just as I do not trust Gorgias' plan," he added, a quizzical expression on his face.

Syrus did not know what to do. This was the perfect opening. If he were going to tell Nicanor of the one chink in the plan—an escaped prisoner carrying information from Gorgias' mouth—this was the time to do so. The dizzy moment hovered over the conversation and Syrus opened his mouth to speak.

Nicanor's sharp tone interrupted the moment. "See, Colonel? What an old man's ridiculous musings can do?" His laugh vanquished the opportunity completely. "Second-guessing the strategies of Gorgias, one of the greatest military minds of our century! What in Zeus' name was I thinking?"

Syrus laughed too, but with less certainty.

Chapter Seventy-five

Into the twilight sky, the distant flame pulsed. "There it is. They are coming," Judah said to the men. "Have the civilians left the camp?"

"Yes, Commander," Asher said. "They are safely away. The villages round about have also been abandoned, just in case. The Greeks will have no civilians as fodder for their swords this day."

"Good, good. Now we must light the lanterns. We will leave only a skeleton force with Avram here to keep the lights burning. Not one lantern must be allowed to go out."

"It shall be as you say," Avram said, holding up his torch in the direction of the camp. "This area will stay alive with fire. I fashioned sturdy lanterns that hang from iron poles—they will withstand even a full gust of wind."

"Good," Judah said. "That is good. Yehonatan, John and Simon, we will keep our fighters together on the same ridges until we come to Jabel hill. We will rest there and organize, then we will descend into their camp, attacking at dawn."

"That is a difficult route," said Yehonatan. "I remember taking it with father, but it took us two days."

"It is the only route that will get us there by dawn, but on a forced march. I want to accompany the sunrise into their camp. The sun will blind them to our attack."

"As well as the surprise," said Aulus. "I now see why you wanted the Greeks to know we were here at Mizpah. Bait for Gorgias, if Ephraim's intelligence is correct."

"I trust his intelligence—it is too expensive to disregard," said Judah, thinking of his friend's broken body. "Are the men ready?"

"They are impatient," Asher said, grinning. "They wonder why the commander keeps them waiting: perhaps he has lost his nerve."

"They will wish Judah had such a loss if this attack goes wrong," Aulus grumbled. "It will take only one cough, or one Greek patrol and we are all dead, all the rituals notwithstanding."

Asher slapped the Roman on the back. "Oh, quit murmuring. Even you were caught up by the ritual, you must admit that it was moving."

Aulus shook his head. "Yes, it was moving. I was bored asleep until that blasted horn blew me out of my skin. I moved pretty fast, then."

"Heathen."

"Hellenist."

"Pagan."

"Stop it you two," Judah said, knocking Aulus' and Asher's heads together, lightly since they were not helmeted, yet. "Keep the epithets for the Greeks. And, I want both of you to make sure my younger brothers know what they are doing during the attack."

"Judah, we know what to do," said John, turning churlish.

"John, make your decisions and if they are right, then Asher will let you act upon them. But, you *will* listen to Asher," said Judah, severe. "Is that clear?"

"Yes," John said.

"Little Brother," Judah said, easily. "This is highly irregular, a man taking his first command at your young age. You are an able warrior, it is true, but inexperienced. The same goes for you, Simon. You are to listen to Aulus."

"I am glad for his help," said Simon. "I do not feel ready for this assignment."

As Judah looked in his youngest brother's face, for the first time that day he saw fear. Simon was younger than John but more sophisticated in the way he looked at things. He, more than the more brutish John, saw the danger of this campaign because he understood strategies and had studied where some of them had failed: Thermopylae, Pyrrhus, Magnesia and even some of the ancient battles of King David when he fought Saul. Judah gently put his hand against the side of Simon's face, the respectable beard belying his youth, and said, "Simon. Aulus will school you. You will learn much about battle. A little too soon, and a little too fast, but you will learn. Listen to the Roman. We are blessed to have his advice. He learned at the feet of his father, one of the greatest fighters in the Roman legions. And a Roman legion is the greatest war machine in the world."

Aulus harrumphed loudly, seemingly moved. Judah grasped him by the elbow and arm and said, "This Roman is at the core of the success of our rebellion. May the Lord G-d bless him and his generations forever!" The two old friends embraced amid the commanders' murmurs of approval.

"Let us march," Judah said. "I will set the pace. You all know these ridges. This is our country: we know its contours so let us move quickly. We will have about ten hours of darkness—that is more than enough time to get to Jabel and rest for a couple of hours before we attack."

"Is not there a chance that we will meet Gorgias?" One of the men asked.

"No," Judah said. "He will be plodding up the Beit Horon pass to get to our camp here at Mizpah. It is better traveled than our route, for all the difficulty the Greeks have had with that pass. Let us on."

Laughing at Judah's reference to Seron's debacle at Beit Horon, the commanders followed him down to their camp. They gathered up their units and, as far as the trickling rivulets of 5,000 men into the western slopes of the Jerusalem hills would allow, double-timed it out of Mizpah.

Chapter Seventy-six

Gorgias said, "Ask the collaborator if this is the way."

I am sitting right here, Nadab thought with irritation. *Why do you not ask me yourself, you great Greek oaf?* He said nothing, however, and waited for Syrus' question.

Syrus turned in his saddle, and with his back to Gorgias, simply smiled, not voicing the question at all.

Syrus' amusement increased Nadab's irritation, but he decided he had better not play games and said, "Yes, this is the way. You will find Mizpah just around that ridge. In fact, can you see that glow? That would be the fires of their camp."

"Excellent," Gorgias said. "We will ride down to that last ridge and dismount. We will get as close to their camp as possible, then mount up and attack. Syrus, send the word along to the rear."

Nadab watched Syrus salute and wheel his mount around; he disappeared through the horsed mass leaving Nadab alone with the general.

Small talk was impossible as the general seemed to eschew his presence, so Nadab just sat quietly and stared at the faint light that was the camp of Mizpah. Their night march had taken them past the very village where Nadab had been raised. Beit Horon had been sleepy enough when he had lived there, but when they had passed it earlier in the evening, it looked comatose. He guessed that the people there had evacuated after Seron's battle. The general had been about to dispatch one hundred of his fighters to scout the village and slaughter its inhabitants to ensure the secrecy of their march, but Nadab, through Syrus, was able to convince Gorgias that the village was dormant and no danger to them.

As Nadab looked about him, every ridge and turn of the road was an intimate reminder of his childhood. Against that outcropping he, his brothers and cousins had built a primitive stone fort—long since collapsed—and played King David and his tens of thousands. There was the ridge where he had hunted for the first time with his father. And over there he saw the stumped remains of trees from a night he and his brothers had been lost. In desperation they had cut down the scrawny cedars to build a fire to keep warm, thinking they were close to death. He chuckled at the memory. In their confusion brought on by the hysterics of youth and lack of sleep, they had not realized they were not ten cubits from the road. Ever after, during their subsequent boyhood jaunts he and his kinsmen laughed whenever they traveled this way and saw those ridiculous stumps. Gorgias' haughty stare brought him back to the present and he coughed to obscure his chuckle.

Syrus clambered up with his horse and amid the great snorting and pawing of his mount, said, "Sir, the men are ready. At your command."

"We will ride down to the ridge yonder. When they see me stop and dismount, have them do the same."

"It shall be as you say."

The thousand lantern lights filled the men with great lust for battle and they eagerly hushed their horses as they led them toward the Jew camp. Their advance was as water, smooth and steady, the only sound the hooved stumbles of their beasts over rocks and scrub. At last, they would surprise the Maccabee. At last. At last. Finally, the command came from Gorgias to mount up and charge the lights.

And that is all they were. Lights upon lights. The men milled about, bumping the lanterns, angrily stomping out the fires, and raging against the trick. The Maccabee was not there. There was not one Jew against whom they could slake their fury. Their horses pounded the earth in vain. The Maccabee was not there.

Gorgias rode up with Syrus to a small rise above Mizpah. Nadab hung back, more nervous than his skittish horse. The advisor to the high priest of Jerusalem watched the two Greek commanders converse, then sighed when in the faltering lamplight he saw Syrus abrupt beckoned to him to join them.

"Well, advisor," Syrus said. "What happened here?"

"He was here, commander. Of that I am sure," Nadab said. "My agents actually described the ritual—an ancient affair reminiscent of the old days of the kingdom of Israel under the prophet Samuel. Ram horns, breastplates and the like."

"I do not care a fig about your ancient rituals," Gorgias barked. "Where is the Maccabee, now?"

As Nadab felt the question was rhetorical, he did not answer. How could he know?

But he did know. Syrus' outward quaking of rage at the trick of lanterns covered an inner shiver of fear. The prisoner, Ephraim, must have survived and had told Judah about the Greeks splitting their force—information that came directly from this fool Gorgias' mouth—and the Maccabee was in Emmaus at this very moment attacking Nicanor.

And the Jews had the full advantage of surprise.

Chapter Seventy-seven

A s they had done so many times before, Judah and his men crouched behind a ridge, the Greek host below completely ignorant of their 6,000-strong, silent presence. Judah had been preparing and preparing for the time that his men would have to meet the Greeks in a frontal assault, and he was always surprised when he was able to avoid that happenstance. The enemy always seemed to fall into their hands by series of eerie coincidence. This latest was a marvel: their altruistic rescue of Ephraim had served as an important factor in their knowledge of Greek movements, again perhaps staving off the need for open battle against a seasoned enemy.

"Have you seen the signal, yet?" Asher whispered, scrambling over the mounds of recumbent men to Judah's position. "Avram said he'd send the signal over the mountains when Gorgias arrived in Mizpah."

"Not yet," Judah said. "It is yet three hours to dawn. We will wait and make our assault when the signal fire appears on Shaalbim Ridge over yonder."

"What if it does not appear?" Asher said, worried. "What, then?"

"It will appear," Judah said simply. "We will wait."

"Your arrogance is astounding, Judah," said Asher. "How can you be so sure?"

Judah shrugged. "I do not know."

At the end of the watch, the signal fire did flare on the ridge and the men made ready. The Maccabee and his brothers arranged their ranks and crouched a final time.

Finally, Judah's hand rose and fell, and the silent warrior mass moved over Jabel hill toward the ridge saddle that directly overlooked the Greek camp. As many men as possible crowded astride the stony saddle, standing up with the sun that rose behind them. They hid no longer, but made their force massive for the Greeks to see.

Chapter Seventy-eight

Emmaus, Judaea   The 2nd day of *Tishri* 3596 (September 11th 165 B.C.E.)

Nicanor lay on his cot, sensing the dawn. Another boring day waiting for Gorgias to return. He almost wished the Jews would attack. At least it would be something to do. But, that would never happen. Even with his reduced force, he could still handle an incursion by the Hebrews, but no one knew that Gorgias had left, least of all the Jews. And the Maccabee would never commit his valued countrymen to an attack—

What was that roar? Nicanor sat up and craned his ear toward the sound. Shouts brought him leaping off his cot, yelling for his adjutants.

They appeared immediately, their faces ashen, all of them shouting at once. Finally, Nicanor had to silence them with his commander's bark to make sense of what they were saying. "Just you, Dorus! Tell me!"

"General! It is the Jews! They are coming from the southeast saddle.Thousands of them!"

"Rouse everyone with the trumpets—do not bother with reveille, but sound the attack note! Hurry! Coriolus! Help me with my armor!"

As his slave threw the armor about him, Nicanor cursed himself. He never did feel good about Gorgias splitting their force and now he was meeting an ambush right in his own camp with only half his complement. Madness! *Hades*!

Pandemonium greeted him when he broke out of his tent, sword in hand. His lieutenants were bawling out orders, none of which seemed to have hearers. Infantrymen were running this way and that, cavalrymen were leading their horses through the sea of armored flesh and the phalangites were doing their best not to skewer each other or their fellows with their wicked pikes.

Nicanor had not heard the trumpeters so grabbed one of his lieutenants and yelled, "Find the trumpets! That is the only way we will establish order in this accursed soup. Hurry!"

As he pushed his man away, he sheathed his sword and shouted individually to his lieutenants, establishing a ripple of order that overtook the mayhem immediately surrounding the command tent. The men ceased their aimless scatterings and settled into a defensive position until they could find a void in the enemy ranks to launch an offense.

The void never materialized. There was no room to swing a sword, let alone move forward. The Jews had the advantage of space and momentum and they were using it to lethal advantage. Nicanor heard death advancing upon their position and took his sword out again to assuage his feeling of impotence. Away in the distance, barely audible for the sound of war around them, the Greek trumpet blew the attack blare. Too late in coming, the ludicrous note died quickly.

"General! We must get you out of here. The hill behind us has not been compromised. We can make our way up over the ridge and flee to Gezer."

Nicanor raised his hand to strike his lieutenant, thundering, "Flee? I cannot leave my men. And you will not either. We will stay our ground—"

A massive wall of armor and weapons swept them back, rendering Nicanor's blow and argument useless. The ground would not be stayed, and the Jewish onslaught had already pushed them to the ridge. In spite of himself, Nicanor found himself hauling himself backward up the hill, a terrace of Jews pushing up the mound and engaging his men just under him. His adjutants were acting as his retreat bodyguard, fighting off the enemy so the general could make good his unwilling escape.

At the top of the hill, Nicanor allowed himself a last look at the overrun camp. Disheveled Jews had supplanted Greek positions, so what had been an orderly, even elegant camp now was a quagmire of flesh, dust, and trampled, bloodstained tents.

"General! We must go! This way!"

As Nicanor followed Lieutenant Dorus and a handful of Greek survivors into the cover of Cedar, his legs trembled with the ennui of defeat.

* * * * * *

Overruling some of the elders' disapproval, Judah had made sure many in their company had brought shofars, and the blowing of the ram's horns had the expected effect: the noise had both signaled their charge and inspired confusion in the ranks of the enemy. From the very beginning, it was clear that the Greeks were frozen by the shock of the attack. They did rally somewhat near what Judah suspected was Nicanor's command tent, but the Jews' pressing numbers had flattened out any defense the Greek may have been able to muster in the face of the surprise.

Battle was hard work, and the joy Judah's men experienced at their easy spill into the Greek camp soon dissipated at the sheer labor of cutting through human flesh. John and Asher swept to the northeast, battling not only dismounted cavalrymen but also their horses that some thinking Greek had loosed, spooking the beasts toward the charging Jews. Yehonatan pressed northwest, his men mowing down the tentative pikes of the phalangite camp. Southwest was the direction that Aulus and Simon thrust, that being the heart of the camp where the command tent reigned. Judah himself plunged his men south to neutralize the dangerous Greek infantry.

The reputed barbs of the formidable Greek defense were no match for the Maccabee's use of shock in his attack, and the Jew's hard butchery was rewarded with a total enemy rout. Not many Greeks escaped, and the few who disappeared over the jutting rock saddles to the west and south were greatly outnumbered by their comrades who fell under Jewish swords.

"Nicanor! Have you found Nic—?" Judah panted when he found Aulus directing his men outside the Greek command tent. He stopped mid-query and grasped Aulus' elbow and arm, embracing him. "Are you yet alive my friend? You are wounded." Judah grabbed at the temples of Aulus' helmet, pried it off his head and peered at his brow. "We must dress that."

"A scratch," Aulus said dismissively and pulled his helmet back down. "And, no, I have not found Nicanor. I have had my men do a check for command armor on the corpses, but we have not found the general."

Judah patted the Roman's arm and tried not to show his unseemly disappointment. In the face of this great triumph, he could not allow himself to feel any frustration at having missed the Greek commander. "How does your force? Have you lost any men?"

"A pittance, although I am sure you would say that is the wrong word. We did very well in numbers, indeed." He looked around at the Greek carnage and nodded. "Especially compared to these chaps."

Simon came rushing out of the Greek command tent itself. "Judah! You have got to see this! Come! Come!"

Smiling at Aulus, Judah followed his little brother into the tent although he knew exactly what Simon had found. "Ah, yes, little grubs. It appears that you are rich."

At this, Aulus, who had followed them into the tent, laughed and joined Simon at one of the chests. "I am surprised Nicanor had this much gold with him. I had thought that Antiochus had every shekel with him in Antioch. He still owes us Romans 2,000 talents in tribute from the old war. Perhaps I should send this to Rome. The senate would reward me greatly."

"Was not a lack of gold the reason for Antiochus' journey toward Parthia and the East?" Judah asked, bemused at the wealth before him. "If so, it seems that his very commanders are holding out on their 'divine' emperor. Even the trusted Nicanor."

Aulus considered this for a moment, then said. "Every general must hold back some wealth for himself. I suspect if they relied on Antioch for every shekel, they would not be able to run their campaigns effectively."

"You call this effective?" Judah laughed and gestured about him.

Aulus chuckled and went on, "And you know yourself, Judah, how much it costs to outfit an army properly."

"Well, this gold will go a long way to outfitting our army 'properly,' as you put it, and no, you may *not* send it to Rome," Judah said. "Simon, that reminds me. Put a detail of your men on stripping armor from the Greek corpses. Then, after we have all the revenue organized, I want this camp in ashes. Get help from Yehonatan and John if you need it." His heart warmed at the prospect of more safety for his men, and as he scanned the plunder again, he breathed, "The Lord of Hosts With Us."

Chapter Seventy-nine

Mizpah, Judaea   The 2nd day of *Tishri* 3596 (September 11th 165 B.C.E.)

Nadab gnawed on the hardtack "Why do you not tell him yourself?" He asked, surly. "He will not listen to me. He barely acknowledges me." In distaste, he spit the offending biscuit out into the dust.

"You must try." Syrus urged, knowing he could not tell Nadab the real reason for his reluctance to urge Gorgias to return to Emmaus. He could not act like he knew too much about why the Maccabee was able to anticipate their arrival here in Mizpah. An escaped prisoner, after hearing from Gorgias' very mouth about the Greek plan to split forces, had alerted the Maccabee. Syrus had gambled that the prisoner, Ephraim, would die before that intelligence got to the Maccabee. It seemed he had lost the gamble. The empty camp attested to it.

"I will do my best. But I do not think it will do any good. Not only that, but you have already asked him to speak to me and he refused." Nadab shrugged. "If the old fool cannot figure out that this was a ploy to keep him away from Emmaus, I do not think I will be able to do much to convince him."

As Syrus labored with Nadab up the ridge to the command tent, his mind worked furiously. Gorgias' inattention to the ramifications of the empty camp here was troubling. As soon as he saw the Jews were gone, the general should have ordered his force to double-time it back to Emmaus with the understanding that the Maccabee had designs on attacking Nicanor, but it seemed that the old man's strategic acumen had been stunted either by laziness or by the shock of the empty camp.

Syrus stooped to clear his boot of brambles as he tried to think. Before he left on this accursed march, he should have told Nicanor that during his interrogation the prisoner Ephraim had heard Gorgias' pronouncement about splitting the forces. Now it was too late to do anything about the failure of his gamble.

This debacle at Mizpah stung him even further when it became obvious that the rebel had set up this folly of lanterns to fool Gorgias into staying away from Emmaus even longer so Nicanor would be more vulnerable. They had wasted an entire night thinking the enemy was hunkered down among the flickering lights ripe for their scythes. Now, getting Gorgias back to Emmaus as soon as possible was the only way Syrus could atone for his mistake. It seemed, however, that Gorgias' inert demeanor would add to Syrus' failure. Nadab was his only hope.

Syrus waited for a moment or two to approach General Gorgias. The General, his head in his hands, was sitting in front of his command tent at the top of the ridge. The colonel paced for a moment or two, anxious to prod the general, but his gumption failed him.

The vantage afforded them by the placement of the command tent at the top of Mizpah ridge was vast, but useless. There was nothing to see. The Jews were gone. If the general had lifted his head, all he would have seen was an empty camp. It was bad enough that they could hear the lanterns taunting them, the creaks a steady cadence in the morning breeze. Finally, Syrus screwed up his courage.

"General?"

Gorgias forced his gaze out of his palms. "Yes, Colonel, what is it?"

"Advisor Nadab would like a word," Syrus said. "He has been waiting for an hour to speak with you."

"As I said before: I have nothing to say to that collaborator fop." Gorgias stretched his legs and sighed. "Send him away."

"You may be interested in what he has to say," Syrus said, trying to keep the eager strain out of his voice.

At Gorgias' glare, Syrus looked down. He had to get Gorgias off his fat arse and back to Emmaus, but he had to do it delicately. The wind worried the lanterns and the creaking increased.

Gorgias looked away from the young colonel, then down at his swollen leg. "This gout is a misery," he grunted, then was silent.

Syrus still waited, attentive, polite, but as his anxiety rose, he became more lightheaded. It would be bad form for a colonel to insist that a general talk to a lowly collaborator, so he forced himself to wait. At last, the general stood. "All right. Send that damned Jew to me. I would like to hear what he has to say before I have him executed."

"Executed?" Syrus asked, feeling the blood drain from his head. "May I ask the cause?"

"He led us into this decoy, knowing full well that the Maccabee was not here."

"But, your honor," Syrus protested. "He has nothing to gain by a Maccabean victory. He is a collaborator, and the Maccabee kills collaborators."

Gorgias grunted again and turned away, and Syrus took advantage of the tacit dismissal.

Syrus left out the allusion to execution when he fetched Nadab. "Now, remember what we discussed. You must make him understand that Nicanor is in danger."

"I still do not see the point in this audience!" Nadab said. "He will not listen to me!"

Syrus was wondering the same thing himself. The general's grasp of the situation was uncharacteristically flaccid. The Maccabee was in Emmaus, probably attacking Nicanor at this very moment.

The two men approached the general who had taken to rubbing his leg. Gorgias did not look up. "So, Jew. What did you want to say before I strip you of your head?"

Even as Syrus kept a stoic gaze fixed on the general, he could sense that Nadab was doing his best not to reel. He felt rather than saw Nadab's stark look of shock.

"General," Nadab said carefully. "I believe that the Maccabee is planning an attack on Nicanor at Emmaus."

"Why would you think that?"

"Because," said Nadab, "It sounds like something the Maccabee would do. As you probably know, he and his men still are not ready to meet you and your forces straight on. He still has to rely on subterfuge and trickery."

Gorgias still did not look up, so Nadab went on. "Your Excellency. I am a Jew and I know how the Maccabee thinks. If I were he, I would use such a deception to avoid a head-on battle." Nadab had not wanted to rely on such an undignified allusion to his race, but Gorgias did not look as if he were responding to the previous argument.

Gorgias considered for quite a few moments. Ignoring the men, he tugged at his tunic, repositioned his greaves and put on his helmet. He straightened, then stood, adjusting his breastplate. "Call the men in from these damn hills. The Jews are gone. There is no one left to hunt, here. Make ready to return to our base camp at Emmaus."

Bald triumph on his face, Nadab looked pointedly at Syrus. For once, Syrus was happy to let the Jew gloat and even hoped it might be enough of a win to allow Nadab to keep his head.

Chapter Eighty

The Road from Mizpah to Emmaus, Judaea   The 2nd day of *Tishri* 3596 (September 11th 165 B.C.E.)

T he grit of the march clung not only to Nadab's skin, but also his sensibilities as a court gentleman. He was not used to life without a daily bath and oiling. If he had wanted to live as a barbarian, he would have stayed in his hometown of Beit Horon among his smelly people. Not only that, every bark from Gorgias' mouth caused his heart to speed abnormally. He was certain that his health would never be the same because of it. Gorgias and his like were the very reason that Nadab had not joined the military but had opted instead for the political machinations of government. And now here he was, conscripted for service in the Greek army. Although he was here only as a consultant, he still felt set upon. He was no more suited for military life, even a temporary one, than he was for living as a desert Jew. Now, because of this expedition, he was doing both, badly.

He and the Greeks were double-timing it back to Emmaus to save Nicanor and his men from a stealth attack by the Maccabee. Given Nadab's present disgust with all things Greek, Nicanor's well-being and that of his soldiers meant less to him than his rump that was sore from bouncing up and down on his horse.

Syrus rode alongside him, although Nadab could not help but notice that the Greek's backside did not pummel the saddle as his did. He had always avoided horses at every stage of his life. His butt and even his testicles attested to that avoidance.

"How fare you, advisor?" Syrus asked.

"As well as can be expected for all that I am inhaling desert with every breath and every bone in my arse feels as if it is afire."

Syrus laughed and said, "Emmaus is just over the next hill."

"You said that seven hills ago," Nadab said.

The eighth hill, however, did prove to be the last before Emmaus, as Syrus had said. But, there was no rescuing to be done as the forward Greek scouts galloped back in a fury to keep the Greeks from crossing that hill with a report that Jews were now occupying the Greek camp. Emmaus had fallen to the rebels.

Gorgias, Syrus and Nadab huddled with the rest of the commanders behind the hill and watched the smoke rise.

"The bastards are burning the camp," Gorgias muttered. "We are done, here."

"But General," Syrus said. "Surely we can attack and drive the Jews out. There is time—"

"Time, perhaps," Gorgias said, nodding. "But numbers? We cannot drive the Jews from a wedge that we created. That is why we chose Emmaus as a site. It is entirely defensible. And, we have not the numbers to take the camp back. The only reason the Jews were able to succeed in taking it is through abject trickery: by sending us on a false chase to Mizpah. No, we are finished here. We must retreat back to Jerusalem, while we still can."

"General—" Syrus began.

"That is enough, commander. And if you want to remain a commander, you will be silent. I am no more mood for entreaties than I am in a useless battle."

The Greeks withdrew from the hill and massed quietly over the ravine, filling their skins with water, but not resting. Gorgias ordered a quiet march back the way they came, intending to veer off to the south out of the hills toward the Jerusalem road.

Nadab filled his skin along with the rest, but drifted away from Syrus. He found a small defile, deeper down the ravine and waited. It took quite a while for the army to dissipate, more than an hour, in fact. Nadab was patient, however, and when the last of the Greek army had winnowed away over the hill in the direction of Jerusalem, he took a different route. Pointing his horse's nose south, he set his face toward Idumea and the house of his wife's family.

Chapter Eighty-one

Gophna, Judaea   The 6th day of *Heshvan* 3596 (October 15th 165 B.C.E.)

T he fingers were impossibly stiff. He tried to do as Avram and Miriam said, flexing them as often as thought willed, but it was almost like being tortured all over again.

"That is good," Miriam said as she patted out the Shabbat bread. "Yes, I know it hurts, but you could get the use of your fingers back if, that is, you can work through the pain".

Ephraim disliked being fussed over, but as he could do nothing for himself, there was no help for it. Miriam had appointed herself his attendant and spent all her daylight hours cooking for him, changing the dressings on his feet and cleaning his camp. A young student was assigned to help Ephraim with the more private necessities, but even he was under thrall to Miriam, a fact that she never let the youth forget.

It was not that Ephraim was ungrateful. In fact, he marveled at her energy and brute organization. But he was wearying of her constant presence, a fact that induced his teeth-gritting finger calisthenics that moment. As soon as he got his hands back, she would leave his camp. At least he hoped so.

"I thought I would visit to see if the stories were true."Ephraim and Miriam looked up. Ephraim was much more excited than Miriam to see Shoshanna. He was so overcome with relief that he stood to bow, forgetting the condition of his ruined feet. The student came out of the background and aided his lurch to the ground.

"What stories?" Ephraim gasped as the youth settled him.

"That the great spy, Ephraim bar Naphtali, is being ruled by a mere woman."

Ephraim did not dare look at Miriam to see her reaction. He even winced his eyes shut to prepare for it.

Nothing happened. Miriam choked out an innocent giggle, but that was all as she resumed her bustle over the bread.

"It is no matter," Shoshanna said, laughing. "I have no doubt that you will be dancing at the next wedding feast."

"Not if I can help it," Miriam growled. "His feet need to heal first. Here, sister. Help me with this bread."

As the women worked the dough into the intricate braid, Ephraim sat back and watched. Miriam seemed happily at ease, and he wondered why. He had heard stories of her jealousy over Shoshanna's pregnancy—that it had caused friction in the tent of the Maccabee.

He decided to find out. He was a spy, after all. He turned to Miriam's sister-in-law. "*Nu*, Shoshanna. When is the happy event? I am sure that Eleazar is fighting the sin of pride every time he looks at you."

Shoshanna's dimple accompanied an embarrassed gulp. She did not seem displeased, however, for all that she lowered her head in a demur nod. "Three moons."

"Really, Ephraim," Miriam said, scandalized. "You should not be speaking so."

Ephraim watched Miriam's face carefully. He was surprised that the only sentiment there was her embarrassment at his familiarity, as men did not usually speak of pregnancy or childbirth, even with their own wives.

Miriam turned to Shoshanna and said, "Do not listen to this heathen, Sister. He has been among the collaborators and Greeks so long he has forgotten how to act." There was no hint of jealousy in her tone; indeed, she was rather jolly.

"The midwife is clucking over her already," Miriam went on. "Shoshanna has but to show her face in any circle of women in Gophna, and—well, you think you are fussed over, Ephraim! It is nothing compared to the birthing preparations for Shoshanna."

Miriam prattled on in the same vein, regaling him with an increasingly graphic sampling of midwifery fact and myth. Ephraim felt his stomach turn with the lurid descriptions.

"Sister," Shoshanna, her eyes on Ephraim, interrupted. "The shewbread is ripening."

Ephraim blessed the wife of Eleazar as Miriam turned her attention to the rebraiding of the bread, its plaits having loosened with the engorged dough. He felt that one more birthing story would have made it impossible for him to fight down the bile that threatened his recent meal.

Shoshanna dimpled at Ephraim as she led Miriam away, the women sharing the weight of the great paddle filled with the elegant challahs for the Shabbat meal. As he watched them go, he could almost smell the future wafts of baking bread.

He leaned back and closed his eyes and thought again on Deborah. Judah and his other rescuers would never know it, but he resented their rescue. As rancid as his experience of torture in the Akra was, the closer he came to death, the closer he felt to his beloved Deborah. Her face and soft arms beckoned him as his body was brutalized, and in his delirium, he almost blessed the torturers for her presence.

Now, as he lay here, trying to evoke her form, her eyes and her laugh, he realized that something else happened during his torture. The guilt that had consumed him since Deborah's death was no more. It was as if the impossible pain he had endured washed him of the need for atonement for her death. He had slain her, it was true, but something, or, as he chose to think, someone, had given her quiet assurance that all was well with his soul. That her death would not be laid to his charge.

After Miriam's rather lengthy and graphic treatise on childbirth, Ephraim's thoughts found a natural channel to children, his and Deborah's children. What would they have looked like? How many? What genders? His face slackened and great happiness filled him at the thought, although why, he did not know. Deborah was dead. There would be no children.

He shook himself. All these women around him all the time! He was thinking like one himself. Since when did a man think on such things? Suddenly he sat up as straight as his broken body would allow when he thought of something. Why was Miriam taking such a prating interest in Shoshanna's impending confinement? Miriam, the no-nonsense martinet who shunned such conversations. Miriam, the bulwark of feminine strength for the rest of the women in Gophna. Miriam, the childless wife of the rebel commander—

Ephraim's hand went to his cheek. Suddenly he was overcome by a thought that stopped his breath for a moment.

Miriam entered the camp. "Shoshanna would not let me help. Is that not ridiculous? What is the matter?"

"I know why she would not let you help." Ephraim said, becoming the spy again. Miriam's hand drifted down to her stomach, craft overcoming her features.

"Why? What do you mean?" She asked carefully. Then an embarrassed smile crept to her face.

Ephraim smiled, too. He said, "Because the wife of the Maccabee is with child, the heir to the throne of King David."

Her widening smile told the truth. Ephraim lay back and closed his eyes, and for the first time in weeks, he wept with something other than pain.

Chapter Eighty-two

Eupator held the stray cat down, delighting in its death struggle. The slave stood by. When the cat expired, the slave asked, "Shall I get you another, highness?"

"Oh, yes!" Eupator said, delight filling his face. "But you must hurry. Lysias is coming to visit me and he—well, he doesn't like all this." The young prince gestured to the six small feline bodies arrayed about him. Each cat had died in horrible, yet creative manner.

A distant, "Lysias, Regent of the Divine Antiochus!" set the slave to gathering the carcasses and Eupator said, "Oh bother. Crix, would you put them in the usual place? I want to study them later."

"Of course, your majesty."

"I wonder what he wants, now?" Eupator sighed. The lessons were increasing in their ferocity now that his father was away in Parthia. And Lysias was a stern schoolmaster. The regent was not like his other tutors, likable scholars who soothed the prince's ego and pronounced his meager efforts at learning, stupendous. Lysias was a martinet whose task was to forge a king even if it took a refiner's fire to do it.

The prince struggled to his feet as the clacking footsteps loomed near; when he heard a shadow of footfalls following the regent, his interest was mildly piqued. He eased himself into his chair and assumed as regal a bearing as his nine-year-old frame would allow. Lysias had at least been successful in teaching him the protocols of receiving visitors of state.

All protocol was forgotten when Eupator saw who was accompanying Lysias. "Nicanor! General Nicanor!" The prince devolved into a boy as he ran to his favorite member of court. Folding himself against the armor of the general, he chirped, "General! I have missed you. Shall I show you what I have been working on?"

Nicanor stepped back and Eupator ran to an ornate ebony chest against the wall behind the chair of state and returned with a wooden sword and round hoplite shield. Nicanor stepped into a stance to defend against the immature choreography of thrusts and parries effected by the prince. The bout ended with Nicanor pushing the prince to the ground with a studied plant of his boot to the royal rump.

"You cheated!" Eupator said as Nicanor heaved him up by the hand. "That move is not a recognized parry."

"Anything that keeps one from death is a recognized parry, young majesty. Do you not remember any of my lessons?"

Eupator felt rather than saw Lysias' scowl and turned to the regent to acknowledge him. "Welcome to my chambers, Regent. It is good to see you."

"Prince." Lysias responded with a curt bow. "Nicanor has returned from Judaea with a report. You must accompany us to a debriefing. May I remind you that you are not to speak. You are to listen and learn and not offer any suggestions or insights."

"But I am the next king! They will want to hear what I have to say."

"Of course they will, your majesty," Lysias agreed, "but the only way you can increase your knowledge of warfare is to listen to experience. Nicanor would agree with me."

"Listen to the regent," Nicanor admonished. "He is right in this regard. In this room, you will be surrounded by the greatest military minds in the civilized world. You would do well to be schooled by them."

"Oh, very well," said the disappointed prince. "But I think this should count for my lessons today."

Lysias bowed. "Of course, highness."

* * * * * *

"The greatest military minds, indeed," Lysias said to Nicanor as soon as they were seated at the command table. Eupator was safely out of earshot wedged in a seat between two guards. Seated on a dais at the room's head, the prince was already looking bored as he dangled his feet from the immense throne.

Nicanor gazed at the prince for a moment, knowing that this meeting was not going to be a pleasant one. He had come back to Antioch to report on the disgraceful defeat at Emmaus; part of that job was going to be enduring endless barbs from the regent.

"Yes," Lysias drawled. "The 'greatest military minds in the world' cannot even win one battle against these ridiculous Jews. Is that how you would typify our progress in Judaea, General? General."

But Nicanor was in deep reverie, watching a golden Antiochus from long ago. This hall was the very place where he and Apollonius had sat all those years ago and first realized that the divine emperor was insane. Antiochus had been dressed all in gold and had given a frightening, mad address. He could still see Apollonius' face, tightened with a mixture of amusement and worry—

"General!"

Nicanor straightened and coughed. "Yes, Excellency?"

"Judaea, General, Judaea."

"We had a failure of intelligence, Regent."

"Obviously. Well. I would like you to give a full debriefing today after we are assembled."

"Yes, of course," Nicanor agreed, but did not feel very agreeable. He especially resented Gorgias for weaseling out of the trip to Antioch. A convenient attack of dysentery laying him low, Gorgias had been most apologetic, but had been adamant that a trip to Antioch would be impossible and would Nicanor take care of the debriefing?

Again outfoxed by Gorgias, Nicanor tried to become a politician as he designed his report during the long trip back, but as politics were not his realm, the report came out irritatingly truthful. He simply did not know how to describe the debacle at Emmaus with any other word other than "debacle."

The faces at the table as he delivered his report were hard, but still respectful, for Nicanor was highly regarded in this circle. Most of the commanders present knew Gorgias' penchant for avoiding responsibility and Nicanor's sole presence here was a testament to both his integrity and Gorgias' lack of it. They asked difficult questions, but Nicanor did not flinch. He was straightforward, not explaining away fault, but accepting his part in misjudging the wiles of the Maccabee.

After Nicanor sat down, Lysias stood. "General Nicanor. I am sure I speak for our divine emperor and his son when I say you are to be commended for your honesty. If nothing else, we can depend upon the general for that."

The commanders looked at each other, then at Nicanor, his face inscrutable. If they dared, they would have harrumphed at this slight of the revered general. Instead, they set their faces.

"But perhaps," Lysias went on, "the fault is mine for not attending to the situation myself. With our dear emperor in Parthia, I had other duties of state to attend to." At this, he bowed to Eupator, who was paying enough attention to incline his head in return. "Now, the time apparently is appropriate for me to take a force to Judaea to deal once and for all with this issue. Nicanor, you will accompany me back to Judaea. You will advise me on what complement of cohorts would work best with the royal guard of Antioch. It is true that Antiochus took most of the crack troops with him to Parthia, but there are enough left that we can still defend our capital and deal with the—what did you call the rebel leader? I can never remember his name."

"The Maccabee, Excellency, the Maccabee."

Apollonius would have been able to tell him what variety of flower it was. Nicanor bent down to inspect it alabaster petals for a moment, then stood, his body creaking, to survey the royal expanse of garden. In Antiochus' absence, the upkeep of the gardens had suffered somewhat, but the seasonal organization of blooms still astounded Nicanor. His own garden in Apamea seemed to sprout only death, as almost all of his flowers bordered on the funereal. On his visits before his death, Apollonius' able advice had little effect on Nicanor's floral ineptitude. Here, however, sprays of every hue and phylum covered the ground. It did not matter what month he happened to be in Antioch, the beds were always laden with blossoms.

Apollonius. He clasped his hands behind him as he continued his walk through Antiochus' palace gardens and wished that Apollonius could have attended the meeting with him. His younger friend would have lightened Nicanor's dour report. He rested against one of the columns that ringed the garden. Ever since Apollonius' death at the hands of the Maccabee, Nicanor's soul seemed as if it had one foot in the underworld. His career had always been one of death, and he wondered at this sudden obsession with nostalgia. Why did Apollonius matter so much?

"Because he was the best friend and comrade I ever had," he muttered and immediately felt foolish at talking to himself.

He found a bench, sat and brushed his hands of pollen. He sneezed and rested with his forearms on his knees, clasping his hands. If he and Apollonius had been together at Emmaus, the outcome would have been different. Apollonius would not have thought it wise to split the troops as Gorgias had done in his futile chase of the Maccabee. Apollonius would not have relied upon collaborators for intelligence. He always insisted upon using infiltrator Greeks as their fealty was less suspect than recruits from the local population.

"Old friend, even as the Maccabee bested you, he has bested all of us," Nicanor said wistfully. Why did speaking to Apollonius make him feel better? "Lysias thinks he will be the savior of the empire, but mark my words, the Hammer will pound him even as he has pounded Timotheus, you, me, Gorgias and Seron. I fear our empire is at an end. He sat erect. Now, what in the name of Zeus, Hermes and Dionysus does this idiot want?"

Nicanor stood and assumed his General's military bearing. Teman's little feet were in such a hurry that gravel sloughed to the left and right as he pattered toward him.

Nicanor wondered why Teman was here in Antioch and not with the mperor in Parthia. With a quick thought, for that is all the time he would allow his brain to dwell on the doings of such a creature, he assumed that Teman was conducting business for the emperor in the capital city. He had no intention of clarifying that fact with a question; he did not care.

"General!" Teman said with a cursory bow. "His highness, Eupator, summons you. You hurried off too quickly after the debriefing for me to catch your attention. Would you attend?"

Nicanor had no intention to accompanying the androgenous advisor through the palace and said politely, "Tell his highness that I will along in just a moment."

"But—"

"I said—'in a moment,' advisor." Nicanor used only a little menace with Teman, as that was all that was necessary to set him scurrying away.

He sat roughly back down. He did not mind Eupator. In many ways, he found the young prince rather engaging, but he also found him to be as dangerous and unpredictable as his father. What could the prince want? His eyes found a ravishing narcissus and he surveyed it with interest. Apollonius would have touted its symmetry, its translucent yellow. All Nicanor saw was a nice flower, its stem somewhat scrawny, but nice.

"Well, Apollonius," he said. "Let us see what our little Narcissus wants, shall we? It might be interesting." Zeus! He did not know what was worse, talking to himself or talking to the dead.

The child was nine. But age was deceptive. This child would one day rule the Seleucid Empire. The degree of his smarts and political acumen would determine how quickly he would cast aside the regent, Lysias, after Antiochus' death. The prince sprawled stomach down, his royal robes splayed out to either side, the youngster's attention totally consumed by his hands working a pat of clay on a small marble slab. As Nicanor watched him, he was pleased that the boy was exhibiting such a high level of concentration, for he neither acknowledged the general's entrance into the arboretum, nor stopped his furious working of the lump.

Nicanor did not speak, since he was curious how long the prince would take to see he was there. He waited. He waited. Eupator sculpted happily, giggling and chortling to himself, rolling the clay, piecing it off into smaller chunks, then molding it as one again. At last, Nicanor became weary of the wait and he harrumphed slightly.

The prince jerked up, howled and reared back until his eyes found Nicanor's. Eupator's eyes could not have been wilder than his own, the general recoiling with fright at the prince's loud reaction of surprise. Nicanor became further alarmed when the howl crescendoed into shrieks and animal moans and chitterings, all of which continued for quite some time. He could do nothing but step away, horrified at the sight of the nine-year-old completely losing his wits.

A slave rushed past Nicanor and pushed Eupator to the ground where the prince writhed and shrieked, twisting his body like a snake in its death throes. Another slave, then another entered, all taking what seemed to be a preordained hold on one of the prince's limbs. Nicanor stepped further back when the ceremonial robes of Lysias swept by in a flourish, the regent stooping with anxiety beside the prone child, whose stuttering body had finally relaxed, but whose face had taken on the gaunt look of coma.

"What happened? What happened?" Lysias hollered into the faces of the slaves, then followed their furtive eyes to where Nicanor stood.

"General," Lysias said, real surprise coloring his face. "What are you doing here? Did you have anything to do with this?"

"I—uh," Nicanor felt more than foolish, he felt guilty. But that was ridiculous. He had done nothing wrong. "I seemed to have interrupted the prince while he was at play." Nicanor shifted from one foot to the other, then added lamely, "I guess I surprised him."

"You guess you—" Lysias said, a wild accusatory glance burning into Nicanor's gaze. "Did you not know the prince has the falling sickness?"

Dumbly, Nicanor shook his head.

"One should never sneak up on one who suffers from the fit."

"I did not sneak up on him!" Nicanor became indignant. "He summoned me, and I did not want to interrupt his sculpting."

"Oh—Ahhhh."

A small rasp from the prince averted attention from Nicanor and everyone crouched near Eupator started fussing, brushing at him, removing his coronet, tight clothing and anything else that might inhibit his comfort.

"All of you leave me," the prince moaned as he struggled to sit up. "Except you, Nicanor."

"But, your highness," Lysias protested. "You must sleep off the fit. You do not look well."

"You do not look so well, yourself, Regent!" Eupator said churlishly. He amended his tone. "I will take a nap in a while, I promise," the prince said, weaving slightly as he sat up. "Just give me a moment with Nicanor."

"Oh, very well," Lysias said with frustration. "But only a moment, your highness."

The slaves, heads bowed, trailed out of the room, followed by a glowering Lysias, clearly loath to leave Eupator.

The prince watched them go and after the door had closed behind Lysias, turned to Nicanor and said, "Well, what do you think?"

Nicanor now had replaced the slaves and Lysias in a crouch next to the prince. He was attempting to rearrange Eupator's discarded robe underneath him so the prince could have a smooth place upon which to sit when he looked up. "Eh?"

Eupator hopped up and said, "You may rise, general. Again, what do you think?"

"I think you should take it easy, my prince," Nicanor said. He was confused. He had seen men in the field with the fit upon them and none had bobbed up so quickly after being in its clutch. "You have had quite a day."

"Oh," Eupator said easily, "it was not a real fit. I stage them all the time. It is very amusing to see everyone run about like squawking chickens. Not only that, it gives me an idea about who my friends are. And my enemies," he added.

Nicanor stood, clasped his hands behind him and cleared his throat. His tongue almost lashed out as it would one of his own sons had he pulled a stunt like this. Another impulse begged him to close his fingers around the prince's scrawny neck, and yet another told him to spank the royal bottom. His soldier's discipline served him well during those impulsive moments: He did not move, and he remained silent.

"Oh, general," Eupator giggled. "I know you do not approve." He donned the clothing that the slaves had removed and smoothed himself until he seemed to feel regal once again. "But, like my father, I know I can trust you. My father has often told me, 'you will always be surrounded by sycophants and traitors, but there is one man upon whom you can rely—General Nicanor.'

Nicanor bowed because he did not know what else to do. The eerie prickles shafting up his spine were reminiscent of those he experienced while dealing with the child's father, Antiochus the IV. Antiochus was forever and always staging exhibitions of this type to test his courtiers. It was during one of these moments of drama that Nicanor had administered to Antiochus when the rest of his courtiers looked idly on, reveling in what they hoped was the king's death. The old general forced himself to breathe, calming himself. Only then, did he trust himself to speak. The venom of this young viper was certainly as virulent as his father's.

"Your highness. Such displays as these are unnecessary. You are surrounded by men who may not love you, it is true, but your well-being is very important to them."

Eupator nodded. "Thank you for not lying to me. I know they do not love me. I do not even know whether father loves me, really. I know I am important, though."

"Yes, you are." Nicanor stooped into a crouch and looked the prince full in the face. "Believe me, Lysias has your best interests in mind and he is a wily politician. If anyone can protect you from court intrigues, he can. I feel you can trust him." Nicanor rose to his soldier's height. "But if you ever feel the need, you can summon me. As long as I am alive, I will come. I serve your father, and by extension of his royal blood, I also serve you."

Eupator rose also, but was no longer the schemer. The loyalty and stature of his father's general dwarfed him into a little vulnerable boy. For the first time ever, Nicanor saw the prince cry.

Nicanor pounded Eupator with an awkward pat on the back. "There, there, your highness. You will be well cared for. I will see to it."

"Thank you, General," Eupator sniffed. "And you will ever have your lands, holdings and titles. I will see to it."

Dismissed by the prince, Nicanor strode through the arboretum out into the great hall. As always, the two monolith griffins crouched guarding the throne room, their sentinel glare bearing down on the general. Nicanor glared back and said, "Oh shut up. I know he is no more fit to rule than Antiochus." Absently he ran his hand along one of the knuckles of the black marble paw. "But he is all we have."

Chapter Eighty-three

The men had been gone for a long time as they manned the Jerusalem corridor. It was not that Brita missed Aulus. On the contrary, she enjoyed the solitude of the camp without the blustery Roman and his demands. She often wondered why she enjoyed being alone so much. Maybe it was true that her kind from the north were a solitary people, their warmth for others extinguished by the cold land from which they had come: other slaves she had encountered on her infrequent travels with the Auli family had told her as much after commenting on her yellow hair.

As she sat on her bluff day after day observing the Jews in their lives and struggles, Brita became more and more intrigued by their human interactions. These people seemed to seek each other out. They would embrace, gossip, commiserate, and even argue or fight. As she had never had the opportunity to form connections, she watched these little dramas with ever increasing interest, but content that she was not involved. Perhaps she was missing something, but she did not care. There was plenty to do in the camp. Feeding herself often took all day: there were traps for the coneys to be set, skinning, cooking, drying, not to mention baking the little cakes that helped to augment her diet. Also, part of daylight each day had to be devoted to laying up stores for the coming winter. She already had a large supply of dried meat, but other sundries she hoped Aulus would bring back. She needed cloth, rope, tar and other basics or she would have to go begging to the Jews. She did not want to do that.

She shifted so that the tree obscured her. Shoshanna, the wife of Eleazar, was bearing small pallets of bread dough to the ovens. She was great with child and although Brita had never met her, she knew her story. Shoshanna was the one who had been kidnapped by the Greeks. And from what she heard, the Jewess had not had an easy time of it while with her Greek captor, nor when she returned to the village. There were many who thought the woman should be turned out of Gophna. Apparently, that time was past, for she had married Eleazar, carried his child and the pregnancy was going well. That brought Miriam, the wife of the Maccabee to her mind. She did not know if the herbs she had given Miriam had worked. That was the only problem created by her isolation: there was no way for her to gather verbal information. She learned much from her distant observations of the camp, but not as much as she could have by listening to conversations..

She shifted further behind the tree, for the Jewess seemed to be looking up. Now the woman smiled, and her look seemed to be that of recognition. Brita stood and hurried back to her camp.

The slave busied herself with rearranging the strips hanging over the fire. The meat from the coney she had trapped the day before was almost dried.

"We know you watch us."

Brita froze. She did not look up.

"Some do not like it, but I do not mind. You do not have to be afraid."

Brita still said nothing, but turned around to look at the Jewess. The face was friendly, open, beckoning a response. Brita did not know what to say.

Shoshanna sat on one of the logs that had been arranged in front of the campfire. "Is it all right if I sit down? I am a little weary after climbing your hill."

Shoshanna's need for hospitality set Brita into action. She was a slave. She fetched a broth that she had stewed the night before and hung the little pot on the cooking tripod over the fire. "This will be warm in a moment." She reached for a skin and poured some water into a cup and offered it to the Jewess. "Drink this." Brita stepped away and sank to her haunches, the servile position a comfort.

"No, come and sit here by me," Shoshanna said, patting the log next to her. "I want to talk to you. I have some news that I think will interest you."

Brita's heart felt like that of a trapped animal. A similar look must have surfaced on her face, for Shoshanna patted the log again and said, "Please. I will not hurt you."

Except for her meeting with Miriam and her subservient interactions with her mistress, Julia Macro, Aulus' mother, Brita had not had much experience with the conversation of women. Her master often had had men around the camp. Men, she knew. Women were an enigma to her.

It was Shoshanna's sheer force of benignity that drew Brita closer. Finally, she sat next to the Jewess.

"Miriam is with child," Shoshanna said, simply. "Your herbs worked. She is very happy."

"You know of this?"

Shoshanna nodded. "Miriam shares some things with me."

Brita was not surprised at the news. "I know of the herbs' great successes," she said, "not first-hand, but an old slave of the Auli Macros taught me. She was an old Persian woman. She died many years ago."

"You do not come down to our camp."

Brita again could think of nothing to say, so just looked down at her feet.

"You would be welcome, you know. Our people are not used to strangers, but we know you and we are grateful to Aulus for his help. And now that you helped Miriam—"

"You must not tell anyone about that. You must tell Miriam to tell no one else. Especially not Judah."

Shoshanna put her hand on the slave's arm. "But, why not? Judah would be especially grateful. Every man wants issue."

Brita looked at this woman, astounded at her naiveté about her own people. How could Shoshanna, who had been captured and used by the Greeks, be so innocent? Even Brita, as an outsider, knew enough about the Jews to know of their mistrust of strange arts, especially herbs and potions. They had their own remedies, and if they knew Miriam had received a fertility brew from the German 'witch' as she knew some called her, there would be trouble. She said only, "I do not think Judah would be pleased at this intrusion of his privacy. I do not think your priests and their women would understand, either." Brita looked down at Shoshanna's hand on her arm, but she did not shrug it off.

Shoshanna gave Brita's arm a slight squeeze before removing her hand. "I think I understand. But that was a wonderful and giving thing you did. I just would like our people to know you."

Brita's hands went to one of her long braids and she fell to plucking absently at its tail. "I think it would be better if people thought your god was responsible for her condition. Perhaps he is, at that. Please say nothing."

"It shall be as you say, of course," Shoshanna said, smiling. But I would be honored if you would come and visit me in my camp for Shabbat dinner one day—"

"That would not be possible," said Brita, in real alarm. She calmed at the surprise in Shoshanna's face and amended her tone. "I do not think it would be wise, but thank you. It is a gracious offer."

"Please consider it an open invitation," Shoshanna said. "My campfire is yours."

As the Jewess left, Brita sat for a moment, considering. She stood and called, "Mistress!"

Shoshanna turned. "You must call me Shoshanna. That is my name." But, she smiled.

Brita returned a smile that was crooked from disuse, and although she was confused by this woman's familiarity, she said, "And my campfire is yours."

Chapter Eighty-four

S hoshanna said, "You should not talk that way about her. She helped you."

"No, the Lord of Hosts helped me," Miriam retorted. "She is still a witch."

The sisters-in-law were batting out the stalks, dumping the grain kernels into stone grinding bowls. Shoshanna had not seen the harm in mentioning her exchange with Brita the day before. She had ignored Brita's warning about mentioning the herbs, but now wished she had not. Since Miriam had been the one to receive the tea, Shoshanna guessed that Miriam was exempt from Brita's admonition.

Shoshanna pounded the stalks a little too hard and Miriam said, "If you are not more careful, you will get some in the bowl." She gathered a few more straggly lengths. "All I said was that she was Aulus' whore, and that you should not talk to her. Any woman who allows herself to be used like that should not—" she interrupted herself with silence.

Shoshanna heard an apology in the silence. The "whore" and "allow herself to be used" comments brought back the unfortunate memory of her captivity in the Greek quarter for almost ten months two years ago. She had been sequestered by her rapist until he had been killed when the uprising began in Modiin all those months ago. In a strange coincidence, it had been Eleazar, Shoshanna's then-betrothed, who had done in the Greek Apelles.

Shoshanna busied herself, but was not aware of the task. Her mind sought Apelles and found him in one of the guilt-worn recesses of her memory. She saw him in his armor and did not want to acknowledge the pang she felt when she remembered his wooing after the violence. She never felt this vulgar pang with Eleazar. When her husband took her in the night, it was not how she remembered it with Apelles. In disgust, she pushed the unseemly recollection away. Her task became visible again and she cupped her hand over the stone bowl, to keep as many of the kernels under control as possible.

"Grain and more grain," Ephraim said as he walked haltingly into the camp, leaning on the young student. "I wonder that we do not all turn into immense loaves of challah ourselves, after eating all this bread."

"'In the sweat of thy face shalt thou eat bread, till thou return unto the ground,'" Miriam murmured.

"Or as the Egyptians said to Joseph," Shoshanna reminded him, "'Give us bread: for why should we die in thy presence?'"

Ephraim smiled. "I do not want to die from lack of bread, but that does not mean I have to like it. Oh!"

Ephraim's foot hit a root and his body lurched off balance. He stumbled away from the arm of the youth and was about to pitch over on Miriam. Before the boy could right him, Miriam reached up and took Ephraim's full weight into her arms that were raised in reflexive defense against his fall. Fall he did, a heavy plummet, right into Miriam's lap.

The injury was apparent at once, for Miriam's face became a wince and she doubled over, a moan escaping her lips.

"Sister Miriam!" Shoshanna cried. "Help me!" She urged the youth.

Ephraim, unhurt, rolled off of Miriam. The woman and youth were so busy attending to Miriam that they did not notice his miserable impotence as he watched the ungainly scene unfold. His hands were useless, and he could not rise without the boy's help. So, he sat and watched.

The youth's obvious discomfort at touching a woman, a pregnant one at that, filled Shoshanna with rage. "The stricture at touching does not exist when it is an emergency," she rasped, not knowing if that were the truth or not. "Now, help me!"

"Help!" Ephraim hollered, finally finding a way to aid the women. "Help us! Someone! At least I can yell," he muttered to no one in particular. "Help!"

Finally, Avram's stout wife came from her hearth two tents away, dragging her two stout daughters with her. The youth gratefully stepped aside and allowed the women to spirit Miriam into her tent.

"Fetch the midwife," Shoshanna said to the youth before she stepped into the tent. "Ephraim. Are you well?"

"I am well," he whispered. "See to Miriam."

As the youth loped away, Ephraim watched him go, then, shaking, lay back and put his arm over his eyes.

Chapter Eighty-five

Gophna, Judaea   The 14th day of *Heshvan* 3596 (October 23rd 165 B.C.E)

J udah said, "It was in this valley where Timotheus camped all those months ago." He handed Aulus a piece of hard tack. "The fearsome Greeks. Do you remember?"

"I will never forget it. You were a green youth, not blooded by battle—"

"Not so fast, Roman," Judah interrupted. As I remember it, the only Aulus who had been 'blooded by battle' as you put it, was Aulus *Maior*, your father. "You were a youth, greener than I."

Aulus boomed his huge laugh and swatted at Judah, who danced his horse away. "I shall look forward to sparring with you again. The Greeks have not proved a very formidable opponent. The Maccabee will have to do, I suppose."

Judah laughed, and turned his gaze up at Gophna. "It will be good to be home. I have missed Miriam's nagging."

"And I have missed Brita in my bed," Aulus sighed. "Again, I say, Judah: you can have her whenever you want. I know she fancies you. And, I believe you fancy her."

Judah did not want to be drawn into this conversation again, so he hummed the first tune that came to mind to chase away his lewd thoughts.

Nearby, Asher heard the humming and took up the tune, adding words. Soon the men around him were singing.

> *The hammer we follow*
> *With the hammer we fight*
> *Judah the Maccabee*
> *Will put Greek to flight*

The song embarrassed Judah, but it was too late to stop the men, after all, he had started humming what he thought was an innocuous tune. He had not figured on Asher's wit with rhyme and lyric. He just hoped the tune would be spent before they reached the heights of Gophna.

The song did expend itself long before they reached the summit, but the men's spirits were still high. Once again, they had bested the Greeks. The enemy kept sending better and better generals against them, but it did not seem to matter. The Lord was with them in this fight and the Greeks could not prevail against Him.

It was true that they had never met the Greeks in open battle, yet. That all their victories had been by stealth and wile. It did not matter, anymore. Judah had told them so, right after the Greeks were driven from Emmaus. "Why should we scorn our singular gift of strategy? Our gift of stealth?" he had asked. "As long as we drive the Greeks out of *Eretz Israel*, what does it matter? And, who knows? Our strength is increasing! Perhaps we shall yet meet the Greeks in a great battle that will feed the stories of our people for years to come."

The chests of bullion that were now a part of their baggage train back to Gophna would also go far in building their strength. Many men could be outfitted and fed on future marches and campaigns against the enemy host with all that revenue.

"The eighth commandment did not apply to Greek bullion, I hope?" Avram remarked to Judah.

"The eighth commandment does not apply to anything Greek in our land," Judah said, laughing. "One cannot steal while in his own house."

The men stopped their horses, reining them against the ridge wall so Judah and his commanders could take their places at the head of the mounted column. Judah had tried to demur, saying that they deserved to ride in ahead of him, but his fighters insisted that he follow this new protocol and lead them into Gophna. It would be thus ever after.

Judah sat up straight in his saddle. He and his men had gotten good sleep the last few days as they spiked farther into northern Judaea. This was their territory, and the Greeks held sway here no longer. Every Greek stronghold had been cleared out by the Faithful, and the Jews controlled the trade and harvests as in the days of Saul and David. The Greeks were confined to their only remaining enclave, that of Jerusalem, and Judah had decided after rescuing Ephraim and seeing the horrendous state of the capital, that the City of Gold would be their next mission. The Greeks had no right to Jerusalem as it was, and their neglect only intensified that fact—Judah would wrench it from them.

Judah saw the familiar rock formations that landmarked their way to the center of camp. The villagers were starting to emerge from tents and tasks, and the word spread: the Maccabee had returned.

Eyes, though, were averted. The people were happy to see the fighters, but a strange reserve seemed to pale the people of Gophna. They turned their faces to the Maccabee, patting his horse and reaching out to him, but their eyes—their eyes were wrong.

They could not bring their horses all the way into camp, so Judah made the sign to dismount, the men then milling among themselves to find family and loved ones. Judah saw Shoshanna first and slapped Eleazar's arm so he could direct his brother's earnest eyes to those of his wife. He watched for Miriam.

Out of the corner of his eye, Judah saw Shoshanna greet Eleazar with a sedate kiss. He turned away to give them privacy but was surprised when Shoshanna immediately sidled over. Where was Miriam?

"Judah," was all Shoshanna said.

Cold gripped his stomach and he knew then that the eyes of the people who had greeted him upon his ride into camp had said true. Something was very wrong.

Shoshanna silently led Eleazar and Judah to Judah's camp. A huddle of people had congregated there in a posture of waiting. Judah did not wait for an explanation, but powered through the tent flap, Shoshanna accompanying, Eleazar waiting outside.

Miriam lay on their skins, one tucked up under her chin. A glisten of sweat sheened her face and she was pale and motionless. Judah crouched beside her while Shoshanna stayed at the door.

"Miriam."

At first, she did not move. When Judah said her name again and added, "Little Mare," her eyelids fluttered and weak, hooded eyes met his.

"Judah. I am sorry. I lost him."

Judah turned to look at Shoshanna, who said, "Judah, she was with child." Her mouth grimaced with apology and she withdrew from the tent, leaving them alone.

"No. It is I who am sorry," Judah murmured, lying down beside Miriam and embracing her carefully over the skins. "I should have been here." He buried his head in her shoulder. "I should have been here."

"Do not be ridiculous," she said weakly. "There was nothing you could have done and anyway, the problem is solved. The evil influence has been exorcised," she said, her voice trailing off so that this last was barely audible.

But Judah was not listening but just reveled in his wife's nearness. Miriam's need made him need her. As he caressed her neck, his mind was filled with her. His wife.

"Judah, Judah," she murmured weakly.

He heard this only because his ear was near her mouth. They lay together for a time, and Miriam fell asleep. It was then that he succumbed to the grief, and he lay sobbing for a long time. Finally, although he would have preferred to sleep beside his wife, he roused himself. Duty required that he see to the camp, regardless of his personal sorrow. The men would be safely in their families' arms by now, but he wanted to make sure all was as he left it: rock defenses, look-out rotations and training for the adolescents. He did not want to disturb anyone with questions, but did not feel he would have to. His eye would tell him everything.

He blinked at the glare that the late sun carved into that eye and brought up his hand as an awning. He would check the look-outs, first. He decided to head in the direction of the setting sun and survey the western ridge. It was not a solitary walk. Wherever he went, children, especially young boys, would accompany him. A herd soon pressed upon him, because of his long absence, he supposed, and questions left and right assailed him. "Commander, how many Greeks did you slay?" "General, is it true that we are rich, now?" "Judah, will you come to training tomorrow? Gad is too mean to teach us—he makes fun of us."

Judah bantered with the children for a while until one of them said, "General, is it true that the German witch caused your wife to lose the child and that is why the women destroyed her camp?"

"What?" Judah crouched to eye level of the little girl. "What do you mean?"

"My mother is there even now," the little girl said smugly. "She is getting some trinkets from the Roman's camp!"

Judah broke from the children and, with all his warrior's speed, hurtled toward Aulus' camp. "Please make it idle chatter," he breathed aloud. "Oh Lord of Hosts, make it not be so."

The catastrophic mess that met him forced him to sit down. He could not even enter the camp, but remained on the ground, his legs in an ungainly splay on the dirt. The tent leaned at a crazy angle to the left, barely supported by the askance center pole. Cooking tripods were upended and pots lay strewn. A few women were picking over some of the pots, ladles and even some of Brita's dresses. A few were squabbling over a blue dress. Judah stood and one of the women looked at him, a faint shadow looming. The other took advantage of her adversary's inattention and wrenched the dress, tearing it with a great racking rend.

"No!" Judah cried. He remembered that dress. He remembered when Brita had worn it on that day long ago during his visit to Aulus' camp. He had brought a deer the day before the visit and Brita had dressed it and fed him stew.

The women dropped the ruined dress and fled. Judah plunged after them, yelling and cursing. He had not removed his armor from the trip yet and ran, a behemoth warrior, at the women. They were cornered in the copse of trees to the north of Aulus' camp and in his mind's eye, he saw Greeks. Still raging and now foaming at the mouth, he raised his sword, ready to bring it down.

"Judah!"

The scream brought him back and he froze. Whimpers were all he heard as the women cowered, waiting for the death blow from the Maccabee.

"Judah! Stop!"

Shoshanna's voice brought him fully back to himself and finally he saw his quarry for who they were. Shaking, he looked up at his sword, the magnificent *kopis* of Apollonius, and he looked at the women again. The shaking increased and he threw the sword from him.

The women disappeared into the trees and Shoshanna approached him. Eleazar was with her.

"What has happened?" Judah, still trembling, managed to say.

"Oh, Judah," Shoshanna said. "Miriam, during her travail, cried out many things. That she had failed you and the new kingdom of Judah; that this was G-d's punishment for her touching a man."

"What man are you talking about?" Judah said, his voice rising in frustration. "No one has told me anything. How did Miriam lose the baby?"

"Miriam and I were in your camp," Shoshanna said patiently, grabbing Eleazar as she sat upon a nearby rock. "As you know, Ephraim was staying there as Miriam was nursing him. Ephraim stumbled and the youth who had been steadying him lost his grip. Ephraim fell against Miriam, who then tried to steady him. But, Judah, he fell against her stomach."

The child. Judah mourned again for the lost child that he had not even known existed. Then reason claimed his thoughts and the illogic of the ruined camp consumed him.

"All this?" Judah gestured around him. "For an accident? How on earth did Ephraim falling on Miriam lead to the destruction of Aulus' camp? It does not make sense!" By now, Judah was roaring.

Shoshanna had dwindled into weeping, so Eleazar said, "Miriam's delirium sent her somewhere else to find blame—the German witch—as she called her."

"Brita?" Judah asked.

"Yes.Shoshanna tells me that Brita gave Miriam a tea to help her, to help her, ah—"

"—to help her conceive a child," Shoshanna finished for him. "Aulus' slave was only trying to help. And then the miracle happened: Miriam was with child. It happened just before you left—"

"When else would it have happened?" Eleazar said impatiently to his wife. "Judah. Miriam, in her pain, babbled that Brita had hexed the potion, that its properties caused Ephraim to fall against her, and furthermore, it caused her to go against our traditions and touch Ephraim, a man not her husband. The midwife spread that among the women. They took it upon themselves to remedy the situation."

"To remedy—Where is Brita? Where is Aulus?"

Shoshanna and Eleazar averted their eyes, their faces terrible masks of sorrow. Judah shook his head. "No! Oh no." Running from the copse of trees, he cried, over and over again, "Aulus! Brita!" Finally, he found them. They were near the western ridge.

Aulus had Brita in his arms, his body a tender bow over her. Sobbing, he clutched at her, and begged her to rise, to open her eyes. Stones littered the ground around the little slave, and her body was punctuated with bloody score marks, the skin discolored by livid bruises.

As Judah staggered toward the impossible scene, he fell into a crawl and was barely able to drag himself over the rock-strewn ground.

Weeping, he touched the side of Brita's head, cradled by Aulus mammoth hand. A great wound had lacerated the scalp, and blood had woven itself into the yellow hair, even down into the braid that obscured the young girl's face, brutalized by the stones hurled by the outraged women.

Aulus, insensible of his presence, did not let go of the dead slave. He only murmured over and over, "*Cur? Cur?* Why? Why?"

"O Lord of Hosts," Judah mumbled into the dirt. "What are you doing?"

Chapter Eighty-six

Menelaus sounded indignant. "The coward! Imagine leaving us to the Maccabee."

"I do not know if I would call Regent Lysias a coward, High Priest," Syrus said, idly fingering the leather threads at the shoulder of his cuirass. "Jerusalem is full of Greek ears; ears that widen when a Jew speaks against Lysias, or any other Greek, for that matter. Oh, and I mention that I am Greek?"

Syrus watched comprehension slowly dawn on Menelaus' face and sighed. It was likely that the high priest had thought he was conversing with his old advisor, Nadab, who had fled to his home in Idumea. Menelaus seemed to forget that a Greek military advisor such as Syrus could make great trouble for him if he reported a seditious comment like the one he just heard to those in Antioch or even Syrus' superiors right here in Jerusalem. And Menelaus seemed to be full of seditious comments, but Syrus believed that the high priest was not being treasonous, only talkative. At least that is what he chose to believe: it saved him from writing tiresome missives reporting the behavior. Not only that, he sensed a laxity from Antioch ever since Antiochus' death. Missives were few and far between and dealt with such inane topics such as the census and taxes. Not that those issues were pressing. Holed up here in the Akra, he had few to count or tax. It was as if his superiors had forgotten all about Judaea. And him.

Two months before, Lysias had come from Antioch to engage the Jews where Nicanor and Gorgias had failed at Emmaus. And during the past year, all readiness had gone into the preparation for what was going to be a crushing annihilation of the Jews. A great battle ensued at the little village of Beit Zur. Then, Lysias, in mid-battle had gotten word of Antiochus' death by fever in Persia and immediately withdrew his troops from the fight—likely fomenting a great confusion among the Hebrew combatants, who were on the cusp of a terrible defeat. When Lysias had ordered Syrus to stay in Jerusalem to help Gorgias and Philo oversee the Greek interests in the city, the insurgent Jews had become so emboldened by Lysias' departure, especially after the previous year's Jewish victory at Emmaus, that it became too dangerous for the Greeks and their collaborators to conduct business in the city streets. In fact, Syrus' march into Jerusalem had been so harried by Jewish guerillas with arrows and slings that his small detachment had barely made it into the Akra, the tower that had been built for surveillance, but was now being used for refuge.

Syrus allowed himself a bitter glance at the high priest. Menelaus, muttering, was pushing tablets and parchment around his desk. But for this stupid assignment, he would be back in Antioch with his wife and mistresses. He had been here in Judaea too long. It had not occurred to him to be insubordinate and voice his regret at his orders, but now he often wished he had had the guts to do so. After watching Menelaus perform his banal machinations for a few moments, Syrus stretched and stood. "Remember to keep a civil tongue in your head, your honor. Lysias is now the most powerful man in the empire. He is regent to the new king. And, I assure you, he is no coward."

"Nonsense," Menelaus said, seeming to forget Syrus' warning. "When he turned tail and ran for Antioch, he fully earned that title. Well, what are we supposed to do, now? The Maccabee will now storm our gates. We are defenseless!" The high priest, whining and pacing among his expensive furnishings, all of which had by now been moved to his new quarters in the Akra, moved to a window and peered out. "And, this accursed tower has no light."

Syrus said nothing, but for the hundredth time, mentally cursed Nadab for fleeing to Idumea. As far as he was concerned, Lysias was not the only coward. For a while he and Menelaus had assumed that Nadab had perished in the battle of Emmaus, but then word trickled back to Jerusalem that the advisor had sought refuge in Idumea with his formidable in-laws. Syrus had enjoyed the banter with Nadab and the two had worked together to provide concert between the Greek army and the Jewish collaborators. It had been a productive liaison, but now with Nadab gone, Syrus was finding the job of overseeing Greek interests difficult if not impossible. Menelaus was a buffoon who had no business administering the affairs of anything, let alone a valuable commodity such as Judaea. Well, Syrus thought, his mismanagement and our underestimation of the Jewish resistance is why we pinioned in this accursed stone phallus. He idly watched Menelaus strain for a ray of light from the meager window. He had not understood Nadab's constant cryptic complaints about working with the high priest. He understood now, all too well.

"You should thank your gods for this tower," Syrus said dismissively. "It is what is keeping your pompous hide intact. We will be safe here until Lysias returns with his cohorts. Then the Maccabee will trouble us no further."

"No, perhaps not, but we are prisoners, now," Menelaus said, reaching out in his agitation to stroke one of his tapestries. "And you hate this tower even more than I do. I know of your aversions to heights."

It was true that Syrus kept well away from the windows and balconies of this refuge, but he would rather eat dung than admit as much to this Jew. "That is none of your concern," Syrus said. "And if you mention it again, I assure you that I will overcome my aversion just long enough to throw you over one of 'this tower's' parapets."

Syrus' gaze bore down upon Menelaus until the high priest veered back to the previous subject.

"Did you hear that those rabble out there are actually are calling themselves 'Maccabeans' and have made incursions into the Greek quarter?" Menelaus asked, stooping a little under Syrus' stare. "They have been expelling Greeks from their homes and are moving their own families in. It is a disgrace."

Although all that Menelaus was saying was true, Syrus was tired of hearing it day after day. And he was tired of Menelaus. He did not like living in the dank Akra any more than the high priest did, but his acrophobia aside, it was onerous having to be shut up in this rock with this whining Jew. They were truly under siege. No one, not even the most carefully disguised slave, could venture into the market for supplies, anymore. The streets were empty of Greeks now; they either buttressing themselves here in this tower, booking passage on ships at Gaza that were headed north to Tyre, or fleeing south over land to Idumea.

Following the yellow Nadab, Syrus thought wryly as he peered at his wax tablet and wrote down the new duty roster for the archers. At least calculating the rotation for the archers on the parapet look-out kept him a little busy. Not busy enough, but it kept his mind away from this untenable situation at times.

"The death of Antiochus could not have come at a worse time." Menelaus was whining again. "The great, divine Antiochus! Some god! He could not even stay alive long enough to enable Lysias to shore up Jerusalem. And it was his silly edicts that got us in all this trouble in the first place."

Although he felt like striking the Jew for his derisive comments regarding the dead emperor, Syrus instead focused upon Menelaus' pacing feet for a while. Finally, he excused himself, grinding his teeth at Menelaus' parting utterance, "Well, at least Nadab abandoned his collection of scarabs. They are very hard to come by, as we are at odds with Egypt right now. . ."

As he entered the maze of the Akra, the familiar closeness of the walls seemed to clear his mind. Although Syrus disliked the thought of the high void outside the tower, its interior was not so bad. Many joined high priest Menelaus in complaining about the claustrophobic corridors of the tower, but Syrus did not find them so. When he wandered the stone entrails of the Akra, as now, he was able to clear his mind and attempt to form the necessary strategies to counter the siege.

The siege seemed impossible, indeed. Syrus did not want to wait for Lysias to rescue them. If he could figure out a way to deaden the influence of the Maccabee, it could go well for him in his ambitions to climb higher in Greek ranks of soldiering.

"Climb higher," he said aloud.

A strange thought accompanied his words. He found himself drawn to the stairs that led to a small parapet that looked out to the west. He immediately started to sweat, but found that he was walking, one tortuous step at a time, toward the small doorway that arched over the stairs. His mind protested. It seemed foolish to follow a nebulous order from his thoughts, but he was now climbing, nonetheless. His legs were leaden weights, but upward they propelled him.

He shut his eyes and let his feet feel their way up. Pressing his hands against either side of the ascending corridor of steps, he steadied himself for a moment, then continued upward. Then, the sweat on his face chilled and his feet found no more steps. He opened his eyes.

Nadab had brought him here once. This was the same parapet where the advisor had taunted him all those months ago. He closed his eyes again and edged out to the outer wall. His hands groped until they made purchase with the chest-high balcony stone. Heaving a great sigh, he opened his eyes. He grasped the limestone and looked out toward the north where the Maccabee and his troops were said to patrolling in an effort to squeeze Jerusalem. The effort was proving good, as staples were becoming harder and harder to come by and no Greek would venture to the north into what was now indisputable Maccabean territory. With Lysias gone, it was only a matter of time before the rebels would storm Jerusalem; Menelaus was right about that.

Syrus forced himself to stand thus for many minutes, and not always with his eyes closed. Willing a steel gaze, he surveyed the view and allowed himself to be astounded by its beauty. This really was a stupendous land. Barren, yes, but majestic in its generous sweep of hill and wash of blue sky. Emboldened by the spectacle, he backed into the tower and found another set of stairs. He steadied himself at the archway and climbed again. This time, his sweating labor up a dizzying spiral of steps brought him to the higher parapet that scanned out to the south. This view was also stunning, but even more barren; Idumea was that way, many furlongs down over the rock-embedded hills of Bethlehem. Nadab was in Idumea, with his wife's family. As Syrus thought again about his old associate, he was surprised that he was worried about him, knowing that Nadab had now been branded by Menelaus and the Greeks as a traitor. If they ever went to the trouble of seeking him out, it would not go well for him. At least the collective Greek mind was occupied with the Maccabee at the moment. That preoccupation would keep Nadab safe for a while, but not the rest of them who were stuck here. For, he thought, if the Maccabee gets into Jerusalem, it will not go well for us. Unless, that is, I can think of what to do.

He looked out toward Idumea and Bethlehem for a moment and felt buoyed by the victory over his fear. Perhaps this boded for a good outcome. As he conquered the height today, in like fashion he might be able to work against the odds and have a hand in conquering the Maccabee. A sudden gale rose against the tower, causing him to shiver violently. "I have conquered enough for today," he said to the wind and finally allowed himself to obey his old malady and withdraw into the warm bowels of the Akra.

Chapter Eighty-seven

Beit Zur, Judaea   The 6th day of *Kislev* 3597 (November 2nd 164 B.C.E.)

T he black mood had been upon him for almost two days and he did not know why. Lysias was gone. 5,000 of the enemy had been killed. Hunched on a camp stool, Judah surveyed the ruined topography of Beit Zur while carrion crows hovered over the battlefield. The ravenous kites were still at their gruesome work even though it had been two weeks since the Greeks had departed, abandoning their dead.

With the year gone since their victory at Emmaus over Nicanor and Gorgias, the Jews had enjoyed the relative peace of savoring that success and taking back the governance of most of the land. Until this battle, that is. Lysias had staged another incursion into Judaea, and the battle had occurred here, in Beit Zur. It had been a pitched, bloody proposition for the Jews, and during the battle Judah had despaired of their cause. They were losing so many men against the prodigious numbers of Greeks that a miracle was needed to save their little nation. Of a sudden, the Greeks withdrew. The rolling course of the battle had ceased as if a great sea wall had fallen from the heavens, and just as the Hebrews thought they were drawing a collective last breath, the tumult stopped. They did not know why.

It had been left to the rebels to dispose of the corpses, burying their own and burning the enemy's. It was a formidable task. 500 men had been lost: too many for their small numbers. But where, for centuries, they had been singing dirges over victims, now they could sing hymns of victory over the bodies of warriors. These hymns mitigated some of the rebels' grief at losing 500 of their men. The comfort of ritual also removed some of the onus.

Not for Judah. The victory songs sounded hollow to him, the burial ritual, trite. His commander's brain wondered how his numbers would ever recover from such a setback. 500 trained men. 500 who had slept, ate, sparred and rode with him and followed him. It did not matter that he and his men had killed 5,000 of Lysias' troops; the smoke of those bodies rose even now from the fire-stoked trenches that he had ordered excavated. He rubbed his temples with his calloused fingers. Perhaps his black mood came from the oily stench of the ugly boiling clouds that had once been Greek human flesh. For the rest of his life,that smell would stay in his memory, never purged by the most horrendous tragedies or joyful elations that he would experience later.

"Judah, Issachar has returned from Jerusalem."

Judah had not even heard the approach of Shimon's horse. He looked up, startled, the blackness turning to annoyance at the interruption. "So what?" he muttered. "I do not feel like talking to the bookworm right now."

Shimon sat down next to Judah on a vacant camp stool. "He has very important news. He has learned why Lysias left so quickly."

"Bring him then," Judah murmured stonily. "But tell him to be quick with his news and not to drag it out with one of his endless preambles. I cannot stand it today."

Judah idly watched the smoke rise from the trenches until Shimon had fetched Issachar and they had climbed the knoll where he sat. They stood before him, obscuring the view.

"Yes, what is it? Why do you trouble the great commander?" he asked, his tone ironic.

He felt rather than saw the exchange of a glance between the two men at his sarcasm, as he had stood and walked slightly away from them so he could keep his eyes on the trenches. Seeing his men toss body after Greek body into the makeshift furnace made him feel a little better. "Well, what is it?" He repeated, harsher this time.

"Antiochus Epiphanes is dead, Commander," Issachar breathed.

Judah's mind almost closed itself to the news. Reality simply did not take such forms as this. "What did you say?" He whispered.

"Antiochus, our enemy, is dead," Shimon said. He shook Judah's shoulder and peered into his face. "Tears, brother? This is a time of joy!"

Judah did not answer. Thrusting the heels of his hands into his eyes, he crouched to his haunches. The smoke spiraled from the trench. "Where did you hear this?" he asked quietly. "Is it reliable intelligence? I must know."

"Most of the Greek haunts that Ephraim used to frequent are no more, Commander," Issachar said. "Lysias' departure has emptied Jerusalem of Greeks, it seems. But I did run into one rebel from my own hideout who had ties to Janus of Menelaus' court. I think he was his brother, or brother-in-law—"

"I do not care about his family tree," Judah snapped. "Get on with it, man!"

"Yes, well," Issachar said quickly, "he said the entire Greek guard and all the collaborators had retreated into the Akra. He also said that that Lysias had announced that he could offer them no protection because his master was dead, and he must return to Antioch to see to the succession. The insurgents who act under your name are in control of Jerusalem. Their control is rather ragged, to be sure, since they have no command capabilities—they are used to quick guerrilla strikes and are jealous of each other, but it is said that their commander, Benyamin Bar Eli—"

"Enough! Shimon, you are to take a patrol and ride north to Jerusalem and our other holdings and corroborate this news. I must move on Jerusalem, but I must be sure that this information is right. I cannot spare any more fighters in a pitched battle with the Greeks. If Lysias has laid this as a trap, I want to know about it." Judah paced for a moment, then stopped, once again mesmerized by the smoke. "Also," he went on, "send out our other scouts to Jericho to see if the caravan merchants can confirm Antiochus' death. I want a report from all patrols in two days. Now, ride!"

Shimon had already mounted his horse, obeying his brother amid an immediate dusty clamber of hooves down the knoll.

"You!" Judah barked at Issachar, who had started a pedestrian retreat following Shimon's horse.

"Yes, commander?" Issachar said.

Judah's mood had lifted and with it, his compassion for the timid Issachar. He could actually see the scholar-turned-spy's knees knocking. He thumped him on the back, amused at Issachar's startled jump. "Good work, scholar! You are becoming quite a spy. Ephraim would be proud of you."

Issachar's retreating grin inspired one in Judah, and as he watched the Levite descend the knoll, he started to pace again. This pace was more one of swagger than agitation, and the smoke continued to rise in billows from the trenches of Greek dead.

Chapter Eighty-eight

Antioch, Syria   The 18th day of *Kislev* 3597 (November 15th 164 B.C.E.)

L ysias floated among the celebrants, his face easy and affable. Nicanor stood, his arms drawn back, ending in his usual hand clasp behind him. This day, he harrumphed even more than usual, as such displays as this curdled his soldier's stomach. Eupator's ascension ceremony had been scheduled to occur as soon as Lysias returned from Judaea and Antiochus' ashes returned from Parthia. Today was the day, at last.

Festoons of gold boughs webbed the black griffins, and golden garlands draped the massive entrance to the throne room. The opulence was stunning. Even Nicanor had to admit that the décor was a fitting accompaniment to a crowning. He and his adjutants stood as guards to the affair of state, witnessing its correctness and seeing to its order.

Eupator had commissioned a special black armor for them, its scored-black bronze inlaid with golden scenes from the lives of the gods and famous mortals. Nicanor had snorted at the motif chosen for him: a depiction of Achilles besting Hector at the penultimate battle of Troy. His lieutenants had similar reactions to the armor chosen for them, wanting to rebel at the foppish breastplates. They took their protests to Nicanor.

"How can I wear this?" One said. "Theseus slaying the Minotaur? Look, the Minotaur looks like—" "Your wife," another finished for him. "But look at mine! I do not want to wear Atlas. He holds up the earth, yes. But he is a disgraced Titan." Another, "I have never worshipped Hermes," and another, "I have to wear a woman? Even if she is Athena, I do not want to wear a woman."

Nicanor listened to their clamoring for a few moments, then pointed out to them that he had no intention of taking their concerns about their wardrobe to anyone, let alone their new king. "But," he added, "If any of *you* would like to take it up with the young Eupator, I am sure he would be delighted to hear your denigrations of his taste."

The lieutenants had been sullen, but the protests ceased. Forming up in their parade ranks, they adjusted their helmets and the dandified breastplates. In their march through Antioch on parade, Nicanor and his men received more than their share of adoration and acclaim. The people cheered the famous general and the lieutenants following him, who would, the mob was sure, be as famous as the general one day.

Now Nicanor and his men watched as the new king and his regent marched past them into the throne room. Snaking into the entrance with measured step, the royal procession assumed the appropriate gravity associated with the responsibility of crowning Antiochus' successor.

Finally, it was the soldiers' turn and to Nicanor it seemed that they assumed more of a military demeanor than usual to counteract the ridiculous armor. He suppressed his smile and led them under the huge garland into the throne room.

If Nicanor had ever wished for a double-timed march, this was the moment. The procession was agonizingly slow and when he and his men had settled into their places at last, there was an even longer wait for the lesser courtiers and diplomats from allied nations to file in.

Nicanor felt a sharp jab in his ribs. His heart leapt back into the proceedings. Untold years of soldiering had taught him to catch sleep whenever possible, even in a stand-at-attention. Although his first lieutenant's poke interrupted his doze, he saw the standing nap was not enough: the ceremony was not finished yet. Damn.

The now ten-year-old king-in-waiting had an impossible list of titles attached to his name and the priest of Zeus intoned the litany as slowly as the ponderous occasion warranted. So slowly, in fact, that Nicanor felt like pacing, and it was only his soldierly restraint that kept him from crying out, "Get on with it already!"

The diadem finally found its way to the young king's head and Nicanor exhaled, realizing that he had forgotten to breathe for a few moments. There was something about the actual coronation that transcended the boredom of its prelude, and Nicanor found that his eyes were slightly wet. He nodded his approval with the rest of the celebrants as the young king slid into the gilded chair where his father, Antiochus the Great, *Epiphanes*, had sat. Perhaps young Eupator would overcome the royal legacy of madness that his father had made part of Seleucia. Maybe a great new age of Greek domination had begun where their provinces and holdings would be governed with intelligence and order.

Nicanor and his men stood at attention in their silly breastplates for almost an hour while the new king ruled on matters brought to him by Regent Lysias. He even gave a token ruling, part of the coronation protocol, where he settled a matter with two litigants arguing a border dispute. The ruling was fair and earned more nods from the convocation. Finally, Eupator rose, the coronation ceremony complete, and descended the dais to leave the throne room and retire to the banquet tables, gravid with culinary opulence.

The young king looked neither to the left or the right as the procession of nobles and priests ferried him out. When he passed Nicanor and his lieutenants, he paused, seemed to consider and whispered something to Lysias, who had crouched to meet the king's height. Lysias straightened out of his stoop and looked at Nicanor. Eupator's eyes followed Lysias' gaze to Nicanor's face. The young king's visage was as full of merriment as the regent's was of vague disapproval. But the regent nodded and Eupator, with all the dignity of a new monarch, approached Nicanor.

Although his men did not move, he could sense their pride, or was it apprehension, at the king's detour toward them. Eupator kept his kingly mien, but an arch cast shone in his eyes. Nicanor had not been worried until he saw that look of mischief.

Finally, Eupator was close enough and his intent to address the general obvious enough that Nicanor sank to a dignified knee to keep the king from having to crane his royal neck upward. Nicanor felt like smiling but bowed his head, instead.

"Faithful General," Eupator's voice reeded. "Nicanor, I am pleased that you and your men were able to attend." The child leaned toward Nicanor and whispered, "You all look splendid. Did the men like my gift of armor?"

"Yes, My King. They have been raving about it for days. They will be happy I had the opportunity to thank you in person." Nicanor bowed his head. "Thank you, Divine One."

Eupator's eyes widened and Nicanor blanched a bit. The specter of Antiochus' madness had informed the regent's and his advisors' decision to not fill the young king's head with ideas of godhood. Nicanor was aware of this policy; his appellation was an extreme breech of protocol.

Eupator recovered more quickly than Nicanor and a mischievous smirk lit up his young face. "Divine? Perhaps not yet, General, but soon. Soon." The mischief was gone, and a strange determination had replaced it. Then, Eupator leaned toward Nicanor again and said, "We must speak soon about Rome and the tribute. I have plans for Judaea. My children must be taught a lesson."

"Of course, Your Majesty." Nicanor bowed and the audience was at an end, Eupator having joined the recessional out of the throne room.

General Nicanor watched the trailing procession and shook his head.

Chapter Eighty-nine

Asher said, "I appreciate a great metropolis as much as any man, but are you sure this is Rome? All my life I have heard, 'Rome this' and 'Rome that!' If this is Rome, give me Judaea any day. Pah, Rome is not so much. And, the stench!"

He was sorry as soon as he said it. Aulus was not as prone to jokes as he had been in the past before Brita's death. Although it had been more than a year since the stoning, Asher was surprised that the Roman was still trying to help the rebellion.

"Oh, and Judaea does not stink?" Aulus snapped. "The fragrance of the Gophna latrines in mid-Quintilis come to mind. Do not speak to me of Rome's stink."

Asher sighed. The months following Brita's death had cast a dark pall on the camp. Although its inhabitants had studiously ignored the little slave while she was alive, now it was as if her spirit harried them, teaching them the folly of hatred. But they did not understand. Their clannish ways had inured them from the outside influences that could have taught them tolerance. His people were a good people, but too many generations of mistrust toward the civilizations around them had turned them inward. Not that Asher blamed them. History had been relentless toward the Jews—since King David's day, they were forever being carried away into captivity, harried and tortured because of their race. Brita had been a victim of that mistrust and had paid for its effect with her life. Well, Brita was receiving her due, now. Gophna was experiencing an unusual swath of tragedy, ennui and upheaval, and if Asher didn't know better, he would ascribe it all to her little ghost exacting her revenge from—well, beyond.

Of course, it all started with the loss of Miriam's baby after Ephraim's unfortunate fall against her. The horrific stoning of Brita followed close after, after which three babies exited their mothers' wombs stillborn and Rebekkah's little Tovah fell into her family's hearth. The child died in terrible manner of her burns.

Luckily, there had been a lull in the fight against the Greeks or the low morale caused by these tragedies would have likely ensured a defeat in one form or another. As it was, word had filtered through their intelligence that Lysias was on his way to Judaea with a large force, but that the logistics in getting his troops to Judaea would delay a confrontation for many months. Judah had told Asher that he was grateful for the extra time to prepare, but the frightening development of Lysias marching again on Judaea was why Asher and Aulus were here in Rome. Judah had sent them as envoys so see if they could get political if not monetary support from the Roman republic.

After Brita's death, Aulus had been more brooding, taking offense where he had not before at the usual slights of the Jews toward him because of his 'infidel' status. Before, he would laugh off the rude remarks and general shunning. Now he had taken to violence "to teach the Jews some manners." This was his quote to Judah and Asher one day after he had walloped Avram in the mouth when the big Jew had made fun of the Roman gods, saying that they were as randy as coneys in a hutch. While they watched Avram spit out a number of teeth, Judah and Asher knew they had to get Aulus away from all the reminders of Brita or the Roman would either depart the cause, go mad or kill someone.

Asher and Aulus had been traveling for six months now and as much of their travel had taken them through Greek holdings, they had to make their journey as inconspicuously as possible. As a result, they did not dare ask much about the goings-on in Judaea, so they had no idea what form the preparations for the fight against Lysias and his troops were taking, or even if the fighting was going on as they trudged toward Rome. That lack of insight made them uneasy and restless on the journey, thinking they should not have left their comrades.

Silently, the men made their careful way through the dirty streets of Rome. Aulus had his toga pulled up to his knees and Asher was clutching his robe to his hip to keep it out of the open sewer that ran down the middle of the street. The wood and plaster buildings loomed together overhead so that not much sunlight reached the dank streets where they walked. When Asher craned his neck to look up, he saw that long wooden poles had been wedged between the buildings to keep them apart. He loosened the clutch of robe to give him more mantle for his shoulders against the winter wind that iced through him like frozen daggers. Where did this Publius Africanus live, anyway?

Rome was a city of steep hills and gentle ravines. As they were moving up a steep incline, Asher decided to try another stab at humor to lighten Aulus' mood. "And these hills—the Seven Hills of Rome, indeed," he panted. "Who builds on seven hills? Which hill is giving me the heart attack, now?"

"That would be the Aventine, Aulus said sourly. We are heading to the Palatine, the next hill over. Gear up, woman. We will be there soon. The forum is on the Palatine and so is Publius' estate."

When they finally reached the forum, they were able to drop their hems and Asher did his best not to look impressed. The marble-columned business center teemed with togate men gesticulating wildly, running in and out of the elegant structure like ants. Clerks sat at desks among the immense columns in the open-air temple of commerce and conducted their transactions with an array of wax tablets, parchment and abacuses, all the while attending to various customers lined up out into the plaza of the forum itself.

"What is that?" Asher pointed to what must be a temple as it dwarfed the immense commerce building. A huge cube of columns held aloft a triangular pediment that was barely visible because of its height. Asher actually had to step back many cubits, widening his vantage so he could view the temple in its entirety. It was bigger than any of the Greek structures at Lydda.

"The temple of Castor and Pollux," Aulus said proudly.

Asher did not believe in the heathen gods of the Greeks or Romans anymore, so could not account for the warmth spreading in his vitals. Perhaps it was nostalgia. In his Greek days, before he had come back to the One True G-d, he had been the famous wrestler, Eupolemus. Castor and Pollux, the brothers of Helen of Troy, had been his gods of choice, especially Pollux the boxer. The old tales showed Pollux to be as prodigious with using his fists as his brother Castor was with handling horses; Asher revered them both, sacrificing to them often in the old days.

"This way," Aulus said, dragging Asher. "Publius' house is over there. His messenger gave me directions."

Reluctantly, Asher allowed Aulus to pull him away from the temple. At least its immensity ensured Asher a good long look at it as Aulus led him out of the forum, the men still ascending the Capitoline.

Asher's appreciation of the fineries of life could not prepare him for the opulence of villas that graced the area. No sewers fouled the streets here and the state-owned slave sweeping at the gates of one estate did not look up as they approached.

"Here it is," Aulus said, standing at the gate where the slave had been sweeping. "*Estne casa domini tui*? Is this your master's house?" he asked.

The slave, whose broom was now motionless, looked up at last. "*Ita. Est Casa Publi Africani. Expectatne vos*? Yes, this is the house of Publius. Is he expecting you?"

At Aulus' affirmative, the slave opened the gate and motioned them inside. Another slave ushered them up a meticulous gravel walkway, lined with a cunning array of shrubbery, trees and flowers, and led them into the atrium of the Villa Africanus.

Obvious delight on his face, the old man said to Aulus "So, you belong to Aulus Licinius Macro. My father spoke of him, you know. He regaled us often with tales of Magnesia. But I was not one for the military. I enjoyed business and commerce, not soldiering and politics."

Publicus Scipio Africanus *Minor* seemed a man of contentment. The easy way that he adjusted his toga and smiled showed an utter lack of ambition. "Father died almost twenty years ago, and I can still remember his disappointment at my lack of interest in war or government. I did serve as praetor with my brother ten years ago, but after that, I kept to my importing business, and my brother, to his vineyards." The old man straightened, and his smile widened. "Ah, son! Here you are. There is someone I would like you to meet."

Asher looked at Aulus. If this old man was not in politics, then what were they doing here? A Roman merchant was not going to do them any good. He kept staring at Aulus who ignored him. But, when Aulus stood, he did also.

"This is my son, Publius Aemilianus Scipio Africanus, one of the youngest men to ever stand for election to the senate," said Africanus *Minor*. "My fortunes have increased ever since I adopted young Aemilianus, so I know that the Lares of my fathers, especially Africanus *Maior*, are pleased at his political aspirations. Aemelianus, this is Aulus *Minor*. His father fought at Magnesia with your grandfather."

The young Roman before them had the stature of a man much older than twenty-three years. The severe angles of his face waxed soft by gentle, yet shrewd eyes, and as he took their hands in greeting, the grip was that of a soldier.

When Aulus finally returned Asher's look, it was one of relief and satisfaction. To Aemilianus, he said, "It is a pleasure to meet you. My father greatly honored your grandfather. He spoke of him often."

Amelianus bowed toward Aulus, then turned toward Asher. "And who is this? You are not Roman."

Asher inclined his head. The face of the young senator was smooth with youth and guile, but the observation did not seem malicious. "I am a Jew,"Asher said, "and one of Judah the Maccabee's lieutenants."

"He is also the great wrestler, Eupolemus," Aulus said, smirking at Asher's embarrassment. "He was well-known in the Hellenic empire as one of the most gifted athletes in all of Seleucia."

"I have heard of you," Aemelianus said. "Your name is known in Rome." He nodded at Aulus. "Your commander did well in sending the two of you. The son of a Magnesia veteran and the Great Eupolemus would be heard with almost any message they bore. Please sit and refresh yourselves."

"We have been sent by our commander to ask for support from the Roman people in our struggle." Asher said carefully, sitting down on an elegant ebony curule chair next to Aulus, hoping he had not plunged into the topic too soon. "He hopes to reach an understanding with your republic."

Aemelianus looked thoughtful.

Asher hurried on, "It is well known that Rome has no love for Antiochus Epiphanes. We would like to be a stronghold for the Romans in Judaea. If we could count on your help, the alliance could be mutually beneficial."

Aemelianus nodded, but shrugged. "I am but a junior senator. I do not have much of a voice, yet." His emphasis on the last word brought a knowing smile to his father's lips. "But, I will bring your cause before the senate when we next convene. I will have the rostra by next week. I will speak of the matter at that time, but I am sure that Rome looks kindly upon your efforts. They are as interested in subduing the empire of Seleucia as you are."

Asher said, "Thank you. I and Aulus will be acting as envoys for Judah. We plan to stay in Rome for a time."

"You will be interested in a report that I just heard by courier in our senate proceedings, then," Amelianus said, excitement replacing the guile in his features. "Lysias has fled Judaea."

Asher sat forward in shock. "Lysias was in Judaea?" He asked weakly.

Aemelianus looked from Asher to Aulus. "I am sorry. I thought you would have heard. Lysias was in Judaea two weeks ago. He had 30,000 troops with him."

"We have been traveling in secret through Greek territory," Aulus explained, glancing over at Asher. "We had no idea he had even arrived."

Africanus *Minor* gestured for a slave and whispered something. The slave disappeared.

"Apparently he was giving the Jews a rough time of it. What town did the courier say he was besieging?" Aemelianus tapped his temple in thought. "The Hebrew tongue escapes me, but I believe it was Beit Zur."

"Beit Zur!" Asher and Aulus said together.

"Yes," Aemelianus said, more sure this time. "I am sure that was it. He inflicted many casualties on your people. From what I hear, however, the Jews gave him as good as he got. But is the place significant?"

"It is our southernmost border that we share with the Idumeans, our enemies," Asher said and then in an aside to Aulus, "I am sure he used their help to approach Judah from the south." He worried for a moment, then remembering, he said, "But you said Lysias fled."

"Yes. That was the word. He is on his way to Antioch even now."

"But, why would he flee?" Aulus said. "That does not make sense. He had 30,000 with him. Judah was talking about being able to muster only 10,000."

"As I said, The Jews were formidable. They killed 5,000 of Lysias' men."

Aulus whistled.

"But, more important than that, it is said that Antiochus the Great has finally died. A fever took him in Parthia," Aemelianus said. "It is said that Lysias had to hurry back to Antioch to solidify the succession of Antiochus' son, Eupator.

Asher stood slowly, an intake of air taking away speech. Aulus, seeing his friend sway, put his hand up in an instinctive gesture to steady him. Aemelianus looked over at his father and smiled.

Asher raised his hands as if to pray, then thought better of it. Clasping his palms together he brought them to his forehead as if to wrench control away from his emotions. He looked at Aulus. "Our great enemy is dead. The Lord of Hosts with us!" He swayed again.

Aulus stood and grabbed Asher in a rough embrace. The Roman said, "The Lord of Hosts with us!"

Aemelianus joined them, thumping their backs. "I am so happy to be the one to bring you the news of the Crazy One's death. You Jews have had a rough go of it with that war monger. I only hope that his death proved long and painful. Ah! Appropriate timing. Here is the wine."

The slave poured the wine with great ceremony, seeming to sense the gravity of the news.

Old Scipio raised his goblet and held it out to Aulus, Asher and his son. "A toast to the new kingdom of Judaea," He said. "May she thrive!"

"May she thrive!" Aulus, Asher and Aemelianus said, returning the salute with their goblets.

Chapter Ninety

Jerusalem, Judaea   The 24th day of *Kislev* 3597 (November 20th 164 B.C.E.)

The streets and buildings when the Maccabee had rescued Ephraim two months before had been shabby and spent. But now, things were worse, much worse. Where before, the cobbles had lain sedately in their pavement mortar, now they were upended, and vast swaths of street had been ploughed up by some monolithic force. It seemed that the same brutal force had reaped the buildings, for nary a wall stood that had escaped the unyielding scythe. Sheets of vines intertwined with noxious weeds infested the ground and buildings alike. Errant shrubbery invaded every spot of earth in the stonework, and every cranny of masonry was plugged with filth. Tumbleweeds, trash, human and animal dung, discarded furniture and other unimaginable offal littered the bosom of Jerusalem.

This shambles was an impossible breach of Israel's stewardship. This was the Jews' city. This had been the Hebrew seat of religion and government since David had conquered the Philistines eight hundred years before. This was the city given to them by the Lord through his prophets. As Judah and his men rode through the alleyways of Jerusalem, he was sure that the prophets Samuel, Micah, Habakkuk and all the others were writhing in their graves at the sorry state of the holy city. And, he felt ashamed.

When Judah and the Men of Modiin launched Ephraim's rescue, Judah did not think it possible that the city could devolve into a worse state of dishevelment. But now, as he looked about, he decided that the ruin was not only physical, but spiritual as well. The evil pall that now blanketed the city must have hidden it from the heavens, for as the men rode through its streets, they glanced about them, uneasy with the ominous air that hovered. It was real; it was thick; they tugged their cloaks tight against it.

"I feel cold," Avram muttered.

"With that great bulk?"

But Eleazar's whisper of a joke fell as lead to the ruined cobbles under the weight of the dense air.

Avram insisted, "The city is not itself."

"No," Judah agreed. "It is not." He sat higher on his horse and hailed the men to stop. "The city looks deserted, it is true," he said to the restive men, "but you must shake off your nerves and proceed boldly. The Greeks likely noted our entrance into the city and are waiting around any corner, in any square or neighborhood. Be cautious and remember that we are here to take back Jerusalem." He sat back on his saddle and peering at a particularly squalid vein of rubbish running across the stones, added, "And, make her whole again."

He signaled them forward. They clattered tentatively toward the Greek quarter, then Judah stopped the men again and motioned John to take a patrol in.

"It is as deserted as it looks," John said when he and the patrol emerged after a swift reconnoiter. "Not even a yellow dog to wag its tail. Where have they gone?"

"To the Akra, you idiot," Simon said. "If you would listen to the scouts' reports, you would know that the Greeks and the collaborators who did not flee Jerusalem are holed up in the tower."

"I do listen," John protested, "but who has time—"

"Stop it you two," Judah said. "You are commanders. Act like it. Simon, I want you to take your men through the Jewish quarter. Find those who have been directing the insurgency here in Jerusalem and tell them I want to meet with them tonight. We will house ourselves in the deserted apartments round about the temple mount. Tell them that they can find me there."

Simon nodded and with a triumphant glance at John, galloped away with his men into one of the narrow maws of the city.

Judah turned to John again. "John, I want you to enter the Greek quarter with the rest of your men and make doubly sure it is deserted. Be wary, for there may be pockets of Hellenists waiting to disrupt us. If you encounter any resistance, send a courier and I will send you reinforcements. But, if you and your men can handle it on your own, so much the better. I do not know what awaits me at the temple mount and I may need all my troops there."

"We will not need any help," John said defiantly. "Any Greek we meet will be as chaff before us."

Judah smiled as he watched John lead his troops back into the Greek quarter. "Reap well, brother," He said as he directed the remaining troops forward.

Judah's words of encouragement notwithstanding, the men rode hunched against their saddles. It was as if every new vision of detritus in the streets weighed them down further and further, and by the time they found themselves in the vicinity of the temple, they found that they could barely sit upright.

"Through those gates is the temple courtyard," Judah said to Eleazar. "I have not seen it for many years. I fear to look upon it now in light of all that is said to have occurred there."

"Do we dare to bring all our troops in?" Eleazar wondered aloud. "After all, it is consecrated ground."

"The blood of pigs has been sprinkled throughout the enclosure and the courtyard. Whores have cavorted upon the altar," Judah said, his eyes becoming wet. He paused and bowed his head for a moment. "This ground is consecrated no longer," he said, lifting his head and motioning the men toward the gate.

He dismounted, patting *Tiklit*, and stood before the gate. "Let us go in," he said to the men in as hushed a tone as he could manage. "Men of Modiin, we will be first. The rest of you wait and if it is safe, you will hear Eleazar's shofar. Then you may enter the temple compound."

He placed his hand on the right half of the massive gate and pushed. He leapt back, the gate swinging away from its lower hinge, then dangling against gravity on the upper bolt. After a few uncertain moments where the gate shuddered under its own weight, the pull of the earth won out and it crashed to the cobbles, its timbers coming apart in cataclysmic splinters.

Judah looked up at his men, and with a frown stepped over the rubble of wood and entered the courtyard. The Men of Modiin followed.

Unsure of whom or what they may find, the men fanned out throughout the enclosure. Swords drawn, they inched over the stones in a crouching walk, starting at every kicked pebble, blanching at every flock of birds that flew overhead. The temple doors loomed ahead, and they were ajar. Judah groaned within himself. It was such a simple matter to close the doors of any dwelling against harm. The yawning doors were not a good sign.

He edged through the doors into darkness. A loathsome odor assailed him, and he reeled back. Holding his cloak up over his lower face, he ventured farther into the darkness. His men followed, some breaking away from the group to the windows that were covered with heavy drapes. With a great clanking of metal against rod and a great exhale of dust from fabric, they drew aside the curtains.

The pyramids of light that thrust down from the windows blinded the men for a moment. As they became accustomed to the ambivalence of vision, they moved farther into the temple.

Blinking against the intruding beams, Judah's eyes debated his mind's wish to focus on the altar, and instead fastened themselves to the golden colossus to the left of the altar. No sound or movement except for Judah's footsteps assailed the huge room. As he came closer and closer to the altar and the colossal image of Antiochus, his feet became more faltering in their approach, finally stopping altogether. It was then that he tore his eyes away from the statue and forced himself to look at the altar. It was dark with blood and a blackened carcass lay across its stones. The desiccated snout of the animal made its identity unmistakable.

Sinking to his knees, a great wail arose from Judah's throat. His fingers found the shoulder straps of his breastplate and unbuckling them he wrenched the guard from his chest. His hands clawed at the collar of his tunic until with one rend, he tore the cloth from neck to navel. He drew his palms over the floor that was thick with dust and gathered as much as he could in his shaking fists, dousing his shoulders and head with the dirt.

"No, Lord of the Universe!" He shouted. "Let it not be so!"

Sobbing, it was as if he had burdened himself with the consciousness of all Judaea. The sorrow for the abomination of desolation weighed down upon the Maccabee. No longer mighty, no longer indomitable, he trembled like a child.

He was not alone in his devastation for long, for as soon as the Men of Modiin saw the statue and the befouled altar, great rendings of cloth and moans filled the once-holy cavern.

The mourning exercise was too grueling for their bodies to sustain for long and soon they lay motionless on the floor. Finally, Judah staggered to his feet, drew his sword and struck it, flat end, against the carcass. The putrefied flesh slid off the altar and across the stone floor until it came to rest against the feet of Antiochus. Judah yearned to hack the filth to pieces, but restrained himself, unwilling to spread the offending flesh further.

Finally, the spent men exited the befouled temple and rested on her steps. Heads in hands, they gently rocked to and fro in their grief.

"Judah. What are we to do?" Avram wiped his face with the neck of his tunic and shook his head, repeating, "What are we to do?"

"We will cleanse it, of course," Judah said wearily.

"We? We are men of war," Eleazar said. "I am a priest, it is true, but I have shed the blood of the enemy. I am not fit—we are not fit to perform the ordinances of purification."

"Then we will get someone who is fit," Judah said. "Give me the shofar."

Shaking his head, Eleazar withdrew the Ram's horn from the folds of his robe and handed it to Judah.

The long, low blast trembled throughout the courtyard, its bass keen an eerie sound in the walled enclosure. Slowly, the rest of Judah's forces ebbed onto the temple ground, the shock on their faces at its overgrown and sullied state mirroring that of the Men of Modiin of a few moments before.

"Issachar!" Judah rumbled. "I need you!"

The bookish clerk stumbled out of the mass of fighters. "Yes, commander?"

"You are a Levite. You are of the landless tribe. I need more of your numbers. We must rededicate this ground."

Issachar glanced around at the temple enclosure and nodded thoughtfully. "There were many with me during the insurgency. If I can find them, they can help me perform the ritual."

"Avram, go with him. Take your force into the city and find his compatriots."

Since Asher was still away with Aulus in Rome, Avram had taken temporary command of his troops. "It shall be as you say, commander. Come on, you clerk," he said good-naturedly to Issachar. "Let us find your Levites."

One of Judah's men screamed. The chaos of scattering men and arrows dashing against stone filled the courtyard.

Crouching, Judah gazed up and saw the Greek archers. They were perched like hawks along the balustrade of the Akra raining death on the Jewish fighters. "*Mehercle!*" he gasped. I forgot about that accursed tower! Take cover! Take cover!" He yelled, and pointing to the men who had taken arrows, "And, drag them to safety!"

The walls of the courtyard were high enough that the men were able to escape the arrows by crouching behind their stones. As Judah hunkered down with them, he consulted with Eleazar. The arrows did not stop their Stymphalian rain, and Judah listened to the snap of their shafts against the cobbles.

Eleazar mopped his brow with his head covering. "Well, Commander," he said. "What do you suggest?"

"I do not know, Commander," Judah replied in irritation. "What do *you* suggest?"

"The tower cannot accommodate enough archers to do us much harm," Eleazar said. "But they can make our task at hand extremely tedious."

"Do you really think so?" Judah asked in irritation, pulling at his beard. "The scholar here thinks those arrows are tedious." Ignoring the dark chuckles of his men, he took a moment to survey the entire enclosure. "See that parapet off the wall over there? If we station our archers there, do you see—"

"Our men will force their archers to retreat off that balustrade," Eleazar finished for him. "I will see to it, brother, for all your derision." He stood and saluted Judah.

"If you do not like my derision, do not leave yourself so wide open to it. But, stay down."

The enemy archers quickly left the tower parapet rather than be picked off by the Hebrew arrows and soon the fighters were able to move about freely in the courtyard.

It was true that being sullied by war, Judah's men could not perform the rituals, but they could set to the task of cleaning up the unwholesome piles of garbage that littered the holy site. This they did with grim relish, and soon the men had scoured most of the offending refuse from the enclosure, piling it into a huge bonfire they had ignited in the outer courtyard.

Judah had just pitched the last splinters of the smashed temple gate into the fire when he heard one of his men call out, "Here come the Levites!"

The robes looked moth-eaten, but the unmistakable Levitical stripe signaled the priestly lineage of those who trooped solemnly into the enclosure. Marching among the rest of the Levites, Issachar had shed his warrior tunic and gear and looked much more at home in his priest's robe. In fact, being the only one among them who knew the Maccabee, he led the procession, the rest following uncertainly.

Judah's men stopped their various tasks and stood, assessing the priests who now stood before their commander. No one spoke for many moments.

Finally, an old priest stepped out of the Levite throng and asked, "Are you truly the Maccabee?"

Judah brushed his hands and came away from the fire. As the flames gnawed at the garbage, he stepped before the old priest, then knelt on one knee. He looked at the rest of the fighters and nodded; soon, obeisance rippled through the hardened gathering of soldiers, only the archers on the parapet keeping military vigil.

"We are in need of you," Judah said humbly. "We are men of war, not of ritual. We have shed much blood."

The old priest took Judah by the shoulders and pulled him to his feet. "Arise, Judah the Maccabee," he said, "for it is we who should make obeisance to you. What is the state of the altar? I have not been within for many years. I, Eli of Bethlehem, was an aide to the temple high priest, Gideon, who was slain in the Kidron caves. I am ashamed to say that we presided over the defilement. Menelaus forced us. After that terrible day, we did not come back to the temple.

"The altar is drenched in swine's blood and the statue of Zeus still stands," Judah said. "Tell us what to do."

"I will set my priests to finding or hewing stone for the altar, for that must be done by one consecrated to the priesthood. You and your men may take down the image and remove the defiled altar."

"What about a Menorah?" Judah asked. "Do any of you in Jerusalem know what happened to it? What about the other vessels for sacrifice? What about oil?"

Eli looked thoughtful. "I am afraid that Antiochus, the Greeks and collaborators took everything of value, especially the gold. We have not seen any of the accoutrements for many years. We believe that the Greeks bore all back to Antioch. But I wonder. . ."

The old priest looked over at Issachar. "Issachar. Come with me to the old apartments of Gideon. They are in the smaller courtyard through that gate." He pointed to a small wooden gate through the northern wall behind the temple. "Commander, you may accompany us."

The smaller courtyard through the gate was not in as bad a state as the main courtyard. The invaders and revelers must have overlooked it.

"Gideon was a very resourceful man," Eli said as he opened the doors to Gideon's rooms. "He and his son, Hezekiah, may have tried to preserve some of the vessels."

"I have heard these names," Judah said. "My man, Ephraim, told me about the temple high priest Gideon. Hezekiah was his best friend. In fact," Judah paused for a moment before remembering, "He was going to marry Deborah, Gideon's daughter. But they were butchered—"

"—In the Kidron Caves, yes," Eli finished for him. "I should have been there, but had to stay in Jerusalem to attend to a death in my family. I survived the massacre."

Judah saw a tremendous flinch of pain, then guilt, cross the old man's features. He said nothing, but rage burned in his breast as he helped Issachar move an old chifferobe away from the wall.

"Hezekiah told me once that there was a false wall in these offices," Issachar grunted as he helped Judah move the cabinet. "Perhaps—but no, it is probably too much to hope. . ."

"Hope?" Judah asked. "Hope for what?"

"For this! Look!"

The three men stood and marveled at the unmistakable outline in the stone. It was indeed a door.

"Help me," Issachar panted as he strained against the stone. "It is too heavy."

Judah gently took Issachar by the shoulders and set him to one side. He summoned the rage that he had felt before, using it and his natural heft to push against the door. After a moment or two of intense effort, the stone yielded. Judah stepped back.

"In case the vessels are within, I cannot enter," Judah said. "I am not worthy to touch them or even be in the same room with them."

Eli nodded, regretful agreement in his face, and disappeared through the door. Judah and Issachar, who had also hung back, heard rustlings and scrapings as the old man fumbled in the dark. Hopeful, they waited, almost expecting a yell of triumph when Eli found the candelabrum. Instead, they looked at each other when they heard a small clink.

The old priest finally emerged. In his hand was a small, sealed pottered cruse. "Oil," he said. "It is still sealed; its consecration is still intact. But, it is not enough."

"Enough?" said Judah. "Enough for what?"

"This oil will last only for one day," Issachar explained sorrowfully. "We need oil for eight days to properly rededicate the temple."

Judah became impatient. "We do not even have a menorah," he said. "What good is oil without a menorah? You are not making sense."

"One of our tribe is a gifted metalsmith," Issachar said. "He can smelt a menorah in no time at all. Oil is another matter entirely."

"We are lucky the olive harvest just finished," Eli said. "But we will have to wait for a few days to rededicate the temple. We cannot process the oil fast enough to have it ready for the purification rite. Pressing the olives into oil will take at least a quarter moon. We must wait."

"We cannot wait," Judah said. "We must start the rededication today, tomorrow at the latest."

"But we cannot hurry the preparation of oil," Eli said, scandal in his voice. "The ritual cannot be compromised by speed."

"We have oil," Judah said stubbornly. "And I have an idea for a makeshift menorah. A ritual candelabrum has six arms, with one *shamas*. Is that not correct?"

"A makeshift menorah? That is unheard of," Issachar said. "We must have a proper lamp for burning the oil, and since the temple is defiled, we cannot burn the lamp within. Not only that, but it is prohibited to use a menorah outside the temple."

"How long will it take to make more oil?" Judah's voice became more forceful.

"Eight days are needed to harvest and press the olives." Eli said, hesitation in his voice. "But even if we are able to fashion a menorah—it cannot burn outside of the temple.

"Come with me," Judah said, plunging out of the door. "And bring the oil."

Judah smiled as he listened to the two muttering Levites following him as he hurried back to the temple courtyard. "What does he expect?" and "One cruse of oil? What good is this to us?" and "They do not call him *The Hammer* for nothing! Such a hard head!"

"Avram!" Judah bounded into the courtyard, calling. "I need you!"

The call went up among the soldiers. "Where is Avram? The Maccabee has need of him! Find Avram!" Finally, Avram answered the relayed summons and stood before Judah.

Judah clapped his old friend on the shoulder. "My old master. It is time you return to the forge. I need a smithy."

Chapter Ninety-one

A ulus said, for what must have been the twentieth time, "The son of Scipio Africanus, a merchant! I lay odds that his old man is mourning even as he cavorts in Elysium."

Asher said, "Here it is, the Western Gate. Thank all your gods we are here, for if I have to hear that one more time, 'the son of Scipio Africanus. . .' I will tear your head off."

"What?" Aulus shrugged. "I only meant to say—"

"Yes, yes." Asher said. "But, do not say it again. That is, if you value your head. As I pointed out before, for the hundredth time, at least the general's grandson followed in his footsteps. Aemelianus seems like a good man."

"I only wish we could have stayed to hear his remarks about us in the Forum. I would have liked to hear how our appeal was received," Aulus said.

"Aemelianus said he would send word if the Senate wanted to help us in our effort," Asher said. "And, you and I agreed that we could not stay in Rome after hearing of Antiochus' death. The old fool's demise could intensify the Greeks' design on Judaea. Judah is going to need us."

"I would think it might weaken the Greek design on Judaea," Aulus offered. "Epiphanes only wanted your sorry strip of land because he was crazy."

"Hilarious," Asher said in exasperation. "Listen, Antiochus' death in Parthia means that all those crack troops that accompanied him there will be on their way home. They may be in Antioch even now, preparing to march on Judaea."

"But, Antiochus' son Eupator is only a child. Surely he does not care about Judaea."

"The new King Eupator will care about what Lysias tells him to care about. And Lysias just invaded Judaea."

"Lysias fled Judaea," Aulus said. "Aemelianus himself said that the Jews drove him out."

Asher scoffed. "Lysias left because he had to see to the succession of Antiochus' son. He was regent, after all. From what you have told me of Lysias—your own words—'he does not run away from a fight.'"

As they made their way farther into the city, Aulus looked around him. "Your Jerusalem is not so much. What a dirty city! And, the stench!"

Asher smiled at Aulus' joke, for Asher had said those exact words about Rome. "Well, Roman. You would be dirty, too if Greek soldiers had been ravaging you for the past thirty years."

"I would at least try to pretty myself up."

"Perhaps that is what Judah is helping her with," Asher said. "That trader on the ship told us as much."

The two men carefully crept through the streets, cast with night shadows. Asher and Aulus had done their best to glean as much intelligence on their trip back as possible, but had still been leery of attracting Greek attention. And what if Amelianus' information about the battle at Beit Zur had been incorrect? The city of Jerusalem could be teeming with increased Greek strength if Aemelianus' report about Lysias abandoning Judaea was wrong.

Upon landing in Joppa, the Judaean port city now held by those loyal to the Maccabee, the two men received word that Judah had the Greeks and collaborators holed up on the Akra and that Jerusalem was under his sway. They had even heard that Judah and his men were setting about purifying the temple, but Asher found that hard to believe. He doubted that even the Maccabee would be able to scare up enough Levites to perform the purification ritual, let alone the religious implements they needed. Antiochus and the Greeks had pillaged the temple so thoroughly over the years he doubted that even if a Levite were found, he would be hard-pressed to find a menorah that had not been defiled for the ritual. At best, perhaps Jerusalem was a little safer for a Jew and a Roman roaming her streets. And if that were true, this silly creeping gait they employed now was not necessary. Still, they did not dare to brazen their way through the city and had their swords drawn, jumping, even lunging sometimes at errant noises.

"This way," Asher whispered. "Let us approach the temple mount from the Jewish quarter. If Judah is indeed here, that would be his center of operations."

Asher was not nearly as familiar with Jerusalem as were most Jews and the two made many wrong turns. He could tell that Aulus was becoming more and more frustrated, as he could hear the Roman grinding his teeth and tsking. At last, he heard murmuring voices and saw a glow of light against the deepening dusk. This area seemed familiar to him, but he could not tell if it were indeed the Jewish quarter—there was too much rubble to be sure of landmarks. The noise and light that increased as they approached seemed friendly enough and they drew near, cautious yet hopeful that they would at least be able to rest and get something to eat.

Nevertheless, they stayed hooded under their thick traveling cloaks, unwilling to shed either the disguise or the warmth they offered against the chill *Kislev* night.

The voices belonged to a group of men seated in a tavern booth. There were so many of them that they had spilled out into the street and were seated on stones, ruined beams that once held up houses, and even discarded pieces of furniture. They seemed unconcerned with their noise, as if all of Jerusalem belonged to them. The voice of one stood out and Asher found himself running toward the group.

"Avram! Reuven! Gad!" Asher threw off his hood and ran at the men, soldiers who were now standing, alarm in their faces. The warriors in them had drawn their swords at the unexpected approach of the two cloaked figures. The swords were quickly sheathed, though, when Judah's men recognized Asher and Aulus.

"Back, already?" Avram's good-natured voice boomed. He hugged first Asher, then inflicted a gentle head-butt against Aulus' brow. "How does Rome? Did she listen to us?"

"Rome does well, for all that she stinks like a sewer!" Asher said, grinning at Aulus, then clapping him on the back. "But she is full of men as honorable as Aulus, here. Senator Aemelianus received us and said he himself would take our diplomatic concerns to the Roman Senate."

The rest of the soldiers at the establishment whooped their approval and clashed their earthen mugs against each other's in a toast. "The Lord of Host with Us," they shouted.

"So, obviously, Judah has Jerusalem," Asher said, sitting down to the mug of ale set before him. "We encountered no Greeks in the streets."

"Nor will you," Avram said, a knowing look on his face, "unless you break into that silly tower of theirs. There they cower and will not venture out."

"And it is not for a lack of invitation," Reuven said solemnly. "We have asked them again and again to come out and talk." He looked around at the others and added, "For some reason, they refuse."

After the laughter rose and fell, Asher said, "So it is true. Now that he has it, what does Judah intend to do with Jerusalem?"

"Make it our seat of government, of course," said Gad. "And he has begun the purification of the temple."

The men became hushed and exchanged significant nods.

"Then it is true," Asher breathed. "That is great news!" But the hushed undercurrent of mood of the men around him intrigued him further. He asked, "What is going on? Has something happened?"

A mass clearing of throats was the only answer he received for a moment until Avram said, "Yes. Something wonderful has happened—is happening." He looked around, inhaled, then exhaled, seeming uncertain of how to continue.

"Well?" Asher said. "Are you going to tell me, or do I have to beat it out of you?"

Asher was smiling, but something about the faces of the men around him made him stop. He glanced over at Aulus who shrugged and shook his head.

"What?" Asher finally asked.

"It is a miracle," Avram said simply.

"A miracle? What are you talking about?" Asher gestured for another two ales from the proprietor, giving one to Aulus.

After he saw that the two men were comfortable with their drinks, Avram started speaking.

"It started when we entered the temple. How Judah cried! The rest of us did, too. The defilement of the altar was more terrible than any of us had heard." Avram shook his head. "I cannot speak of that further. It is too—anyway, Judah, Issachar and the Levite High Priest went looking for the ritual artifacts. They found nothing but one paltry cruse of oil. They looked for more, but none was to be found, no, not in all of Jerusalem."

"But I thought you said that they had started the purification," Asher reminded him. "How can they purify anything with just one cruse of oil?"

"Well, there it is," Avram said. "They cannot. But they are."

"What do you mean? You are not making sense!"

"I mean," said Avram patiently, "that the oil has been burning for three days and has not burned itself out, yet."

"One cruse of oil lasting for three days," Asher said, mocking. "That is impossible! And you said yourself that they had no artifacts. What are they using for a lamp to burn the oil? The ritual menorah was carried off by Antiochus. This is ridiculous. Someone is playing a joke on you, old friend."

"This is no joke," Avram said solemnly. "Under the priest's careful eye, I showed a Levite metal worker how to fashion a Menorah out of hollowed-out spear shafts and the Levites blessed it for use in the purification."

"You fashioned a menorah! Everyone knows that a menorah can only be used inside the temple—and the temple is defiled! So how—"

"Judah figured out a way around the stricture," Avram patiently explained. "This menorah has eight oil reservoir holders: seven wells with one shamas. He did not want to wait until the new oil could be pressed. The metallurgist was able to pound down the shafts into oil wells and they held the oil right nice. Then something told Judah to start burning the oil, and he did. And," Avram went on meaningfully, "one day of oil has now lasted for three days! You will just have to see it for yourself."

"I intend to," said Asher lightly. "Hollowed out spear shafts, indeed. Where is Judah?"

"He is in the temple enclosure with the others. They are singing songs."

Asher had been attacking a flat of bread the proprietor had placed before them. He stopped mid-chew, highly bemused. "Judah the Maccabee singing songs," Asher said, laughing. "This is a sight I want to see, although I am not sure I want to hear it. I heard him sing, once. Come on Roman," he said, dusting the crumbs of the bread from his hands. "This should be interesting."

"Perhaps you should not be so dismissive, Asher," Aulus said as he rose from the table following the Jew into the street. "I have never known Avram to lie or make sport. Perhaps he is being truthful. Not only that, if it is true, the gods do not like irreverence."

"What, you too? A Roman believing in miracles? Since when?"

"The Roman republic's birth and survival itself is evidence enough of miracles, but there are many others—Jupiter allowing Baucis and Philemon to die on the same day, Actaeon sprouting antlers after displeasing the goddess Diana."

"Myths and legends," Asher scoffed. "That is what those stories are."

Aulus shrugged and stopped walking. They had just arrived at the old Greek quarter. "Here is where I leave you." At Asher's inquiring look he said, "I do not want to horn in on your 'miracle.' I am only an infidel, after all."

"Don't be stupid!" Asher sputtered. "Judah will want to see you—"

"And he shall," Aulus interrupted him. "I just have some business to attend to. Aemelianus wanted me to check on possible investment opportunities in Jerusalem. The abandoned Greek quarter seems like a good place to start. I shall see if there are any properties that are worth his attention. It may help our dealings with the Romans if I can find something with which to line their palms."

"But—"

Aulus put a hand on Asher's arm. "Believe me, *amice*. It is better this way. Tell Judah I will join him soon." Aulus turned and started walking down the alley that led to the Greek quarter, then suddenly stopped. "Oh, and Asher—"

"What?"

"Again, do not dismiss the 'miracle' too quickly. Wait until you talk to Judah. See what he says. Then you can decide. We are mortal and do not always understand the workings of the gods."

Aulus' earnest words silenced Asher but not his skepticism. Judah will tell me the truth, he thought. And I know that Judah believes in strategy and deeds, not miracles.

But when he entered the temple enclosure his disbelief faltered, for there was Judah the Maccabee, among the Levites, kneeling and singing before the temple entrance. The smell of burning oil was strong even in the open air outside the temple, but through its doors, which had been flung open, he saw a low mound of light. The open courtyard of the temple, its stones usually quiet, was busy with Jews building *sukkot*, the little booths the Lord ordered the Israelites to build to celebrate His bringing them out of Egypt. Asher had been gone a long time, away from the calendar of his people, but he was sure it was not the time of the year to celebrate *Sukkot*. That happened in spring. It was now the middle of winter.

Another wafture of smell assailed Asher's nostrils, and it was not the pleasant smell of fired oil of a moment before. It was then that he heard the bellows and bleats and realized that the courtyard was now smelling more like a barnyard. Sure enough, when he looked over to his left, away from the booths, he saw Levites leading huge oxen, rams, and bullocks, baaing kids and lambs. Most of the livestock were placid enough, but one of the priests was having a horrible time with one of the bulls that was rearing and plunging, disrupting the line of animals.

Asher glanced at Judah again and saw he was still immersed in his oblations with the priests, so decided to put off his greeting. The light through the open temple doors arrested his interest, but he hesitated. For all that he had shed his Greek ways a long time ago, he was still an impious man of war. Because of the blood he had let, entering the temple never crossed his mind. He was even nervous about approaching the holy edifice, but that light! Curiosity drove him to sidle up to its open doors and peer in.

The Maccabee was immediately at his side, embracing him. "Welcome back! What say the Romans?"

"They say. . ." Asher trailed off, concentrating on his squint so he could see into the dark interior of the temple. "Judah, what is that light? It is behind the altar." He looked at Judah. "I thought the altar was defiled."

"That light is the Lord's offering blessing our freedom," Judah said, keeping his arm around his friend. "And that altar is one new-hewn by the Levites." He must have misinterpreted Asher's look of bewilderment for one of indignation, for he said, "All is well. It has been duly consecrated and rededicated to the Lord."

Asher asked carefully, "So, they found more oil?"

His eyes joyful, Judah turned toward Asher and exclaimed, "That light has been burning for three days, Asher! All on one tiny cruse of oil. One cruse! The shamas well stays full—it does not deplete."

"What about all this livestock?" Asher asked. "The smell is terrible."

Judah laughed. "The livestock is here for today's sacrifice. We are in the third day of dedication for purifying the temple." Judah turned solemn. "This has been a week of miracles."

Asher looked at Judah. The light that had glittered in his friend's eyes now had spread to the rest of his face. All the hardness and bitterness that the war had melded into Judah's features over the years had fallen away, replaced by a sweetness that Asher found discomfiting. "Someone must be sneaking in and replacing the oil," Asher murmured.

"There is no more oil to be found," Judah said. "My men not only turned Jerusalem upside down, but also Bethlehem to the south, Azareyeh to the east and Moza to the west in their search. There is no oil," he repeated. "And it takes eight days for the olives to be pressed and their juice to be consecrated. But," he added cheerfully, "You may keep vigil with the other skeptics to make sure the 'miracle' is real. Their presence is to ensure that no one else 'sneak in and replace the oil.' And something tells me that this oil will last until the new press of olives is ready in five days."

Asher followed Judah's gesture and sure enough, the booths that had been assembled the moment before were populated by a number of people, including some Levites. All were sitting in postures of expectation.

"What, are they trying to make another festival? Another *Sukkot*?" Asher asked.

Judah smiled. "There are many who believe our regaining of our city, our temple and our freedom warrants an observance of some kind. What better holiday than

Sukkot? I think Moshe would approve, for like Yehoshua, we have fought for the promised land. And because we have been fighting, for two whole years we have not been able to build booths for our families to celebrate Moshe's Exodus. I know it is early for *Sukkot*, but I do not think the Lord of Hosts will mind." Judah gazed around the enclosure, craning his neck. "Is Aulus with you?"

"No. He is looking for some property in the Greek quarter with which to bribe the Romans." Judah's face turned stony and Asher went on, "Judah, I know that look. It is something we may have to do."

"I did not take Jerusalem just to turn it over to the Romans in some smarmy land deal."

"We are a nation, now. And with that nationality goes politics," Asher said. "Your sense of ethics must give way to politics. But," the light in the temple drew Asher's interest once again, "how can a lamp burn without oil? That cannot be real. In fact, it is impossible that one day's oil can last for three. I do not understand."

"Perhaps you should stay here and watch," Judah said, a smile replacing the stony scowl of a moment before. "Maybe your sense of reality must give way to faith."

Asher considered Judah's parry of words. "Then I shall sit also, and watch, and wait." But as he drifted away from Judah to appropriate the materials to build his own booth and sit among the witnesses, it was his turn to scowl.

Chapter Ninety-two

A nd Asher sat. For five more days, he and the rest of the faithful, the Men of Modiin joined by the Jerusalem insurgents, stayed in the mélange of booths that littered the temple courtyard like so many market stalls. Under the shelter of the *Sukkot* huts, they slept, ate, read *Tanakh*, discussed strategy and watched the temple doors to verify the miracle. Day after day, more booths sprang up in the courtyard, indeed, throughout the streets, as more and more Jerusalemites gathered themselves to the Maccabean warriors, helping them to celebrate their errant holy day. What did it matter, they said to each other, shrugging, if the observance of Moshe's departure from Egypt is a little early? The Maccabee has given us our own Exodus.

Eli, the high priest and a few select Levites were the only ones to enter or exit the temple. Daily, they performed the purifying rituals with incense, sacrifice and prayer, cleansing the temple of the influence of the Greek defilers. Blood once again stained the altars within, but this was not the corrupt blood of swine, but rather the blood of clean sacrifices as set forth in the Law of Moshe.

As the warriors crouched in their huts, their women made their way down from Gophna to Jerusalem, for the word had spread: the Maccabee has taken Jerusalem; the Maccabee is cleansing the temple; the Maccabee has routed the Greek invader. The roads to the north were safe for Jews, now. The roads to the north belonged to the Jews, now. Nevertheless, the Gophna women traveled with a healthy contingent of fighters, although it was more for pomp than for expediency.

On the eighth day of dedication, the final day of purification, the wives arrived, entering a Jerusalem that again stood as capital of Israel, for the Maccabee had made it so. Miriam, wife of Judah, Shoshanna, wife of Eleazar, and all the other warrior wives of Gophna entered their designated place in temple courtyard amid much joyous keening, the women of Jerusalem having turned out in as great a number as their depleted population would allow. Their ululations filled the city while Hebrew archers from their parapet maintained the Greek tower in their bow sights, able to keep their women safe, at last.

Judah emerged from his *sukkah,* kissed his wife and gathered his people in the courtyard so that as many as possible could witness the last of the rites renewing their temple. Flanked by his family and friends, he looked out over the multitude. His people were not so vast as the crowd Moshe must have gathered in Goshen for their departure from Egyptian bondage. And, perhaps his mandate was not as valid as Moshe's had been, for Judah never pretended that G-d had spoken directly to him. But yet, he was sure that Moshe's Israelites could not have faces as full of hope as those whose eyes were on him now.

The tower rose in his view behind the temple wall. It was the only blemish on the spectacle of today's celebration. The Greeks and the collaborators huddled in the stone monstrosity could yet make trouble for the new kingdom. As he gazed at the obscene monolith, Judah vowed that he would not rest until he had dismantled it stone by stone, razing the foundation to the ground.

"Judah, say something," Eleazar urged through the side of his mouth. "The people want to hear from you. The last bullock has been sacrificed. The priests are waiting, too."

For a moment, Judah had forgotten his new status as the political leader of his people. He was not sure he was comfortable with that new role. For the last two years, he had only had to focus on the strategies of war. Now it seemed he would have to shift his attention to the strategies of government. For a moment, he quailed, almost trembling at the prospect. How does one rule? Not with the sword. Evil Antiochus had shown him that. But Judah's comfort was his sword. His hand went to his hilt. He calmed down at once at the feel of its sturdy grasp. The calm deepened when he realized that the war was not over.

He straightened. "We have Jerusalem," he said simply, and the crowd roared. He reveled in the intense noise for many moments then spoke into the expectant silence that returned. "But we must keep it." The crowd nodded and murmured. "Lysias will return. The fight is not over. We must steel ourselves for what is to come." He considered the crowd and they, him. Judah smiled. "But for today, let us celebrate our new temple!"

As one, the crowd answered him. "The Lord of Hosts With Us!"

"Let us celebrate our G-d'! Judah roared as the Lion of Israel.

"The Sword of the Lord!" the Hebrews shouted.

"And, let us celebrate our Freedom!" Judah the Maccabee rejoined.

"The Lord of Hosts With Us!" The crowd offered the warrior shout to each other, their commander, and their G-d.

The End

FREE BOOK

As thanks for reading the second book in the Judaean Revolt Series, please accept as a gift my free novel entitled Asher's Story, a prequel to Judah the Hammer. Read about Asher's struggle to discover where he belongs: in the staid Jewish world of his upbringing, or the seductive freedom of a Greek life. To receive a downloadable copy, click on the book funnel QR code below:

Thank you for reading my second book of **The Judean Revolt Series**. To help other readers discover the Maccabee's world, please go to the link below for *Judah the Hammer* and leave me a review! Thanks again!

Start reading the next book in J.D. Sonne's

The Judean Revolt Series

Legacy of the Maccabee

The Third Book in **The Judean Revolt Series**

(excerpt)

*****

Miriam was matter-of-fact. "The Blackness has settled upon him again."

"Well, tell him he has got to get over it!" Asher cried. "Lysias is heading another expedition. He wants to finish what he started last season. And, our siege of the Akra provoked him into an immediate march."

Miriam shook her head. Asher always seemed to be the one to bring bad news. Especially when her husband, Judah the Maccabee, was in one of his dark moods. "I cannot tell him to get over it. *You* tell him to get over it. It is not so easily done—his getting over it. It sometimes takes him days."

"I need to see him. Aulus just received a missive from Aemelianus in Rome," Asher said. "I need to show it to Judah."

"Is it not in Latin? Since when can you read Latin?" Miriam said. "And, since Judah cannot read Latin, this whole exercise is useless; therefore, I think we can leave him alone."

"Woman. If you were not the wife of the Maccabee, I would take you over my knee. I have a translation, of course. Now let me by."

"No, Asher. You must leave him alone when he is like this. Come back later."

"Miriam, this cannot wait."

"What. What? What!"

Both turned uneasily at the slurred interrogative. Miriam turned a look upon Asher as full of invective as she could manage.

Judah was shuffling into the atrium. "I was sleeping, damn both of you. Be silent and leave me alone!"

"Husband! I am sorry. Do you need anything? Asher was just leaving."

"Woman, tend to your business, and let Asher tend to his. Asher. Did she not say you were leaving? *Nu*. So, go away!"

Miriam did not move. Judah looked terrible. His eyes were halos of dark gloom and his drawn face forbade discussion. These moods did not necessarily coincide with bad news. At the moment, they, the Jews, were on the cusp of self-rule. Lysias' departure from Judaea precipitated a great coup for the rebel forces, for they were able to take Jerusalem, purify the temple and stage a real siege against those collaborators and Greeks that were still wedged in the Akra tower. Judah had vowed that the tower would come down and the last enemy would at last be banished from Judaea. Now, for the first time, it looked like that miracle could indeed be possible. But Judah had retreated to the palace room four days ago and had not emerged until this moment. Miriam found that the longer she allowed him to stay in his dark place, the sooner he would bring himself out of it. But, if she intruded, more than just leaving food and drink outside his bolted door, the mood could endure for weeks.

*****

Can Judah see the fight through? Scan the link below and order the final book in **The Judean Revolt Series** to find out!

QR to *Legacy of the Maccabee* on Amazon.com

Also by J.D. Sonne

A Fitting Tomb
A Fitting Tomb: The Shoot

The Maccabee Series
Book I: Birth of the Maccabee
Book III: Legacy of the Maccabee

Medieval Rain

Bred for Harvest

Acknowledgments

This series has enriched my life for the past twenty years, and there are many to thank for my enduring to the finish. Prior to personal shouts-out, I first must mention Professor Bezalel Bar-Kochva of Tel Aviv University of Israel, whom I have never met, but whose Books on the Maccabean Rebellion, specifically *Judas Maccabaeus* and *The Seleucid Army*, provided a great foundation upon which to write this story. Historians who keep these stories alive through their meticulous research are the real heroes, as they make it possible for these epic struggles to be read and re-read by those in the world who understand the value of freedom. Then, my parents, who didn't burden me with chores during my childhood, but rather encouraged me to write, draw, play music and waste time with friends, allowing me an idyllic upbringing; My brother, who was also a writer, musician and artist who kept me from trusting the world too much; My son, who as an infant and toddler watched me pounding away on my novels at my old Apple II GS, and became a writer who now continually inspires me with his profound grasp of literary rhetoric and advice on the writing process itself; My editor, Carrie, who helped me get rid of some of my self-important magniloquence (as my son would call it); My book group of long ago: Brittany, Alice, Eliza and Dawnell, who kept me writing with their not-so-faint praise; My friend, Tawna Hutchison, who showed me the important final step of publishing; And finally, my helpmeet, strong-arm and loving partner, Mark, who at this moment makes me a wordsmith with no words.

Author's Note

A perplexity of discussion exists on the actual date of the first Hanukkah. To calculate the dates for my chapter headings, I lifted information from a few different sources that put the Julian year of the occurrence between 162 and 170 B.C.E. *Kislev* 25 of the Hebrew calendar is generally thought to be the actual date when the temple purification commenced, and by studying Bezalel Bar-Kochva's works, *Judas Maccabeaeus* and *The Seleucid Army,* and looking at his extrapolations, I decided that the year of the first Hanukkah may have occurred in 164 B.C.E. Therefore, *Kislev* 25, 164 B.C.E. is the day and year that I use at the end of Book II, *People of the Prophecy*, to denote the first day of Hanukkah. The remaining dates in the series, forward and backward from that event, come from other historical sources and make up the rest of the timeline.

J.D. Sonne

Made in the USA
Monee, IL
15 September 2023

42810523R00215